Mr. Rowl

©2020 Spire Books
Historic Romance Book #4

Hardcover ISBN 13: 978-1-5154-4366-7
Trade Paperback ISBN 13: 978-1-5154-4367-4

Mr. Rowl

by D. K. Broster

Contents

Part IV. A Month of Miracles

Part I
The Happy Valley

"Le Jeune et Beau Dunois"

"Here is neither labour to be endured nor danger to be dreaded, yet here is all that labour or danger can procure or purchase. Look round and tell me which of your wants is without supply: if you want nothing, how are you unhappy?"—Rasselas, chap. iii.

It was quite likely that at an earlier stage of the afternoon the youthful and lively little company in the drawing room at Northover had been playing forfeits, or something equally childish. But when Mr. Ralph Bentley, the owner of Northover, strolled along the terrace about half-past five o'clock with a couple of companions, they were making music, for a very pleasant tenor voice came floating through the windows, which, because it was a fine mid-March day, were slightly open. The voice was singing "Since First I Saw Your Face."

The middle-aged gentlemen outside stopped to listen. "Very tuneful, egad!" observed one of them. "Who's the minstrel, Bentley?"

"Judging from the 'r's,' I should say it is our captive friend des Sablières," responded the master of the house with a smile. "Don't you think so, Ramage?"

"'The sun whose beams most glorious are,'?" sang the voice, but the brow of the gentleman just addressed in no way resembled that luminary.

"What right has a French prisoner to be singing English songs?" he growled. "If he must sing at all, let him keep to his own jargon!"

"But surely one should admire the Frenchman's enterprise," objected the first speaker. "And he sings the old song very well. How did he learn it, I wonder?"

"Better ask him, Sturgis," replied Mr. Bentley with a twinkle, as the unseen singer declared that where'er he went he would leave his heart behind him, and applause greeted the end of the song.

"I had almost asked you, Bentley," said Mr. Sturgis, who had only that day arrived on a visit to Northover, "what a French prisoner was doing singing any kind of song in your house, having forgotten for the moment that Wanfield was now a parole town. You have a good few of Boney's officers here, I expect?"

"Only about eighty—not nearly so many as at Reading or Oswestry. Wanfield is quite a small place, as you know."

"Eighty too many!" remarked Mr. Ramage, who seemed possessed by a grievance. "They are a damned nuisance, and Bannister, the agent, is too easy with them. Hardly a week passes but one of them breaks his parole or is up to some dirty trick or other!"

"Come, come, Ramage," interposed Mr. Bentley, "you exaggerate, my dear fellow. We have not really had a case since December, 1812—since last year, in fact—when that major of engineers took the key of the fields, as I believe he would call it. He got clear off, too."

"Yes, and how?" enquired Mr. Ramage indignantly, the very wig he conservatively wore bristling with indignation. "Disgraceful to say, with English assistance! To think what some people will do for money—that for the sake of gain there should exist throughout the country a regular gang of escape agents who live by it as by a trade! But I have got my eye on that man Zachary Miller—pedlar, poacher, and what not—and one day I shall catch him at his nefarious practices! I am convinced that it was he was the go-between with Major Suchet and those even greater scoundrels on the coast."

"Zachary Miller?" enquired a fresh voice, proceeding from a tall, fair, handsome gentleman of about thirty who had come unperceived along the terrace and joined them. "What about Zachary Miller? Not poaching again, I hope? I had him up before me last month, but he managed to prove an alibi."

Mr. Ramage turned eagerly to the newcomer. "Not poaching, no, Sir Francis. I suspect him of something much worse—only there again nothing can be proved against him."

"Ramage thinks he is a sort of escape agent for the prisoners, Mulholland," supplied Mr. Bentley rather quizzically. "That is a somewhat more ambitious occupation than poaching."

"A better paid one, anyhow," observed Sir Francis Mulholland. "If you would tell me what you know about Zachary Miller, Mr. Ramage, I should be greatly obliged to you, for I am tired of finding him prowling in my woods for no apparent reason. But let us remove ourselves for the purpose, since I know that Mr. Bentley finds it hard to believe anything to the discredit of the French prisoners."

"Now, my dear fellow!" protested his host, but Sir Francis, with a smile which seemed to show that he was only jesting, slipped his arm through that of the detractor of Zachary Miller and they walked away, he inclining his head to listen to the gesture-emphasized disclosures of the smaller man.

"That is Mulholland of Mulholland Park, I take it?" observed Mr. Sturgis to his friend. "I did not quite catch his name when you introduced us just now. I seem to remember that he had just succeeded his uncle in the estate when I visited you two years ago, but that he had not yet taken up his residence. The prospect, however, if I am not mistaken, was then causing a considerable flutter among the young ladies of the district and their mammas."

Mr. Bentley smiled. "It was, and the flutter continued unabated until about three months ago, when he ceased to be the very eligible parti at whom they were all setting their caps."

"Ceased? Why?"

"Because he became engaged. And the mortifying thing to the fair of the neighbourhood was, that he laid Mulholland Park at the feet of no local aspirant after all, although—and this perhaps made it the more bitter—his chosen lady was staying at Wanfield at the time, in this house, in fact. Sir Francis Mulholland is betrothed to a very charming young lady, Miss Juliana Forrest, a school friend of my daughter's."

"Juliana Forrest—Lord Fulgrave's daughter?"

"The same. She is one of the party in the drawing room now, for she has been staying with Mrs. Mulholland—though she goes away the day after to-morrow, and then returns, I hope, to visit us here at Northover. Don't fall in love with her if you can help it, Sturgis; I have a fancy that, though he tries not to show it, Mulholland is infernally jealous."

"He could hardly be jealous of an old man of sixty! And so they met here, at Northover?"

"He was accepted last January under this very roof—to be exact, I believe, in the small room off the drawing room where I keep my Chinese porcelain."

Mr. Sturgis looked away for a moment. Sir Francis and his companion had disappeared round the corner of the house. "I should have thought, Bentley," he said slowly—"pardon an old friend, won't you?—that Mulholland and your own pretty girl . . . had you never thought of the match?"

Mr. Bentley showed a heartfree smile on his daughter's account. "Laetitia, my dear fellow, is going to marry her second cousin. And—try to believe that it is not a case of sour grapes—she does not greatly like Mulholland; I can't think why. Possibly because—well, you know what girlish friendships are. Yet hers and Juliana's seems as strong as ever; in fact, I sometimes wonder how Sir Francis likes his betrothed spending as much time at Northover as, I am glad to say, she does, and what he said when he heard that she was going to pay us, and not his mother, a visit in April. . . . Where have he and Ramage got to, I wonder?"

"Some quiet spot where they can discuss the chance of getting this Mr. Zachary Miller transported, I imagine," returned his friend. "It is transportation now, is it not, for helping a prisoner of war to escape?"

"Since last year, yes. But I cannot say that so far the fact has done much to deter escapes, though I suppose it has raised their cost. It is a very surprising thing to me, this inability of the French to respect their parole of honour. My old Royalist friend, the Comte de Sainte-Suzanne, who has been an exile for twenty years and lived here for twelve of them, assigns it all, of course, to the spirit which came in at the Revolution. He says that the majority of these officers are destitute alike of breeding and of military tradition, so what can one expect?"

"Ah, you have a Frenchman of the other party living here?" exclaimed Mr. Sturgis with interest. "Yes, of course, I remember him now. How do the two kinds mix?"

"About as well as oil and vinegar. The Comte ignores any Bonapartist prisoner he may happen to meet. Young des Sablières, who was singing just now, is about the sole exception, and I think he tolerates him only because he is of good family and has a pleasing address. It is a mercy that it is so, for Sainte-Suzanne being such an old friend, and having the freedom of Northover, he and Mr. Rowl meet here fairly often."

"Mr. Rowl?" queried his guest.

Mr. Bentley smiled. "The shop people and so on, who can't get their tongues round M. Raoul des Sablières' family name, call him by that form of his Christian one."

"Is Mr. Rowl the only one of the paroled officers who has the privilege of your hospitality?"

"No; I daresay there are about half-a-dozen others. But he is here the most frequently. A charming fellow, we all think him, even though he is an enemy—and when he was at large, I somehow fancy, a pretty daring one. Not that he ever talks of his exploits. He is a hussar, and was wounded and captured at Salamanca last summer."

They took a turn up and down. Someone was now playing the pianoforte with vigour. "That's Laetitia," said her father. "We might go in when she has finished her performance."

"Before we do, and before the patriotic Mr. Ramage comes back," said Mr. Sturgis, taking his friend by the arm, "tell me something, my dear Bentley. I presume that here, as elsewhere, the prisoners are strictly limited as to where they may go—one mile along the turnpike road from either confine of the town being their boundary, eh?"

Mr. Bentley nodded.

"Well, my dear friend, when last I visited you the first milestone—I distinctly remember the fact—stood a few yards to the left of your entrance gates, between you and Wanfield. Now it is a few yards on the right! Has

Northover shifted its position since 1811? I understand that an earthquake tremor was felt last year in some parts of England."

"It wasn't an earthquake, Sturgis. I had the distance from the town remeasured, and it was found to be . . . slightly incorrect." And as Mr. Sturgis laughed and shook his finger at him the good gentleman added half apologetically: "The poor devils have so few distractions! And as I am a magistrate, and was actually deputy sheriff at the time of the—the correction, no one dared to say anything. Yet some day" (and here Mr. Bentley lowered his voice and glanced over his shoulder), "I half expect to find that Ramage has remeasured the distance yet again on his own account, and laid his discovery before another magistrate—Mulholland perhaps."

"Curious, if you come to think of it," said Mr. Sturgis reflectively, "that all over England and Scotland these French officers on parole are living freely amongst us, and in many cases are received into our family circles!"

"And why not?" asked Mr. Bentley. "They fought clean; every soldier from the Peninsula says that. Well, let us go in; I fancy that Laetitia is drawing to the close of that newest display of fireworks of hers, the 'Siege of Badajoz.' If the actual event was really as noisy as that, I am glad I was not there."

It was a charming scene into which Mr. Bentley ushered the new arrival, for the wide, low room, whose last-century chintzes still survived in this thirteenth year of the new, was brightened by groups in narrow high-waisted gowns and sandals, in long-tailed blue or brown coats and tight pantaloons and frills, the wearers of which, all young and all animated, seemed to be enjoying themselves hugely, and, now that the strains of Mr. Wesley's "characteristic sonata" no longer resounded, were making a good deal more noise than even the pianoforte had done.

Laetitia Bentley, a pretty, fair girl in white and yellow, still sat at that instrument, but she was looking up and talking to another of her own sex. Leaning against the pianoforte, and studying some music outspread upon it, was a young man of about four and twenty who caught the eye at once by reason of his unlikeness to any of the other young men present; and that not so much by his good looks as by his naturally more lively expression, his air of being able to set himself instantly in motion with the minimum of effort, like a well-trained runner or a deer. He was dark-haired, but fair-skinned, with a suggestion of sunburn that had survived captivity and winter; his little moustache, so slight that it was hardly more than a pencilled line across his lip, like that of a Stuart gallant, left the firm but sweet-tempered mouth revealed. Yet its mere presence sufficed to stamp him as not English. "That, of course, is 'Mr. Rowl,'?" said Mr. Sturgis to himself.

The sound of the door opening had been drowned in chatter, but suddenly Laetitia caught sight of her father and rose quickly from the music stool; the young Frenchman too raised his head and saw him, and his face lit up with a very pleasant smile. There was a general chorus of exclamation, and Mr. Sturgis, welcomed a little shyly by his host's daughter, was presented to all the ladies severally, and before long found himself engaged in converse with her whose acquaintance had been specially promised him—Miss Juliana Forrest.

She was a tall, dark, handsome girl with a beautifully modelled head on a long neck, an exquisite mouth, and an air of race—"a typical beauty," thought Mr. Sturgis to himself, "and with all the airs and graces of one too, I'll warrant." But as he chatted to her a little, telling her how he had known her father at Cambridge, he found her not quite what he had looked to find, but more lively, natural, and open, more charming, in short, than he had surmised from his first glance at her.

A little later, after he had been called away by Mr. Bentley to be presented to someone else, he perceived that the young French officer (who, however, was not in uniform) had gone up to her where she sat in her long-sleeved gown of lilac sarcenet, spotted with amber, on a small couch in a corner of the room. She looked beautiful and animated; his face the observer could not see. "Making pretty speeches, of course," he reflected—"a Frenchman's main idea of conversation with a woman."

But, if he could have overheard, he would have discovered the chief subject of the little interview to be quite other. So too might Sir Francis Mulholland who, having just come in, was watching the couple, unobserved, from his place near the door.

"And so you are leaving us on Saturday, Mademoiselle?" the young man was saying.

"Yes, for about a month, Monsieur. But I shall find you here, no doubt, when I return?"

Raoul des Sablières made a little face. "My chance of being exchanged is so small that I fear you will. Pardon my ill manners! At any rate, I have something to look forward to—your return, Mademoiselle . . . I must strive, must I not, that my English, improved, I dare to hope, by the books which you and Miss Bentley have been so kind as to lend me, shall not fall away while you are absent."

"Your English is very good indeed, Monsieur," said Miss Forrest, who had lent the young Frenchman books in that tongue just because, speaking and understanding it so well (he had passed his childhood in England), he could appreciate them. "Ah, that reminds me—how annoying! I had intended before leaving Wanfield to lend you my copy of *Rasselas*, and to bring it here to-day, but I forgot. It is written, you know, in the most excellent style; you could not do better than study it."

"I should be only too delighted," said M. des Sablières with an inclination. "But, alas, I cannot come and fetch it from Mulholland Park, since that is out of bounds."

"So it is," agreed Miss Juliana. "How vexatious! I must send the book then to your lodgings by one of the servants—you lodge with Miss Hitchings, I think? But then I shall not be able to point out to you my favourite passages, as I had designed."

"*Mais celà, c'est désolant!*" exclaimed the prospective reader. "What is one to do?" He could not, of course, suggest that she should accompany the book to his lodgings.

The Honourable Juliana pondered. She was a very high-spirited young lady, accustomed to having her own way, and equally unaccustomed to having that way criticized—much less controlled, as a certain person was trying to control it at present. Still, to inform a young foreigner, whom, after all, she did not know very well, that she purposed coming to Northover to-morrow afternoon to take farewell of Laetitia Bentley, and to apprise him of her homeward route in case he also should be taking a walk . . . no, even with so laudable an aim as the personal bestowal on him of Doctor Johnson's model of style, it would not do. . . .

"I must mark the passages before I send *Rasselas* to you, Monsieur des Sablières," was her conclusion, and Raoul had hardly bowed his acquiescence before a deputation of young ladies was upon him, begging him to sing again—a French song this time, and by preference a new one, since he had sung them so very antiquated an English air; Heaven knew where he could have unearthed it!

"New?" repeated Captain des Sablières doubtfully. "*Mais, chères demoiselles*, where do you think I have been these last three years to learn the new ditties of Paris?"

"Did you never sing in Spain, then, 'Mr. Rowl'?" half mischievously enquired one damsel.

"Yes—hymns," replied Raoul with entire gravity. But before the protesting laughter had subsided he admitted, "*Eh bien*, yes, I know one new song—at least, it was new two years ago. I heard it first on the banks of the Caya—Queen Hortense's ballad about le jeune et beau Dunois, partant pour la Syrie in the time of the . . . the Croisades. I can play the air *tant bien que mal*." Bowing to Miss Forrest, he went towards the pianoforte, the little group following him with questions about the song and its writer, and Juliana Forrest was left alone in her corner, on which Sir Francis Mulholland immediately stalked across to her, his face rather thunderous. But Miss Forrest, if she noticed any meteorological symptoms, did not betray her knowledge, as she remarked evenly, "Ah, there you are, Francis!"

"There I have been for some time," returned her betrothed. "I was waiting until you were disengaged."

His tone was not exactly disagreeable, but neither was it the tone of mere jest. Juliana shot a little glance up at him. That Francis was jealous, and sometimes insanely jealous, she had discovered about three days after her engagement; at first the fact had amused her, but it had soon ceased to do so.

"But that was very unnecessary," she returned cheerfully. "I, on my part, had been wondering where you were got to all this time."

"I did not observe any signs of solicitude. Had there really been any speculation in your mind, you could have seen me standing by the farther door these five minutes or so."

"My dear Francis," returned the girl with a shade of impatience, "you surely do not desire to see me craning my neck in all directions to observe your whereabouts every moment that I have not the pleasure of your society! I would not wish to make either of us ridiculous. And, as you are now happily arrived, pray sit down and listen to the new French song which M. des Sablières is about to sing to us."

Sir Francis did not sit down. The word "ridiculous" had brought a slight colour to his cheek. "I have no desire to hear French songs. I came to ask you to give me a few minutes' private conversation—in the Chinese room over there, for instance."

"Willingly," replied Miss Forrest, "when the song is over. Hush—it is just going to begin. Pray, Francis . . ."

"Partant pour la Syri....e,"

sang Mr. Rowl, seated at the pianoforte,

"Le jeune et beau Dunois
Venait prier Mari....e
De bénir ses exploits.
Faites, reine immortell....e,
Lui dit-il en partant,
Qu'aimé de la plus bell....e
Je sois le plus vaillant!"

And, fidget and scowl though Miss Forrest's future lord did throughout the following three verses, he had to remain beside her. The moment, however, that the last note was drowned in applause, he gave her a significant glance, and going to a neighbouring door, held it open for her. Unhurriedly, the Honourable Juliana rose and passed through it into a little room containing an old spinet, one or two fine Queen Anne chairs, and much Chinese porcelain, mostly imprisoned in cabinets.

She turned on the young man as he shut the door behind them. "So this is to be an interview en règle! We had another in here once!" And she smiled, a delightful roguish smile calculated, one would have thought, to dissipate the most obstinate male sulks. "But what is it that needs such solemn precautions, and that cannot be said when we go home presently in your curricle?"

"You forget the groom," replied Sir Francis rather shortly. He took a turn down the room and then began to study a famille verte vase on its shelf, while Miss Forrest, sinking into a chair, watched him half mischievously. "Juliana," he said at length, not looking at her, "you may not like what I am about to say to you, but I beg you to believe that I must say it."

"If it is a duty, then I certainly would not keep you from its performance," said Miss Forrest equably. "Pray proceed, or we may be interrupted before your task is accomplished."

Thus adjured, the gentleman turned from the porcelain and faced her.

"I desire, I request you, when you return to Wanfield next month, to have nothing more to do with Captain des Sablières."

The colour sprang up in Juliana's cheeks, and her hands went to the short walnut-wood arms of her chair.

"And the reason, pray?"

"Because I do not like him," said Sir Francis with brevity.

"But if I do?"

"I must still ask you to oblige me in the matter."

Juliana returned her hands to her lap. "I find him intelligent, amusing, and well-bred," she announced calmly. "What have you against him?"

"He is a French prisoner—and what does one know of a French prisoner's antecedents?"

"Captain des Sablières is a gentleman—his name alone shows it," observed Miss Forrest.

"His name may not be his own."

"Then his bearing, his manners show it."

"Even that fact does not make him a suitable companion for a girl of your station, Juliana."

"A girl of my station, Francis, is accustomed to judge of that for herself."

"Pardon me, not in the case of a man to whom her future husband objects."

"No, perhaps not—if the man in question were really a 'companion,'?" admitted Miss Forrest somewhat coldly. "But look at the facts, Francis. I have seen very little more of Monsieur des Sablières than of any other prisoner at Wanfield—for indeed it is Laetitia Bentley, and not I, who has had most of his society. I meet him occasionally at other houses, rather more often here, but always in company. As it happens, I have never spoken with him actually alone."

"I should think not, indeed!" commented Sir Francis between his teeth.

Miss Forrest stopped in her discourse and looked at him.

"And of what, pray, would you be afraid if I were to find myself alone with a young man for a quarter of an hour or so? Do you realize, Francis, that you are making very strange and unflattering reflections on my character and upbringing?"

Her betrothed came nearer. "Do not try to misinterpret me so, Juliana," he protested, in a voice of mingled injury and indignation. "You know that I am doing nothing of the kind. But the idea of your being alone with that fellow for any length of time is outrageous. Do you not know what Frenchman are?"

"No," said Miss Forrest. A sprite appeared in her eyes. "But now that you have excited my curiosity I think I should like to find out."

"Juliana!"

She swept on, unheeding the explosion. "But how a young man—even one of these terrible Frenchmen—conducts himself with a lady depends chiefly, I imagine, upon the lady. Do you think that I"—she drew up her long neck and looked like Diana—"that I am likely to allow any man to take liberties with me?"

"Not for a moment, Juliana—not for a moment!" asseverated the jealous lover. "But it is impossible to believe that a man exists who would not try to make love to you if he had the chance."

"Which," completed Juliana with a little smile, "you do not intend that any man living but yourself shall have?"

He stooped over her and possessed himself of a hand. "Can you blame me? No, I do not intend it, and you, you beautiful creature, when you accepted this," he kissed the gleaming ruby on her finger, "you assented to that compact, did you not?"

"Yes," said the girl. "And I have kept my share of it. But in this matter of Monsieur des Sablières——"

"You will do what I ask, will you not, my darling?" he broke in, and made a movement as though to kiss her. Juliana slipped instantly out of the chair. Then she turned to him, and her look was grave.

"No, Francis, it is as useless trying to cajole me as it is to dragoon me. Day by day this ridiculous and quite causeless jealousy of yours is growing more insupportable. Now it is this man, now another; soon I shall be able to speak to none under the age of a grandfather without incurring your frowns. I have tried to be patient, but now I see that it is culpable in me to give way to you, that by doing so I am preparing a sort of slavery for myself. For I am an Englishwoman, and you are not living in Turkey, as you sometimes appear to think."

An attack so direct plainly staggered Sir Francis Mulholland. He seemed to be about to make a fiery retort, then he lost his balance and countered lamely, "So my wishes—*my* wishes—have no weight with you?"

"Yes, certainly they have, when they are reasonable. But to forbid a perfectly innocent acquaintance with a well-behaved and rather lonely young man whom chance has thrown in my way——"

"Lonely!" ejaculated her affianced, recovering himself. "That foreign nightingale in there *lonely*! And chance, indeed! Was the part he took with you in those theatricals last month due to chance?"

Miss Forrest's gravity relaxed. "No, to talent," she retorted. "As he happened to be the only young man in the neighbourhood who did not look uncouth and absurd disguised as a woman——"

"His selection was due to you! Do not deny it!"

"Certainly not. I am proud to think that it was Monsieur des Sablières as the gipsy girl who was the success of the evening."

"Especially in the scene with you! I watched you both, Juliana——"

"I should hope you did! I was told I looked very well as a wood-cutter's daughter. Though if you had condescended to act yourself, as you were requested, Francis, you would not have been under the painful necessity of looking on—if it was painful."

Sir Francis stifled some remark which sounded remarkably like a curse. "Juliana, for God's sake drop this levity, this trifling with a serious question! You are——"

She interrupted him firmly. "You quite misapprehend, Francis. I am not trifling—far from it. It is indeed a serious question. You are trying to impose on me a perfectly unreasonable demand. And, leaving aside that it is unreasonable in itself, how do you suppose that, when I come to stay in this house, I am to avoid meeting a guest who frequents it as much as Monsieur des Sablières does? Stay in my room—by your orders—when this dangerous foreigner is announced . . . or ask Laetitia to have him refused entrance—and tell her why? He would have to be told too . . . and might be flattered at your apprehensions, I imagine."

Sir Francis, darkly red, was gripping the back of a chair. "Juliana," he said thickly, "are you trying to see how far you can go with me?"

"No," answered she, her head very high, "only trying to show you how far you go—to lengths which, three months ago, in this very room, we could neither of us have foreseen, I think."

Mulholland's colour suddenly faded, faded to real pallor. The words seemed to hold a veiled threat. But he had no opportunity of ascertaining this, for (with a good deal of preliminary rattling, it is true) the door leading from the drawing room opened, and their host apologetically put his head in.

"I am sorry, but they are clamouring for you, Juliana, in there, and I could deny them no longer. Do not hate me, my dear."

Juliana went to him and put her hand through his arm. "I think you come at a good moment, Mr. Bentley," she said, and, without a glance at her betrothed, entered the drawing room.

But, as that gentleman instantly discovered, the bone of contention was no longer there.

"Mr. Rowl" Gets into Trouble

"Pride . . . is seldom delicate: it will please itself with very mean advantages."—Rasselas, chap. ix.

After finishing his warmly received rendering of Queen Hortense's ballad M. Raoul des Sablières had removed himself with what speed he might from the neighbourhood of the pianoforte, for he was a modest young man and had no desire whatever to monopolise attention, particularly in the anomalous situation which was his. With the idea of suggesting to Miss Bentley that the time had come for her father to sing them "A-Hunting We Will Go," as his custom was, he sought for her among the little groups, and soon descried her in a corner talking to a very erect old gentleman, at sight of whose back he stopped and bit his lip. But at that moment the old man turned round, revealing a deeply marked, austere countenance with piercing blue eyes. His hair was snow-white; his clothes, spotless as they were, had seen long service. He wore a ribbon in his buttonhole.

"Ah, a French song for once, Monsieur des Sablières, but unfamiliar to me for all that," he said, with a courteous little inclination. "A pretty air, though I did not hear the words as I should have done had I been younger. May I ask what it was?"

The singer's colour rose faintly. "No, you would not know it, Monsieur," he answered quickly. "It is new—only two or three years old. . . . Mademoiselle, I came to ask if Mr. Bentley——"

But Miss Bentley, disregarding his haste to leave the subject, ill-advisedly pursued it. "Monsieur des Sablières ought to tell you about it, Comte, as he was telling us just now, for it is so interesting. The song as written by a

Queen—words and music too—by Queen Hortense."

The old Royalist raised his eyebrows. "And pray who is Queen Hortense?"

The little smile that accompanied the question was so acid that Miss Laetitia realized (too late) what delicate ground she had thus rashly invaded. "I think . . . I forget . . . is she not Queen of Westphalia—or is it——?" she faltered, stealing in her confusion a glance at M. des Sablières, only to find that he, looking fixedly at his compatriot, was frowning—a phenomenon she had never witnessed in him before.

"Your ignorance, my dear Miss Laetitia," said the Comte de Sainte-Suzanne with an intensification of his double-edged manner, "is fully excusable, since I, a Frenchman, share it. But Monsieur des Sablières can no doubt enlighten us—if indeed it be worth while—or rather, enlighten me, since I see your father making signs to you over there."

It was true, and Laetitia, after a rather troubled glance at her two French friends, left them together. Immediately she had gone Raoul des Sablières remarked very stiffly in their common tongue:

"I should hardly have thought it was worth your while, Monsieur, to affect ignorance of the identity of Her Majesty the Queen of Holland."

"I beg your pardon," replied the old man. "The Queen of . . . *Holland*; thank you! But I am, you see, no . . . botanist; I am not well acquainted with the nomenclature of the mushroom tribe."

"Really, Monsieur de Sainte-Suzanne," exclaimed the young hussar angrily, "you exceed the bounds of——"

"And you, Monsieur des Sablières, are obviously aware of no bounds at all! So, lest you should be contemplating rendering any further compositions by the self-styled monarchs of that family, I will betake myself to the library. As far as I am concerned, you will then be free to sing the *Ça ira*, if it pleases you." And, brushing aside the young man's half stupefied protest, he marched to the door, an attempt on Raoul's part to follow him being neatly frustrated by the intervention of two ladies and a very young gentleman who beset him with supplications.

"Monsieur des Sablières, do not go away, please! We want you to give us a translation of the words you sang. Here is Miss Curtis who understood but half, and Mr. Molyneux who understood none" (the very young gentleman blushed), "and I who have but the vaguest idea of what it was all about. The marriage of Dunois—was there not a marriage?—appeared so sudden!"

"It was a reward for his . . . what we call *prouesse*," stammered Raoul, the English word evading him for a moment under the blue lightning shaft which was launched at him just before the door closed on the Comte de Sainte-Suzanne. He tugged angrily for a second at his tiny moustache. Preposterous behaviour—and all for what! Then he recovered himself, and the smile which was never far from it twitched the corners of his mouth. "Sudden? . . . yes, Mesdemoiselles, a little. In war, you know. . . . But I will translate from the beginning."

And, with one elbow on the mantelpiece, he rendered the words of the romance into English, laughing himself when he came to

> *"De ma fille Isabelle*
> *Sois l'époux à l'instant!"*

and unaware of another listener, Mr. Sturgis, who had drifted to that corner of the room, and was thinking to himself as he watched the scene, "Strange how natural and easy they are, these French! Graceful young beggar—pity he's not in uniform . . . no, perhaps on the whole just as well, young ladies are so susceptible. . . . But light, unreliable, of course, like all his nation." For Mr. Sturgis had no great first-hand knowledge of the French.

"Yet, Mesdemoiselles," he heard the expositor conclude, "the English chanson which I murdered to you just now is worth six of '*Le jeune et beau Dunois*,' for it has real feeling; this is . . . pasteboard."

"You are quite right, Sir," observed Mr. Sturgis, coming forward. "I had the pleasure of hearing you sing 'Since First I Saw Your Face,' and you certainly brought out that feeling." There was a little twinkle in his eye.

But the young man was a match for him. He betrayed no sort of embarrassment; on the contrary he observed with a candid smile, "*Mais*,

Monsieur, one must feel what one sings, must one not, even when in truth one does not feel it at all?"

"Oh, Monsieur des Sablières," exclaimed the eldest of his little audience in a disappointed tone, "how unromantic! And we who were thinking while you sang of—of the lady with whom you left your heart over there in France, and compassionating her for your absence!"

"But you need not have done that, Mademoiselle," remarked the young hussar. "She will certainly have consoled herself by now—if she ever existed," he added, with a mischievous smile which showed his even little teeth.

But a young lady at the piano had now begun to play what she proclaimed to be "an adagio and march in the Turkish style," and under cover of it Captain Raoul des Sablières of the Third Hussars slipped quietly from the room with the intention of finding and making his peace with the Comte de Sainte-Suzanne. But he himself could not regard his alleged offence very seriously; indeed if he were not so much the younger man it might well be his to demand an apology. Nor did he think the old Royalist need have hurled the *Ça ira* at him in that ridiculous manner; as if he had ever sung it, or indeed, had ever heard it sung! But *ce vieillard-là* imagined that one was still in the year of blood '93.

Whether this was true of him or no, *ce vieillard-là* himself had something the outward appearance of belonging to that vanished world, where he stood choosing a book from a case in Mr. Bentley's library, the light from the branched candlestick in his hand falling kindly on his silver hair and worn aquiline features. He looked round as Raoul came in, and put down the candlestick, his mouth tightening for an instant.

"I have come to offer my apologies, Monsieur le Comte," said the young soldier, standing rather erect, "for what I am sure you must be aware was a perfectly unintentional offence. And having done so, I would permit myself to tell you, with all respect, that I repudiate the sentiments and associations of the *Ça ira* quite as strongly as you do, and that to credit me with the intention of singing it—"

But M. de Sainte-Suzanne put up his delicate old hand.

24

"I am already ashamed of my speech, Monsieur des Sablières. I have a hasty temper, still imperfectly controlled, I fear, for all my long apprenticeship to adversity. I ask you to forgive my outburst, and, if you can, to forget it."

"Willingly, Monsieur," returned Raoul, immediately mollified. "I hope, in return, that you will believe I never meant to hurt you."

"Nobody can do that now, Monsieur des Sablières." He turned his astonishingly blue, keen gaze more fully on his young compatriot. "But a few, a very few, can make me feel regret—and you are one of them. I do not need to tell you why. . . . If I did not think the climbing rose outside this window here a fine plant I should not be so sorry to see the blight on it summer after summer. . . . My only son, Monsieur des Sablières, was about your age when he was killed twenty years ago at Rülzheim, serving with Condé; and indeed he was not at all unlike you in voice and bearing. But, though life has never been the same for me since his loss, nothing can take away from me the consolation of knowing that he fell as his forefathers fell, and under the same flag which had led them so often to victory. If you had been killed in Spain, could that have been said of you?"

"I should have fallen for France, Monsieur," returned Raoul proudly, "and been glad to give my body for her. None of my ancestors—or yours—did more. Does it matter whether the flag which wraps a French soldier bears the lily or the eagle?"

M. de Sainte-Suzanne made a gesture. "Ah, Monsieur des Sablières, there is the blight I lament! Do you think it immaterial that you can so lightly give the title of Queen to the half-creole wife of an upstart who is barely a Frenchman, when She who last bore the title in France. . . ." His voice sank and died; he turned away, as from the scaffold he could never cease to see.

"But, Monsieur, we are not now in the Terror!" exclaimed Raoul. "Had I been born when your son was born, it would have been very different with me. Should I not also have served that beautiful and unfortunate lady? But, because of outrages and crimes which took place when I was a child of three or four, events of which I have not even a memory, must I be inactive all the best years of my life? I wanted to be a soldier, to fight for my country—for

France of to-day, the new France. Twenty years ago I should have fought for the old. Is it my fault that I am, as you no doubt consider, born twenty years too late?"

The old Royalist turned once more and looked at him as he stood there, young, ardent, handsome, and argumentative, and his face softened a little.

"It is extraordinary the way you resemble him," he murmured almost inaudibly. "*Mais lui, il avait la tête blonde . . . si blonde! . . .* Well, we will not discuss it, Monsieur des Sablières. I am too old to listen to new creeds, and you, I suppose, too young to understand mine. One particular of the old, however, I am glad to think that you observe more punctiliously than some of the new defenders of France, who have made a Frenchman's word of honour worth less than a pinch of dust in England to-day. Every time that I hear of a fresh case of parole-breaking I feel as if I could never hold up my head in an Englishman's presence again."

"And do you suppose, Monsieur," cried Raoul, with his own head held rather high, "that I do not feel exactly the same as you about it? Are you insinuating that I hold lightly a thing which on the contrary I regard with absolute abhorrence—that any soldier must so regard—the breaking of his sacred word of honour?"

"The six hundred and eighty officers who have broken it in the last three years alone were all soldiers—or sailors," observed the Comte drily. "No, indeed, as I say, I do not think any such thing of you. But, with such examples, who knows? . . ."

And, not unnaturally, this qualifying of the testimonial stung the young hussar to a sharper annoyance.

"When you hear that I have actually disgraced myself, Monsieur de Sainte-Suzanne, it will be time enough, will it not, to reproach me? To anticipate that day is only to——" He broke off controlling himself before age and misfortune. "I wish you good evening."

To reach the library at Northover one had to traverse another room, never used nowadays, except for this one purpose. But as Raoul des Sablières emerged into this apartment he was aware of a tall man standing looking out of the far window, though it was almost dark outside, with his hands behind his back and a little the air of waiting for someone; and when he was half way across the rather dimly lighted room this individual turned and revealed himself to be Sir Francis Mulholland.

"Ah, Monsieur des Sablières, good evening," said "le Roi Soleil," as Raoul had christened him among his French associates. "May I have the pleasure of a word with you?"

So it was he who was awaited! Raoul, trying to digest his annoyance with the Comte de Sainte-Suzanne, and at no time particularly desirous of conversation with this gentleman, with whom he had scarcely exchanged ten words in his six months at Wanfield, was obliged to reply, "With pleasure, Sir," and managed to do this with his usual politeness. On that, finding that Sir Francis did not move from the window, he went towards him.

"What I have to say is a little difficult," began the owner of Mulholland Park, scrutinizing him closely. "I trust that you will not take offence at it."

"I am not in a position, Sir, to indulge the luxury of taking offence," responded Raoul non-committally, but wondering what on earth was coming next.

"Ah, your speaking thus of your position makes it easier for me," was Mulholland's next remark, though his manner did not suggest that he was finding difficulty of any kind. "Since you already realize, then, Monsieur des Sablières, that it is not quite that of . . . of the other guests at Northover, perhaps the merest hint that you might with advantage carry that fact still more in mind may be enough."

Raoul looked at him, three-quarters bewildered.

"To what end am I to carry it in my mind?" he asked shortly.

"Well, to take an example," said Sir Francis, with a little smile which he perhaps intended to be deprecating, "we all realize that you have a pleasing voice, but it is possible, you know, to have too much of a good thing."

Raoul coloured. "You mean that I talk too much?"

"I should not venture to express an opinion on that point," returned "le Roi Soleil" with an air of diplomacy. "I was referring rather to your vocal gifts, in the exercise of which—forgive me!—you are certainly not sparing. Two songs in the space of half an hour—and neither of them, if I may say so, in the best of taste, all things considered."

"Monsieur, I think you are impertinent!" said Raoul, sharply.

Sir Francis shrugged his shoulders. "I warned you that my errand was unpleasant."

"Errand!" Raoul took him up. "Who sent you on that errand? Not Mr. Bentley, I am sure."

"No, I have no commission from Mr. Bentley, though I think that, for your own sake, he would approve of what I am saying. For my only desire (if you would but believe it) is to present you, out of good-will, with a hint."

"I do not take hints from you, Sir, whatever prompts them!" said Raoul, drawing himself up. But Sir Francis from his superior height looked across the embrasure at him with an olympian air which was hard to stomach.

"That is a pity, Monsieur des Sablières, because it would really be better, again for your own sake, that you should reflect whether your very frequent presence at Northover is not putting too great a strain even on Mr. Bentley's hospitality."

Naturally sweet-tempered as he was, Raoul began to feel that this was too much. "The day that Mr. Bentley himself——" he began warmly, but Sir Francis bore him down.

"Mr. Bentley, as you well know, is too kind-hearted ever to suggest such a thing. Let me put another consideration before you, then. Do you suppose that it is a source of satisfaction to the gentlemen of this neighbourhood to find a person of your nationality present at almost every gathering, and usually in a position of prominence which his own better feelings should have led him to avoid?"

Now this indictment, wounding as it was, might, for all the young Frenchman knew, have some truth behind it, though he had never observed the slightest signs of ill-will towards him among the local gentry, with many of whom he was on excellent terms. And he had always been most careful not to push himself forward. Still, if there were one or two who disliked him . . .

But while he stood silent, honestly trying to face such a possibility, Sir Francis saw fit to follow up his advantage by adding, in the most openly insolent manner: "You are only here at all, you know, on sufferance!"

Raoul could not suppress a little gasp. "Thank you for the so courteous reminder!" he said. Then he gripped the edge of the card table in the window and became dangerously quiet. "You will tell me, please, whether in doing me this kind office you are speaking for yourself alone, or whether you have been deputed by others to insult me?"

"And I also should like to be informed on that point," said a level voice behind them, and both, turning round in surprise, beheld the Comte de Sainte-Suzanne on the threshold of the library. "I take it, Sir Francis," he continued, coming forward a little, "that the recommendation you have just so tactfully made to Monsieur des Sablières applies to me also, a Frenchman, an exile and an habitué of Northover. I am only sorry that my reliance on Mr. Bentley's ever-ready welcome has led me, like my young fellow-countryman here, to offend Mr. Bentley's other guests. You may be sure that I shall make him and them the profoundest apologies."

If the young fellow-countryman had been in a laughing mood he might have enjoyed the stupefaction and then the patent alarm of his aggressor. "Monsieur le Comte," stammered "le Roi Soleil," leaving the window, "I beg of you . . . my remarks were of course not meant . . . I was not aware . . ."

"Then if you do not wish Mr. Bentley to know how unjustifiably you have been trying to dictate to one of his guests in his house," said the old man sternly, "I suggest that you immediately apologise to Monsieur des Sablières for your last very gross observation."

"No, no, a forced apology is of no use to me, Monsieur de Sainte-Suzanne!" cried Raoul quickly. "And, for my part, I would point out to this gentleman that since he so much dislikes my visits here, the remedy is simple—he can cease his own."

"You impudent——" began Sir Francis, taking a step towards him; but the old man broke in sharply:

"Monsieur des Sablières, look at the clock there! You have but just time to take leave of the company and to reach your lodgings before curfew. That obligation takes precedence of everything else at this moment."

Raoul's eyes had instinctively followed his pointing finger, and he saw indeed that the tall clock in the corner marked twenty minutes to seven, and by seven he must be back under the roof of Miss Eliza Hitchings in the little town.

"Thank you, Monsieur," he said to the old Royalist with a mixture of real gratitude and of regret at having to quit the field of battle. "And thank you still more," he added in his own tongue, "for your generosity just now in classing yourself with me; I shall not forget it." He bowed to him, looked at Sir Francis in no pacific fashion, and remarking "We must finish this conversation, Sir, another time," left the room.

He was excessively angry, but it was imperative to bottle down his wrath for the moment, since he must return to the drawing room and make his farewells without an instant's delay. As he hurried towards that apartment he rejected the idea of slipping out of the house without taking leave, not only because it would be discourteous, but also because Sir Francis, if he heard of it, might draw very incorrect conclusions as to the effect of his admonitions. No; good manners at any cost, even if he all but burst with the constraint he was putting upon himself as he opened the drawing-room door.

Afterwards he was to think how differently things might have gone if he had not made that sacrifice to politeness and pride.

His re-entry into the lighted drawing room was hailed with questions as to where he had been and reproaches for his absence. Smiling, shaking his head, and reminding his critics that a good prisoner had to be home by seven o'clock this month, and that he should have to run most of the mile to the town as it was, he made his way to Miss Bentley and apologized for his hasty leave-taking.

"All right, my boy," said Mr. Bentley, coming up from behind and clapping him upon the shoulder. "Letty quite understands. Off with you—but be sure you come extra early on Tuesday to make up, that's all."

"Yes, you have not forgotten Tuesday, I hope, Monsieur des Sablières?"

enquired Laetitia anxiously. "The concert, you know."

No, it did not seem as if the Bentleys, at all events, felt that he trespassed too often upon their hospitality.

Nor that Miss Forrest, the most beautiful girl in the room, resented his presence there, alien though he was. ("The sun, whose beams most glorious are, rejecteth no beholder.") For as, his farewells over, he made for the drawing-room door, she chanced to be standing near it, alone—or at any rate she was near it, alone.

"I must bid you a long, a month's, farewell, Mademoiselle," said the young man, with lightly feigned solemnity. But the words of the song wove themselves unuttered about his own as he looked at her, though he hoped that that "sweet beauty past compare" did not cause his gaze to be too bold. "Do not, I pray you, forget your kind promise to send me the romance of Doctor Johnson to make that month seem less long."

To this, looking him in the face, Miss Juliana replied calmly: "I have been reflecting about *Rasselas*, Monsieur des Sablières. To-morrow afternoon I intend to come to Northover again, to take farewell of Miss Bentley. I will put the book in my pocket, just in case I should be walking back, and should come across you—should you, for instance, by any chance be fishing near Fawley Bridge, where I think I have heard you say that you do fish sometimes."

The young Frenchman dropped his eyes, not to show his surprise. Did she know what she was doing? She seemed extraordinarily composed about it. And why was she doing it—she, "le Roi Soleil's" betrothed? But it was not for him to hesitate.

"You are quite right, Mademoiselle," he replied without a perceptible pause. "Although it is off the highroad, I have a special licence from Mr. Bannister to fish for a mile from the bridge. And as it happens"—he looked at her again, and his eyes were sparkling now—"I had already arranged with myself to go and fish there to-morrow afternoon, so that if by chance you should be taking that way back to Mulholland Park. . . ." He left the sentence unfinished, and added: "For I believe that path which mounts the steep field from the bridge goes to Mulholland Park, does it not?"

"It does," answered Miss Forrest, looking at the carpet for a moment. "It is a short cut." She then added, in a highly negligent manner: "It is of course quite uncertain whether I shall return that way."

But Raoul des Sablières, bending over her hand and murmuring that he at least would be there, was conscious of a distinct hope that, whatever motive had prompted her to this unconventional suggestion, she would be able to carry it out.

And when, rather out of breath, he reached Miss Hitching's doorstep just as the first clang of the prisoner's curfew smote the air, it was evident that the smothered wrath to which he had promised himself to allow free play as he hurried towards the lights of Wanfield had occupied him but little, or his first action on opening the door would scarcely have been to tap the weatherglass in the little hall.

How Juliana Asserted Her Independence

"Even the Happy Valley might be endured with such a companion."–Rasselas, chap. xiii.

Mr. Rowl's unspoken petition had certainly been granted. The nineteenth of March was an even finer afternoon than its predecessor–a thought too fine, indeed, for a fisherman whose heart had been set wholly upon sport. (But then Mr. Rowl's heart was not so set.) The stream sang as it rippled under the little stone bridge whose presence almost raised it to the status of a river, and the birds were singing too in the coppice that topped the meadow on the farther side and then flung down a tributary line of thicket almost to the water. And all over this thicket, and everywhere else, the green was breaking in varying degrees of eagerness–a promise of what would reward the eye if one came again in a week or so. . . .

The young man on the bridge at present, however, had his back turned to all this display, since, leaning his arms on the parapet, he was looking meditatively down at the water. His fishing rod rested against the same support, for M. des Sablières had really been fishing conscientiously (though fruitlessly) in order to delude any one who might witness it (or possibly even himself) into the belief that this prearranged meeting with Miss Juliana Forrest was just a chance encounter.

If Miss Forrest came, that was; for to-day she might think better of her design. Of course, the conventions were not quite so easily outraged for an English girl as for a French; he knew that. Besides, she might have her lawful escort with her, since it was not likely that Sir Francis would allow her to walk back from Northover unaccompanied. In that case, did she intend to make the gentleman wait while she pointed out to a French prisoner her favourite passages in *Rasselas*? If so, having regard to his recent conversation with that prisoner, there might be interesting developments.

More possibly she meant to come unescorted, which, if "le Roi Soleil" learnt afterwards of their open-air study of English, might lead to more interesting ones still. Almost undoubtedly for his own sake, just possibly for Miss Forrest's too, it would have been well to decline this encounter. But how could he put such an affront upon the lady who, whatever her motive, had been kind enough to propose it? Such a proceeding, especially after Sir Francis's attempt to read him a lesson, would have been of a prudence to make M. Raoul-Marie-Amédée des Sablières blush all the rest of his life at the remembrance.

If *le gros* Mulholland accompanied her—and Raoul really did not see how on this, her last afternoon at Wanfield, she could avoid his escort—dare he throw that gentleman into the stream, as, after yesterday's impertinence, he would so greatly enjoy doing? He dallied with the idea, leaning there on the bridge, knowing perfectly well that he could not do such a thing in Miss Forrest's presence. *D'ailleurs*, Sir Francis was much the bigger of the two. But what a souse he would make going in! The poor little river would be completely dammed by *le gros* Mulholland . . . unfortunately it was not deep enough to drown him. . . . It was all very well to indulge in these pleasant fancies, but what of his future relations with Sir Francis, quite apart from any possible complications which might be imported into them by this afternoon's interview with his ladylove, if he came to know of it? On one thing, however, Raoul was determined—that he was not going to be bullied by him out of his footing at Northover.

In the midst of these reflections he caught the sound of a light step approaching, and turned eagerly. In another moment Miss Juliana Forrest came round the corner of the bend . . . and she was unaccompanied.

Raoul swept off his hat and went to meet her at the end of the bridge. Miss Forrest wore a long close-fitting coat of cherry colour, edged all round and up the fronts with ermine, but from just below the bosom, where it was tied about with a ribbon, it fell a little apart, and showed her white cambric walking-dress. She was looking very charming, the more so that her own colour was undoubtedly a trifle heightened.

"Miss Forrest, as I live!" exclaimed the young man. "What pleasant surprises Fate can give an unlucky fisherman after all!"

Miss Juliana smiled, and coloured yet more at this disingenuous address. "You have not caught anything this afternoon, then, Monsieur? I am sorry."

"You have no cause to pity me, Mademoiselle," returned Raoul, looking at her and smiling too. He was still bareheaded; the breeze lifted his fine, dark, loosely curling hair, and the sunlight showed the laughter and vitality in his grey eyes with their rims of still darker grey. And suddenly Miss Forrest seemed to find the little bridge too bright a place to stand and talk with a young man, for she began to move across it.

"Mademoiselle," said Raoul, moving with her, "you were going to point out to me the beauties of le docteur Johnson. But remember that I cannot accompany you up that path to the little wood. Only by the river may I disport myself—and that solely by permission of the good Mr. Bannister."

She hesitated and looked down the stream. It was clean out of her way. Raoul read her thoughts quite well.

"I have never been along that path," said the Honourable Juliana.

"You would find it quite dry," observed Raoul, glancing at her thin footgear.

"Then I think I will take a turn there."

"And I may have the privilege of accompanying you?" enquired Raoul. "Since Monsieur le docteur comes too," he glanced at the reticule upon her arm—"and I have my fishing rod," he added, laying hold of it.

Under the tutelage of these two chaperons, therefore, they left the bridge and started along the little track by the river bank, which was just wide enough for Juliana's slender feet in their kid half-boots. Under Raoul's the grass swished pleasantly, and for a moment or two that was the only sound the couple made.

Could Juliana Forrest herself have said what had caused her to do this thing? Hardly. Pique, a desire to show her betrothed that he could not dictate to her—a desire, in short, to read him a lesson? But it is of no use reading a person a lesson unless he is aware of the process, and Juliana, being conversant with Sir Francis's movements this afternoon (which she had had no small share in determining) knew that he would not pass by Fawley Bridge. But she always had it in her power to tell him of what she had done, if she saw fit . . . since not for one moment did she regard this as a clandestine proceeding, to be hushed up. Miss Juliana Forrest did not condescend to behaviour of that sort; nor, certainly, had she been the least in the world in love with M. des Sablières, or he with her, would she have suggested handing over *Rasselas* in this manner. M. des Sablières was a friend, in whom she took a friend's interest and whom she might meet whenever it seemed good to her.

So, after they had gone a short way, she opened her reticule and held out a small volume.

"Ah, the famous book!" said Raoul, and read off the title: "'*Rasselas*, Prince of Abyssinia.' *Il était donc prince, le héros du bon docteur?*"

Miss Forrest assented, and Raoul tucked his rod under his arm the better to examine the book as they walked slowly along.

"But he was a captive, then, in the hands of his enemies, this prince?" enquired the young Frenchman after a moment.

"A captive, but not in the hands of his enemies," replied Miss Forrest. And she explained how, according to the author, it was customary for the children of the royal race of Abyssinia to be confined in a delightful valley until they should succeed to the throne.

Her hearer listened attentively, but he did not fail to mark at the same time the fineness of her profile, and the way her lashes lifted themselves after their downward sweep. How green the boughs were behind her head—and how good the air smelt!

"Well, this *Rasselas* cannot have had a pleasanter captivity than mine," he observed at the end of this exposition. "You are all too kind to me here, Mademoiselle." "All except *le gros* Mulholland," he added to himself.

"Then I hope," said Juliana gently, "that you can sometimes forget your captivity."

In the flash of an eye the mobile visage had changed. "No, Mademoiselle, I never forget it," said the young hussar quite simply.

"Yes, the restrictions are ridiculous," agreed Miss Forrest sympathetically. "What is one mile along the turnpike to a man? You must often long to walk in the fields. And then that curfew. . . ."

They were at a standstill now. "It is not those little things," said Raoul, shaking his head. "You, Mademoiselle, will understand me, I think, when I say that I did not put on the Emperor's uniform in order to use this"—he indicated his fishing rod. "Every day I become older, is it not, doing nothing. Eight months have gone by——" He broke off.

"Eight months," repeated Juliana, struck by his tone. "Eight months since Salamanca, your last battle—and the most terrible, perhaps?"

And there by the stream she looked at him with new eyes, realizing that he was, after all, a soldier, and, amusing and accommodating though he might be, evidently had a preference for a soldier's life, with all its hazards.

"No, Mademoiselle," he now replied, "not the most terrible. Salamanca, where I was taken prisoner, was the greatest battle in which I had the honour of participating, but Albuera, the year before, was more bloody."

"Albuera!" exclaimed Juliana. "Was it not at Albuera that there was that terrible cavalry charge which almost wiped out I forget how many of our regiments in a few minutes—or so I have heard?"

"Yes," said Raoul. "There was a sudden violent hail-storm . . . which helped us." And he added, looking away: "You must try not to hate me too much, Mademoiselle—but I was in that charge."

Juliana was not conscious of any violent aversion. "But I am sure that you, Monsieur des Sablières, were not one of the lancers who afterwards rode down and massacred our wounded! No, I forgot, of course you are not a lancer."

"I hope," said the young man, with rather a wry smile, "that is not the only ground on which you are sure of it?" Then he faced her squarely. "To tell the truth, Mademoiselle—and I am glad to be able to tell it—it was not French troops at all who were guilty of that atrocious conduct. It was the Poles who had just charged, the Lancers of the Vistula. But I cannot deny, to my shame, that it occurred. I—I was able to intervene in the case of one officer, and I was fortunately successful; but the Lancers were beside themselves, and it was not very easy. . . ." He broke off, looking meditative—back, Juliana could see, on the field of battle again.

"Oh, Monsieur des Sablières," she exclaimed, "how grateful that officer must have been to you! Did you know his name?"

"We had no time to exchange cards, Mademoiselle," said Raoul smiling. "He was, of course, made prisoner, and I did not see him again. I do not even know his regiment, except that it belonged to the brigade we had just charged. But do not let us talk of battles, since in doing so we must realize that we are enemies. . . ."

"Must we?" asked Juliana with a smile. "Even here?—Do you know, Monsieur, that from every officer returned from Spain whom I have ever met—and I have met not a few—I have heard the same praises of—the enemy?"

"Mademoiselle," said Raoul bowing, "*vous me rendez confus!* May I say that that sentiment was not confined to one side? Yes, one exchanged courtesies—gifts sometimes; one even had one's friendships with the foe."

"As in the times of chivalry!" said Miss Forrest with sparkling eyes. "When I read those wonderful poems of Walter Scott's—I wish I could lend you Marmion—I feel that if I had been born a man I should like to go to the wars.

But there must be much hardship as well as glory. Tell me, Monsieur des Sablières, how long had you been in Spain before your capture?"

"About a year and eight months," replied Raoul. "I joined my regiment, the Second Hussars, at the end of 1810; it was part of the First Corps, Marshal Victor's, under Soult. And I was fortunate enough to be present at the battle of the Gebora, in February, 1811. Perhaps you may not have heard of it"—he permitted himself a rather malicious smile here—"for it was an undisputed French victory—against the Spaniards, bien entendu. At the Gebora—it is a river, Mademoiselle—we destroyed the army of Estremadura, and then Badajoz surrendered to us. (Oh, yes, I know that you have stormed it since Salamanca, but we had held it against you for more than a year.) Then came Albuera, of which I have spoken; then Marshal Soult joined Marmont, and both armies lay for a fortnight on one side of the River Caya, with Lord Wellington on the other. How I used to long for the attack!—but the day never came. At the Caya I was transferred to the Third Hussars, which formed part of Curto's Light Cavalry Division in Marmont's army, and being thenceforward with Marmont instead of with Soult, I came to be at Salamanca, and so—find myself here at Wanfield."

"You were wounded at Salamanca, were you not?" asked Juliana. "I hope you received proper attention from our surgeons?"

"I was very well cared for indeed, thank you, Mademoiselle. And my wound was not serious; I was lame for a little, that was all."

"And how did you come to England? It could not, I fear, have been an agreeable voyage."

M. des Sablières' mouth tightened a little. "No. It was horrible. We were crammed on the transport like sheep, and battened down most of the time. But at any rate it came to an end; and the conditions could not be helped; you took so many prisoners, alas, at Salamanca. But I gained some idea of the horrible conditions—which you must pardon me for saying could be avoided—under which so many of the less fortunate of us are rotting in your hulks to-day."

"The hulks!" said Miss Forrest with a shiver. "Do not let us speak of them.

38

I have heard things . . . no, too horrible! If they are true, they are a disgrace to us, to England!"

Raoul, touched that she could feel for misfortunes which she had never witnessed, and which in any case were suffered by enemies, was about to say something of the kind when he became aware that a man was walking along the more frequented path on the opposite side of the stream, and that he was not unobservant of them. He looked across and saw the Comte de Sainte-Suzanne.

Miss Juliana Forrest saw him too. For the second time since her coming her colour rose a little; for the second time she took an added beauty from it. She acknowledged the Comte's salutation and Raoul did the same, unable to decide whether he could detect on his compatriot's face, across the width of the stream, an indication of the surprise which he was probably feeling. In silence they both watched him continue his path away from the bridge, and Raoul suddenly remembered that at the beginning of this interview he had half expected somebody else to break in upon it, and realized too how completely he had since forgotten that anticipation. . . . As for Sainte-Suzanne, he was not the man to go gossiping.

"Tell me, Mademoiselle," he said, for the sake of saying something, for a shadow of constraint seemed to have fallen across them both, "does this *Rasselas*," he touched his pocket, "ever escape from his Happy Valley?"

"Yes," replied Juliana, beginning to move in the direction of the bridge, "he makes a way out, and leaves it in the company of a sage and a lady.—But the lady is his sister," she added, with the suspicion of a smile. "Do not expect to find a romance of love in so edifying a work as *Rasselas*. If you want that you must ask Miss Bentley to lend you Richardson."

"But surely Monsieur le docteur Johnson could have rendered even a romance of love edifying?" protested the student. "Yet, perhaps, for purposes of escape a sister would be a more suitable companion. That is, some kinds of a sister—one like mine, for instance."

"Ah, you have a sister, Monsieur?"

"Yes, Mademoiselle—*au plus haut degré même*. I mean that I have a twin sister."

Miss Forrest was much interested; she had never met a twin, and said so. "Does your sister resemble you very much?"

"Not so much, perhaps, as one pea another in the same pod, which I believe is expected of twins," answered Raoul, laughing, "but we have changed clothes, Adrienne and I, in our younger and wilder days, and no one has been much the wiser." He smiled as at some reminiscence, and Juliana knew that he was thinking of his home. Presently, indeed, he began to speak of it a little: of his father, who was old, and old-fashioned in his ideas, not moving with the times but regretting the past—"yet a better father no one could have, Mademoiselle"; of his mother, loved by everyone who came near her, "and not least by me, as you can imagine. . . . I have not seen her for nearly two and a half years," he went on. "I had leave from Spain once, in the winter, but there was not time to get farther than Bayonne—and we live in the Orléanais! My little mother was ailing; she could not undertake the journey; my father was anxious, and stayed with her. It was a great disappointment. But Adrienne came; she travelled all by herself across two-thirds of France, in the snow; the diligence broke down too, at Dax, but it would take more than that to stop her. So we met in Bayonne, on the jour des Rois, and were very happy—for twenty-four hours."

They walked on in silence after that, Miss Forrest thinking how simple and modest he was under his lively exterior—this terrible Frenchman who had not made the slightest attempt to take advantage of her rashness—which proved that she had not been rash! So it was a great thing to him to meet his sister; but she could not help wondering a little whether there were not any other lady whom he would have liked to meet in Bayonne, on Twelfth Night.

The bridge was nearly reached again when she said suddenly, "Since I am going away to-morrow, may I ask you what I fear may sound an impertinent question?"

"Pray ask me anything, Mademoiselle. It could not be impertinent."

"I have had it in my mind for some time," confessed Juliana, looking down and playing with her reticule. "And now, the sight of old Monsieur de

Sainte-Suzanne has revived it. How is it, Monsieur des Sablières, that you, a gentleman of a family no doubt as old as his, find yourself. . . ."

"Find myself an officer of the Emperor's?" completed Raoul as she hesitated. "Mademoiselle, if when you say 'find yourself,' you think that it was due to an accident, or to necessity, I must tell you that it was not Fate but my own choice which has made me serve the greatest soldier that even France has produced. And I am not singular in that. He has many better-known names than mine on his rosters."

"But when the choice has made you—though surely without your recognizing it or willing it—the enemy of your own class, your own traditions, your own King?"

Raoul looked intently at her. It was a strange coincidence to be taken to task for this delinquency two days running. Yet it was flattering that this young English lady should be sufficiently interested in him to demand an explanation when the action evidently caused her some embarrassment.

He tried to explain his position. They were at the bridge again by the time he had finished.

"France is young, Mademoiselle," he urged in conclusion—"always young, although she is old! There is sap in her veins, even springing up. And it comes up, up from the root. My family is not a newcomer—not a graft on that tree; the new sap runs through it also. Now Monsieur de Sainte-Suzanne, though I respect him deeply for what he has suffered, I cannot but think of him and his fellows as dead boughs—dropped off. The Bourbons too—a withered branch; France does not need them any more. It is sad. I regret it—though less than my parents regret it, yet more than my sons will regret it when their time comes. *Tout tombe, tout pousse à jamais; c'est la loi de la forêt.*"

"Yes," said the girl thoughtfully. "I understand a little better. You forgive the question, I hope . . . And now, I must go on my way."

She held out her hand. Raoul des Sablières kissed it. "You have been, in everything, too good, Mademoiselle. I shall, I promise you, read every word of *Rasselas* with the care it deserves. I wish you an agreeable journey to-morrow."

"Mr. Rowl"

"The best I could wish you, Monsieur des Sablières," said Juliana, looking at him with great kindness, "is that on my return I should find you gone on a journey across the Channel! But I suppose there is small chance of that?"

Raoul shook his head with a smile. "Yet there are consolations in every lot. I shall be able to restore your book to you."

He assisted her over the stile, and watched her progress up the sloping meadow path, where he might not accompany her. When the cherry-colour and ermine had vanished over the brow he returned to the bridge and started to take his rod to pieces. But he had hardly got the first joints apart when he heard a faint scream from the direction of the meadow. Raoul did not wait for its repetition, but, dropping his rod, vaulted over the stile and ran up the path like a hare.

The cry came again as he ran, and joined to it his own name. "Je viens! je viens!" he called out, and burst into the thicket to find a rough-looking man struggling with Miss Juliana Forrest for the possession of her reticule.

"Fortune Favours the———"

"Your ignorance was merely accidental, which, being neither your crime nor your folly, could afford them no reason to applaud themselves; and the knowledge which they had . . . they might as effectually have shown by warning as betraying you."–Rasselas, chap. ix.

All this while Sir Francis Mulholland was returning towards his mansion and his betrothed in no sunny frame of mind. And he undoubtedly had a grievance, for Juliana, on this, the last afternoon of her stay, had absurdly insisted on going yet again to Northover to take a final and solitary farewell of her dear Laetitia. After yesterday's scene, and the ominous words with which it had concluded, the lover thought it better to affect complaisance. He obtained the privilege of at least escorting his lady to Mr. Bentley's door, though he was not allowed to enter, nor to wait, nor to call for her, being given to understand that the exact moment of her return was uncertain, and that Mr. Bentley and Laetitia would perhaps walk back with her. He could occupy himself, he was told, by going on to Stoneleigh to see the horse for sale there, as he had several times said he was anxious to do.

Not too enthusiastically, Sir Francis had agreed to this, and was even now returning from a long interview with the quadruped in question. His shortest way home from Stoneleigh lay by the turnpike road, and by the turnpike alone he would have proceeded thither, had he not fallen in at the crossroads with Mr. Ramage riding, or at least sitting on his old flea-bitten cob taking his usual afternoon's airing. And Mr. Ramage had implored him to accompany him a little on his homeward path, which, though it lay at an angle to the coach road, would not take Sir Francis very much out of his way if the latter continued by the short cut over Fawley Bridge. It appeared that Mr. Ramage had something about which he wished to consult him.

So Sir Francis consented, and all the way down the lane Mr. Ramage confided to him his suspicions that Morris the tallow chandler's prisoner had a habit of leaving his lodgings at six o'clock in the morning (which was strictly against regulations), and his own conjectures as to why he so left them . . . It could not be to find mushrooms in March. "Tell Bannister about it, then," counselled Sir Francis, rather bored. "That is what he is here for, to keep an eye on the prisoners." Mr. Ramage retorted that he greatly feared one, at least, of Mr. Bannister's eyes was a blind eye; but that he himself was certainly going to do his duty and warn him about the suspected activities of Zachary Miller, whom this very afternoon the speaker had seen with his own unobscured vision, sitting in his pedlar's cart talking to two of the French prisoners near Four Oaks Farm. Why?

But Sir Francis Mulholland, beginning to regret his yesterday's interview with this zealous gentleman, concealed a yawn and, having come to a convenient point, bade the suspect-hunter farewell, and resumed his solitary course and his ruminations about Juliana.

In his own fashion he loved her, and he prized her even more than he loved. And the more valuable an object the more acute is one's apprehension of loss. He was inconsistent, no doubt, in his violent and at times all-embracing jealousy, for he had far too good an opinion of Sir Francis

Mulholland to imagine that his destined wife could prefer another to him—least of all this foreign Other whom he had made his latest subject of torment. Lord Fulgrave's daughter was not in the least likely to fall in love with a penniless if good-looking French prisoner. But it enraged him that she should even allow the Frenchman to talk to her, while to have the audacity to confess that she found pleasure in his conversation, and to refuse to abandon the acquaintanceship . . . ! Acquaintanceship, indeed! It was more than that! What of those damned theatricals last month, with that cursed foreigner in a petticoat and shawl, sheltered by Juliana, the wood-cutter's daughter, in her cottage, and then turning out to be a man after all . . . some ridiculous romantic farrago it was, everybody with a name ending in o or a; its only merit that at least the petticoated young man was not the titular hero, and did not make love to Juliana, a proceeding which was very stiffly gone through by that nincompoop Elwell, of whom not even Sir Francis could be jealous. . . . And that ball at Wanfield Assembly Rooms in January, shortly after their betrothal, at which, for the first and only time, des Sablières had appeared in his dashing hussar's uniform, confound him, and had danced twice with Juliana, confound him still more—because it was useless to deny that the silver-grey and scarlet set off his looks and figure to great advantage, and one knew what women were about regimentals, and Sir Francis had overheard plenty of appreciative comments that night from some of the ladies . . . if not from Juliana.

Damn it all, was there no way of getting rid of that hussar fellow while Juliana was away? His attempt to put a spoke in his wheel yesterday evening had been worse than a failure. If only he could use a little quiet influence to get him transferred to one of the other parole towns! But that, preëminently the wisest course, was also preëminently the most difficult, because des Sablières never misconducted himself, and Bannister, the agent, had a strong regard for him and would never lend himself to intrigue against a well-behaved member of his not always amenable flock.

But, though as yet he knew it not, Sir Francis was under the guidance that afternoon of some tutelary spirit. By sending Mr. Ramage across his path this dæmon (good or bad) had withdrawn him from the highroad, and forced him to take the route by Fawley Bridge and the short cut up the meadow to Fawley Copse. Not content with guiding his steps, it had also timed them to the best advantage. Yet even when Sir Francis saw a partially disjointed fishing rod lying by the parapet of the bridge he was not aware of this; he merely wondered who could have left it there.

When he was half-way up the sloping path, however, he saw a man coming out of the copse. As there was a right of way through it the sight did not surprise him. But in another moment his pulses gave a leap. Surely that was des Sablières himself who was coming so unconcernedly towards him! It was, it was—Bannister's model prisoner, out of bounds at last! What luck . . . what unbelievable good luck!

Des Sablières' head was bent, for he was twisting a handkerchief round the knuckles of one hand, and so he did not at first see who was approaching him. But when he raised his head and did see, it was obvious, to Sir Francis's gratification, that he was by no means pleased.

"Good afternoon, Monsieur des Sablières," said the Englishman, grimly polite. "So your fishing licence has been extended to cover Fawley Copse! I hope you had good sport there?"

The offender met his gaze quite boldly. He did not look at all ashamed of himself, but rather hot and untidy, and his neckcloth was disarranged.

"I know that I am, strictly speaking, out of bounds," he replied coldly. "But I assure you that I had an excellent reason for it." And, stepping off the path, he passed his enemy.

But he was not going to get away so easily! Sir Francis turned round after him. "Then I should like to hear that reason, Sir."

The Frenchman slackened his pace, but did not stop entirely. "It does not concern you, Sir Francis Mulholland," he observed over his shoulder.

"Ah, but I think you will find that it does! You forget, perhaps, that I am a justice of the peace, Monsieur des Sablières!"

This time des Sablières did stop, and faced round. "No, I know it quite well," he retorted. "But that fact does not justify you in questioning me. If I have to give an explanation I shall give it to the proper person. I wish you good afternoon." And, turning on his heel, he resumed his progress down the slope.

Sir Francis watched him go. "Yes, you will be asked for that explanation, my fine fellow," he said under his breath, exhilarated by his good fortune. "And, by George I think you will find it devilish hard to give!"

Turning on that very quickly, as one struck by a brilliant idea, he ran up the rest of the slope, plunged into the copse, and searched it from end to end. But there was no one there, least of all Mr. Zachary Miller, whom he was hoping that some further grace of the gods would enable him to find. Nevertheless, some half hour later Sir Francis was back in Wanfield and entering the private residence of Mr. James Bannister, the agent responsible to the Transport Office for the prisoners of war on parole in that place.

Raoul meanwhile had gone straight home with his fishing rod to his little room off the High Street, under the roof of Miss Eliza Hitchings, that acidulous-looking female, of whose cold eye he mendaciously declared himself to be in perpetual terror. This apartment was not a palace, and he was without the means to render it more attractive (for which he consoled himself by the reflection that he would not have dared to do so if he could). He had at present nothing but the weekly sum allowed by the British Government to officer prisoners of war, because, on its recent augmentation from ten and six-pence to fourteen shillings, he had promptly forbidden his family to send him any more remittances, as he was now living in affluence—which was far from being true. But though, when in straits, he would sooner cut down the expenses of his commissariat than endanger the irreproachableness of his outward appearance, and would tell Miss Hitchings that such and such a purchase need not be made that week, only hoping that the good lady would not guess the reason, Miss Hitchings of the unsmiling countenance had much better ground, on her side, for being sure that "Mr. Rowl" had not the faintest suspicion of how many loaves of bread and pats of butter he was never charged for at all.

It was not often that "Mr. Rowl," being popular, returned home before he was obliged to do so by his parole regulations, which, in the present month of March, demanded that he should be indoors by seven, as the Comte de Saint-Suzanne had reminded him yesterday. From May till June he was looking forward to being free till nine; the three winter months, however, had seen him driven to his fireside by five o'clock. So Miss Hitchings was a little surprised when she heard him come in now, the clock marking only a quarter past five; and by the fact that he did not run upstairs as he usually did.

Raoul was in fact rather worried as he mounted that narrow staircase and came into his ugly little room. What devil of ill luck had sent Sir Francis up the path just at that moment? As far as Raoul himself was concerned, it would have been less damning if Mulholland had come on him a few minutes earlier by the bridge, conversing though he were with Miss Forrest; the Englishman might have disliked that, but he could not urge it against him as a crime. On his way home the prisoner had in fact debated whether he should not do well to go and inform Mr. Bannister that he had for a short space gone out of bounds, and why. Bannister would believe and absolve him, he felt sure. For the matter of that, Sir Francis must have absolved him, too, if he had told him the reason. Perhaps he had been foolish to give him no inkling of it, since indeed Mulholland, far from blaming him, ought in the circumstances to be deeply grateful. Raoul did not, however, feel sure that he would, exactly, for he had an intuition that Miss Forrest had somehow manipulated circumstances—in other words, her betrothed—in order to return alone by Fawley Bridge. At the moment, with no time to spend on weighing pros and cons, it had seemed natural to cover Miss Forrest's traces. Sir Francis would probably hear soon enough what had happened in Fawley Copse.

He might even have come on the tramp or poacher or whatever he was, though to be sure the latter had vanished very quickly indeed after he had picked himself up. . . . Proceedings, it was true, had opened with a somewhat scrambling *corps à corps* encounter after Raoul had torn him away from Miss Forrest, but the end had been more in style, though he himself had broken his knuckles over it. . . . Miss Forrest had been shaking so much when it was over that he had been obliged to support her to a tree stump, on which she had sunk down, while he knelt beside her and fanned her—it was the only treatment he could think of—with his hat. And really she had looked almost more beautiful when she was as white as a lily. But she was never near swooning, he thought, except, perhaps, just for the first second or two after he had disposed of her assailant—that first second or two in which she had clung to him . . . moments which, neither at the time nor in retrospect, were at all disagreeable ones. . . .

In the end he had escorted her to the boundary of the Mulholland domain. And just before they parted she had said, in a voice full of emotion, "Will you . . . would you care to . . . keep my little *Rasselas* for your own . . . in memory of my undying gratitude?"

So Miss Forrest's book was now his, a memento of an episode which would have been wholly pleasurable to contemplate if it had not been for the encounter with Mulholland—on top of yesterday's, too! But Raoul now put Sir Francis resolutely from his mind, and, ensconcing himself in his one fairly comfortable chair, took out the book in question from his pocket. By the absence of any sounds from the room above, where lodged another prisoner, a naval lieutenant named Lamotte, he surmised that the latter was not home yet. He had invited him to partake that evening of a hare recently presented to him, which, as its arrival almost coincided (of course, unknown to the British donor) with the second anniversary of the birth of the little King of Rome, would be treated as a commemorative feast on the eve of the event, combining in one both dinner and supper. It was a pity that Miss Hitchings had insisted on cooking the animal to-night, on the ground that it would keep no longer, for the birthday was not till to-morrow.

As every well-conducted reader should, Raoul began at the first page; and the stately and beautifully rounded exordium impressed him as much as Miss Forrest herself could have desired. "Ye who listen with credulity to the whispers of fancy, and pursue with eagerness the phantoms of hope; who expect that age will perform the promises of youth, and that the deficiencies of the present day will be supplied by the morrow, attend to the history of *Rasselas*, Prince of Abyssinia." And soon he was reading of the delights of that blissful place of captivity, the Happy Valley, with its remarkable floral and zoological riches, and the even more remarkable juxtaposition of the latter, since "on one part were flocks and herds feeding in the pastures, on another all the beasts of the chase frisking on the lawns; the sprightly kid was bounding on the rocks, the subtle monkey frolicking in the trees, and the solemn elephant reposing in the shade." A momentary reflection that the Happy Valley must have been rather like the Jardin des Plantes in Paris, and the student, struck with the justice of these last epithets, repeated them several times to himself. Then he went on to read of the human inhabitants, who "wandered in gardens of fragrance and slept in the fortresses of security," and by six o'clock had reached the passage in the fourth chapter where *Rasselas*, carried away by a day-dream of that outer world which he has never seen, actually pursues the imaginary robber of an imaginary damsel whom he pictures as appealing to him for help, until he is brought up short by the foot of the impassable mountain hemming in the Happy Valley.

"Here he recollected himself, and smiled at his own impetuosity. Then, raising his eyes to the mountain, 'This,' said he, 'is the fatal obstacle that hinders at once the enjoyment of pleasure and the exercise of virtue. How long is it that my hopes and wishes have flown beyond this boundary of my life which yet I have never attempted to surmount!'?"

The incident, in more ways than one, had sufficiently close a resemblance with what had happened to Miss Forrest and himself in Fawley Copse that afternoon to make "Mr. Rowl" lay down the book and smile. But the smile had a spice of melancholy. In his situation, just as much as in that of Dr. Johnson's hero, was "a fatal obstacle that hinders at once the enjoyment of pleasure and the exercise of virtue"—his parole. And it was more insurmountable than *Rasselas*'s mountain. No doubt he was fortunate that his military rank entitled him to the indulgence, but, nevertheless, comparative ease and pleasant society had to be paid for—in the same coin in which *Rasselas* paid. Wanfield was rather like the Happy Valley!

Upon this reflection the door opened, and Miss Hitching's voice observed in a somewhat minatory manner: "Mr. Bannister to see you, Sir!"

The reader jumped up, as there entered the retired chemist who was his very good friend and custodian.

"I was thinking about you, Sir!" exclaimed Raoul. "If I had not been sure that you would have left your office, I think I should have paid you a visit this afternoon."

"Well, you see that I am paying you one," returned Mr. James Bannister rather heavily, as he took a chair. "And I wish I had not to; but I did it rather than send for you. I expect you know what I have come about. You are the last man I thought I should have trouble with on such a score."

Raoul stood looking down on him with a slightly heightened colour. "You wish to know why I was out of bounds this afternoon? On my honour, Mr. Bannister, I could not avoid it. I had to go—as you will acknowledge when you hear of the circumstances. But first, who told you of my crime?"

"You can guess, I should think. Sir Francis Mulholland."

Raoul made a face. "He has not lost much time. Well, I suppose he was able to tell himself that he was doing his duty. But as it was on account of a person in whom he is deeply interested that I had to transgress, his zeal is a little misplaced."

"What do you mean—what person? Sir Francis said nothing——" began the Agent.

"No, no, I told him nothing. The sheep reserves the tale of its misdemeanours for its own shepherd," announced Raoul cheerfully, bestowing a smile on the gentleman in question, and sitting down on the arm of a chair. "*Voyons donc. . . .*" And he proceeded with his tale—a strictly truthful narrative in all but its suppression of Miss Forrest's previous whereabouts.

By the end of this recital Raoul's shepherd looked decidedly relieved. "No, my dear fellow, you certainly could not have done anything else. But why the deuce didn't you tell Sir Francis about Miss Forrest?"

"Because he had no right to demand an explanation of me," replied the champion. "I said that to the right person I would give one, if necessary."

"But you see, you hothead, if you had done it there and then he would not have lodged information against you for breaking your parole!"

"Breaking my parole!" exclaimed the young soldier, indignantly. "How dare he suggest. . . . But I suppose I was breaking it—in a sense!" he finished in some dismay.

Mr. Bannister laughed. "Technically, perhaps, but certainly not in the spirit, if that is all you went out of bounds for."

"I hope you do not think it was for any other reason, Mr. Bannister?" rejoined Raoul rather gravely.

"No, no, I take your word for it without reservation," said the Agent. "But Sir Francis, who does not know you as well as I do——"

"Yes?" enquired Raoul, with an odd light in his eyes.

"Sir Francis suspects—now pray don't run away with the idea that I suspect it—he imagines that you had gone into Fawley Copse to meet some escape agent or other."

Raoul gave a short, angry laugh. "He has an imagination, that one! Certainly I had a meeting with a man in the copse . . . and I think he will remember the fact, but not pleasantly. I myself also." He showed his grazed knuckles.

Mr. Bannister got up. "Well, I am only too glad that you can give me such a satisfactory explanation. And as Sir Francis must by now have received from the lady concerned her account of your chivalrous conduct, I hope we may think of the incident as closed. But till he formally withdraws his charge—which, as he is a magistrate, I am bound to take rather seriously—you would make things easier for me if you would engage not to leave your rooms till I tell you that you are free to do so."

"But with pleasure," agreed Raoul, "I will constitute myself the prisoner of Miss Hitchings."

"I will see Sir Francis and get the matter cleared up with him—to-morrow morning if possible. You have taken a weight off my mind, des Sablières. I have so much to try me, one way and another, between your countrymen and my own. But I have always felt that you were one of those whom I could fully trust," concluded Mr. Bannister.

"Thank you," said his charge. "I shall try always to deserve that opinion." They shook hands, and the Agent departed, leaving the young Frenchman to reflect with indignation upon Sir Francis's action. He saw his game quite well: he had seized on this opportunity to do him an injury because—as yesterday's collision had made abundantly plain—he resented his presence in Wanfield society. However, when he knew the truth he would find this weapon broken in his hand. Moreover, as Raoul's own conscience was clear, and the Agent did not—could not—regard the matter seriously, there was nothing that need cloud his and Lieutenant Lamotte's enjoyment of the commemorative hare, upon which they very cheerfully supped, nor of their game of cards afterwards, in which Raoul lost with equal cheerfulness (since to-morrow was pay-day) the whole of his remaining weekly income, namely, one shilling sterling. And his mimicry of an imaginary scene in which he, Raoul, went on his knees to Sir Francis Mulholland to beseech him to sing "Rule, Britannia," and Sir Francis condescendingly sang it—out of tune—while the Francophobe Mr. Ramage played the accompaniment at sight, reduced Lieutenant Lamotte to such helpless laughter, and Miss Hitching's old spinet to such a condition of discord, that Miss Hitchings herself appeared, to deprecate the holding up of that patriotic air to ridicule lest the neighbours should hear; and had to be calmed by Raoul's assuring her, with his hand on his heart, that no disrespect was intended to the majestic lady who rose from out the azure main, only to those who murdered so fine a song. But he did not tell Lieutenant Lamotte why he had selected Sir Francis Mulholland as the murderer.

"Broke-Parole!"

"The suddenness of the event struck me with surprise, and I was at first rather stupefied than agitated."–Rasselas, chap. xxxviii.

"Shall you be going out this morning, Mr. Rowl?" enquired Miss Hitchings of her lodger not long after breakfast next morning.

"Yes, I expect so," responded Raoul rather vaguely, not raising his head from *Rasselas*.

"At what time, then, Sir, if I may make so bold?"

"What time?" repeated the young man. "Oh, about—no, truly, I cannot tell you just when. Does that inconvenience you, Miss Hitchings?"

"Not in the least, Sir," responded Miss Hitchings, in a tone signifying exactly the opposite. "I suppose that one more day for the carpet to lie there, so full of dust as it is, don't signify."

"*Mon Dieu*, were you going to take the carpet up?" cried Raoul, with every symptom of alarm. "Is it one of those days when everything is *dessus dessous*—one of the days of tornado? I am desolated, chère Miss Hitchings, for truly I cannot tell you when I shall be able to——I mean," he pulled himself up firmly, "when it will suit me to go out."

For he was not going to confess to her that he was a prisoner in the house, though he had mentioned the fact to Lamotte over the hare the night before, adding that his confinement need not be taken very seriously.

Indeed, he hoped that it would not be long now before Mr. Bannister sent word that he was at liberty. Time to read some more *Rasselas*—though, as the book was now his own, he had plenty of leisure for that pursuit. And to think that Miss Forrest had not shown him her favourite passages yesterday, after all! They had been too much immersed in conversation, he and she. As he returned to his reading he recalled the look in her beautiful eyes up in the copse—that thrilling look of deep, deep gratitude and admiration. . . .

Ciel! it was already half-past eleven, and still no word from Mr. Bannister! Perhaps he had not been able to get hold of Sir Francis. Raoul rose, and sat himself down at the table with pen and paper and began a letter home—one of those letters whose composition never failed to irritate him a little, for one reason because it was so difficult to find anything new to say, for another, because no letter was private. To-day he was writing to his sister.

"*Ma chère Adrienne: As-tu pensé à moi hier, car j'ai un peu parlé de toi? Ah, si tu étais ici, je m'ennuierais moins; nous attrapperions des truites ensemble, comme autrefois. Nous lirions aussi le chef-d'œuvre du célèbre docteur Johnson, l'Histoire de Rasselas, que je suis en train d'étudier pour perfectionner mon anglais. . . . Mais un jour, sans doute, nous le lirons ensemble, car on m'a fait cadeau du volume."*

He broke off to mend his pen, beginning softly to whistle, "Since First I Saw Your Face," while he did so. And before he had finished he was singing the second verse under his breath:

"'The sun, whose beams most glorious are,
  Rejecteth no beholder;
And your sweet beauty, past compare,
  Made my poor eyes the bolder.
When beauty moves, and wit delights,
  And signs of kindness bind me,
There, oh, there, where'er I go,
  I'll leave my heart behind me.'

"*Ah non! je suis trop prudent pour celà!*" he observed aloud, shaking his head. . . . Yet if he were not poor, and an enemy, and a foreigner, and a prisoner . . . and Miss Forrest were not rich, and English, and affianced to "le Roi Soleil" . . . but in the existing circumstances (though he admired her and was grateful to her for her friendly kindness) there was no use in contemplating impossibilities. He returned to his letter.

"Pour le reste, rien de neuf. Je suis, comme toujours, en bonne santé, mais aussi, comme toujours, fixé ici, aussi immuable qu'une épée rouillée dans son fourreau, ou une statue dans sa niche, figé comme du lait caillé—"

"Mr. Bannister has sent word to say would you kindly go round to his office at once, Mr. Rowl," came the voice of Miss Hitchings.

"With all my heart," exclaimed Raoul, springing up. "In fact, I fly." He hastily put aside his unfinished letter, snatched up his hat, cried, at sight of the bandanna tied round his landlady's head and the broom in her hand: "Now you can do your worst in here, Britannia!" and went down the stairs two at a time.

Mr. Bannister's office was full in the High Street, and a very short distance away. Yet by the time that Raoul reached its respectable columned entrance he had already wondered why the Agent had required him to come there instead of merely sending him a line of release. Perhaps he had been too busy to put pen to paper.

Raoul knew the office well, since he had to go there to report himself twice a week, and to draw his allowance on Saturdays. He came briskly round the bookcase which stood at right angles to the door, making a kind of screen, and said, "Here I am, Sir." Then he perceived that the Agent was not alone, and that the tall man in riding costume, standing with his back to the room, looking out of the window, was Sir Francis Mulholland. He stopped, displeased.

Mr. Bannister himself was standing by his writing table, not far from the same window, turning over some papers in a perfunctory fashion. He was looking so grave that Raoul felt suddenly apprehensive. Had anything gone wrong!—but nothing could!

"I have sent for you, Monsieur des Sablières," said the Agent, and his voice was not the voice of yesterday, "so that you can in person repeat your explanation of your action in going out of bounds yesterday afternoon."

Raoul stared at him. "Why should I repeat it, Sir? I have nothing to add or to take away from what I have already told you."

"Because I should like Sir Francis Mulholland," said Mr. Bannister, glancing for a second at the back of that gentleman, who had not turned round, "to have an opportunity of hearing it from your own lips. It is only fair."

"Fair!" repeated Raoul rather stormily. "Fair to whom? And what has Sir Francis to do with the matter—beyond having denounced me to you? I should have thought that even a magistrate might have been satisfied with that!"

"Monsieur des Sablières, I beg of you——"

"Oh, I am not saying that he exceeded his duty. But he certainly exceeds his rights in being here in the capacity of a judge—and I refuse to recognize him as one."

At that Sir Francis turned round and faced the young Frenchman.

"I am not here, Sir, as it happens, in the capacity of a judge," he remarked coolly. "I have not the slightest desire to encroach on Mr. Bannister's province. I am here, as any man might be, in the rôle of a witness."

"Unnecessary, Sir," said Raoul sharply. "Mr. Bannister knows that I instantly acknowledged having been for a short space out of bounds yesterday."

"I did not mean as a witness to that physical fact," replied Sir Francis imperturbably. "It would certainly be of small use your denying that!"

"Sir Francis means, I am sorry to say," interposed Bannister, looking more and more distressed, "as a witness to the truth of your explanation of the fact."

"No, no, Bannister!" Sir Francis gave a short laugh. "As a witness to its falsehood, if you please!" And as Raoul stared at him, momentarily bereft of speech, he addressed him directly. "Now listen, des Sablières, and correct me if I misrepresent what you told Mr. Bannister yesterday. You asserted that at half-past four Miss Forrest passed you at Fawley Bridge, where you were fishing, that immediately afterwards you heard a scream, rushed up the field to the copse, found that a vagabond was attacking her, and beat him off. Is not that what you asserted to Mr. Bannister?"

"It is."

"Then let me tell you, as I have already told your Agent, that your 'explanation' is a tissue of lies. No vagabond or any one else could have attacked Miss Forrest in Fawley Copse at half-past four o'clock, just before I met you, because Miss Forrest was not there to be attacked."

"Not there—Miss Forrest not there!" stammered Raoul, thinking he had not heard aright.

"Miss Forrest returned from Northover yesterday afternoon by the turnpike road, reaching Mulholland Park at four o'clock. She did not go out again. It is therefore impossible that she should have passed you at the bridge or been in Fawley Copse, and the using of her name in this unwarrantable fashion to cloak whatever you were doing there is very far, let me assure you, from being of assistance to you!"

For the first moment or two Raoul was so staggered that he merely said slowly:

"Who told you that lie—that Miss Forrest returned by the highroad?"

"I had the information from Miss Forrest herself."

Raoul's head whirled. "And she . . . when you mentioned the tramp she——"

"Why should I mention the tramp to her? You forget, you told me nothing about one, when I met you coming out of the copse—had not yet invented the story, perhaps."

"Invented!" cried Raoul hotly. "It is as true as that I am standing here! Mr. Bannister can witness——"

"Mr. Bannister can witness that that was the story you told him yesterday, certainly. But what does that prove?" enquired Sir Francis evenly, and sat down in a chair by the window.

"You see, des Sablières," said the Agent, with a wrinkled brow, "there is only one person who can prove that you are speaking the truth—though I freely admit that yesterday I thought you were. I mean, of course, Miss Forrest herself. And you hear what she says?"

"I do not for one moment believe that Miss Forrest—" began Raoul, and then stopped. For in a flash he saw that it was perfectly possible she had told that taradiddle about her return by the highroad in order to shield herself from Sir Francis's jealous expostulations . . . only, surely, she had told it without dreaming of the position she had got him into! And by this time she was gone from Wanfield and would never know it!

"Come," went on Bannister persuasively, "you cannot stick to that story against the lady's own testimony, can you? I am not at all anxious to go to extremities with you, des Sablières—won't you tell me what you were really doing up in the copse?"

"You had better ask the tramp—if he can be found," answered Raoul defiantly.

"Exactly—if he can be found," observed Sir Francis, crossing his legs. "I have my own ideas about that tramp. We will come to that presently. For the moment, as Miss Forrest's future husband, I ask you to withdraw your use of her name."

"I will do that only at Miss Forrest's own request," said Raoul, looking him in the face.

"A safe offer," commented Sir Francis. "Miss Forrest, as I expect you are well aware, left Wanfield this morning, and does not even know that you have taken the unwarrantable liberty of using it. And could you not," he continued with the most galling air of distaste, "have cloaked your proceedings by somebody else's—some village wench's, if you must be a squire of dames?"

Raoul's eyes flashed. Mr. Bannister interposed, clutching at this suggestion. "Is it not possible that Monsieur des Sablières was genuinely mistaken in the lady's identity?" He turned to Raoul. "Might it not have been some other lady, resembling Miss Forrest, whom you defended in the copse?"

"No," said Raoul stubbornly, "it was Miss Forrest herself and nobody else." But he could have met these attacks so much better if he had not had to think hard all the time, to try to puzzle out while he spoke what Miss Forrest really had said—what she would wish him to say. Had she really kept silence about the tramp?

"Do not press Monsieur des Sablières unduly, Mr. Bannister," said Sir Francis with suavity. "Where there was no lady, and no tramp—at least in the form of a tramp—it is putting too great a strain on his powers of invention to call on him to provide another female in distress!"

The taunt went unheeded. Raoul, his eyes following the pattern of Mr. Bannister's worn carpet, was thinking furiously, while up from the street below floated scraps of an animated conversation between two of his compatriots. The subject seemed to be the price of meat. . . . Was Sir Francis speaking in good faith, or was it conceivable that he was deliberately lying? In either case, if he, Raoul, chose to reveal the fact that Miss Forrest, shortly before the episode, had been neither walking along the turnpike, nor safely ensconced at Mulholland Park, but in his company by the stream, Sir Francis would not have a leg to stand on. And though, in Miss Forrest's absence, that fact would no doubt be disputed, he had it in his power to prove it beyond question. It was lucky, after all, that Sainte-Suzanne had seen them.

He lifted his head. "What would you say, Mr. Bannister," he asked crisply, "if I told you that I had a witness, an unimpeachable witness, to the identity of the lady, and to her whereabouts just before the occurrence?"

"I should rather want to see the witness before I expressed an opinion," replied Mr. Bannister with some acerbity. He at least was plainly not enjoying himself. And Sir Francis Mulholland had suddenly turned in his chair and was gazing out of the window as at something of great interest in the street. The movement attracted Raoul's notice, and he kept his eyes fixed on him, for he felt that if he could only have seen his face at that moment he might have got some light on the game he was playing. Was he, or was he not, alarmed at the prospect of adverse testimony? When, after a minute or so, the Englishman turned round again, his face, unfortunately, betrayed nothing. But his tongue was biting.

"You really propose, Monsieur des Sablières, to call a witness to prove that the lady to whom I have the honour to be engaged is telling a lie? I thought you claimed to be a gentleman!"

"If I call him," retorted Raoul, throwing back his head, "it will certainly not be against Miss Forrest."

"You mean, I presume, that it will be against me, then. It is the same thing. I speak for Miss Forrest, and Mr. Bannister is satisfied that I do. Produce your witness!"

"The whole question is," said Raoul in a low voice, eyeing him, "whether you do speak for Miss Forrest."

Sir Francis surveyed him for a moment, and then shrugged his shoulders. "Then we will leave Miss Forrest out of the matter into which she has so improperly been dragged. Who is this witness whose word Mr. Bannister will take before *mine?*"

Raoul studied the sunlit carpet once more. If he called the Comte de Sainte-Suzanne the whole affair would come into the light of day, would have to be elucidated somehow. It would clear him, certainly. But what would be the result? Perhaps merely to show that though Miss Forrest had seen fit to hide her meeting with him by means of a fib—and even, just possibly, had done so to shield him from the effects of her betrothed's jealousy—he, of all men, had been unchivalrous enough to drag the cloak off her shoulders. And even if the testimony proved it was Sir Francis who was doing the lying, yet, in the *esclandre* that must ensue, all Wanfield would know that he and Miss Forrest had been seen, not just conversing openly on the bridge, but some way down the stream, conveniently remote from the public gaze and by no means on the route to Mulholland Park. For though Raoul felt, as he had felt at the time, that the Comte was too well-bred and too discreet to blazon abroad his knowledge of that fact, once his testimony to it was demanded, it would not be much of a step to the discovery of an arranged meeting, of manœuvres on Miss Forrest's part. . . . He could not bring that upon her. No, his feet were entangled every way.

"Well, who is it?" demanded Mr. Bannister with some impatience.

"On reflection, I shall not call him," said Raoul slowly.

"You are well advised," observed Sir Francis. "English law—you may not know it—does not smile on perjury. And now, having disposed of your fictitious companion in Fawley Copse; let us—let Mr. Bannister, that is—hear what you were doing there with your real one."

Raoul gave an impatient movement and turned his back on him. "I have nothing more to say. Mr. Bannister, cannot this farce come to an end? Even though I am not believed when I tell the truth, I am not going to invent falsehoods to stand a better chance of pleasing Sir Francis Mulholland."

"But, des Sablières," said his shepherd very gravely, "on Sir Francis's showing, you have already invented them! This is not a farce; I have every right to ask you for the real explanation of your presence in the copse, out of bounds."

"I have already given it to you!" said Raoul with suppressed passion.

"As Monsieur des Sablières suggests, this farce *had* better end," put in Sir Francis. "I will give you the real explanation, Mr. Bannister. He was there to meet an escape agent, and I can tell you who the agent was—Zachary Miller, the pedlar."

Raoul laughed. There seemed nothing else to do. "Why not suggest that I went to meet the Emperor himself in Fawley Copse?"

"That is only a suspicion of yours, Sir Francis," said the Agent, shaking his head. "You cannot prove it, I think."

"Not yet perhaps. But I may be able to. Zachary Miller was seen near Four Oaks Farm at three o'clock yesterday afternoon, talking to two Frenchmen, and he can give no satisfactory account of his movements between that time and half-past four. And, as you know, he rests under very strong suspicion of being concerned in the escape traffic in these parts, though nothing can be proved against him."

"Two points that cannot be proved," observed Raoul mockingly. "You are not altogether lucky, Sir Francis, in your efforts to get rid of me!" He was becoming reckless.

"What do you mean, Sir?" demanded his enemy, turning on him angrily. "Do you suggest that I am allowing personal motives to weigh with me in this matter?"

"I don't suggest, I know!" retorted Raoul. "The only question in my mind is to what lengths you have gone in that direction. Of that your own conscience is the best judge."

"Will you allow me to speak to Monsieur des Sablières alone?" asked Mr. Bannister, intervening rather hastily at this point. "I think it would be better."

Sir Francis immediately took up his hat and riding whip. "I will withdraw altogether, my dear Bannister. My unpleasant task is done. I have shown you that Monsieur des Sablières' alleged reason for going out of bounds is a pure invention, and a clumsy one at that, besides not reflecting much credit upon him, and in my capacity as a justice of the peace I warn you of what I am convinced was his real reason. However, as I understand it, the mere fact of broken parole is in itself sufficient. . . . I have every confidence that you will do your duty. Good morning." And the door shut behind him.

"Well, are you going to do your duty, as Sir Francis orders you?" enquired Raoul after a moment. But Mr. Bannister was walking up and down with bent head and did not answer. "Why did you say you wanted to see me alone?" went on the young man. "I have nothing different to tell you, nor, since Sir Francis has poisoned your mind against me, would you believe it if I had."

Mr. Bannister stopped his pacing. "My mind is not poisoned against you, des Sablières. I am more grieved and disappointed over this affair than I can say. But how can I take your word against Sir Francis Mulholland's? If you had only been frank with me——"

"I have been—to very little purpose!"

"How can you call that being frank," asked the Agent reproachfully, "to tell me an impossible and yet specious story about a lady and a tramp which the very next day is unmasked as a falsehood? If you had said straightforwardly that you had yielded to a not unnatural temptation to go out of bounds for a few moments I might have stretched a point and let you off with a fine, but the motive which requires so preposterous a tale to cover it. . . . He paused.

"Yes, I see," said Raoul bitterly. "Next time that I am in a difficulty I must remember that the one thing not to do is to tell the truth. But I suppose your kind intention is to deliver me now from the possibility of getting into any more such difficulties?"

And, though he threw out this feeler with a certain airy defiance, his heart was beating pretty rapidly.

"I cannot help myself," returned the Agent shortly. "You have broken your parole and will not tell me why. The interpretation which Sir Francis puts upon your action cannot be proved, but, since you will give me no other that satisfies me, it always remains a possibility. I should not, therefore, be worthy of the trust which I hold if I let you continue at large. In accordance with the standing orders which I have received from the Transport Office I must send you to Norman Cross depot, if they have room to receive you, which I shall ascertain without delay—if not, to Stapleton Prison or elsewhere. Meanwhile," he approached the bellrope on the wall, "I am afraid that I must send you to the lock-up here."

Raoul had turned a little pale, but at that the colour swept over his face again. "Could I not go back to my lodgings till you—till you hear from Norman Cross?" he asked. "I would give you my word, as yesterday, not to leave them."

"I cannot take your word now, I am sorry to say," replied Mr. Bannister sadly; "and as you are no longer a prisoner on parole I am unable to grant you that indulgence. I have a militia guard here; the best advice I can give you is not to cause a disturbance. You shall not stay in gaol an hour longer than is necessary; that I can promise you." But still he did not ring the bell to summon the guard.

He was giving Raoul a last chance before the net closed about him; the young man was conscious of that. He had only to mention Sainte-Suzanne's name. For a moment he hesitated, struck by the idea that he might make some kind of compromise—tell Bannister of the interview by the stream but say that he did not wish the information to go further. For it was a real grief to him to lose his shepherd's regard—and needlessly. But Bannister was too honest a man to send him to prison if he believed him innocent, yet, if he did not, the Agent would be forced to justify his action to Sir Francis at least, and the whole meeting by the stream would become public after all. If he could only be sure that Miss Forrest had not fibbed, that it was Sir Francis, incredible as it seemed, who was lying? Yet, because there was the chance that she had done so, there was nothing for it but to uphold her and take his punishment in silence. For, though Sir Francis Mulholland affected to doubt it, he did claim to be a gentleman.

"Thank you for that promise, Sir," he said, and shut his mouth rather tightly.

"And is that all you have to say?" asked Bannister, his hand on the bellrope.

"Mr. Rowl"

"That is all," said Raoul; and the Agent rang the bell.

So, a minute and a half later, Mr. Rowl went through the door of that well-known office for the last time, and presently afforded all Wanfield the spectacle of yet another French officer being marched off under arrest. The thronged High Street stared and sniggered, while from all quarters came joyfully clattering small boys crying out that epithet which he had vowed should never be applied to him—"Broke-parole! Broke-parole!" . . . And outside the post-office, for the last drop in the cup, was standing the Comte de Sainte-Suzanne, leaning on his cane. Their looks met, for Raoul flung up his head defiantly. A fleeting expression, which began as sorrow and ended as scorn, went over the old man's face. Then he turned his back on him.

Fiat Justitia, Ruat Cœlum

The Bassa was carried in chains to Constantinople, and his name was mentioned no more.—Rasselas, chap. xxiv.

Fragments of a correspondence exchanged at the end of March, 1813.

From Miss Laetitia Bentley to the Hon. Juliana Forrest

Northover, March 24

My dearest Juliana, when she pays her promised visit to Northover next month will, I feel sure, sadly miss one *agreeable presence* from our little gatherings and *one very pleasing voice* from our musical diversions, and she will be distressed at the reason for it. Captain des Sablières, sad to say, has been sent as a prisoner to the dépôt at Norman Cross in Huntingdonshire, for breaking his parole under some mysterious circumstances which Mr. Bannister will not reveal, but which are given out to be particularly discreditable. Your Laetitia cannot believe this latter charge, nor Papa either, who says, however, that since Mr. Bannister is a perfectly honest man, and was formerly very well disposed towards M. des Sablières, it is clear that the latter must have committed some breach of the parole regulations. It is said that he had all but completed his arrangements for escaping. If that should be so, how were we deceived in him! But no—I do not, will not, credit it!

. . . . Is it true that everything in London at present is à la Russe, and have you, my Juliana, observed any real élégantes wearing the hair, in evening or opera dress, "flat on the sides, and in waved curls in front, and confined in full curls at the back of the head, with an apparent stray ringlet falling on one shoulder," as I have read is the mode? Pray be sure to bring back all the fashionable intelligence of this kind. . . .

From the Hon. Juliana Forrest to
Sir Francis Mulholland, Bart.

Grosvenor Square, March 27, 1813.

My Dear Francis:

I am greatly distressed to hear that M. des Sablières has been sent to Norman Cross prison for breaking his parole, since I cannot but connect it with his coming to my rescue in Fawley Copse, as I described to you. But surely he could not have been convicted for an act so plainly one of chivalry—yet still less can I imagine his having transgressed the obligations of his parole. I am deeply uneasy about the whole matter, and implore you to relieve my anxiety.

From Sir Francis Mulholland to the Hon. Juliana Forrest

Mulholland Park, March 30, 1813.

My Dearest Juliana:

Sorry as I am to lower the high opinion in which I know you hold M. des Sablières, I must, as you urge me, tell you the truth of the matter—or at least so much of it as is known to me. It was not his having gone to your assistance in Fawley Copse (which could, in the circumstances, easily have been overlooked) that was the cause of his committal to Norman Cross, but a much more serious happening which came to light immediately after your departure. Bannister refuses to reveal the circumstances, but as far as I can gather, they must be very black: it is generally understood that the

Frenchman had all but completed the arrangements for his escape when they were discovered.

I look back, my dear Juliana, with regret to the thought that we could ever have had a difference of opinion over so unworthy an object, nor do I wish to lay stress on the fact that it is not I who am proved wrong by the sequel. You will, I am sure, be glad now that you gave me your promise that last evening here not to say a word to any one of your encounter with the tramp: as much as I myself will you wish to preserve your name from association with that of a man who has violated his word of honour.

You cannot guess how I count the days till your arrival at Northover, where, I hope, Miss Bentley will not find me too assiduous a visitor. . . .

Spring was a fact, not a promise, when Juliana came back to Wanfield, and Northover welcomed her with pear and apple blossom. As for Laetitia, she and her dearest friend might have been parted for a year instead of a month, so rapturous was her greeting. Sir Francis Mulholland's also was everything which a young lady could desire of her swain, and when he paid his first visit to Northover the day after Juliana's arrival, Laetitia thought him strangely improved in manner, and commented upon the fact to her Papa, who opined that somehow or other Miss Juliana, when last at Wanfield, had given him a fright, and that he was walking delicately in consequence.

It was true that Sir Francis had need to walk delicately, but it was more on account of his own actions than of Juliana's. He had been—he was still—playing a terribly risky game, but he had taken precautions.

When, on returning to Mulholland Park that evening after laying information against des Sablières, he heard from Juliana herself the reason of the Frenchman's rushing up to the copse, he was greatly chagrined, both by the check to his newly formed plan of getting rid of him, and by Juliana's openly displayed gratitude and admiration for his timely succour. On top of this—for it did not take much to bring out what Miss Juliana had always half intended that he should know . . . for his own good . . . came the stunning intelligence that she had previously met her rescuer, by appointment, at the bridge.

The shock convinced her betrothed that his apprehensions were far from being idle. Drastic action was absolutely necessary now. But he behaved to the transgressor with a circumspection of which he was afterwards to reap the reward. By the exercise of really praiseworthy self-control he contrived to avoid making a scene over this mortifying discovery, confining himself to pointing out the patent results of having returned home unescorted. And Juliana, worked upon by this moderation as she would never have been by reproaches, admitted to having been at least foolish, and gave her affianced without much difficulty the promise that she would not only abstain from mentioning the clandestine meeting even to Laetitia Bentley, but that the tramp episode also should be buried in deep oblivion. For she was sufficiently ashamed now of the one and shaken by the other to agree that it was not desirable to have her name coupled in Wanfield gossip with her rescuer's, since blame might thereby accrue to Sir Francis, who certainly could not with justice be accused of having willingly let her return home unescorted.

After this interview Sir Francis spent a good part of the night weighing the risks of the all-too-tempting course open to him; and, with this revelation of Juliana's self-will before him, decided to take them. It was quite useless for her to declare (as she had done) that the Frenchman had not attempted in the slightest degree to make love to her, or that he was not jointly responsible, at the very least, for the meeting; Sir Francis simply did not believe her. Yet without Juliana's early departure next morning he could hardly have carried through his unscrupulous design. His one really uncomfortable moment in Bannister's office was when his victim threatened to call a witness of Miss Forrest's whereabouts; but, since he did not do it, and Juliana had said nothing of any one having seen them together, Sir Francis decided that this threat was mere bravado. Bannister's mouth he subsequently shut by the very reasonable-sounding request that he would abstain from mentioning in Wanfield the ground on which des Sablières had been sent to prison, because Miss Forrest's name had been brought—though unjustifiably—into the affair. The one risk against which it was impossible to guard was that of the Frenchman's writing from prison to Juliana in person and asking her to corroborate his challenged statement; indeed, it was not until Sir Francis received Juliana's own letter of enquiry that he knew for certain that this had not happened.

After that it remained only to provide against Juliana herself making inconvenient investigations at Wanfield on her return, and this, too, the ingenious gentleman had devised a means of preventing. He put his plan into practice when, on the third day of her stay at Northover, she drove, with Laetitia Bentley, to call on Mrs. Mulholland, bearing with her for the old lady a large shawl of Siberian wool edged with sealskin.

Juliana's future home, which stood upon an eminence, had been Grecianized and stuccoed over at the end of the last century, and one looked from between an intolerable number of pillars down a good mile or so of park-like distance which included fallow deer. The other two ladies tactfully remaining in the drawing-room (from which indeed Mrs. Mulholland rarely stirred), Sir Francis drew his betrothed through the pillars on to the terrace.

"You have very much improved the view from here since I last saw it, Francis," remarked Juliana with appreciation.

"I am so glad that you think so, my dearest. I hoped it would please you." He took her hand and carried it tenderly to his lips.

He was to-day much more the man who had swept her off her feet in January, strong, self-confident, handsome, smiling, yet lover-like, and as she looked at him Juliana began to feel that she had been unduly hard on him that afternoon in the Chinese room at Northover, that it was she, perhaps, who had exaggerated his care and devotion into jealousy. He had behaved so well over the test—Fawley Bridge!

But what of her companion that day by the stream? Her face clouded. Sir Francis, watching it, felt that he knew on what subject she was about to embark, and welcomed the topic, for the finishing stroke had to be put to his own security.

He was right. "Francis," she said in a troubled voice, sinking down on a stone seat which faced the view, "this sad business about Monsieur des

Sablières? I cannot believe what is said of him! I want to go into the matter more fully—I want you to institute enquiries. I am certain there is a mistake somewhere. Yet you told me in your letter that Mr. Bannister will not say a word, and Mr. Bentley, I find, knows nothing, distressed as he is about the affair. And you know nothing. . . . But I am determined to find out. You must recognize that gratitude alone——"

"Oh, yes, my dear, I recognize that, and I quite agree with you," said the follower of Machiavelli. "But since I wrote to you Bannister has told me the story—the whole story. My lips, however, are unfortunately sealed, even to you, Juliana, for it involves the honour of someone of consequence." (He was not referring to himself, but to some entirely mythical personage.) "No good to des Sablières, I assure you, could come of investigation, and it would only bring shame on this other person—if you succeeded, that is. So I implore you, my dear one, to give up the attempt."

This man, the lover of four months ago, she would listen to, and so she looked at him mutely, impressed, and with no thought of doubting what he said.

"You realize, Juliana, do you not," he went on gently, "that des Sablières, who was undoubtedly a favourite of Bannister's and had received privileges from him, would never have been sent off to a prison without strong proof of his guilt?"

"And you know the story," said Juliana slowly, looking at him as if she only wished she could read it on his face. "Can you not assure me, at least, that it was not very disgraceful—from M. des Sablières' point of view?"

How she fought for him! But the shade of Machiavelli inspired Sir Francis to his best stroke. Instead of replying, in the style of Mr. Ramage, that it *was* disgraceful, scandalous and disgraceful, he said temperately: "I suppose, Juliana, that one must make allowances for a poor devil of a prisoner who is tempted to regain his liberty at the price of his honour. Perhaps we, who are perfectly free, have not the right to blame him very much."

Juliana Forrest sighed and looked away at the long vista, and her betrothed looked at her. The doubt had already begun to work, perhaps? If she thought the fellow had really behaved ill, he believed she had too much feeling for him (curse him!) ever to set to work to unveil the details of his misconduct.

"And the other man involved?" asked Juliana after a moment.

Sir Francis slightly smiled and shook his head. "I have given my word to Bannister that not a syllable shall pass my lips. You, surely, are not the woman to tempt me to break it, my Juliana? . . . Will you look at the new shrubbery before we go in again?"

She assented, and in the shrubbery allowed him to kiss her.

*

"Did you have an agreeable talk in the garden, Francis, you and dear Juliana?" quavered old Mrs. Mulholland when, some half hour later, her son returned from handing the ladies into the Northover barouche. "I thought the dear girl looked a little sad when she came in, but you seemed in such spirits that I daresay I was mistaken and I had mislaid my spectacles. . . . Dear Laetitia Bentley and I had such an interesting discussion about woolwork while you were out there."

"We had a very satisfactory conversation indeed," replied he, "and she quite approves of the new shrubbery."

"Dear Juliana has very good taste," rippled on Mrs. Mulholland, gazing fondly at her new acquisition. "This exquisite shawl—so warm, too! I wished to ask her if she liked my new cap, but I feared that it might be crooked and thought it better not to draw her attention to it."

"It is certainly crooked now," observed Sir Francis. "I will put it straight for you." He did so, and gave his mother a kiss—a somewhat rare event. But when a man has just brought off a very delicate stroke of diplomacy, he is naturally rather expansive.

*

So Juliana became once more a part of the merry little gatherings at Northover which, as the weather grew warmer, tended to overflow from the drawing room and the pianoforte into the spring-decked garden. Another French officer or two had superseded Raoul des Sablières, whose name was practically never heard there now, for the discussion of the crop of black surmises raised by Mr. Bannister's determined refusal to give even a hint of why he had been sent to prison was dying down by this time. Yet Juliana had declared to her friend that she did not believe one of the damaging conjectures which were repeated to her, had even declared it once or twice vehemently in public; after which she never spoke of the young Frenchman again. Only Laetitia noticed that on the day when young Mr. Curtis from Stoneleigh Manor sang "Since First I Saw Your Face" in her hearing she made an excuse and slipped from the room.

But inwardly Juliana still told herself that she never doubted there had been some misunderstanding; indeed she could not, illogically perhaps, quite rid herself of the feeling that after all the rush to her succour had had something to do with the business. But she could do nothing now, after what Francis had said. And perhaps there had come to "Mr. Rowl" some sudden violent temptation . . . he had said that day something significant about his inactivity . . . Francis, who knew the truth, had suggested that he should not be blamed overmuch . . . that was so generous of Francis . . . so different from Mr. Ramage, who on the same theme was intolerable. Knowing the sentiments of M. de Sainte-Suzanne on the subject of parole-breaking, she was careful never to mention Raoul's name before him; but the topic of his disgrace did come up one day in the Comte's presence, and he behaved in an unexpected and inscrutable manner, puzzling her not so much by what he said as by what he did not say.

Meanwhile there began to be talk of her wedding, some time in the autumn. It was to take place from her father's house in Grosvenor Square. Every time she went over to Mulholland Park Mrs. Mulholland reconsulted her about her headgear for that occasion, and Juliana and her betrothed, in the new communion which seemed to have sprung up between them, smiled together over her anxiety.

*

The pear blossom fell; the apple blossom was at its zenith. In a certain wood not far from Wanfield were reported to be great quantities of bluebells; and there, on the twenty-eighth of April, the young people proposed to partake of a cold collation. Sir Francis Mulholland (on horseback) and Mr. Bentley were also to be of the party. But early on the morning of this expedition Juliana, who was without her maid, discovered that the dress which she designed to wear on this occasion was in need of a new tucker, and since there was plenty of time to supply this want, she and Laetitia ordered the barouche early and drove into Wanfield.

Just before they alighted from the carriage in the High Street Juliana observed a French naval officer salute Miss Bentley, and enquired who it was.

"It was Lieutenant Lamotte," replied her friend. "I have met him at the Curtises. He lodges with Miss Hitchings—where poor M. des Sablières used to lodge."

At the mention of that name Juliana's face had clouded, but she said nothing, and in another moment they were descending at the door of the linen-draper's shop. But, as they were on the point of entering, they heard hasty steps, and turning, saw the young Frenchman hurrying towards them.

"Miss Bentley," said he in his own language, "I have a commission—that is, if this lady is Miss Forrest, as I think, and if you will be so obliging as to present me? The commission was entrusted to me by my comrade, Captain des Sablières, before his departure."

Juliana coloured. Lieutenant Lamotte was presented, and thereupon addressed her directly.

"Captain des Sablières entrusted me, Mademoiselle, with an English book to return to you. If it is not improper, would you allow me to discharge the commission now . . . provided it would not be burdening you . . . for Mulholland Park is out of bounds for me."

"But Miss Forrest is not—" began Laetitia, and was too much arrested by the expression on her friend's face to finish.

"I lent M. des Sablières no book, Monsieur," said Juliana slowly.

"But yes, Mademoiselle! You have forgotten your kindness. *Rasselas*, by the Doctor Johnson. If you will allow me—as I see that you are on the point of entering this shop—I will run meanwhile to my lodgings and get it and wait for you here."

"Do, pray," said Juliana. She was looking oddly grave and discomposed, and in the shop paid but small attention to the choice of a tucker.

When they emerged there was the young man awaiting them.

"This is the book, Mademoiselle. When Captain des Sablières came out of gaol he was allowed a short time in his room to get together his effects, and he charged me with it. I was to give it to you in person with the expression of his regrets that in so short a time he had not been able to finish reading it."

Juliana, now colouring deeply, took the book. Why had Mr. Rowl returned it? She had given it to him to keep—he knew that. It surely was not possible that he felt himself unworthy?

"I suppose," she said falteringly, "that M. des Sablières was not allowed to take his possessions with him to Norman Cross?"

"Oh, yes, Mademoiselle; he took what he had—it is true it was not much. I think this book, being your property, was the only thing he left behind . . . and he charged me most particularly to return it to you in person at the first opportunity."

Juliana looked down at the little calf-bound volume, and was back nearly six weeks in time, and heard the stream ripple again and the thrush call, which he who had been with her then could hear no longer.

"And that was all the message?"

"Yes, Mademoiselle, that he regretted he could not finish the book in the time. In effect," said M. Lamotte as if to excuse his compatriot, "he had only that one evening before he was sent to the gaol here."

"Which evening was that?" asked Juliana quickly.

"The evening when, coming to sup with him, I found him deep in that book; and he told me that he had only just received it that afternoon. I remember observing the title—a strange one. And when I saw him again three days afterwards, under guard, he gave me the book for you, as I say."

"He—he did not say then why he was being sent to Norman Cross?" asked Juliana with a beating heart.

"No, Mademoiselle. But I suppose it was for the same cause which had led

Mr. Bannister to put him practically under arrest on the evening to which I was referring. Mr. Bannister had been to see him, and bade him not to leave the house; Captain des Sablières did not tell me why, only that it was on account of some misunderstanding which would be put right in the morning. Certainly it did not trouble him much that evening," said Lieutenant Lamotte reminiscently. "But yet in the morning it was not put right."

Fawley Copse . . . her rescue . . . *Rasselas* had been there, too . . . oh, was it Fawley Copse which had ruined him? "Oh, Monsieur, if you could but tell me which evening that was! Forgive me—but the exact date is so important! I—I know something which might help M. des Sablières to clear himself, for I have never believed that he broke his parole."

"Nor I, Mademoiselle," said the sailor simply. "And I do not need any effort to remember the date, as it happens. It was on the evening before the birthday of the King of Rome that des Sablières was confined to the house—Friday, the nineteenth of March. The birthday itself, which is on the twentieth, the poor des Sablières spent in gaol, but for a certain reason we had celebrated it the evening before, the nineteenth. I am quite certain of that, Mademoiselle."

"The nineteenth of March—the Friday—the same day!" said Juliana, apparently speaking to herself. "So it had to do with that—it was not something which was discovered later! Thank you, Monsieur," she added, "and forgive my questions. Your friend has had a great injustice done him; it must be put right at once!"

Her voice was firm, but she was very pale. Lieutenant Lamotte bowed and took himself off. Laetitia put her arm through her friend's.

"What is the matter, dearest Juliana?" she asked anxiously. "You are unwell! Let us go back into the shop."

But Juliana shook her head. Clutching *Rasselas* to her she said solemnly: "Letty, I shall never, never play with fire again! It is other people who get burnt. I am sure it is all my fault that he was sent to prison—but if it is I am going to repair it. Please desire your coachman to set us down at Mr. Bannister's office without delay."

D. K. Broster

Three quarters of an hour later the barouche was bearing back to Northover two very different damsels, not only from those who had set out upon that brief shopping expedition, but even from those who had entered the office of the astonished Agent to set right an injustice . . . and had discovered and fired a mine. Laetitia was frankly crying; Juliana, shivering with a strange inner cold, sat staring straight before her. It had needed only her initial remark to Mr. Bannister—"I fear it is on account of the service he rendered me that day in Fawley Copse that M. des Sablières got into difficulties with you?"—to bring down like a pack of cards all Sir Francis Mulholland's elaborate edifice of lies. But the effect of the fall on Bannister and themselves had been like that of a landslide.

As they came in sight of the gates of Northover Laetitia dabbed her eyes.

"Oh, Juliana, what shall we do? We cannot go to the wood—at least, I feel too wretched . . . and what will Papa and everybody say if we do not?"

"I am going to the wood," responded Juliana firmly. "I want to see . . . Sir Francis . . . at once. He joins us there, you remember. And you must come, Laetitia, because you must, if necessary, contrive an opportunity for me to see him alone. Do you understand? Pull your bonnet down a little, and perhaps no one will observe that you have been crying."

Her resolution and self-command amazed the weaker spirit, who made haste, however, to obey her. Fortunately, they were so late—Mr. Bentley was already waiting on the doorstep, and two other carriages full of laughter and expostulations were in the drive—that there was no time for any one to notice discomposure, and if the two young men who drove with the just-returned young ladies observed anything unusual, they had perforce to keep their speculations to themselves.

The bluebells were even bluer and more numerous than had been expected, the collation was voted excellent, the weather perfect. But Sir Francis Mulholland, if no one else, noticed that his bride-to-be looked pale and distraite, and himself made the opportunity she wished for by suggesting, soon after the company had risen from their cold chicken and ham, that they should take a stroll to see more bluebells.

Juliana assented, but almost inaudibly, and she did not take his proffered

75

arm. Side by side they walked away from the others.

"I am alarmed about you to-day, my love," observed Sir Francis solicitously, as they went. "You are so pale; you tired yourself, I fear, by going into Wanfield, as I hear you did, this morning."

The moment had come—so soon. Speech was not easy. Juliana fixed her eyes on the stump of a tree, and the words came out slowly and heavily. "Yes, I had a great shock in Wanfield this morning. . . . I do not imagine that, however long I live, I shall ever receive a greater."

The colour left her lover's face, too. "What were you doing in Wanfield?" he asked uneasily.

"I went to Mr. Bannister's office." She heard him give an inarticulate exclamation. "I do not need to tell you what I learnt there—what an incredible story of deceit, of mean revenge, came out." She turned her beautiful, accusing eyes on him. "Francis, Francis, how could you do it—how *could* you descend to such inexpressible baseness!"

"Because you drove me to it!" he cried wildly. "You scorned my entreaties, my warnings! And what of your own deceit? After your meeting him like that at Fawley Bridge I *had* to get rid of him. And I did nothing so very blameworthy, after all; Norman Cross is the best of the war prisons . . . and he was a prisoner in any case; it cannot have done him much harm. If you had listened to me——"

The inward cold grew and spread till Juliana's very heart seemed frozen with disgust. "Then, if I can drive you to such an act as knowingly to take away an innocent man's honour, and to say that you have not hurt him—and to such monstrous lies to cover it—it is my duty as well as my wish to sever our relationship!" And she slipped the ruby from her finger. "Pray take back your ring, for our engagement is at an end."

He would not take it, and finally it dropped between them among the croziers of the young fern. He blustered, he raved, he pleaded; he even went on his knees to her among the bracken and the bluebells. "Juliana, have mercy! It was because I loved you so . . . I'll do anything—retract what I said, write to Norman Cross—"

"Mr. Bannister is already doing that!"

Sir Francis got to his feet; his face was patched and chalky. "I shall be ruined if this gets about!"

She surveyed him with deeper contempt. "And what of the man you have ruined?"

"It can be undone, Juliana—I swear I'll reinstate him, whatever it costs! You don't know how you maddened me. . . . For God's sake, think better of it! Put that ring on again and I will never be jealous of you again in my life. . . . Where is the ring?" He stooped and began to fumble with shaking hands among the dead leaves and sand.

"Jealous!" exclaimed Juliana. "It is the lies, the subterfuges—the chain of subterfuges! . . . Why, I should never be able to believe a word you said to me as long as I lived. And once I thought . . . Oh, Francis, Francis——" The tears came over her own lost happiness, and the ideal figure she had been rebuilding—on a foundation of mud. And for the sake of what she once had thought him she promised, before she left him, that in the rehabilitation of his victim he should be spared as much as possible, that she would ask Mr. Bannister to say locally that there had been a mistake . . . misunderstandings . . . anything to cover his disgraceful conduct. For she, too, felt humiliated to the dust.

And finally she went away from him rather stumblingly, and a little later was found by Mr. Bentley crying at the foot of an oak tree, and that good friend, after letting her finish on his shoulder, had the carriage brought up and sent her home alone with Laetitia, on the plea of sudden illness.

But the ruby ring, after exercising the wits of a number of ants and beetles, was found next year by Zachary Miller as he was putting a ferret down a rabbit hole, and, cautiously disposed of at a distance, contributed not a little towards his marriage and the consequent begetting of a number of assistants and successors to carry on his activities in the Mulholland woods and elsewhere.

Part II
The Cost of a Whim

Forgotten?

It was divided into many squares or courts . . . according to the rank of those for whom they were designed. . . . This house . . . was built as if Suspicion herself had dictated the plan.—Rasselas, chap. I.

The mild blue sky was covered with the most delightful little fleecy clouds in motion. Raoul des Sablières, his head tilted back against the eight-feet high palisade of the officers' enclosure at Norman Cross, watched them rather abstractedly. One seemed to be outstripping the others: he wondered how long it would take to traverse the great camp, and what it saw as it sailed over the heads of more than five thousand prisoners.

He knew pretty well, although, as an officer, he was confined to one small section of the town—for Norman Cross dépôt, though set in the middle of fields, was almost a town. For a moment or two Raoul idly imagined himself voyaging on the cloud over Yaxley or Stilton Barracks (the prison was rich in these three names). Now he was poised above the octagonal wooden blockhouse in the centre, with its projecting guns dominating each of the four courts or "airing-grounds" which so symmetrically surrounded it—each court a couple of acres in extent, and each containing four blocks of wooden buildings placed side by side at one of the outer edges. Every block was calculated to hold five hundred men, but in the northeastern court three had been taken over as a hospital, and, of those in the southeastern, the endmost facing east was the officers' prison, in the small separate enclosure of which the imaginary voyager sat at this moment. The two English militia regiments on guard were quartered outside the walls altogether.

Raoul and his cloud would, he knew, see a good deal of activity going on in those forty-two acres, and more especially in the twenty-two of the prison proper. There misery and cheerfulness, improvidence and industry jostled each other daily, for while some of the prisoners persistently gambled away not only their clothes and their bedding but even their rations, others turned out little articles of beautiful workmanship in straw, bone, or paper, of which they were able to dispose at the market regularly held at the eastern gate. One object alone they might not legally manufacture and sell—straw plait; so that highly paid commodity was generally smuggled out by soldier accomplices.

It was Saturday, the first of May, and Raoul had now been for nearly six weeks a member of this captive population. His immediate companions, with a very few exceptions, were all "broke-paroles" . . . like himself. Raoul had come by now, on the surface, almost to class himself as one, but underneath there was still the same indignant repudiation of the stigma. At first he had kept somewhat aloof from the other officers, until he saw that his attitude was resented, until he was, in fact, asked rather roughly what he had to give himself airs about—and had bitterly put the same question to himself. . . .

For the first month at Norman Cross he had been sustained by the hope that when Miss Forrest returned to Wanfield she would discover his absence, realize her share in the disaster which had befallen him, and set about having the injustice righted. Even if she had told the untruth attributed to her, surely when she discovered what it had involved for him. . . . In his very uncomfortable and depressing detention in the lock-up at Wanfield he had been strongly visited by the temptation to write directly to her and ask her whether she *had* declared that she had returned from Northover by the highroad. But that would have been to force her hand; it was practically begging her to save him at whatever cost to herself, and it was of small use to be quixotic (if he had been quixotic) in the semi-publicity of Mr. Bannister's office if, at the first taste of the consequences of his attitude, he was going to cry for mercy. So the letter was never written—though another was.

But, though he would not put pressure upon her, "Mr. Rowl" might legitimately hope that Miss Forrest would, of her own free will, take some action on his behalf. Yet the days stole on, monotonous and unpleasant, and nothing happened. He was forgotten; just one more "broke-parole."

Raoul was not, however, of the temper to spend his time idly brooding over his situation, and from the first moment of his entry into Norman Cross his dominant idea had been how to get out again. And at last, after weeks of planning, there seemed a chance of realizing this ambition. It was true that in the sixteen years of its existence as a war-prison (for which it had been specially built) very few captives had succeeded in escaping from the dépôt. But chance had thrown Raoul into close contact with two others as determined as himself to get away—a certain Lieutenant Clairet of the 26th of the line, and a Captain Dumont, commander of a St. Malo privateer, the *Indienne*. The shortage of accommodation in the officers' quarters at the moment of his arrival had caused Raoul to be thrust at night into the cupboard—it was scarcely more—which was inhabited by these two men, and in this proximity was hatched the scheme to which that very proximity had given rise.

The first problem was that of procuring three suits of civilian clothes; this, with the greatest difficulty, they had succeeded in doing. The next was that of getting undiscovered out of Caserne No. 8, the officers' block. Their tiny sleeping apartment had no proper window, but there was a ventilator in the roof, and this could be gained by an active young man assisted by his friends, and the same young man, at the cost of abrasions, could just squeeze himself through it, and enlarge the exit by removing portions from outside. For the last three nights Raoul had been working away at this task, and on Monday the three adventurers counted upon scrambling out of this aperture and then climbing down in the dark as best they could into the enclosure. They had already contrived to bore a few small holes in the high stockade, and into these, when the moment came, they intended to thrust some long nails to give them a foothold. But, since it was out of their power previously to approach and prepare the great brick wall which surrounded the prison, they had to trust to aid from its other side. Cautious negotiations, conducted by the English-speaking Raoul, with a venal sentry of the West Kent militia, then on duty there, had resulted in the agreement that on the Monday night the latter, being on guard outside near the south gate, should throw a rope over the wall, fastening it to some projection or other at its foot. Once over, and if they had the luck not to be seen by a sentry on the farther side, the fugitives could easily find their way to the Peterborough road, which practically bordered the camp on the south. Thereafter, trusting to their wits, they must make either for the shores of the Wash or for the northern coast of Norfolk; they had a rather pathetic faith that, once arrived at the sea, Dumont, as a master mariner, would find some means of conveying them over that element.

*

Raoul's cloud was gone now—melted into the blue; but that did not grieve him, for he had already forgotten about his aërial journey. A young man a few years his senior had detached himself from the groups strolling about the enclosure and was coming towards him in a purposely nonchalant manner. It was Lieutenant Clairet.

He sat down on the bench by his fellow conspirator, who affected to take little notice of his arrival.

"You looked just now as if you were trying to learn the stars by daylight," observed the newcomer jestingly, and then, lowering his voice, "I expect they are all we shall have to steer by. I can't get hold of a compass anywhere."

Raoul just glanced at him without removing his head from its resting place on the stockade. "The question is rather whether Dumont has succeeded in getting that map," he returned equally low. For as yet they had nothing of that nature to guide them on their way to the coast, though they had for some days been trying to buy a smuggled map from a fellow prisoner. "Yet, map or no map, we must start on Monday, because of Marwin's being on sentry duty that night. His next turn is ten days later, and by that time the moon will be full."

"Dumont knows the canals, of course," said Clairet doubtfully, "because he was brought by water from Lynn, but we cannot use them except as rough guides. It would not do to follow them closely."

"I expect he will succeed in getting the map out of Parisot in the end," observed Raoul. "Parisot never intended to use it himself, and, fortunately for us, Dumont is pretty flush of cash."

"Yes, the old pirate! I think," said Lieutenant Clairet, "that when I reach

France I shall resign my commission and ship on board a privateer. . . . Talking of privateers, I hear that some of the men in Caserne No. 4, who are mostly sailors and privateersmen, are getting rather out of hand, and Captain Hanwell has stopped the whole block from selling their wares at the market this week. As a consequence, more unruliness, and he threatens to get the worst black sheep sent to the hulks."

"Poor devils!" said Raoul. "Ah, there is the postman."

A turnkey with a leather bag had just come through from the Superintendent's office, which was not far away. Clairet got up and went toward the crowd of which the man immediately became the centre. After a moment Raoul followed him, more because he snatched at anything which relieved the tedium of captivity than because he was any longer expecting a letter, and he waited, only half attending, on the outskirts of the group.

To his surprise he heard his name called, and elbowed his way through the throng to find himself staring, with somewhat quickened pulses, at a letter bearing the Wanfield postmark. The handwriting was a lady's. He slipped back to his bench, his heart now beating really hard.

The letter had, of course, been already opened . . . and it *was* from Miss Forrest. He read:

Dear Monsieur des Sablières:

I do not know how to write to you. I know the truth now, in spite of the measures which have been used to keep me in the dark, and which did keep me in that condition until yesterday. No words of mine can express the shame, the burning indignation, which fill me. I implore you to believe that I knew nothing of the duplicity which has sent you to such an unmerited captivity. I did not utter the lie which I find has been attributed to me: on the contrary. I gave that evening an exact recital of what had occurred in Fawley Copse and of your gallant behaviour there. Yet, from the sequel, you must have been convinced that I had shielded myself at your expense. Oh, believe me, such an idea never entered my mind—would that it had never entered another's!

I am not, however, wasting my time in idle lamentations. I am determined that this intolerable injustice shall be repaired, and that you shall be liberated as soon as possible. I am writing to my father to ask him to use all his influence with the Transport Office: Mr. Bannister, on the strength of my evidence, has already communicated both with the Commissioners and with Norman Cross. Meanwhile also I am seeing to it that all Wanfield knows how unjustly you have been punished. Mr. Bannister's relief is great to find that you are what he always thought you, Mr. Bentley's and his daughter's likewise. I do not think the two latter ever doubted it, nor did I, in my heart, though circumstances had been made to look very black against you. Strangely enough, it was your returning of *Rasselas*—a proceeding which cut me at the moment, as shewing, I thought, your opinion of me—which led to the discovery of the truth.

I have only this to ask of you, Monsieur, that you will keep up your spirits and your patience, and believe that she who, as she sadly feels, is really responsible for the wrong which has been inflicted on you, is doing her utmost to procure its reparation.

Your friend,
Juliana Forrest.

Postscript. Since you will hear it when you return—as I trust you will return—to Wanfield, I think it better to inform you now that my engagement is at an end.

Raoul leant against the stockade and put his hand for a moment over his eyes. Now that what he had hoped for and then ceased to hope for had really happened he felt almost bewildered. The ordeal was over; he was cleared, and his friends at Wanfield need no longer be ashamed of him!

And Miss Forrest had never told even that venial lie! Generous girl, to act, to write as she had done! Since he had never for a moment believed that she would have sacrificed him knowingly, he had afterward regretted that, piqued and sore as he was at being so unjustly used, he had given way, on leaving

Wanfield, to a hasty and not very intelligible impulse, and thrust *Rasselas* into Lamotte's hands with that message. But now it seemed, by its results, that his rather unworthy little action had been happily inspired. It was that, evidently, which had led her to make enquiries, to find out that Sir Francis—

But here Raoul suddenly sat down on the bench, and Juliana's letter fluttered to the trodden earth of the prison enclosure. He had never fully thought out what, to a girl of the disposition which he attributed to Miss Forrest, might be the result of discovering that her betrothed had stooped to a baseness and a malignity really incredible in a gentleman. Well, now he knew what it had meant, and his breath was somewhat taken away by the knowledge. He bent down, picked up the letter and re-read the postscript. There was no doubt of it. She had broken her marriage over this business—it had changed the course of her whole future life.

As a Frenchman, accustomed to the extremely binding nature of a French betrothal, and the difficulties of untying it, Raoul was a little horrified. Her discovery of the truth had certainly been bought at a heavy price. No; his thought changed—no price could be too heavy to save a woman of upright instincts from marrying a man capable of what Sir Francis Mulholland had shown himself capable of! Miss Forrest was, in the event, fortunate in her escape, and in this country, with her position and her looks, she would have no lack of other suitors. And he doubted whether, from what he had seen, she would cry her eyes out for the lover whom she had so promptly dismissed. Yet, what an upheaval!

He sat, with the letter in his hands, staring unseeingly at the hated contours of Block No. 8, not spending any thoughts, even thoughts of triumph, on the situation which must now be Mulholland's at Wanfield, but thinking solely of the girl. Yes, she would soon console herself, with a better match, even—some rich English lord, no doubt. He gave a quick sigh, and put the letter carefully into his pocket.

As he did so Raoul saw the large form of Captain Dumont tacking towards him. Captain Dumont *had* a little of the pirate about his appearance, and was reported to display on emergency the class of temper and linguistic acquirements indispensable, no doubt, to one of his calling, but his usual bearing was that of the typically bluff and jovial seaman. He was one of the few officers there who were not "broke-paroles." As the *Indienne*, at least when captured, carried less than fourteen guns, her captain was not entitled to the privilege of parole—from which, indeed, he had self-sacrificingly cut himself off by throwing three overboard to prevent them from falling into the hands of the enemy.

He now winked a blue eye set, as to its outer corner, amid innumerable creases, and said cheerfully, "Fine morning, des Sablières! Had a letter? Lucky dog! We are all in luck . . . for I have got *it*. So . . ." He rolled on, repeating the wink. The unfinished sentence meant, "There is now nothing to keep us back from Monday's venture."

But Raoul remained staring after him without moving or replying. He had quite forgotten that he was to escape the day after to-morrow. . . . But to try to escape now would be insanity—more, it would be ingratitude. Yet . . . could he withdraw at the eleventh hour? He got up at last from the bench with a face vastly more troubled, for all the advent of Juliana Forrest's letter, than that with which he had watched his cloud an hour ago.

That evening, in their close little sleeping apartment, he soon learnt from his comrades that he could not withdraw. The idea of the escape taking place without him was received by them with incredulity, with consternation, and then with an indignation which, in Captain Dumont's case, began very soon to warm into anger. And Clairet was not conciliatory.

"And so," he exclaimed, "you are content to wait while strings are pulled for you—to wait indefinitely, perhaps for ever? What has come to you, des Sablières?"

"I am not afraid, if that is what you are thinking," retorted Raoul, firing up a little. "I have told you exactly the position I am in. Is it so difficult to understand?"

"No," said Dumont starkly. "It's not. Everyone for his own skin, and I'll call no man white-livered unless he has given better cause for it than a natural wish to care for that. But there are two of us, and only one of you, Captain des Sablières, and I reckon two skins are worth more than one. Or perhaps, seeing that you are a noble by birth, and we ain't, you count it quits, me and Lieutenant Clairet against you?"

"You know I think nothing of the sort, Captain Dumont!" answered Raoul hotly. "And my birth has nothing to do with the matter!"

"Come," put in Clairet pacifically, "all this is off the point. I'm sure that if des Sablières thinks it over—"

"Thinks it over! He don't need to! Why, I believe, damn my eyes," said Captain Dumont with an angry laugh, "that neither of you youngsters has seen the real reason why we must have him, willing or unwilling. He's the only one of us who speaks English!"

And when, by the way in which both young men gazed blankly at him, the master of the *Indienne* saw that he was right, he slapped his knee with delight, and the threatened simoon blew over.

"I've got you there, young fellow!" he said to the recalcitrant fugitive, and slapped him next. "You can't back out when you know that Clairet and I might just as well lie snug in our beds on Monday night as start through two English counties without you to do the parleying."

"Yes," said Raoul, swallowing down with as good a grace as he could his irritation and disappointment. "Yes, you've certainly got me there. I confess I never thought of that point. Of course I will come, and willingly. Forget that I ever proposed anything else."

Captain Dumont made a large gesture. "It is already forgotten," he said magnanimously. "And if you supply the lingo, des Sablières, I can supply a fist." He doubled that formidable object as he spoke.

"Which will not, I hope, be required," put in Clairet quickly. "The last weapon we want to employ, Captain, is violence. It is a very undiplomatic one in the hands of a fugitive."

"You wait, my lad, till you are in need of it, and you won't think it undiplomatic then! Well, this little matter being settled, I shall turn in."

Clairet lingered a moment by Raoul's bed as the latter also began to undress. "You know," he said in a low voice, "it is really much better, for your own sake, to come with us. There have been other cases here for whom representations have been made to the Transport Board—poor Mazard, for instance; he has been waiting nearly three years for their result."

Raoul at this moment was pulling his shirt over his head and made no immediate answer. When he emerged he said briefly: "I have no doubt you are right. At any rate, I am coming with you."

*

It was the question of a letter to Miss Forrest, not this imminent adventure, which chiefly engaged his thoughts next day. He could write and thank her, it was true, but he could not possibly say the thing he wanted to say—that, ungrateful and foolish as he must appear, he was only carrying out this escape because he was already committed to it, for in a letter which would be read by the authorities he could obviously make no reference, even veiled, to a project of flight. In the end he decided that he would wait to write until he was clear of Norman Cross.

But it was plain that he would never see Juliana Forrest's face again. Reinstatement and release, such as she was working for, might have meant return to Wanfield, but successful escape meant leaving England altogether . . . and unsuccessful would mean Norman Cross for ever, or removal to another prison—perhaps to one of the big new dépôts in Scotland, Valleyfield or Perth. If he were retaken he would certainly never be allowed out again on parole while his captivity lasted. Yet the more he knew that it was impossible, the more keen was his desire to see her once more, not only to thank her from his heart for what she had done, not only to ask her to let him have back as a memento (really to be kept this time) that book which, indirectly, had been the cause of everything, but . . . just for the sake of seeing her.

Yes, he would like to talk to Juliana Forrest once again. Not by the stream; in the garden at Northover, where they had spoken once or twice when the daffodils were out under the cedars. He wondered what flowers were blooming there now—one knew nothing of flowers here. . . . He would like to see the garden at Northover again, and now he never would.

But at this point Raoul pulled himself up. He, a soldier, regretting his captivity because it had been pleasant! He was indeed growing soft! Here, with the chance before him of breathing once more the air of France, he was sentimentally thinking of the charms of England . . . and of an Englishwoman! But surely he had the right to wish to thank her who had championed him, and the most fervid Anglophobe could not blame him for that desire.

The chosen day, Monday, dawned at last. Raoul, waking early, looked in the dim light at his sleeping companions and wondered where they would all be by next morning—if they were all three still alive. It was quite on the cards that one of them would get a bullet through the head, for the sentries were numerous, and armed with ball cartridge.

It was a day of tension for all of them, and passed with cruel slowness—but it did pass. Dumont was unusually noisy and cheerful at supper, the more so that there was a rumour going about that the sentries were likely to be doubled that night in the vicinity of Caserne No. 4, the mutinous block, and he thought that in consequence the officers' quarters might be less closely guarded. But Raoul and Clairet pointed out that the Brigade Major (who, and not the Agent Superintendent, was responsible for the military arrangements of the prison—a dual control not always of the most happy) had plenty of men to post as extra sentries. And if he did withdraw any from their corner of the dépôt, might not Marwin conceivably be one of them? If so, what of the rope for which he had made himself responsible?

. . . Five hours later, when they were actually stealing in the dark along the ditch at the foot of the great wall, that was indeed the vital question. To Raoul, the foremost, feeling vainly along the brickwork for that indispensable adjunct, it seemed a cruel irony to be baulked at the last stage of all after having overcome their other difficulties—after having squeezed through the ventilator, climbed safely down the rickety pipe outside the caserne and over the pointed palisade, and after having avoided (more by luck than skill) the many sentries posted between it and the wall. And then, suddenly, his hand encountered what he sought.

It was a good stout rope, knotted at intervals. He gave it a hard tug. It seemed securely fastened to something on the other side, and in a whisper Raoul communicated this information to his comrades.

It had been arranged that he was to go last, because, being the lightest, he would probably have least difficulty in swarming up the rope when its end was free; so he was first to steady it for his heavier companions. As the wall was only nine feet high on its outer side (its greater height on the inner being due to the excavation of the fosse at its base) the fugitives, once up, could drop the distance. Dumont the sailor went first, and had soon arrived at the top, in spite of his corpulence; yet, dark as the night was, his bulk seemed to Raoul to be plainly visible against the sky on the crest of the wall, and his arrival on the ground the other side was announced by a rather telltale thud. Clairet followed quickly; his drop was inaudible. Then Raoul went up, the rope spinning as he climbed, straddled the wall, saw their upturned faces very dimly below him, and dropped lightly beside them. There was no sign of Marwin, nor, at the moment, of any of his comrades. Surely some sentries had been removed!

"Don't wait!" whispered Raoul, his mouth at Clairet's ear. "I will overtake you in a moment. I promised not to leave the rope about."

He hauled the slack over the wall to him, and, as the others vanished, stooped to feel in the darkness how the end was secured at its foot. He could easily have cut it off without ascertaining this, but in that case the knot, remaining, might perhaps bring complicity home to Marwin—a serious business for a sentry. Moreover, he had given his word.

Confound the fellow, whatever was this he had fastened it to, right down in the grass at the base of the wall? The essential need of haste made Raoul's fingers clumsy. He would have to cut the rope, after all. Kneeling on one knee, he put his hand into his pocket for a small knife which he had contrived to retain in spite of regulations . . . and the next instant was almost blinded by the glare of a suddenly opened lantern.

"Mr. Rowl"

The Shadow of Huntingdon Gaol

"I knew not to what condition we were doomed, nor could conjecture where would be the place of our captivity, or whence to draw any hope of deliverance."—Rasselas, chap. xxxviii.

The voice said, "No, not to-day. To-morrow, perhaps. I will let you know, Sir."

Streaks and circles of alternate light and darkness swirled incessantly under Raoul's closed lids. The light was of a reddish tinge. "Not to-day . . . not to-day . . ." the words went on reverberating in his brain—but only as sounds. They had no meaning. "To-morrow, perhaps, . . . to-morrow . . . to-morrow. . . ."

What was "to-morrow"? And this sensation in his head, what was it? Had he always had it? But who was he himself . . . and where?

A feeling as if he were floating upward brought the conviction of water . . . . drowning. Yes—the crossing of the Gebora in the mist of a February morning before the battle . . . his horse must have been swept away . . . the river had been in flood the previous day. But there was no water in his mouth or nostrils—he could breathe.

He could see! He found his eyes open and lay blinking. But he was not seeing what he expected—sky, the cork-trees, the slope where Mendizabal's army lay. He saw white-washed walls, with highset windows, and beds, rows of beds, mostly empty. It was in a bed that he lay himself. Hospital, then . . . . but where? Salamanca?

He tried to lift his head a little in order to see more, but the pain (now localized at the back) became so acute that he drew a sharp breath and desisted, and involuntarily shut his eyes again. But after a moment he put up a hand to this head and found that something was tied round it. Was that why it hurt so? He was inclined to think that it was.

His mind began to grope backwards, and gradually he came to the conclusion that he could not be in Spain because he remembered coming to England . . . being at Wanfield . . . then at Norman Cross. That was where he was, then. But of recent events at Norman Cross he could recall nothing since a certain supper when Dumont had been so hilarious. Was it possible that he himself had got drunk on that occasion, whenever it was? But there had been nothing to get drunk on, that he could remember. He was beginning to explore his head more carefully, when he heard steps approaching him, and opened his eyes once more.

A lanky, sandy-haired young man came and stood looking down at him, and finally took hold of his wrist and felt his pulse.

"How does your head feel now?" he enquired after a moment.

"It hurts," answered Raoul. "Why is that? And if I move it . . ."

"There is a very good reason for its hurting," replied the young man. "Don't you remember it?"

Raoul incautiously tried to shake his head on the pillow, and succeeded only too well. He gave an exclamation. But his mind continued to grope.

"Am I still at Norman Cross?" he asked, gazing fixedly at his visitor.

"Yes, in the officers' hospital."

"Why?"

"Good Lord, you ask why? . . . Because you were attempting to escape last night and—and got a thundering knock on the head in doing so. You must possess a remarkably hard skull, or it would have cracked," said the lanky young man in a tone of admiration.

"Perhaps I do," agreed Raoul unenthusiastically, and knit his brows in a fresh effort to remember. "Escaping . . . Was I alone?"

"I say," ejaculated the young man, "have you genuinely forgotten? . . . No, there were two others with you, and, so far, they have got away. I don't know their names, but they were your room-mates at No. 8. You are supposed to have got out by the ventilator. You remember that, surely?"

"No," replied Raoul. "I remember nothing since supper last night—if it was last night?"

"Perhaps that is as well," said the young man to himself. The tone struck Raoul, but he did not enquire into its meaning.

"Are you the doctor?" he next asked.

"No, only his assistant. My name's Wanklin. But Doctor Walker was here himself a short time ago—you did not hear him speaking to Captain Hanwell, I suppose, for you seemed to be still unconscious then. They were at the foot of the bed, however."

"The Superintendent himself! What was he doing here?"

"Well, you see, he's . . . he wants to ask you some questions."

"Oh," commented Raoul wearily. "Not much good, is it, if I cannot remember anything?"

"That, of course, is what Doctor Walker said. At least, he said that you would not be fit to answer them to-day, though he did not, naturally, know that you had lost your memory. So the Superintendent had to go away again. We of the hospital staff, you know," added Mr. Wanklin, smoothing his carroty locks with an air, "are not technically under his control. We have our warrants from the Sick and Hurt Board, not from the Transport Office."

"Then I hope the Sick and Hurt Board will not allow Captain Hanwell to pester me with questions about the other two, because I shall tell him nothing . . . and my head aches," finished Raoul rather peevishly.

"I don't think it is about the other two that he wants to ask you questions," said Mr. Wanklin, and again his tone was so odd that Raoul this time was about to ask him what he meant, when a voice from a distant bed was heard summoning the budding surgeon, and he hurried off. And, in a little, Raoul, after vainly beating that blank brain of his, and realizing that the worst had happened—unsuccessful escape—drifted off into a comfortless sleep.

When he woke again it seemed by the light to be a good deal later. The pain in his head was much less, but still he could remember nothing of the actual escape. But now his mind was invaded by another subject, Miss Forrest's letter; and mingled with thoughts of that came crowding in the often-discussed details of that plan of escape which, evidently, they had put into practice last night. . . . Yes, he remembered now the endless debates, the feverish preparations. . . . Well, the other two had been lucky, but he—he had indeed defeated all Miss Forrest's plans for his welfare! And France, freedom, his parents were all as far off as ever.

An attendant came with some food—a little meat and potatoes—and placed it on a chair beside him, and Raoul realized that he was hungry. He fed himself with some difficulty, though if he moved his head cautiously he no longed suffered such shoots and stabs of pain. And soon after the plate had been removed he observed an individual whom he judged to be the surgeon himself walk down the ward and come to his bed. He was about sixty, grey-haired, upright, somewhat severe-looking.

He bent over Raoul, felt his pulse, looked into his eyes, and then sat down beside him.

"I understand that you speak English, Captain des Sablières?"

"Yes, Sir."

"Is your head still troubling you?"

"Not nearly so much—very little if I keep still."

"I am glad to hear it. Mr. Wanklin tells me that you can remember nothing since supper last night.

"No, Sir."

"Have you made the effort?"

"Yes."

"You can recall nothing of the circumstances of your escape?"

"No, Sir, nothing."

"You were found unconscious on the outer side of the wall. How did you come there?"

"I have no recollection. I remember how we—I—planned to surmount it . . . but I have no recollection of doing it."

"Nor of what happened on the other side?" The doctor was looking at him very searchingly.

"No. I suppose I was stunned by a blow—or did I fall?"

"You were stunned by a blow from a musket—eventually. It is a great pity that it did not happen at once."

Raoul stared at him in bewilderment. What was this mystery at which Mr. Wanklin, too, had hinted? "Why do you say that, Sir?" he asked. "It would be very kind to tell me exactly what happened on the other side of the wall, for I have not the slightest idea. I daresay you do not believe that, but it is true."

"As a medical man, Monsieur des Sablières," replied Doctor Walker gravely, "I am inclined to believe that you are speaking the truth. It will, therefore, I am afraid, be all the greater shock to you to learn that you are in danger of having to stand your trial for murder, and, but that you are obviously unfit for it, ought properly to be either in the Black Hole of this dépôt or in Huntingdon Gaol."

"*Murder!*" gasped Raoul, like one suddenly immersed in water. "In God's name, whose murder?"

Doctor Walker looked at him very keenly before replying.

"The sentinel's," he said at length. "The sentinel who came up and discovered you. There was a struggle, in which you bayoneted him, and were then felled yourself—for that is more probable than that he dealt you the blow first. At any rate, the man is in a most critical state, and if he dies——"

"But it is impossible!" exclaimed Raoul, horror-struck. "I never bayoneted any one, I swear it!——" He stopped.

"I thought that you did not remember anything!" commented Doctor Walker drily.

There was a long silence. Raoul, after staring at him as if he could not remove his gaze, put a hand to his head, then, with a sound like a groan, covered his eyes with it. The colour flared up hot in his face, then died as suddenly away.

"Do you think, Sir, that I can have done it and have forgotten?" he enquired at last, in a strangely submissive voice, visibly very pale now that the hand was removed.

"To be perfectly frank with you," replied the doctor, leaning back in the chair in a somewhat judicial manner, "I think there are great difficulties in the way of your having done it at all. It is highly improbable that you could have run the sentinel through after a blow from which eight hours' unconsciousness and partial loss of memory have ensued. On the other hand, if you did it before you received the blow, then it is almost equally inconceivable that the unfortunate man can have had sufficient strength to wrest the musket from you again and to deliver one so heavy. I know, of course," he went on, "that you had two companions, and common-sense would point to their having stabbed him and made off. For you must understand that no one witnessed the affray; when the other sentinels, attracted by this man's feeble cries, came up, they found you both lying there, you quite senseless, and he nearly so. But, unfortunately for you, Captain des Sablières, the wounded man was able, before lapsing into an unconsciousness from which he may never emerge again, to make a fragmentary statement by which it appears that it is you, and not either of your companions, whom he charges with the deed. If he recovers sufficiently this statement can be sifted, but if he dies, I am afraid it will go hard with you."

A second silence fell. This was worse than any mere recapture—worse than anything Raoul could have imagined. He gripped his hands together hard under the bedclothes.

"What would happen to me?"

"You would have to stand your trial at Huntingdon Assizes. Killing and forgery—even in the case of military prisoners—come under the civil law."

"Then . . . if I were convicted . . . I should not be shot?"

"No," said Doctor Walker gravely, "you would not be shot."

A little involuntary shudder ran over the young officer, and he turned his bandaged head away.

The doctor bent forward and put a hand on his shoulder. "You are not in Huntingdon Gaol yet," he said. "This is not the moment that I should have chosen to break such serious news to a patient, but I thought it right to let you know how you stand, before Captain Hanwell questions you. I may as well warn you that he is, not unnaturally, extremely incensed, and the Brigade-Major likewise, so much so, indeed, that I had considerable difficulty in saving you from the Black Hole, unconscious as you were—for you are no doubt aware that an officer caught trying to escape is liable to be treated exactly as one of the men. However, I would not have that, nor, I promise you, shall I allow you to be interrogated before I consider you fit for it, and, if possible, not until your memory has returned—which I think may occur at any moment now."

"You are much too kind to me, Sir," said Raoul moved. "If I have done what the man says . . . and perhaps, in a moment of madness, I may have done it . . ." His voice stuck in his throat.

"Tut, tut!" said Doctor Walker with a little smile. "You see, I do not believe you did—not from any acquaintance with your character, but because I think it is physically, impossible. Now if your companions are recaptured——"

"Oh, I am sure they could not have done it!" cried Raoul, alarmed. "They would never have been so foolish . . . I remember hearing Lieutenant Clairet strongly deprecating violence."

"Ah, you can remember something on behalf of a friend, can you?" remarked Doctor Walker, with a little note of appreciation in his tone. "Still, theory and practice are two different things, and, as one of you three must have done it, I think that you personally would be in a better position if they were recaptured, and I should pray for it, if I were you." And he went away without giving Raoul time to reply.

Murder! They said he had done, or attempted, murder! And, for all he knew, they might be right. Alternately panic-struck and unbelieving, Raoul spent the rest of that miserable day trying to batter down the closed door of memory. One or two of the other prisoners in the ward addressed him and condoled with him, but the place was unusually empty, and most of the occupied beds were too far away for conversation, and some of their occupants too ill. The successful escape of Dumont and Clairet afforded general gratification, though it was considered very unfortunate that des Sablières had been left to pay the penalty of their assault on the sentry—for those who had overheard the doctor's opinion shared it, and one patient told Raoul that he had never seen a man who looked less capable of bayoneting anybody than he when he was carried in about midnight. "I thought the dead-house was the proper place for you," concluded this observer.

*

"It must have come back in my sleep, Sir," said Raoul with animation.

96

"When I woke this morning I found I remembered everything."

"Everything?" queried Doctor Walker, standing beside his bed. It was the following morning. "How much does that include?"

"Oh, not what the authorities think," replied the young man, almost cheerfully. "The last thing—but one—that I remember is the flash of a lantern in my face as I was kneeling at the foot of the wall trying to—well, kneeling there; the last thing of all is a smashing blow on the back of my head before I had time to rise. I must have gone down like a log. And there it ends—though I daresay Captain Hanwell will not believe me."

The surgeon looked down at the bright and candid eyes below the bandage.

"You will be able to put that to the test very shortly," he said. "He is coming up here to interrogate you at half-past nine, unless I pronounce you unfit for it."

"Please let him come, Sir," urged Raoul. "I would rather get it over . . . if I may know two things—how the injured sentinel does, and whether my two companions have been recaptured?"

"The sentinel is still alive; that is all one can say. No, your comrades have not been taken, so far. And, if you are not, one of them is guilty."

"Oh, not necessarily," said Raoul stoutly. "Another sentinel may have bayoneted the poor man in the darkness, or he may have impaled himself on his own bayonet."

Doctor Walker went away shaking his head, but Raoul had the temerity to submit this last hypothesis to Captain Hanwell when he, with the Brigade Major, came to interview him about an hour later. He meant it as a real contribution to the problem, but it seemed to be regarded as culpable persiflage, and he could see that it had done him no good in the eyes of the frowning authorities, particularly in those of the military one. His emphatic denial that he had attacked the sentry, his asseveration that the latter, on the contrary, had put him out of action before he could even think of defending himself were, as he had half expected, treated as negligible against the testimony of the injured man himself. And his case was not advanced by his refusal to give, not only any information about his escaped comrades' probable whereabouts (which, to do them justice, the inquisitors seemed scarcely to expect) but about his supposed accomplice in the garrison either—as yet, apparently, undetected, in spite of the telltale rope.

It was a rather exhausted offender who lay back on the pillows when this ordeal was over. But the unspeakably blessed relief of knowing that the blood of the unfortunate militiaman did not lie at his door had upborne him wonderfully, and he could not believe that, if the latter died, the supreme penalty would really be extracted from an innocent man, even in an enemy's country.

So when Wanklin approached him afterwards, his large pale-blue eyes full of a somewhat horrified interest, Raoul observed with a jocularity that was only three parts forced:

"I suppose you feel that you are enjoying the privilege of looking at a condemned criminal, Mr. Wanklin?"

"If you really did not do it, des Sablières, you are in a devilish tight hole," responded this Job's comforter with so much of simple awe in his tone that one could not credit him with malice.

"Are you of opinion, then, that I should be in a more enviable position if I *had* done it?"

Wanklin scratched his chin. "No, not exactly. But if a . . . if a man's got to swing it might as well be for something."

"I had not thought of that," returned Raoul quite gravely. "In that case I had better——"

"You know, I daresay," went on Wanklin without letting him finish, "that about five years ago a prisoner was condemned at the Assizes over a matter like this—only it was a turnkey in his case—and he was hanged . . . hanged *here*, too. It was quite an occasion, I believe—all the garrison under arms, all the prisoners made to be present. He was an officer as well—name of Boucher or something of the sort."

"Well, I hope that you will secure a good place when I afford Norman Cross a holiday of that kind," returned Raoul. "Though I gather that you will then harbour regret that I had no fun for my money, only a knock on the head."

The good Wanklin looked uncomfortable. "I don't think you ought to jest about it, des Sablières—indeed I don't."

"Why, what else is there to do?" demanded Raoul.

What, indeed, as he privately asked himself, when the other two, who had coerced him into flight by the plea of their dependence on his knowledge of English, were, evidently, getting on out there quite well without it, while he was left behind to bear the brunt of their ill-usage of the sentry! Not that Raoul blamed them; the turn of affairs was just the fortune of war, but he could not be blind to its irony. Even if he escaped the dock, he would certainly be punished somehow, and never would he see Wanfield again, however much that kind and generous girl exerted herself on his behalf. And by evening he learnt that the sentry, though still alive, had not made any different deposition about the identity of his assailant. Yes, it was an ironical, though hardly a mirth-provoking situation.

*

Next morning Raoul asked if he might get up, and, having received permission to do so for a while in the afternoon, arose and dressed himself with the assistance of a French hospital orderly. He was obliged, of course, to resume his uniform. Too giddy to walk about, he contented himself with sitting in the stiff chair beside his bed and observing the ward and its occupants, which he was now in a better position to do. He counted eighteen beds each side, of which only ten were filled. All but two of the patients, moreover, were asleep. Wanklin was sitting beside one of them, and there was not a sound in the long room save the buzzing of an imprisoned blue-bottle.

Suddenly the big door of the ward was flung open and an officer came briskly in followed by a sergeant who, however, remained at the door. Raoul tried to stand up, and succeeded for a second, but was obliged to sit down again on his bed, his head swam so. The officer marched up to Wanklin, now in the middle of the ward.

"As the prisoner des Sablières is not to be sent to Huntingdon Gaol for the present he may stay here, on account of his condition," he announced. "He is, of course, to be treated strictly as a prisoner—as a dangerous prisoner."

"But I can't be responsible for him, Captain," replied Mr. Wanklin rather helplessly.

"Oh, your task will be made as light as possible," said the officer. "Sergeant!"

The sergeant advanced, pulling from his tunic something that jangled. The officer made a gesture, and the other wheeled and came down between the beds to Raoul. But Raoul, when he saw the handcuffs, started up and away until he was stopped by the chair and the wall.

"Put them on!" said the officer sharply, and, coming to the foot of the bed, addressed Raoul in person. "It is a concession your being allowed to stay in hospital at all. But if you prefer the Black Hole you have only to say so."

"No," said Raoul faintly; and, overcome by a double nausea, he sat down on the bed again and held out his hands. A wave of scarlet ran over his colourless face as the manacles clicked into position about his wrists. The officer watched the sergeant lock them, and then without more words took himself off again, followed by his subordinate.

Raoul sat stupidly on the side of the bed and watched them go. Then he looked down at his fettered hands. He remained so long in this posture that Wanklin came up and touched him on the shoulder.

"Lie down on your bed again," he counselled. "You'll get used to those things—though it is a shame to put them on—you'll find that you are not by any means helpless in them."

Raoul raised the same rather stunned white face, and after a moment clumsily obeyed him, and lay there shivering—not with cold. Wanklin fetched a blanket and spread it over him, and he lay huddled up, his hands clasping each other as though to assure himself that their close proximity was voluntary. The touch of those abhorred irons brought home to him what he was now—no longer a prisoner of war but a criminal. He knew that there was a murmur of sympathy and indignation among the awakened occupants of the ward, but it did not help him. He was degraded in his own estimation.

That he knew himself innocent did not help him, either; in fact, a cold doubt of his innocence, of the value of his own memory began to invade him.

When Doctor Walker heard the news that evening he looked grave.

"I don't like that done in the hospital," he said, displeased. "But I am afraid that in this case it is the only alternative to the Black Hole."

"Could I not," asked Raoul, with his eyes on the floor, "could I not have them taken off for part of the time—at night, perhaps—if I gave my word not to take advantage of it? I would give you my word of honour, Sir?"

The elder man looked at him half pityingly, half sternly.

"I have no power to accept it, Monsieur des Sablières. And have you a right to expect any one to take it?"

Whether or no he were referring to his lost estate as a reputed parole-breaker, Raoul was utterly silenced by this rebuff, and when Doctor Walker had gone away he rolled over and lay with his face hidden in the pillow.

The others, respecting his mood, did not speak to him. His supper was taken away untouched. He was too sore in spirit to make the first attempt to eat in his shackles before the eyes of the other patients, ludicrous as he felt the spectacle must necessarily be. And as the evening wore on he lay fighting down the mad impulse to try to tear the links apart by main force. It surged over him in waves, and he knew that if he gave way to it he was lost. Yet when, hours later, he had got the better of it and sleep was beginning to come to him, he would move and the constraint catch his wrists and rouse him afresh to the realization of what he wore.

When he woke in the morning he was lying on his back with his hands crossed on his breast after the fashion of a dead man—as he would really be, perhaps, after he had made a spectacle, like that other officer, for Norman Cross.

But the morning light had brought a hardening of resolution. He told himself that he had behaved like a child yesterday—like a guilty man, it might be. Whatever was coming on him he would face with more courage than that. He forced himself to eat his breakfast, clumsily as he did it; and afterwards, observing to Wanklin that, if he had to go as far as Huntingdon, it was time he learnt to walk straight about the ward, rose up and essayed to do so. He staggered a little at first, but after a few turns found his head much steadier. Subdued congratulations greeted him from the other beds, and he acknowledged them; the doctor, too, when he came, approved of his perambulations. He also told him that the sentry was slightly better.

Just before he left he came up to Raoul, now sitting patiently by the side of his bed again, and asked him whether he would like to do a kind action, and when Raoul looked astonished at the request, said, walking meanwhile with him to a door at the end of the ward; "There is a poor young fellow in this little room who will never come out of hospital. I put him in here because it is quiet, but I am afraid that it is sometimes too quiet for him. He is dying of consumption. Would you like to go in and see him? It pleases him to have visitors—when he is fit for it."

Raoul looked down at his wrists. "But a visitor in handcuffs?"

"I have told him about that," said Doctor Walker.

"Will you tell him also, please," said Raoul very quietly, but looking the surgeon straight in the face, "that I am not a 'broke-parole,' for all that I was sent here as one?"

Doctor Walker evidently understood very well that this pronouncement was meant for him rather than for his patient. He gave a little dry smile. "Would it surprise you to hear that that has already been done, Captain des Sablières." And before Raoul, rather taken aback, could answer, he had opened the door, and the visitor went in.

He forgot his fettered hands when he looked at the bed, at the young, virile, but inexpressibly wasted face on the pillow, whose lips gave him a faint and sweet smile like autumn sunshine and spoke in a voice like the whisper of autumn leaves.

"How kind of you to come! I have books—Monsieur le docteur is so good to me—but not many visitors. Will you not sit down? I have heard of your misfortune, but I am sure you——" A fit of coughing shook him. He made or seemed to make a motion towards a glass on the table and Raoul gave it to him—with both hands.

"You see how clever you are, Monsieur!" resumed the phantom voice. "Now, talk to me, if you will be so good . . . about yourself . . . about France. I am from the Pyrenees. And you?"

Soon they were deep in converse, and the thin fingers straying over Raoul's irons. "You will be free—yes, you will be free before very long. But I think I shall be free before you . . . I am so much better, and when I am well enough to travel I am going to be exchanged; the cartel is already made out. And I shall see the mountains again, and the colour of the gaves that tumble down them—there is no water in the world like theirs—and the snows . . . and the little Templar church up at Luz, where I was born. . . . Yes, I think I shall see them."

He was seeing them now, his bright eyes fixed on the bare wall. When Raoul left him, he found tears in his own.

That evening, as he sat on the side of his bed trying to nerve himself to another night of discomfort, Wanklin came up to him with an air of great mystery.

"Would you like to have those handcuffs off for the night, des Sablières?"

"Would I like the moon, Mr. Wanklin?"

The young man sat down beside him on the bed, and showed in his palm a small rusty key, at which Raoul stared uncomprehendingly.

"I picked it up months ago—had no idea what it was—don't know why I kept it. I suddenly remembered it this afternoon, and it looks so much like the one the sergeant . . . Let me see." He bent over Raoul's wrists and inserted the key. It fitted.

But Raoul drew his hands away. "No, no—you will get into trouble if I am found with these off, and I might be."

"Not in the night! Come now!"

"A guard might come for me then, or early in the morning. And it might be traced to you."

But, with a resolution which one would not have expected of him, Mr. Wanklin seized the prisoner's hands again. The key resisted, turned, and the liberator wrenched one of the handcuffs open.

"What have you done?" said Raoul, half aghast.

"Diddled the Transport Office," replied Mr. Wanklin in high glee. "Of course, I should be glad if you would give me your word not to—you know!"

"I swear not to move from this bed. You're a good fellow to trust me, Wanklin." He cautiously stretched out his cramped arms. "My God, it's like heaven!—What, the other one, too?"

The bliss of being able to thrust a hand anywhere under the pillow that night without the other's having perforce to follow it! Excellent, foolish, good-hearted Wanklin! Raoul fell asleep and dreamt that he was trying to induce that bold spirit to follow him out of the ventilator in Number 8.

But when his accomplice came to lock his fetters again next morning his exhilaration seemed to have evaporated; in fact, he looked distinctly glum.

"What is the matter?" asked Raoul, discreetly tendering him his wrists under the bedclothes. "I hope you have not been getting into trouble over this business already?"

"Oh, no," responded Mr. Wanklin. "Nobody knows about it. There is nothing the matter."

But Raoul, unconvinced, supposed that he had some private vexation, the more so that, his mission accomplished, Mr. Wanklin hurried away and did not come near him again. Doctor Walker was late in making his rounds that morning, and evidently pressed for time when he did appear, but, though he did not visit Raoul, the latter was aware of the rather strange glance which he cast upon him as he hurried out of the ward. When he was gone it occurred to the prisoner to wonder very uncomfortably whether the sentry whose condition kept him in such continual uncertainty were worse. The orderlies, being prisoners themselves, would not know, and now Mr. Wanklin, too, had vanished. Well, if the man died he would hear it soon enough!

The sound of coughing coming through the door at the other end of the ward reminded him of Lenepveu, the consumptive, friendly and lonely in there, so he went in to pay him a visit and forget his own uneasiness. The dying man looked ghastly this morning, but he was more full of hope and plans than ever, and talked of the day, now so near (he said) when he should land in Brittany—for Morlaix was the cartel port with England—and of what route he should take to the Pyrenees. . . .

"And your affairs, Monsieur, how do they go?"

"I do not know," answered Raoul. "But I think I am not yet free of the shadow of Huntingdon Gaol."

Lenepveu shook his head with an air of knowledge. "Ah, no, you will not go to an English gaol. I think of you—I see you—on the sea. Yet I shall be free before you. . . ."

At this moment Mr. Wanklin put his head into the room.

"You are wanted, des Sablières. A guard has come to take you to the Superintendent at once."

"Why?" asked Raoul.

"I don't know!" replied Mr. Wanklin.

("You do know!" said Raoul to himself.) "The sentinel's worse, I suppose . . . dead, perhaps?"

"No, no, he's not dead," said Mr. Wanklin with such haste that Raoul was certain he was lying. He got up and straightened himself.

"Good-bye, Lenepveu," he said gently, taking his hands. "Remember to greet France for me when you get to Morlaix!"

The brilliant, wasted smile followed him out into the ward where the corporal's escort was waiting for him.

Two Remorses

"She had lost her taste of pleasure and her ambition of excellence: and her mind, though forced into short excursions, always recurred to the image of her friend."
—*Rasselas, chap. xxxv.*

"Hallo!" exclaimed Mr. Bentley, rustling the newspaper, "here are fine doings at Norman Cross! Tch! tch!"

The other three persons in the room instantly put aside their occupations; that is to say, M. de Sainte-Suzanne, who was instructing Laetitia in the moves of chess, ceased to illustrate, and she to wrinkle her pretty forehead over the grasshopper-like progress of the knight, and Juliana, who had been doing nothing at all, roused herself.

"Listen, my dears," said Mr. Bentley, and read out:

"'On Monday night last three French officers made the most determined attempt, in which two of them succeeded, to escape from Yaxley barracks. Having climbed out through a ventilator from the building in which they were confined, they scaled the stockade and, by means of a rope supplied no doubt by an accomplice, surmounted the great wall. At this point, however, they were discovered by a sentinel of the West Kent Militia, and an affray ensued, in which we regret to report that this valiant sons of Mars was run through the body with his own bayonet, and left in a very serious condition. But as his assailant was also discovered insensible from a blow on the head, this shocking outrage will be punished as it deserves. It is to be hoped that the other two miscreants may also be captured, though so far they appear to have got away.'—Well, well, what a dreadful thing!"

"Papa," said Laetitia very seriously, after a second or two of silence, "I hope that M. des Sablières was not one of those officers!"

"Now why, my dear Letty," asked her parent, looking at her quizzically over the top of the sheet, "why should you imagine that he would be? If young des Sablières has any sense—and I think he has plenty—he would not risk his chances in an escape now."

Juliana was sitting very still on her low chair. "Perhaps he never got my letter, Mr. Bentley."

"Dear me, Juliana, now you! The riches of the female imagination! You wrote, my dear, did you not, on Thursday in last week, and to-day is Friday. A letter might almost have reached Greenland in that time!"

"But the newspaper says the attempt was made as long ago as last Monday night, does it not?"

"Even so, my dear," said her host kindly—for everyone at Northover was especially gentle with Juliana these last ten days—"even so you have no reason whatever to connect des Sablières with this attempt. I suppose there must be some hundreds of French officers at Norman Cross."

"Yes, I know that I am foolish," said Juliana in a low voice. And M. de Sainte-Suzanne, who was watching her from his place by the chessboard, saw that her eyes had filled with tears.

"Would it not be possible to find out for certain, Bentley?" he suggested. "Bannister might have heard something."

"He might, he might," agreed Mr. Bentley. He, too, was looking at Juliana. "I was thinking of going into Wanfield this afternoon—I'll start at once, and call on him. We cannot have these dark fancies." He got up and patted Juliana's shoulder, and she caught his hand and gave it a little pressure.

Most certainly Juliana needed—though she told herself that she did not deserve—all the sympathy which was hers at Northover. Although—chiefly for Sir Francis's sake—the rupture of her engagement was not yet announced, any awakened eye could see that she was not wearing her betrothal ring, and Sir Francis's absence from Mulholland Park . . . on urgent and unexplained affairs . . . had now lasted for over a week. Very soon the thousand tongues of rumour would all be busy with her and him, and he would be lucky if no connection were established between her dismissal of him and the just-proclaimed innocence of M. des Sablières.

Had Juliana been less high of spirit than she was, she would have fled from Wanfield before her Northover visit was completed. But it was not, she felt, of what she had done now that she should be ashamed, but of what she had brought about by her conduct that March day. The honour of the man who had been wronged through her lay in her hands, and she did not mean to leave the place until she had some assurance that it was to be publicly cleared by his restoration to parole—of which so far nothing had been heard. Moreover, though she did not know how she could look him in the face, yet if "Mr. Rowl" were sent back to Wanfield within a reasonable time, she would wish to meet him. She could not be happy in her mind till she had heard from his own lips that he had forgiven her, and believed what she had said in her letter—that she had not shielded herself at his expense. For *Rasselas*, lying on her dressing table, whispered to her daily that he suspected she had.

And after this her next task would be to placate her father, who, though in general extremely amenable, had exhibited by letter a very lively sense of his only daughter's waywardness, though he lamented rather than condemned the rupture with Mulholland, and promised to throw all his influence on the side of Mulholland's victim. Nothing but an attack of gout had prevented his arriving in person to remonstrate with Juliana; and only expressions of profound penitence from his erring offspring had deterred him (so he wrote) from sending his carriage to fetch her away at once from the locality where she had done so much mischief and earned, or was about to earn, such uncomfortable notoriety.

(But Lord Fulgrave knew in his heart, and Miss Juliana knew, too, that what really deterred him from this exhibition of paternal authority was the conviction that the carriage would have returned as empty as it started.)

*

Almost directly Mr. Bentley had gone, Laetitia discovered that it was time for her to set off to the lodge to read to old Betty as she had promised. Would M. de Sainte-Suzanne keep Miss Forrest company until she or her father returned?

"Most willingly," replied the old Frenchman, "if Miss Forrest will be satisfied with me. I cannot hope for the privilege of teaching her chess, for she knows it already. But perhaps she will accept my arm round the garden?"

Restless and apprehensive—unnecessarily apprehensive, no doubt—Juliana was glad of the suggestion. She liked the Comte, though she was a trifle in awe of him. And since the nineteenth of March she had felt a certain constraint in his presence, while being grateful to him for so unexpectedly abstaining from public condemnation of the unfortunate Mr. Rowl. Now, walking slowly along the terrace with her hand resting lightly on that meagre arm, she suddenly realized not only that it was the first time they had been alone together since her return to Wanfield, but also that the foolish feeling of constraint was ebbing away. That the old Royalist had seen her and M. des Sablières together by the stream that day was surely *now* a bond between them, not a barrier. She even had an impulse to speak to him about it, and when, having paced round the lawn, talking of nothing in particular, they reached the terrace again she was not sorry when M. de Sainte-Suzanne said apologetically:

"But here am I chattering like an old magpie, while you are anxious about that report from Norman Cross. You must forgive me, Mademoiselle."

"I think I should not be so foolish if I had not a bad conscience," said Juliana dejectedly.

The Comte stopped. "Mademoiselle, I wish mine were as clear as yours! Will you allow an old man the privilege of saying how much he admires your courage? I tread on delicate ground, I know . . . but I am so very old!"

Juliana half laughed, though her eyes were misty. She was aware that he knew the truth about her engagement. "I am afraid that you are not very accurate, Monsieur le Comte! And I could not do anything else but what I have done latterly. But oh, if only I had not been so wilful!"

"Wilful?" asked M. de Sainte-Suzanne, raising his eyebrows.

"You do not know the whole story—only Mr. Bentley and Laetitia know that. But, as you saw M. des Sablières and me together that day by the stream, I think I ought to tell you. . . . Shall we sit on this seat? I daresay that when you saw us, however surprised you may have been, you thought at any rate it was a chance meeting?"

M. de Sainte-Suzanne seated himself beside her. "Had I allowed myself to speculate about it," he said with his fine smile, "I should undoubtedly have thought so."

"But it was not, Comte! It was I who . . . suggested to M. des Sablières that he should be there that afternoon. I wanted to give him a book, and I returned to Mulholland Park that way on purpose. So—though I had no thought in my head but to—show my independence" (the words came out very low, and she studied the gravel), "you see that it is I who am to blame for everything."

"But, my dear young lady," said the old man, "though in a sense that may be true—and one but thinks the more highly of you for acknowledging it—still, it was in no way your doing that this vagabond was in the little wood and tried to rob you, and so brought about M. des Sablières' intervention."

"Ah, yes, it was," said Juliana, "because if I had not—had not acted so, the vagabond might have been there indeed, but I should not. I should have gone back the other way, and so M. des Sablières would never have been involved in any difficulty."

"Well, well," said the Comte, "we cannot all be wise when we are young. Nor, even if we live to be old, can we foretell the consequences of our actions—a merciful dispensation, no doubt, of the good God."

He had made it easy for Juliana to talk to him. Now she was looking at the austere profile with her own brows drawn together. "There is one thing which has puzzled me so much, and that is, how M. des Sablières could have forgotten that you saw us together, so short a time before the vagrant attacked me? When he—when his word was doubted as to my being in the copse, why did he not say to Mr. Bannister: 'But the Comte de Sainte-Suzanne saw Miss Forrest near the copse just at that time?' You would have confirmed that, if he had asked you, would you not?"

The Comte inclined his head. "Certainly—if he had asked me."

"It seems so strange to have forgotten," repeated Juliana musingly. "But the whole affair must have been so sudden, such a shock. Mr. Bannister has told me about that interview."

M. de Sainte-Suzanne got up and began to examine the climbing rose just by them, whose new green promise was once more clothing the old bricks of Northover. He picked off a leaf and looked at it.

"You are sure, Mademoiselle, that he *did* forget?"

Juliana gazed up at him, astonished. "What do you mean, Comte? Not—surely—that he believed you would refuse to bear out his statement?"

"No, Mademoiselle, I do not mean that." He dropped the leaf. "It is a beautiful afternoon; Mr. Bentley cannot be back yet; will you do me the honour to walk with me as far as my little cottage, Mademoiselle Juliana? I can answer your question better there."

"Yes, certainly I will come with you, if you wish," said Juliana, her surprise

110

not lessened.

*

The Comte's little house—it really was not more than a cottage—lay a bare ten minutes from the gates of Northover. Juliana had been there once or twice with Laetitia to drink tea with the old man, but she was struck afresh to-day with its impeccable orderliness. He had a wrinkled French servant—perhaps that was the reason. But then the same order pervaded his stiff little garden, which was not in her hands.

"Perrine, bring us your elderberry wine and some biscuits," said M. de Sainte-Suzanne, and in the spotless parlour conducted his guest, with his usual punctilious courtesy, to a comfortable chair; and Juliana, not to be outdone in the same quality, sipped some of the elderberry wine, which she disliked, and looked once more at the pastel portrait of the young man in uniform over the mantelpiece, cut down, as she had heard, by the Republican soldiers in Alsace because he refused to ask quarter, and brought back, after Condé's victory, on the gun he had died to save. Twenty years dead, he was very handsome, very gay; and his sword hung beneath him, and beneath that again a little wreath of immortelles, so dry and shrivelled that to Juliana they only emphasized what they commemorated. Her glance went thence to the tiny garden, with its beehives each exactly the same number of inches apart, and a sense of great sadness came over her. M. de Sainte-Suzanne could have gone back years ago, had he wished, to his estates and revenues in France. But no, that would have involved recognizing and making his peace with the usurper. Rather than belie his convictions he lived on year after year in exile, poverty, and cramped surroundings, his family dead, with nothing to look forward to except what seemed a very improbable desire on the part of his native land for the return of the Bourbons. A dead bough—the words came back to her, and the withered everlastings seemed to lend point to them. And yet . . . decay had its dignity.

Meanwhile the old man had been unlocking a writing table, and came back with a letter.

"Here is the answer to your question, Mademoiselle. I received this, by an unknown hand, from the gaol the day that M. des Sablières was taken thence to Norman Cross. You read French, I know."

Juliana took the missive, written on coarse paper with an obviously superannuated pen, and in an unfamiliar foreign script. One glance at the signature—which sent the colour to her cheeks—and she read:

Wanfield Gaol, March 21, 1813.

Monsieur le Comte:

You saw me on Friday afternoon about four o'clock in converse with a certain lady on the banks of the stream. After she had left me at the bridge the lady was attacked in Fawley Copse by a tramp; I naturally rushed to her assistance, and had the good fortune to beat him off. To do this I was obliged to go out of bounds for ten minutes or so. For this technical breach of parole, and because it is asserted that, the lady in question being elsewhere at the time, the whole story is a fabrication, I am now in gaol and shall probably be sent to Norman Cross.

Since I could have requested you, had I wished, to testify to this lady having been in my company that afternoon shortly before the occurrence, and have not done so, you will understand why I ask you henceforward to forget the fact. The lady has now left the neighbourhood, and, I am sure is ignorant of the turn events have taken. I do not wish her to be caused annoyance nor would you, I am certain, desire her name to be coupled, however innocently, with that of a man on whom you have publicly turned your back.

Raoul-Marie-Amédée des Sablières.

But, by the land which gave us both birth, I swear to you that I did not break my parole—except in a fashion that any man must have done for the moment.

The colour had left Juliana's face. "He *did* not forget, then—he went to prison for a scruple! He could have saved himself! Oh, why did he do it? I was not ashamed of having met him!"

The Comte sat down beside her. "My dear young lady, I am sure he was quite content to go to prison for a scruple of that sort. He is a gentleman, and it was not for him to mention having had the pleasure of a previous meeting with you, especially—may I say so now you have honoured me with your confidence?—especially if it was not a chance meeting. He probably feared that that fact would come to light. No, no, my dear, you must not blame yourself unduly. He did quite right. Yet I, to my eternal regret, when I saw him marched off to gaol, I did as he says—I turned my back upon him."

But Juliana was too much occupied by her own self-reproach to feel M. de Sainte-Suzanne's very keenly. She got up and walked rather agitatedly to the window, pulling out her handkerchief. The outlines of the beehives were no longer quite clear to her.

"I have heard you criticize M. des Sablières because he served the Emperor," she said, dabbing surreptitiously at her eyes. "You said such soldiers had no traditions and no breeding. How could any one have behaved more honourably, more chivalrously, than he has done?"

"Mademoiselle, I have told you that I am full of remorse. But I do not recede from my position," replied the inveterate old aristocrat. "M. des Sablières—one in a hundred of the 'Emperor's' officers—has breeding and traditions, and I ought to have known that they would tell, in spite of his environment. No, I could not have wished Félix"—he glanced for a moment at the portrait—"to have behaved otherwise. I shall welcome the day when I can beg M. des Sablières' pardon for misjudging him."

"But," said Juliana half irritably, "one cannot count on that now. If he has escaped—or if by chance he is the recaptured officer . . . no, I will not believe that, it would be too much ill-fortune. . . . Let us return to Northover, Monsieur, for Mr. Bentley may be back now." She picked up the cloak which she had let slide and her host put it over her shoulders. But as he did so a thought struck her, and she turned again: "Then all this time—ever since M. des Sablières went to Norman Cross, indeed—you have known the truth about him, Monsieur de Sainte-Suzanne?"

"Yes—in confidence. It has been at once a reproach and a consolation to me."

"Then I think you might have shared it with me before!" said Miss Forrest rather indignantly.

"My dear Mademoiselle Juliana, I am not sure that I ought to have shown you that letter even now! Certainly I would not have done so before you admitted me into your confidence about the rendezvous. The whole point of the letter was to bid me forget the fact that I had seen you together, and I endeavoured to do so."

"But——" began Juliana and then stopped, for there were steps in the little hall, Perrine's voice at the door announcing, "Monsieur Bent-lee," and that gentleman himself walking hastily in, too perturbed to be tactful.

"It's true, I'm sorry to say—that is, Bannister has heard that the recaptured officer came from Wanfield, which is sufficient to identify him as des Sablières. And the sentinel has died. . . . Most unfortunate affair. . . . I shall go to Yaxley to-morrow to see the boy and get the facts, then to Peterborough or Huntingdon to interview an attorney. He must have the best possible legal assistance if the case goes to the Assizes. Of course there will be an inquest first and——My dear Juliana, drink this!"

He caught up the half-empty wine-glass as Juliana sank down, white as her dress, upon the nearest chair. She shook her head.

"I am quite well. And if you go to Norman Cross to-morrow I shall go with you. Mr. Bentley, he deliberately threw away . . . Oh, I can't. . . ." She could not, at any rate, finish.

A Better Gift than "Rasselas"

"The violence of war admits no distinction; the lance that is lifted at guilt and power will sometimes fall on innocence and gentleness." "How little," said I, "did I expect that yesterday it should have fallen upon me!"–Rasselas, chap. xxxviii.

"To visit a French officer prisoner, Sir? That rests with the Superintendent, Captain Hanwell. If you will drive round the barracks here you will see the east gate of the prison before you, and the turnkey there will send your card in. I do not suppose there will be any difficulty."

Then this group of buildings was only the barracks; the prison itself was behind that high encircling wall which they had already seen as they approached Norman Cross by the Great North Road. Mr. Bentley had alighted from the chaise and was talking to the officer who had appeared on their being stopped by a sentry; and Juliana, with her heavy heart, had moved nearer to the window to hear better.

Mr. Bentley was now uttering thanks. Then she heard him say dubiously, "I suppose you are not able to tell me, Sir, how matters stand with Captain des Sablières, who is alleged to have fatally injured a sentinel?"

"Oh, is that the fellow you have come to see!" exclaimed the soldier. By now he had evidently become aware of the fair face at the chaise window. "You will be glad to hear, then, that as the sentinel has exonerated him——"

Both Mr. Bentley and Juliana gave an exclamation. "But we understood that the sentinel had died!" ejaculated the former in astonishment.

"He nearly did, I believe. But he is now on the road to recovery, and when, last night, his evidence was taken again, he retracted his former accusation against Captain des Sablières—said, in fact, that he had never really made it, knowing that he had knocked des Sablières senseless at the outset." Here the beautiful daughter at the chaise window showed signs of agitation—lucky dog, this Frenchman!

Mr. Bentley breathed an enormous sigh of relief. "There is then no prospect of M. des Sablières having to stand his trial?"

"None at all, that I can see," responded the young man. "Punishment of some sort, of course, he will get, for one can't encourage escaping, you know, Sir, but nothing—er—condign, I am glad to say." He delicately emphasized the reason for his sympathetic attitude by a tiny bow in the direction of the chaise.

"I am very greatly obliged to you, Sir," said Mr. Bentley. "You have relieved us from a terrible apprehension. What a relief! Juliana, my dear, we are to drive to the prison entrance yonder. I will walk; 'tis not worth my reëntering." And he motioned the postilion forward, while Juliana leant back with her hands over her face.

There followed a wait, which seemed to her endless, in the turnkey's lodge outside the East gate, till at last the messenger from the interior returned, and the turnkey announced to Mr. Bentley that Captain Hanwell would allow him to see the prisoner he named.

"As a matter of fact," he added, "he's interviewing him himself at the moment. If you will follow this man he'll take you across to the Superintendent's office there."

So they went through the great gate, and were in the precincts of the prison to which she had sent her friend. Down a long wide alley in front of her Juliana saw the guns of the central blockhouse, and had an impression of penned humanity. But her mind was in such a turmoil that she was not conscious of much except palisading and sentries everywhere, and over the palisading the chimney-less, almost windowless casernes, roof after roof. . . . Their guide bore to the left across the open space dotted with sentry boxes, and stopped at a low building in a line with the stockade. It was of wood, like all the rest, and appeared to be an office, for within, at a high desk, was seated a clerk who incontinently withdrew himself into an inner room. Then, the turnkey likewise departing, Juliana was able at last to give vent to her relief.

"Oh, Mr. Bentley, let us thank God that the sentinel is alive—and has told the truth!"

"Indeed, my dear Juliana, I do," replied her companion with warmth, "and our young friend may do the same, as I hope he does. If this man had died, I don't like to think what might have happened to the boy."

"But, Mr. Bentley," protested Juliana indignantly, "how could any jury believe so monstrous a charge?"

"'Monstrous,' my dear?" queried Mr. Bentley gravely. "It might very well have been true!"

"What! M. des Sablières bayonet a sentinel!"

Mr. Bentley shook his head. "My dear child, an escaping prisoner is usually desperate. When a young man's blood is up, when his liberty is at stake—however, we need not pursue that subject, but thank God with all our hearts that des Sablières was saved from that extremity. . . . Now sit down, and compose yourself after all this fatigue and anxiety. I understand that Captain Hanwell is interviewing our friend at this moment—I suppose in this very building—no doubt to announce to him the favourable change in his circumstances."

Juliana obediently sat down on a bench against the wall. Her eyes went round the unattractive room, where the paper was peeling from the walls. Through the window she could see an empty enclosure, looking damp and sodden and inexpressibly dreary, and, at the end of a paved path which ran diagonally from the rear of this little building, the caserne, just like all the rest, which their guide had pointed out as the officers' quarters. This was the place to which she had sent him!

But oh, it might have been a thousand times worse! It might have been Huntingdon Gaol on a capital charge! And that would have been her doing, too. But now, cleared of this dangerous accusation, and with all the evidence to hand of his initial innocence, he would soon be released. Perhaps in time he would forget this unmerited captivity and who had brought it upon him. Would he return to Wanfield . . . would he wish to return to Wanfield?

Mr. Bentley, who was slowly pacing up and down with his hands behind his back, now came to a stop, listening, and a tramp of feet was heard outside. Juliana got up, her heart beating painfully.

The steps halted at the door, which began to open. A voice which she did not recognize said in low tones of entreaty, "For God's sake take these things off before I——" and another replied sharply, "Out of the question. In with you!" Then the door swung wide, and there, standing just inside by the wall, not looking at them, was Raoul des Sablières, in the gay, trim uniform he had worn at the January ball. The door shut again.

But it was not the Raoul of the ball, nor indeed he of the stream. For a moment Juliana hardly knew him. His face was nearly as white as the unforeseen bandage round his head, and there were dark circles under his eyes as if from illness. But the expression on his face was one of shock, of flinching. The next second Juliana realized also why he kept his arms in that unnatural position in front of him—his wrists were chained together. She stifled a faint cry and shrank back in her corner.

Mr. Bentley, who also had seemed for an instant disconcerted, now took a step or two towards the unmoving figure and held out his hand.

"My dear des Sablières, I am very glad to see you! I hope the bandage does not mean anything serious?" Then he perceived why Raoul had made no motion to take his hand, and, biting his lip, he dropped it.

"We have come, my dear fellow," he began again, "Miss Forrest and I——"

"Miss Forrest!" exclaimed the young man. His pale face was suddenly tinged with colour; he lifted his head sharply, and saw her indeed in the background. The colour deepened painfully; then it ebbed in a rather startling manner. He made an inclination of the head in Juliana's direction, and after an instant said, still in that voice which seemed someone else's, but was now expressionless, "It is very kind of you, Sir . . . and Miss Forrest. I can say good-bye."

"Say good-bye!" ejaculated Mr. Bentley. "What on earth do you mean? Don't stand there like that, my boy, but come and sit down and tell us the whole story. We have heard some of it—that is to say, the end—and we are happy to know that——"

He did not finish. Raoul had broken into the most disconcerting and mirthless little laugh.

"Have you heard the end, Mr. Bentley—the real end? I think not, or you would hardly use the word 'happy'!"

"Surely you are not going to stand your trial after all?" exclaimed Mr. Bentley in alarm, and again his glance dwelt on the handcuffs.

The bandaged head was shaken. "I wish to God I were! I might have had a chance then . . . for I did not bayonet the sentinel, Mr. Bentley, and I think I could have proved it. And even if I had been hanged for what I did not do, it would have been over quickly. But now . . . it will not be over quickly, for I am going . . . they are sending me——" He obviously found it hard to finish, and, gripping his fettered hands tightly together, bent his head and turned

118

away.

"My dear boy, where?" asked Mr. Bentley, putting a hand on his shoulder.

Raoul swung round again. "To hell, Mr. Bentley. To the hulks at Plymouth."

Juliana gave a sharp cry. "The hulks!"

"Good God!" said Mr. Bentley, horror-struck. Then he recovered himself. "But that is impossible—a mistake! You are an officer—an officer cannot be sent to the hulks!"

"When an officer tries to escape he loses the privileges of his rank," answered Raoul bitterly. "I am going with a gang of mutineers which is starting on Monday for Plymouth, the hulks at Chatham and Portsmouth being so overcrowded at present that even the Transport Board cannot cram in any more."

"Going with the common soldiers—mutineers—you!" said Mr. Bentley. "It is unheard of—outrageous! I shall see Captain Hanwell about it at once!"

"I assure you that it is useless, Mr. Bentley. He will listen to nothing; he has, I understand, his orders. And it *has* happened before to officers. I have taken part in an escape with violence . . . and I am the only one who can be punished. The other two, I am glad to say, got away."

"And it was they, of course, who stabbed the sentinel! Oh, something must be done about this! Captain Hanwell must be reminded that you were wrongly sent here in the first instance. Has he not heard from the Transport Office on that point—has he not received Bannister's letter?—You know, don't you, that it has all come out—that Miss Forrest . . ."

"Yes, I know," answered Raoul, and he looked briefly, painfully, towards Juliana. "I received Miss Forrest's very kind letter."

"But has Captain Hanwell had no official communication?" persisted Mr. Bentley. "That must be looked into. I shall see him myself—I will take no denial! How can I get at him? There's a clerk in there, I believe."

Raoul's eyes dwelt on him in a manner which did not suggest that he had any great hopes from his intervention as Mr. Bentley went to the inner door and knocked upon it and called. He said nothing, and never looked at

Juliana during the short parley which ensued between that gentleman and the clerk whom he did indeed cause to emerge, and who agreed, not very willingly, to take him into Captain Hanwell's own office adjoining.

And so the next minute, the two were gone, and in the dull, disheartening little room were left the girl, looking like some strayed figure of Spring in her pretty white jaconet dress and the cape of green silk slung by a cord across her shoulders, and the young hussar in his silver-grey bravery, with a bandage round his head which might well have testified to a battlefield and its painful honours. But Spring had horror and remorse in her gaze, and the handcuffs made a mockery of the uniform.

Its wearer was plainly only too conscious of that fact. He stood rigid by the discoloured wall, quite silent, his eyes on the floor, his fettered hands, as always, in front of him. "He does not want even to look at me," thought Juliana, transfixed with misery. "He hates me—he knows it is I who have brought him to this. He would rather be alone." But then, as if he had read her thoughts, the young man suddenly lifted his head, looked at her out of his dark-ringed eyes, and said gently:

"It is so kind of you to have come . . . and to have written like that, Mademoiselle. But why do you not sit down—is it too dusty in this horrible place? . . . I wish you need not have been brought here."

And from his tone she felt sure that he meant, "to see me like this." The conviction that he was humiliated by her presence, that indeed, since she had come too late, it would have been kinder to have kept away, brimmed over the cup of her unhappiness, and she sank down on the bench that might or might not have been dusty and put her hands over her face.

"Mademoiselle," came his voice, less unfamiliar and strained, "please do not be so distressed! This cannot be helped, and Mr. Bentley should not have exposed you to—to the . . . *Mon Dieu*, are you crying? Why should you cry?"

What a question! Suddenly Juliana was sobbing helplessly, and then she knew that he was beside her, having moved for the first time from his self-chosen station.

"Please do not cry!" he said, and his voice was now as she remembered it.

"Mademoiselle, if I am guilty of making you do that I do indeed deserve heavy punishment!"

But that observation, and the attempt at lightness with which it was uttered, did nothing to check Juliana's tears.

Raoul sat down on the bench beside her. "Mademoiselle, *de grâce*! You make me so ashamed to have let you see that . . . that I do not like my sentence. You must try to forgive me . . . I had only just heard it; but now I am a little braver. Mademoiselle!"

Juliana Forrest was not readily given to tears, and she found it proportionately difficult to control them now. Yet amid their mingled bitterness and relief she felt that she really was distressing him, and wasting the precious time as well. She made a great effort over herself and presently was drying her eyes. And the question which for twenty-four hours had tormented her came out, not free of reproach:

"If you had my letter, why, why did you try to escape?"

"Yes, I do not wonder at your asking that!" he said, with a little phantom smile. "It was because I was already committed to the enterprise. I tried to withdraw, but . . . my comrades needed me. I knew that my conduct would seem foolish, and worse, ungrateful—but indeed I was not ungrateful, Mademoiselle, only unable to do otherwise. I meant to write to you when I got out. But now . . . I see you and I can tell you myself how divinely kind and generous it was of you to write that letter."

"Generous! I? When it is entirely my doing that you are in this situation!"

"No, not *yours*, Mademoiselle!"

She coloured, and dropped her gaze. It rested on her ringless hand. Then she raised her eyes again bravely. "Yes, mine, Monsieur des Sablières. You know it was my . . . my pique and self-will which brought about all this."

"Mademoiselle——" began Raoul, embarrassed, but she went on quickly: "It is true, Monsieur des Sablières—alas, I wish it were not! But I know that you might have saved yourself with Mr. Bannister, if you had been willing to risk a possible slight injury to the reputation of a girl who did not deserve such consideration. Oh, why did you not call the Comte de Sainte-Suzanne as a witness to my whereabouts? Indeed you were too chivalrous. I had no wish to hide the fact that we had met that day by the stream—had I known what hung on it I would have blazoned it abroad."

"Ah, Mademoiselle. . . ." said the young man. His eyes thanked her. "But . . . it was not so simple as that. It was not that, by calling the Comte, I so much feared for you the revelation of our very harmless little promenade by the stream, as that, for all I knew, you yourself had—and were not to be blamed for it if it seemed good to you—you yourself really had told a certain person that you had returned by the highroad, and had said nothing about Fawley Copse. I know now that it was not so, but I could not be sure of it, then. So how could I call a witness who might prove you . . . a liar?"

"And you went to prison rather than run the risk of that?"

"But of course, Mademoiselle!" He seemed surprised at the question. "How could I repay your kindness by doing such a thing?"

"Kindness!" said Juliana in a low voice. Her lip trembled a little. She looked at him sitting there beside her, pale, injured, fettered—her victim, and yet how immeasurably above her! He was her judge. The thought of her rejected gift returned sharply to her.

"Monsieur des Sablières, I *implore* you to say that you believe I did not lie!"

He turned his bandaged head quickly.

"Mademoiselle, what are you thinking of me? Did you not tell me so in your letter? That was enough for me. Ah, it is I who should be imploring you for pardon that I ever thought you might have done so. But I never, for one moment, thought that you had done it knowing that I was in difficulties—never, never! And I begin to think now," he added on a sudden half-whimsical note, "that since it distresses you so, I had better not have chosen the hospitality of Captain Hanwell. But it seemed the right course to take, then."

That she should be driving him to apologize for his heroism and his chivalry was more intolerable than the other position. She sprang up. "You think I am blaming you!" she exclaimed. "Oh, Monsieur des Sablières, you must hate the very sight of me!"

"That," said Raoul as he rose, with something of his old easy, buoyant manner, "is not very probable, even if I were going to be hanged for what you choose to imagine is your doing, chère Mademoiselle Forrest! And hanging, as you know, is not to be my fate. As for the hulks, perhaps I shall not stay there very long. An old ship and some water——"

The opening of the door stopped him. It was Mr. Bentley, unsuccessful, as was evident from his expression.

"It is of no use," he said dejectedly. "Captain Hanwell expresses regrets, but he has definite orders from London. And he *has* received Mr. Bannister's letter. I do not see what further plea can be brought to bear on him."

"But, Mr. Bentley," objected Juliana, "evidently Captain Hanwell cannot realize that the initial injustice of M. des Sablières' having been sent here at all is being pressed upon the Commissioners at this moment by my father and others. He surely has sufficient discretionary powers allowed him to wait a few days and see the result. I shall go and interview him myself!"

"My dear, I am really afraid——" began Mr. Bentley.

"Do not go, I beg of you, Mademoiselle," said Raoul, looking rather startled. "Even to you I do not think he will listen. I assure you I was not dumb myself." He smiled, half wryly, at the recollection.

"Yes, I must see him," said Juliana firmly. "My father's name should have some weight. If Mr. Bentley did not actually ask for a little delay——"

"No, my dear, I can't remember that I urged that. I argued rather from the premises you mention, that M. des Sablières ought never to have been sent here at all."

"Then I have a sufficiently good reason for an interview," said Miss Forrest, "and I shall not be asking for too much. Will you take me to Captain Hanwell, Mr. Bentley? . . . I shall see you again to take farewell, Monsieur des Sablières."

"God bless you, Mademoiselle," he answered. "But—if they should have taken me away? . . ."

Juliana held out her hand, with a look which proclaimed as plainly as speech, not what she thought of herself and her part in this calamity, but what she thought of his. Rather dazzled, Raoul took the little hand, as best he could, in both his own and put his lips to it.

In his own office, where there was no wallpaper to peel, so lined were the walls with pigeonholes, at a large table heaped with docketed papers and files, Captain William Hanwell, R. N., had now turned from the des Sablières affair, which as far as he was concerned, he considered closed, to his correspondence with the Transport Board on a subject about which that body were just as inquisitorial, namely, the undue consumption and the ultimate fate of the birch brooms in use at Norman Cross.

Captain Hanwell was fairly new to his present duties, having succeeded the late Agent, the popular Captain Draper, just two months before. Like nearly all in his position, he was a naval official, the Transport Office being a branch of the Admiralty. The successful escape of Dumont and Clairet, the attack on the sentry, a certain amount of friction with General Williams and Brigade-Major Mills, the discovery of the complicity of the man Marwin, and some very stiff letters from the Commissioners about the affair were not a particularly auspicious prelude to his third month of office, and it would have been surprising if he had been sympathetic to des Sablières when he had had him before him just now. The culprit had been so stunned by his sentence that it had taken the news of Marwin's prospective five hundred lashes to rouse him. He had then pleaded hard for the unfortunate militiaman, and was told that he should have considered the probable results to the latter before suborning him. Yet Captain Hanwell, if stern, was neither vindictive nor unjust; he had every right to be angry, and he was only carrying out his instructions.

He had just taken up his pen to assure the Commissioners that the old broom stumps should be received back into store as they ordered, when there was a knock at the door, it opened, and there came in a beautiful, tall girl, simply and elegantly dressed, accompanied by the oldish gentleman he had already interviewed.

"Miss Juliana Forrest, Lord Fulgrave's daughter, desires the favour of a word with you, Sir," said this Mr. Bentley; and there was nothing for Captain

Hanwell to do but to jump up and fetch her a chair, and exhibit all the attention proper from a naval officer to a member of the fair sex. But when this attractive intruder reopened the question of the fate of des Sablières he presented an immovable front.

"I do not for a moment doubt your testimony, Miss Forrest," he assured her when she referred to the episode of the tramp. "In substance it is already familiar to me, you know, from a letter which I received from the Agent at Wanfield. But you see, do you not, that to adjudicate on Captain des Sablières' past innocence or guilt never came within my province. He was sent to me as a 'broke-parole', and as a 'broke-parole' I received him, and that past guilt or innocence does not, unfortunately, at all affect the question of the grave misdemeanour he has committed since."

"But all I ask for, Sir," replied Juliana, "is a few days' delay—only that you should not send him to the hulks on Monday. My father and my cousin, the Earl of Chichester, are both interesting themselves in this case; it is impossible that nothing should come of their representations to the Transport Office."

"Again I do not doubt your word, Miss Forrest, but I must point out that there is no trace of this in the instructions I have just received from the Commissioners."

"But by Monday you may well receive different instructions," pleaded Miss Forrest, a bright spot on either cheek. "This place is not very far from London."

"Seventy-six miles," returned Captain Hanwell, with precision. "If I hear from the Board in Captain des Sablières' favour on Monday you may rest assured, Miss Forrest, that he will not go with the draft. More than that I cannot possibly promise."

"You could not, then, yourself write to the Board," suggested Juliana, "and point out that representations are being made to them . . ." She paused suggestively.

Captain Hanwell almost permitted himself a smile. The lady was very persistent for her Frenchman; it occurred to him to wonder whether

Viscount Fulgrave, for his part, were being quite so assiduous in London.

"They must themselves be aware of it, Madam," he replied, "if such influential pressure as his lordship's and the Earl of Chichester's is being brought to bear on them. And to inform them that—er—representations are also being made to me, who cannot move in the matter without their orders, would, I think, prejudice rather than advantage the prisoner's case."

"I think Captain Hanwell is right there, my dear," observed Mr. Bentley, who had wisely left Juliana to conduct this duel by herself.

"But I am sure that you will hear from them," reiterated Miss Forrest with feminine persistence. "If you could only keep him back a few days!"

"Impossible," replied Captain Hanwell rather shortly. "In the first place, I should be disobeying the plain orders of the Board just transmitted to me; in the second, were I willing to disobey them on the chance of the arrival of a counter order, I should be obliged, if no such order came, to incur the expense of a separate escort for des Sablières. And—you must forgive me if I sound unduly harsh—apart from my orders, I cannot personally see why he, who has actually broken prison and been concerned in the shedding of blood, should suffer a less punishment than the misguided ruffians in Block No. 4 who have done neither."

It was, evidently, hopeless. He did not want him to be reprieved.

"And how will Captain des Sablières go to Plymouth?"

"He will march with the rest, Miss Forrest."

"March!—from Huntingdonshire to the extreme limit of Devonshire!"

"Prisoners are only required to do on an average twelve miles a day."

"Then it will take . . . weeks!"

"It is a healthy enough life in fine weather."

"The journey will probably be preferable to what he finds when he arrives, poor boy," put in Mr. Bentley sadly.

"Yes, I think you are right, there," agreed Captain Hanwell with a certain grimness. And he rose, to indicate the end of the interview.

"You think me hard, I am sure, Miss Forrest," he said, as he went to open the door for her, "but you must remember that an unfortunate sentinel has all but lost his life over this business, and another has to be flogged. Pending any reconsideration of their order by the Commissioners, des Sablières must take his punishment, too. And I should not be doing you a kindness if I held out any hope of its being remitted, now. I am sorry. Good afternoon." He bowed, and they found themselves outside in the damp.

"Oh, what a hard, cruel man!" said Juliana. "And I, what have I done—what have I done!"

"You have done your best, my dear," said Mr. Bentley, patting her arm. "You must not be morbid over it. The terrible pity is that the boy tried to escape—especially after getting your letter. I can't understand his doing it. *That* was not your fault."

"Yes, everything is my fault, because I sent him here," said the girl. "He did not want to escape, but the others needed him, it appears." Struggling for her composure she glanced at the door of the other office; the sentry was still on guard outside. "And now we have to tell him that there is no hope of remission!"

"Well, I'll do it, my child," said Mr. Bentley compassionately. "I think you had better not see him again, since it distresses you so."

"Oh, no," replied Juliana instantly. "I *must* see him again—and I think," she added, "that I would rather see him alone."

"Very well, my dear. I will wait for you out here."

*

Raoul des Sablières was sitting on the bench in the far corner, his elbows on his knees, his face hidden in his hands. He did not seem to have heard the door open, for he made no movement, and Juliana was able to stand near it a moment till she was sure she could control her voice. It was only for her sake, then, that he had shown that cheerfulness; when he thought he was alone—— She went and sat down beside him. Even then he did not move.

"Monsieur des Sablières, it is of no use—he will not consent to any delay. But if the Transport Office do not relent, not a day shall pass that I do not work for your release—not a day! I shall communicate with you at Plymouth, and keep you informed. Even if my father and my cousin can do nothing, I shall not rest, I swear it, till I have you out—somehow."

He murmured something scarcely audible about his not being worth so much trouble, and the lifeless tone seemed to indicate that he had little faith in her efforts. Small wonder when already—as she now noticed—his wrists were chafed by those horrible handcuffs. Her eyes filled.

"Say that you trust me," she said in a breaking voice, "or I cannot bear it!"

That brought his hands down—and quickly. She caught them as they came. "Do you trust me—*me* who have harmed you so?"

He tried to smile at her, and as far as his mouth went the result was not unsatisfactory, but out of his eyes, not hidden now, looked something that had no kinship with smiles.

"I do," he replied firmly and earnestly. "I believe every word you say. I doubt if you *can* do anything more, but I would trust you with my life, and I shall think of you every day . . . as you were at Wanfield, and, still more . . . as you have been here!"

He did trust her—he did believe! And she was all he had to look to, in the horrible existence to which he was going, the pit into which she had pushed him, which he dreaded so much that he had not been able to hide his momentary failure of courage. The tide of pity and remorse which every second was rising higher in her heart was swelled by another stream whose existence in herself Juliana Forrest had never guessed, that fount which almost every woman has of maternal and protective for a man. And so she gave him a last and more beautiful remembrance of her, for as he looked at her with those betraying eyes, his manacled wrists clasped round by her compassionate fingers, she suddenly leant towards him and kissed him on the forehead, low down, because of the bandage, almost between the eyes . . . kissed him as his mother might have done. And before he had recovered from the wonder and the surprise of it she was gone.

The Yoke-Fellow

"The angels of affliction spread their toils alike for the virtuous and the wicked, for the mighty and the mean."—*Rasselas*, chap. xxxviii.

128

"There, at the end of the file," shouted the mounted subaltern in charge.

It was nine o'clock on Monday morning. The mutineers destined for the hulks, drawn up just inside the south gate at Norman Cross, murmured and stared as an officer was marched up to join them, and Raoul swept a hasty glance over the double rank of sullen, reckless faces. He had just learnt that prisoners were handcuffed two and two upon the march, and as his escort brought him nearer he beheld his future companion in irons—a big man of forty-five or thereabouts, grizzled and not over-clean, and with the general stamp of a rogue. A droop of the right eyelid did not improve his appearance. His hairy and unengaging right wrist was already encircled by a handcuff, and near him a soldier was waiting with some keys.

"Look sharp now!" said the lieutenant impatiently.

Raoul took his place by the large man and held out his own chafed wrist without a word. His companion looked down at it curiously. The sergeant hesitated.

"Have you got a handkerchief, Sir?" he asked in a low tone. Raoul produced it, and the man wrapped it round his wrist. "Should do that all the time if I were you," he muttered, as the iron snapped into place over it.

"Thank you," said Raoul, and gave him a little smile—all he could give in return for the man's humane impulse, for his small store of money had been taken from him after his attempted escape (though he had been told this morning that it would be returned to him on arrival at his destination) and he had not yet received the allowance of sixpence a day which was made to prisoners on the road for their subsistence.

Five minutes later, marching in double file, the armed escort either side, the officer bringing up the rear on his horse, the string of unfortunates was on the tree-shaded Peterborough road where, a week ago, Raoul had hoped to find himself in very different circumstances. A few minutes more, and they debouched on to the Great North Road, and turned their faces south.

There was life and traffic here—it was strange to see it once more—and they had not gone very far upon its excellent surface before a coach passed them laden with passengers. As it drew abreast of the gang and its escort the horn began fumblingly to bray out the Marseillaise. It was a brutality for which nothing in his English captivity had so far prepared Raoul, and he clenched his hands and swore under his breath.

"Quite a pretty attention," remarked his comrade, speaking for the first time, in a husky voice. "They don't play it very well, though."

"It is an abominable thing to do!" said Raoul between his teeth, as the derisive strains died away in the distance, and nothing was heard for the moment but the dull tramp of more than eighty feet.

The man to whom he was handcuffed laughed. "For me, I have heard that air too often to care who plays it. You are too sensitive, Captain—that comes of being an officer. And, speaking of that, I ought to feel honoured to share this with you"—he gave the short bit of chain a little shake. "I don't suppose you could return the compliment, though. I am not exactly a dandy, am I?"

"But I should not feel flattered even if I were tied up with Soult or Masséna," responded Raoul. "On the other hand, you and I have both fought for the Emperor, and we have both known captivity and misfortune, so there's not much to choose between us."

His companion gave a hoarse laugh. "I've done as little fighting for the Emperor these last years as I could manage," he said with great frankness. "I deserted twice—once in Germany, and once in that devil's own country, Portugal. But I don't think the English officer knew that when he picked me out for you, Captain. It was just chance. I can tell you this, that you are lucky not to be coupled with a sailor, for they don't understand that, to a soldier, once an officer always an officer, and they treat a broke-parole just as one of themselves. You'll not have to complain of that sort of thing from me, at any rate, *mon capitaine.*"

"Thank you for the assurance," returned Raoul rather drily. "And in any case let me tell you that I am not a broke-parole. What is your name and regiment?"

"You'll excuse me, Captain," said the man with a grin, "if in the circumstances I don't tell you my regiment. And my name—well, I'm always called Sarrelouis. I'm from Lorraine."

A little farther and he was enquiring, quite respectfully and in fact admiringly, about his companion's frustrated escape. They had all heard about it, of course, in their caserne; the captain had had hard luck indeed, though not so hard as if the sentry had died. At one time it was reported that he himself was dying from the effect of the blow on the head. Raoul assured him that this had never been the case, and that, though he still had to wear a bandage, the wound was nearly healed. He did not add that to him the chief disadvantage of this adornment (besides adding to the conspicuousness already conferred upon him by his rank and bright uniform) was that he could not wear his tight-fitting shako, but must march bareheaded for the present.

At the village of Stilton they quitted the Great North Road, turning off to the right and making for the Northampton main road through a network of minor roads and lanes. At their first halt Raoul discovered the composition of the party. There were thirty-two prisoners, a guard of eight men, a sergeant and a corporal, and the officer in charge, one Lieutenant Hunter. Besides these, there was the "conductor," whose business it was to ride on ahead and make arrangements for the billeting of the men for the night in some barn or outhouse, and to pay them their allowance of sixpence a day. With such affairs the officer in charge had no concern; his business was to see that no prisoner escaped en route, and he looked as if he would carry out this duty all the more efficiently that he plainly had no fancy for journeying to Devonshire in charge of what amounted to a gang of convicts. Yet life at Yaxley must have been monotonous enough.

For Raoul at least, despite a slow, unhurried progress and frequent halts, Thrapston village on the Northampton road, where they were to spend the night, was not attained any too soon. To a man not long out of bed it had seemed a portentously lengthy twelve miles (which Sarrelouis had informed him was the usual day's stage) and indeed, though he did not know it, it had been nearer fifteen. Raoul had rather liked the narrow lanes, for they seemed to hold out better prospects of escape than the turnpike road, and in one he had seen belated primroses; but as it happened they were never afterwards to engage in such byways.

At Thrapston they were shepherded into a large barn which had been engaged for their occupation, and, to Raoul's relief, were unshackled for the night. He had already been speculating as to his reception at the hands of his fellow prisoners when they were removed from the constraint of their guards. Once shut into the great dusky building—they were not allowed a light—he soon discovered what it was to be.

They began by exhibiting an ironic and exaggerated respect which was in itself insulting. Such cries resounded as "Room for the officer. . . . Make way for the captain of hussars. . . . Now, you wretched linesmen and sailors, out of the way, here comes the cavalry. . . . Will the general condescend to sit on this tub?" Raoul declined, and taking as little notice of their facetiousness as might be, went and sat himself down on a heap of turnips in a far corner, and tried to tear his attention away from this stupid mockery to the wonderful thing that had happened to him on Saturday—which indeed had been with him ever since like a sustaining hand. He might be miserable, but he was—unbelievably—blest as well. As a particularly offensive remark about the honour of officers came to his ears he told himself that not one of these poor devils who were now trying his temper had a single soul in England to care what became of him. But he . . . once again he was sitting on that bench, once again he heard her voice, so deeply stirred, felt her agitated hands, and then, miraculously, her lips on his brow, like the kiss of a saint, which he should have received on his knees. For he had no illusions about the feeling which had inspired it; so might Adrienne have kissed him, had she seen him then.

But he was recalled from that mental place of refuge to the realization that the disorder in the barn was growing, and that, for the sake of the future, it was time to put a stop to it if he could.

"Look here, my men," he said, suddenly emerging from his dark corner, "do you imagine that the English sentinels outside are gaining a very favourable idea of what the Emperor's soldiers are like, because I do not!"

"What? not if they see us in our beautiful new uniforms, you and me,

132

Captain?" mockingly enquired a scarecrow figure, lurching up to the young man and bringing his rags into juxtaposition with the smart silver-grey.

"We was soldiers once; we ain't even deserters now!" growled another voice.

"And most of us never was soldiers," observed a privateersman, and added, "Thank God!" on which there was a nascent scuffle.

"At any rate, we are all French here," went on Raoul, making his voice heard with some difficulty. "It is not that I want to claim any superiority over you or any right to your obedience because I am an officer, for I am only, like each of you, a Frenchman in misfortune——"

"Ah, but you brought your misfortune on yourself, Captain, by breaking your parole," put in someone quickly. "You wasn't in misfortune before that, like us poor devils, for no fault of our own, but living on the fat of the land in a fine house, and free to go where you liked, along of being an officer."

Raoul kept his temper. "How am I to persuade you, mes vieux, that I did not break my parole?"

"Not very easily," sniggered the same speaker. "For if you didn't why were you sent to prison—begging your pardon, of course, for the liberty, General!"

"I was sent there because an enemy bore false witness against me," replied Raoul succinctly. "I will swear that by anything you please. You have therefore no reason for treating me with disrespect, and so giving the English a handle against the Emperor—for that is what you are doing by this behaviour."

A voice declared that the Emperor would feel this burden very little, having enough on his hands without it. And then a prisoner of a waggish turn suggested: "Hasn't the Captain got a demoiselle—for sure he has, a handsome hussar like him! Let him swear by the white hands of his demoiselle that he is not a broke-parole, and I for one will believe him!"

The idea caught the unruly assembly. It seemed an odd and not very suitable way of asserting his position and his innocence, and . . . he had no demoiselle! But surely Miss Forrest, who had been so heavenly kind, would lend him her white hands—in thought? So he swore, thinking of them again as they had touched him, and no doubt he swore with fervour. The shadowy, wolfish crowd acclaimed him, and the same wit who had proposed this ceremony struck up, with bitter and calculated irony, the marching song "A la Première Auberge," and the rest roared out the refrain:

> "*Compagnons, dîtes mé donc, dîtes mé donc,*
> *Dîtes, dîtes, dîtes mé donc,*
> *Si les d'moiselles sont bell' où nous allons.*"

And then, with an odd mixture of bravado and respect, they asked the captain if he would sing them a soldiers' song just to show that there was no ill-will?

So Raoul, seated on the tub, sang them, after a moment's thought, the old air, charming and a little wistful, which had floated round the campfires of Louis XIV and many a leaguer since:

> "*Au jardin de mon père,*
> *Les lauriers sont fleuris;*
> *Au jardin de mon père,*
> *Les lauriers sont fleuris;*
> *Tous les oiseaux du monde*
> *Vont y faire leurs nids . . .*
> *Auprès de ma blonde,*
> *Qu'il fait bon, fait bon, fait bon,*
> *Auprès de ma blonde,*
> *Qu'il fait bon dormir!*"

and they took up the chorus till he came to the seventh verse:

> "*Dîtes-nous donc, la belle,*
> *Où donc est votr' mari?*
> *Il est dans la Hollande,*

D. K. Broster

Les Hollandais l'ont pris.

Il est dans la Hollande,
Les Hollandais l'ont pris.
Que donneriez-vouz, belle,
    Pour avoir votre ami?

Que donneriez-vouz, belle,
    Pour avoir votre ami?
Je donnerais Versailles,
    Paris et Saint-Denis.

Je donnerais Versailles,
    Paris et Saint-Denis,
Les tours de Notre-Dame
Et l'clocher de mon pays."

But before he could finish the remaining stanza someone burst out with a tremendous oath, and Raoul, looking round in surprise, saw that it was his yoke-fellow Sarrelouis, who had taken no part in the previous altercation.

"No more of this, comrades, or one will play the crybaby! Who wants to be reminded of the clocher de son pays here? Besides, you should remember that a few days ago the captain bayoneted a sentry, which none of us had the pluck or the luck to do, and had his head cut open in doing it. You might give him the chance of getting a little rest and sleep, you —— ——!"

"Agreed," chorused the now quieted audience. "We will all go to sleep." They dispersed at once to divide the straw which had been thrown into the barn for them. And one meek-looking little man with a lisp (who, as Raoul afterward discovered, possessed a most murderous disposition) came up to him with tears in his eyes and faltered: "You sing like an angel, *mon capitaine!* Ah, my poor wife at Lons-le-Saulnier, does she ever think of me like that, I wonder?"

"Mr. Rowl"

Ten minutes later Raoul himself was lying in a corner on a double pile of straw, fenced off from the rest by two hencoops and an old trough which Sarrelouis had discovered and placed in position. The march, however, had tired him so much that for long he could not sleep. Persistently there came into his mind the memory of that winter night before the battle of the Gebora, when he had lain with his men in a barn in Estremadura much like this. But they were his own men, and the morrow had brought that victorious charge for his share in which he had been mentioned in the order of the day, had got his promotion, and very nearly the Legion of Honour too. Now he was merely one of a gang of malefactors going to a living death.

On the other side of the hencoops Sarrelouis snored like a pig, another man was cursing steadily in his sleep, and the smell of unwashed humanity and its garments was increasing in volume. But for all that Raoul's last thought, his last sensation, was of Juliana Forrest and her lips on his brow. To whatever depth he was hence-forward to sink, he would always have that memory, that seal.

*

Although the first day's stage was a long and tiring one, the weather had been cool. But next day, as they tramped along the road to Wellingborough, the sun took to shining with unspringlike intensity, and, in spite of the fact that it was a shady road, Raoul's damaged head soon began to ache. By the close of the next day, when they were nearing Northampton, he had had sufficient experience to warrant the theory that it was always likely to trouble him in heat and sunshine, and could only pray that these might not be his portion too often, for he was determined not to complain—and indeed had not much chance of doing so.

The officer in command took no more notice of him than of any other of the prisoners. None of the escort was brutal, but their charges might have been cattle for all the interest that was shown. Sarrelouis the deserter, however, turned out better than Raoul could have believed possible. He never took advantage of his position, he never inflicted on his companion during their hours of enforced intimacy any of the filthy language which he had at his command for others, he made up as good a bed for him every night as was possible and never tried to share it—in fact, he seemed to have constituted himself a kind of orderly. But he could do nothing to make the weather less hot and thundery, though he displayed a genuine solicitude at its results, and on the sixth night—it was at Chipping Norton in Oxfordshire—stirred up the most fiendish tumult in an endeavour to impose silence on the whole barnful because his captain had a headache. It almost came to a pitched battle between the marine and the military sections, and when the fracas had subsided and Sarrelouis, comically crestfallen, came up to Raoul where he lay on some sacks with his hands over his ears, the latter very nearly cursed him for his misplaced zeal.

A burning sun next morning gave promise of an abnormally hot day, and so it proved; and after an hour or two on the road Raoul, in addition to his usual headache, began to suffer from momentary spells of dizziness. Sarrelouis in consequence shoved his elbow under his as a support, which was not very comfortable for either of them, but served to steady the young man when he needed it. The sun got hotter and hotter as they trudged along the high, shadeless road towards Shipton-under-Wychwood, and Raoul began to fear that he might not hold out till the end of the march, especially as it was rumoured that it was to be a long one.

At midday, when they crossed the Evenlode by Shipton, a halt was called, and Raoul and his inseparable companion lay down in the shade of a hedge. Listening to the murmur of the stream, and longing inexpressibly to strip off his hot, dusty clothes and plunge in, Raoul drifted into a doze, from which he was wakened by clumsy fingers spreading something wet and cool on his forehead as he lay there.

"That is delicious," he murmured. "But how did you get it, *mon bon?*" For without dragging his comrade with him Sarrelouis could not have gone to the river-brink to soak the linen.

"I got a soldier to go," responded the Lorrainer, bending over him. "It is your own handkerchief. Mon capitaine, report yourself now to the officer, and fall out. You will not be able to go much further, I think. You are as pale as a winding-sheet."

"No," said Raoul with his eyes shut. "I am not going to do that. And how could I fall out? We have to go on somehow, mon vieux, till we . . . arrive."

"I fell out once in Portugal before I deserted," observed Sarrelouis, lying down beside him again. "But, my God, that cured me of doing it for a bit!"

"You got into the hands of the country people, or the guerrillas, I suppose? If so, you are lucky to be alive to tell it."

"Agreed," said Sarrelouis. "Since you are indisposed, I will not tell you what they did to my companion. My faith, every time I thought of it for days afterwards, when I was hiding, I would bring up what little food I had managed to put into my belly. . . . But if one got away here," he went on musingly, "the country people are not like that devil's spawn of Portugal and Spain—no, not at all, I think. . . . Name of a name, is it time to go on again already? Wait, I'll help you up, mon petit capitaine."

It was Sunday, and the bells were ringing for afternoon service in the great church of Burford as they came down the hill into the little town; but by the time that they were climbing up the wide steep street out of it again other bells seemed to be ringing in Raoul's head also. They had all thought that they were at least going to halt in the old wool-trading centre (which indeed, by mileage, should have been the end of their day's tramp) but, presumably because it was church-time, Lieutenant Hunter would not allow it, and they pushed on up the hill, the escort as much discontented as the prisoners. And when they were up they were ordered to proceed along the turnpike which made for Northleach and Cheltenham, instead of taking the road which made more directly for Cirencester by way of Aldworth, the officer trusting, apparently, to come upon the turning to this later on, whereas they had already passed it, just outside Burford.

Neither Raoul not Sarrelouis was, naturally, aware of this fact from his own topographical knowledge, which was nil, but the nearest member of the escort, who happened to have observed a signpost, was grumbling under his breath, and Raoul understood the reason only too well. They were going miles out of their way, and would either have to retrace it or plod along as far as Northleach and then turn south. And the road still went, though less steeply, uphill, and the sun was hotter than ever. Right and left stretched the great Gloucestershire fields, fading into miles of distance; down on the right, green and inviting, but not for them, was the valley of the Windrush from which they had just ascended.

"I *will* not give in!" declared Raoul to himself; but he kept stumbling.

"Head going round again?" enquired Sarrelouis in his husky tones. "I would put an arm round you if I could, devil knows. *Holà*, Englishman, cannot you give the officer an arm?" he said over Raoul's head to the grumbling soldier next the latter.

"Yes, if he will carry my musket and pack!" retorted the militiaman, soured by his geographical presentiments.

Sarrelouis shrugged his shoulders, and Raoul set his teeth and half closed his eyes. They passed through a double belt of trees, which was a slight relief, but when they came out into the full glare again, he felt quite sick with vertigo, and his brain seemed to be hammering at his skull. The soldier by his side muttered savagely and far from encouragingly, "Going on like this all the way to Northleach, I suppose, eight or nine mortal miles before he finds that we have passed the — turn!"

However, he was saved that test of endurance, for about a quarter of a mile farther on the young hussar captain by his side suddenly swayed violently and pitched forward in the dust, though his fall was broken by his companion, whom he all but dragged down with him. The end of the column immediately stopped.

The officer, looking annoyed, came riding forward from the rear, dismounted, and stooped over the fallen prisoner.

"Undo the irons," he said curtly to the sergeant. "Damnable nuisance, this! Where can we get water?" He himself was unfastening Raoul's collar.

"There is an inn just ahead, Sir," replied the sergeant, preparing to free Sarrelouis, who was kneeling in the road beside his prostrate comrade. "In fact, we are almost there." And no doubt his own thoughts were suddenly gilded with prospects of another beverage than water.

"Mr. Rowl"

It was true. Although it stood on the highway the great elms hid the New Inn until one was within a few yards of it, but there was no doubt about its presence, low, grey and solid, with attendant barns and orchards behind it. Sarrelouis, now on his feet, signified that he could carry his captain so far. Assisted by the sergeant, he got the insensible Raoul up and over his shoulder, and they moved on again.

By the time that the head of the column, with its shuffling, or its military step, had come abreast of the New Inn the whole personnel of that establishment was collected outside. Seeing that there was a wide, low wall in front, Sarrelouis carefully deposited his burden thereupon and asked for water, which request was also repeated more intelligibly by English voices. However, the motherly looking landlady, after one glance at the young man with the bandaged head lying so limply upon her wall, said to the world in general: "You bring him inside at once—this way! And I'd like to know what you sodgers has been doing to him!"

And, before the officer at the far end of the throng filling the road could either give or withhold his consent to this move, Sarrelouis had picked up the still unconscious Raoul with surprising ease and celerity and was following the speaker in. Mistress of the situation, she preceded him through a passage and into a large parlour.

"Lay the poor boy there," she said, indicating an enormous sofa under the geranium-filled window. "And, as I say, whatever have they been doing to him? Marian, fetch some brandy!" She bent over Raoul and began to rub his hands. "Look at this wrist now!" And then, finding the room filling up behind her back, "Now, I don't want all you sodgers in here, thank you! Out you go! What do you suppose the poor fellow can do, laying here like this?"

No, Raoul could do nothing . . . except unintentionally give an opportunity to a very astute philanthropist. By the time it became any one man's business to see what Sarrelouis was about the Lorrainer was nowhere to be found. The hurly-burly which ensued was the first thing that greeted Raoul when he opened his eyes again; but all the commotion was in vain. The deserter must have slipped out of the room unobserved, left the inn by a back way, raced down through the sloping orchards, perhaps swum the Windrush at the bottom, and was either lying perdu or running for his life through the lonely Cotswold uplands. It was unlikely that without money or much of the English tongue he would retain his freedom long, but at any rate he had snatched it now—together with Raoul's only possession of value, his watch. . . .

The officer, naturally, was furious over the business. He accused Raoul of having known of the project and feigned collapse in order to get the chain unfastened. Raoul, sitting bewildered on the horsehair sofa, and really more dizzy than before, with a different kind of dizziness, from the quantity of brandy which the kind landlady had poured down his throat, could only shrug his shoulders. He did not much mind what was said to him provided only that they did not start along that road in the sun again.

Mercifully they did not. Lieutenant Hunter, who had by now discovered his mistake about the route to Cirencester, decided to go no farther that day—and indeed the twelve miles had already been considerably exceeded. Very ill-temperedly—thinking no doubt of the similar arrangements already made by the conductor along the Aldworth road—he settled with the mistress of the New Inn to quarter his charges for the night in one of her barns. Despite her protests, Raoul was removed from the large parlour and the unwonted comfort of its sofa and committed to the same incarceration. But before this happened she had unbandaged and bathed his head, and thrust various excellent small pasties upon him. Moreover, the straw in her barn was fresher than he had met of late, and his companions in misfortune were unusually quiet and attentive, considering that he had deserved well for Sarrelouis' escape, some of them indeed believing, like the officer, that the whole thing had been prearranged. As for Raoul, he wondered with whom he would be conjoined to-morrow; someone less tolerable, perhaps, than his late partner. Judging from the trend of the conversation, there might even be some competition for the privilege. Then he remembered that they were now an uneven number, thirty-one in all, and fell asleep trying to divide thirty-one by two . . . and by some strange process succeeding.

"Mr. Rowl"

Raoul Meets the Devil in Bridgwater

"This, at least . . . is the present reward of virtuous conduct, that no unlucky consequence can oblige us to repent it."–Rasselas, chap. xxxiv.

Probably as the result of the longer rest—for it could hardly be attributed to the brandy—Raoul found his head much better next morning, though in body he did not feel very vigorous. No official enquiry was made as to his condition, nor, indeed, had he expected one. But, to his surprise, after all the other couples in the barn had been shackled together, he was marched out alone, led up to the already mounted officer, and fastened by his left wrist with a stout cord to that gentleman's off stirrup.

The procession started from the New Inn. It was a lovely morning, of a dewy freshness; the road, now level, still ran along the crest of the ridge, and afforded beautiful wide views. Raoul looked at them, hardly thinking about his unusual situation, or the officer whose spurred foot his hand was almost touching. The only thing that mattered was whether he would be able to get through to-day's march without another *faiblesse*.

Yet, annoyed though he was at collapsing yesterday, it had been beyond his power to prevent it; but that afternoon at Norman Cross . . . what sort of an idea of a soldier of the Empire had he given Miss Forrest on that occasion? He had ever since been acutely ashamed of his unmanly display; and yet . . . it was possible that but for it he would never have received from her that angelic assurance of compassion. At that moment she had been as Notre Dame de Bon Secours, to whom one might without reproach disclose one's needs. . . . But since that day no *man*, at any rate, had seen him show the white feather—nor was any man going to.

They had gone perhaps a couple of miles in silence when Lieutenant Hunter said suddenly, "Take hold of the stirrup leather." And as Raoul, surprised, looked up at him he added, just as abruptly, "That will help you along, won't it?"

"Thank you," said Raoul, and, moving his hand a little, gripped the taut thong.

Silence descended for another half mile or so, then the rider demanded: "How did you contrive to time your swoon so well yesterday?"

"One hardly times those events," replied Raoul with a little frown.

"It was suspiciously near the inn, however. If that ruffian had not carried you in there, he would never have got away."

"I knew nothing of any inn," replied Raoul briefly. "I went on as long as I could, that is all."

"We have a long march before us to-day," was the next observation.

"I assure you that I shall not fall out again if I can help it," responded the tethered young man. Then he added politely: "This stirrup-leather will be a great assistance to me."

The officer said nothing, and Raoul returned to his reflections. The lieutenant could hardly continue to believe in his collusion with Sarrelouis if he were to tell him—which he did not mean to do—of the episode of his watch, the absence of which he himself had not discovered till this morning. Yet, after the first shock of disgust, he could almost wish the thief luck of it, for his compassion had been as genuine as his opportunism, and, as the English said, one could not make a silk purse out of a sow's ear. But the loss was more than pecuniary and inconvenient, for the watch had been his father's. . . . What would his father say if he could see him now, tied up to an enemy's saddle! Probably that it was the fitting reward for serving a parvenu like Bonaparte. . . . *Pauvre père*, he would be terribly upset. . . . Luckily, he could not see. He believed his son to be in prison, it was true, but only because the privilege of parole had been temporarily withdrawn from officers, a fiction which Raoul had hoped his family would not discover to be such. Of his latest misfortune they were as yet ignorant; he supposed it would have to be broken to them somehow. . . .

Here the saddle above him gave a creak, he felt fingers about his wrist, and, turning his head, found that the officer was stooping.

"The cord is not loose—not at all," remarked the prisoner.

"I was feeling if it were not, on the contrary, too tight," responded the rider, as curtly as ever. "Were you in irons at Norman Cross, before you started?"

"Yes, for three days."

"I thought so. Why is your hand bleeding now?"

Raoul looked at it. "From my own carelessness, I expect. I must have scratched it against your spur."

"I'm sorry," said the officer with extreme brevity, and the conversation dropped once more. On the whole, Raoul did not regret this; he could better devote his energies to the business in hand—getting to Cirencester. He certainly did not regret that he had the stirrup leather.

*

Northleach at last, and a halt. The officer dismounted and went into the innyard, while Raoul hastily threw his arm over the saddle, and, leaning against the horse, stared very hard at the fine old church in front of him, round whose pinnacled tower the swifts were holding their aërial games.

> *"Je donnerais Versailles,*
> *Paris et Saint-Denis,*
> *Les tours de Notre-Dame*
> *Et l'clocher de mon pays . . ."*

The officer came out again, followed by an ostler leading a saddle horse.

"I am going to mount you as far as Cirencester," he said shortly to Raoul, and began untying the cord.

"You are very kind, Sir," said the young man, greatly surprised. "But, though I would willingly do so, I have no money to pay for the hire of a horse."

"The Transport Board must do that," replied the lieutenant, "if they give me men to conduct who are not fit to march."

And Raoul got up, thankful for the indulgence, whatever were the officer's motive in granting it. He had not been across a horse since the day of Salamanca, when his own beloved Bayard had been killed under him. He was not now allowed the reins, and the cord, still round his wrist, was in the grasp of the soldier who had control of these; but in this manner he voyaged comfortably enough along the Foss Way, the cortège having turned south for Cirencester just beyond Northleach.

Prisoners and escort alike were tired when they got there, and Raoul felt rather ashamed of the privilege of being mounted. One or two remarks of no kindly nature were indeed made about it that night in the stables of the inn, where they were quartered. Next morning, therefore, he got hold of the sergeant when he entered to put on the fetters of the rest, and said that if the officer were thinking of procuring a horse for him that day he was deeply grateful, but that as he was now quite recovered he would prefer to go on foot like the others.

So he was once more attached to Lieutenant Hunter's stirrup; but as this operation was carried through, not outside a lonely inn, but in the middle of busy Cirencester, it attracted some attention and comment. The officer's brow was like thunder, and Raoul himself did not much relish the publicity of it. And the charger, possibly too well supplied with corn in that hunting centre, was unusually mettlesome after they had started, which, though it occasioned no particular disturbance to his rider, was once or twice distinctly uncomfortable for the prisoner, and a shade ignominious as well. He was obliged to hold tightly to the stirrup leather to prevent sudden drags of the cord upon his wrist.

"Be quiet, you brute!" exclaimed Lieutenant Hunter in extreme exasperation, as a wilder plunge almost took Raoul off his feet. "I'll teach you to play the circus horse!" And, by a very liberal use of the curb, he did succeed in subduing his steed, so that by the time they were out of Cirencester the animal's behaviour had become normal again. But his rider's temper had not.

"It is a thrice-damned nuisance, having you strung on to me like this!" he observed angrily to Raoul, as though it were an arrangement forced on him by the latter, and Raoul was moved to retort drily that it was no source of enjoyment to him, either. And then, after a quarter of an hour's complete silence, Mr. Hunter electrified him by saying abruptly:

"Suppose you gave me your parole of honour and marched free?"

"My parole!" exclaimed Raoul. A slow flush burnt his face. "Would you take it? I am supposed to have broken it once."

"I know that," snapped the officer. "No, I have no right to take it, and if you break it I shall get into the deuce of a mess. Perhaps that consideration might have some slight weight with you?"

"No, not in the least," was the young Frenchman's unexpected reply. "My parole, once given, does not depend on 'considerations'."

Lieutenant Hunter looked down at him and then gave a short laugh. "Upon my soul! If you really have those sentiments, then . . ."

Raoul reflected. Tied up or chained up he had no more chance of escaping than if he were inexorably bound by his word, and by one method or the other he must, obviously, be secured. Moreover, he had never seriously contemplated an attempt to escape during the day, surrounded as he was by an armed escort and clad in his very noticeable uniform, but he still hoped that there might come a night . . .

"I will give you my word of honour to make no attempt to escape on the march," he said.

"Ah, you intend to make off during the night, then?"

"I don't say so," replied Raoul. "But I do say that if you also require my parole for those hours when we are all unfettered, you are putting too high a price on the privilege you offer. I will give you my promise for the daytime, and thank you for the courtesy, but otherwise I must refuse it."

"Well, I suppose I must be content with that," said the lieutenant. "You definitely engage, then, to make no attempt to escape during the day, on the march?"

"I give you my most solemn word of honour not to do so," replied Raoul, looking straight up at him.

"Very good," said Mr. Hunter, and lost no time in acting on this assurance. He withdrew his foot from the stirrup, pulled up the iron, and cut the cord with a penknife. "At the next halt I will tell the sergeant about you, and you may march where you please in the column. For the present, however, you had better stay here."

Raoul thanked him. He was puzzled by this treatment; he had made not the slightest attempt to work on the officer's feelings, and after the affair of Sarrelouis had been fully prepared for harsh dealing. Nor did the lieutenant's manner to him suggest leniency; yet first he had procured him a horse, and now was extending to him an indulgence that Raoul had never dreamt of, and which might very well get its originator into trouble if it ever came to be known. He concluded that Mr. Hunter must dislike his society so much that he was willing to go to any lengths to be rid of it. Yet surely, in that case, he could have had him tied up to one of the escort, since regulations declared that he had lost his status as an officer.

"You are welcome to my stirrup leather still, if you wish," said the object of his surmises presently, and Raoul, thanking him, took it again, not wishing to appear churlish. And now that Mr. Hunter no longer had him on the end of a string he seemed to have a weight off his mind also, and became a little more talkative; for the first time addressed him as "Captain," enquired about his military experiences in the Peninsula, and expressed regret that he himself had not seen service there.

That day's stage and the next were designedly short ones, and this fact, together with his having had a mount and the absence of hot sun, worked a remarkable change in Raoul's physical condition. He was no longer giddy, nor did his head ache; indeed he was soon feeling positive benefit from the open air and the exercise which had been denied him at Norman Cross.

But all the while he and his companions were proceeding steadily nearer to their doom. At Chilcompton eight men made a determined effort to escape after dark. Raoul, as it happened, knew nothing of this design—and thinking it over afterwards he suspected that they had been careful to keep it from him, for since he had been paroled they had shown a certain jealousy and suspicion of him, though they had never been openly disrespectful after the first night at Thrapston. But the attempt was frustrated, and one of the fugitives slightly wounded.

Raoul himself still cherished the idea of escape during the night, but he intended his attempt, when he made it, to be successful, and so far he had seen no really good opening. He was mentally hampered as well by a perfectly illogical feeling that his escape would be a poor return for Lieutenant Hunter's indulgence. He knew that this was a ridiculous scruple, yet he almost wished, sometimes, that he had not accepted his offer. But the days went on; Bath, Wells, Glastonbury were behind the pilgrims; soon they would be in Devonshire itself, and the picture of the hulks began to loom more and more blackly. Raoul was not going tamely to them without one final throw for liberty, whatever it cost . . . when the chance came.

It did come, on the fifteenth day—but not as he had expected.

They had just marched through Bridgwater, and were going to make their prolonged midday halt about half a mile on the farther side of the town when Raoul, discovering that he had lost his one remaining pocket-handkerchief, asked the lieutenant if he might go back into Bridgwater and buy one. Mr. Hunter readily gave him permission, warning him, however, to be back in three quarters of an hour, and Raoul walked off, unescorted, as in the days of Wanfield, which now seemed so remote.

Merely for the pleasure of feeling free to do so, he spent some time in the little linen-draper's shop, although they were out of pocket-handkerchiefs. "Yü'm a furriner, zurelye," observed the apple-cheeked old Somerset woman, looking at his uniform, and Raoul admitted it.

"And wheer be gwine tü?" she asked, evidently not having been among the inhabitants who had turned out to witness the passage of the gang a little before.

"To the hulks, mother," replied Raoul. "I am a French prisoner."

The old lady lifted up her hands and exclaimed in horror. "My dear soul! Yü, so comely as yü be, to one of they tarrible plaäces! Jan, Jan, dü ee hear that?" she called out to someone behind, and Raoul had a momentary glimpse of a bearded man in a jersey before he bade her farewell and left the little shop.

He had still, he saw by a clock, plenty of time, and strolled about the town a little, not unnoticed by various small boys. Just by an old inn whose carving interested him he felt a touch on his arm, and turning, saw the bearded man of the linen-draper's shop, with a companion of the same type.

"Us do want a word wi' ee, Zur," he said in a low voice, and impelled by curiosity Raoul went with them a little way up the alley at the side of the hostelry.

"Us do belong to Minehead, Zur," continued the bearded one, "and our boat be here tü the quay, and wi' tide gwine down and wind astern . . . and 'tis only a matter of five mile down the Parrett any day. . . ."

"The parrot—five miles—what on earth do you mean?" asked Raoul bewildered.

The bearded Jan approached still nearer; he smelt of ropes, tar, and a little of fish. "Bain't ee French officer, and don't ee want a boat to the coast, and no questions aasked, lyin' snug under a spare sail?" His eyes twinkled suggestively.

Raoul stared at him as if he were the Serpent compounded with Eve. "I . . . I can't," he said slowly turning rather pale. "I have given my word not to escape."

"Then the more füle yü, aaskin' your pardon," observed the other man.

"Come now," said Jan coaxingly, "once yü'm out of they crazy clo'es, and wi' a jersey on your back, who's to say a word to ee between here and Bridgwater Bay? And once in the Bristol Channel—speakin' the tongue so easy-like—yü've but to work round the coast in a fishing-smack or tü, and in Mount's Bay—full o' smugglers 'tis—yü taäkes——"

"No, no!" said Raoul, backing away from the siren, on which the other took up the tale.

"Is it money, Zur? Us can zee as yü'm a gentleman, and us would trust ee till such time as——"

"For God's sake, don't tempt me like this!" cried poor Raoul, and, pushing him off, literally ran out of the alley, and made as fast as he could along the street, so fast that a spectator might have thought he was really absconding.

And then he remembered that he had not bought his handkerchiefs. He went into another linen-draper's, where he had to wait before he could be served, so that when at last he came in sight of the encampment by the roadside he saw signs of activity and deduced that he had exceeded the time allotted to him. He quickened his steps once more. A boat—the river—the Bristol Channel only five miles away . . . oh, if only he could, if only he could. It was a cruel vision, and he felt that it was going to haunt him.

He came up to the group in the road. But his head was too full of where he might have been to observe the expression on the face of the sergeant as he called out to Mr. Hunter, already in the saddle, "Here he is, Sir!"

"Am I late, Sir?" enquired Raoul. "I am extremely sorry." Then, like a thunderclap, comprehension came to him. They were surprised to see him at all!

"I understood that you had accepted my parole," he said in a hard voice, looking very straight at the young man on the horse.

"I—yes—that is——Oh, damn it, there has been some misunderstanding," stammered Mr. Hunter. "Fall in!" he said sharply to the men, and then swung off his horse and approached the Frenchman where he stood stiffly in the road, clutching his little parcel rather tightly. "You must forgive me, but I thought . . . and when I heard that you had been seen talking to a couple of sailors——"

"You sent a spy after me, then!"

"I told the sergeant to follow you——Put yourself in my place, des Sablières!" cried Lieutenant Hunter, now thoroughly shaken. "I know very little of you, I ought not to have made this arrangement about parole—and when you had gone, it appeared to me that you had created this opportunity for yourself rather too neatly; I felt what a thundering fool I had been—and when the sergeant came back and reported that you had given him the slip but that someone had seen you in conversation with two fishermen, I thought the temptation had been too much for you."

"Well, it was, nearly," admitted Raoul, a queer little smile creeping round his mouth. "You see, it was so unexpected—for my errand, I assure you, was quite genuine, and I had no idea that I was going to . . . to meet the Devil in Bridgwater."

"You mean you *had* the chance of getting away?"

"Since you ask, yes. I suppose I might already be sailing down the river with a curious name—by invitation. But, of course, it was not possible. . . . I am sorry if I have delayed you."

"Will you accept my most profound apologies?" asked Mr. Hunter, studying the road with a noticeable increase of colour on his countenance. "I shall know better next time." And raising his eyes he drew himself up, and saluted his prisoner as he might have done Lord Wellington himself.

No Escape

"His wish still continued, but his hope grew less. He . . . determined to keep his design always in view, and lay hold on any expedient that time should offer."—Rasselas, chap. v.

It was with their arrival at Exeter on the seventeenth day that Raoul realized with a shock that he had only three nights left. He must make his dash for liberty within that space, or never make it at all. And he could only seize flying chance by the skirts, since to plan anything beforehand was impossible, when he knew nothing of the country, nor where the conductor would lodge them each night.

The first night after leaving Exeter they lay at Chudleigh, where circumstances were unfavourable; the second at Buckfastleigh, where they were even less propitious. Next morning Raoul told himself desperately that he must make his attempt that night wherever they were to be confined. If only it might be, as it often had been, some ramshackle and deserted barn!

But their place of temporary confinement turned out to be exceedingly unlike this desired haven, for, to Raoul's surprise, it was a church, standing in a graveyard in the middle of a little town. It appeared that there was no other building in the place capable of containing them with safety, and the conductor had, rather rashly, Raoul thought, guaranteed that no harm should be done to monuments or furniture.

The men laughed as they were shepherded into this unfamiliar kind of barracks, and most of them set to work to explore its possibilities. A few proposed breaking down some of the pews and making a fire in the aisle to dry their damp clothing (for it had been a rainy day) and were deterred from this project much less by Raoul's remonstrances than by the discovery that there was no reliable tinderbox to be had. So, after one of them had delivered a short and ribald discourse from the three-tiered pulpit, and several had scrawled their names, as well as they could see to do it in the gloom, on the mural tablets, they settled down for the night in the capacious pews.

But Raoul still wandered round the walls, a grey shadow amid the greyness, feeling, tapping, shaking when there was anything to shake. The others, talking or snoring, took no notice of him, save once to shout a suggestion that he was sleep-walking, and so, when he felt his way into the small square bell-tower which stood like an alcove at the end of the church, he passed from their remembrance as well.

It was not probable that there would be any separate exit to this place, nevertheless he pursued his slow and methodical voyage round its walls. If there were one it would be like all the other doors, solid and solidly fastened. . . . Sainte Vierge—there was one—his exploring fingers had suddenly come on wood instead of stone: a door, a small door—but a fastened door, of course. There was a lock, but no key. Higher up, as he had already felt, there was a latch, and half mechanically his hand went back to it. It was stiff, and had remained lifted. For what reason Raoul did not know he took hold of it with both hands to pull it down again; and incontinently felt the door tremble with the slight pressure on it, as an unfastened door might tremble. Impossible! . . . But he pulled harder . . . towards him . . . and with only a little reluctance the door followed the pull. It was *not* fastened.

The sweat started out on the explorer as he stood there, the fingers of his left hand stealing round the edge of the little door, the others still on the latch. Now, was he going to share his discovery with the men in the church? No; it would be madness, for they would all troop out instantly, reckless as they were, and be shot down by the sentries outside. On the other hand, ought he to monopolize this startling opportunity? At any rate, he would not summon the others yet; he would slip through and reconnoitre first. Next moment he had done so, and was moving cautiously along the outer wall of the church, his heart beating almost to suffocation.

He had known that he should find no moon, but for all that it was much lighter outside than he had realized, disconcertingly light. Every tombstone was more or less visible, and he certainly would be. He stopped. It would be better to return to the church and wait a little. . . . Too late—here was a sentry coming round the bell-tower; he was already between him and the little door.

Raoul slipped past the next buttress, then dropped to his hands and knees and crawled; and thus progressing among the tombs, this time at right angles to the building, had the satisfaction of getting almost to the cover afforded by a large upstanding family monument when, without the slightest warning, a bullet splintered into it just ahead of him, knocking chips of stone in all directions. Most disagreeably surprised and startled, and paying no heed to the belated shout of "Halt, or I fire!" which now reached his ears, the fugitive then took the perilous course of springing to his feet and running.

In another locality the course might have been a sound one, but a graveyard is no place for a twilight sprint, and so Raoul found. Before he could pick himself up from the flat tombstone over which he had tripped and fallen headlong a sentry was on him, his hands at his throat, and in an incredibly short time was joined by another as zealous as himself. Indeed the vigorous fight which the recaptured prisoner put up was less for liberty than to save himself from strangulation. In the end, breathless, dishevelled, bruised, and generally rather limp, he was taken back through the little tower door, which had meanwhile been discovered and guarded, and thrown into one of the high, roomy pews.

Shouts, shot, and reëntry had roused the rest of the prisoners to excitement, which the soldiers, cursing the author of it, had now to quell. In the middle of the turmoil arrived Mr. Hunter, at whose advent it somewhat died down. He had ordered the little door to be nailed up, and the noise of hammering was already resounding when he unexpectedly appeared at the door of Raoul's residence, with a lantern-bearing orderly behind him—so unexpectedly, indeed, that he took its occupant by surprise, and found him still rather dazed and breathless, sitting in a corner with disordered hair and dabbing at a graze on his temple.

"Are you hurt, des Sablières?" he enquired in an unemotional voice.

Raoul instantly put away his handkerchief and rose to his feet. "Only my clothes, Sir. I have no complaint to make."

The officer surveyed him for a second in the light of the lifted lantern. Some of the scarlet frogs had indeed been wrenched away from the breast of the grey dolman, and the high military collar was gaping after its departed hooks, while the red and white sash round his waist, some of its twisted strands broken and hanging down, was several inches away from the locality prescribed by the Imperial regulations.

"Did any one outside tell you about that door or help you in any way?"

"No one, Sir. I came on it almost by chance."

"Very good," said Lieutenant Hunter, and withdrew; and five minutes later, when lanterns and clattering boots had gone, the church settled down to almost its usual nocturnal silence.

Aching and horribly disappointed, Raoul stretched himself out on the wide seat of the pew, with his head on a moth-eaten hassock. The high wooden walls of his retreat gave him such privacy as he had not known since he left Wanfield, and such as he certainly would not know to-morrow night; and finally he slept, undisturbed by the mice which ran over his legs.

*

Opinions were freely expressed in the church next morning that the Captain, after last night's exploit, would not be allowed to march free for this, the last day's journey. Even Raoul himself felt a little doubtful. . . . But no; he was not to have any slur cast on his word now. Mr. Hunter made no reference to the occurrence, nor indeed did any conversation pass between them. Raoul walked in his usual place, unfettered and rather dishevelled.

It was raining slightly when they crossed the Erme; more heavily when they came to the Yealm, and Raoul pulled his pelisse over his shoulders. One more of these beautiful free-falling rivers that Dartmoor sent as a message to the sea and they would be in Plymouth. But before they crossed the Meavy they halted for the last time, a spot being chosen, for the sake of shelter, where the road ran through a tiny wood. The rain, however, had ceased now, though the trees were dripping, and the air was hot and steamy. Raoul sat down at a distance from the rest on a fallen trunk. He was conscious of every leaf of his surroundings, for something warned him how often he would think of this day, and long for a road, even in the rain—he who had made such a poor use of last night's great opportunity, who could not bring off a successful escape even when *le bon Dieu* had left a door open for him. . . .

As he sat there, his eyes fixed on some narrow ribbons of leaves, shining with wet and exultantly green, which poured themselves forth from between two mossy stones near him, he was suddenly aware of Lieutenant Hunter's presence.

"Don't get up," said the Englishman abruptly. "I want to speak to you." He sat down beside him on the tree, and then said nothing.

It was Raoul who broke the silence. "What do you call that plant in English?" he asked, pointing.

"Hart's-tongue fern—tongue of a deer, you know. . . . I thought we had better say good-bye now, des Sablières, while we have the chance."

Raoul looked at him. "It is very good of you to say it at all, after last night. I am sorry I put you to all that trouble. I hope at least that you had not gone to bed?"

"No," said Mr. Hunter.

"I shall always remember you, and your consideration, Sir," went on Raoul warmly. After all, it seemed to be he who was doing the leave-taking.

"There was not much of that shown you last night, I am afraid," muttered Mr. Hunter, with an eye on his prisoner's uniform. "I can't help wishing——" And there he stopped.

"That I had never found that little door of mine?" supplied Raoul, and looked at him with almost a twinkle in his eye.

But Mr. Hunter, with his teeth in his lip, was mutely studying the wet grass between his boots. After a moment he took up the riding switch which lay across his knees and began to examine that in its turn with close attention.

"You do not need to assure me, des Sablières," he said indistinctly, "that, whatever people say, you never broke your parole before you were sent to Norman Cross. I don't mind telling you that your behaviour at Bridgwater has given me a better opinion of the French officer in that respect than I have ever had before."

"Well, you could not give me a handsomer valediction than that," said Raoul smiling.

And apparently it was Mr. Hunter's valediction, for he now got up, and Raoul did the same.

"You said the other day that you had someone working for your release, I think. I can heartily say that I wish him success."

"Thank you," returned Raoul pleasantly. "I also naturally wish . . . him . . . the same."

Still Mr. Hunter lingered, switching rather savagely at the hart's-tongue fern.

"Oh, don't do that!" exclaimed Raoul impulsively. "You see, it will be there—to-morrow."

Shooting a rather perplexed glance at him, Mr. Hunter desisted. "You make me wish that I could give you back what you gave me that day near Cirencester," he said, colouring in a curious and as it were reluctant fashion. "I mean—without the alternative. . . . But it is too late now."

Raoul was startled in his turn, and touched as well. "It would always have been too late, Lieutenant," he replied. "A poor return, too, that would have been for your kindness!"

"Well, whether your friend succeeds or no, des Sablières, I should like to know when you leave the prison-ship. It would be some compensation to me for—having to take you there. Address me at Norman Cross . . . if you think it worth the trouble. Good-bye." He shook hands and walked towards his horse; and a few minutes later the whole convoy was once more in motion.

Over the Meavy, through the streets of Plymouth with their sailors and their slatterns, and now in heavily falling rain. If only this, the last stage of the three weeks' pilgrimage, could have been prolonged a little! The hapless wayfarers did their best to spin it out; they lagged and had to be admonished. To Raoul that march through the breadth of Plymouth was like being in the grip of a gigantic hand which slowly tightened and tightened . . .

At last they were come to the end of solid ground, for they were in a dockyard, on a quay, where a guard of marines from the hulks was already awaiting them. The conductor was with these, and he and Lieutenant Hunter formally made over their unhappy charges to the lieutenant in command of this party.

"Why is that man loose?" demanded the latter, pointing to Raoul.

"Because he is an officer, and I allowed him his parole, which he has most faithfully observed," replied Mr. Hunter.

"You must know, Sir, that there are no officers, and consequently no parole, here!" was the angry retort. "I'm to have him jumping out of the boat, I suppose. Tie him up at once!"

And in the twinkling of an eye Raoul found his hands secured with naval thoroughness—behind his back this time. He tried to catch Lieutenant Hunter's eye and smile, but the soldier, cursing under his breath, would not look at him.

Soon they were being tumbled into the pinnace which was waiting alongside on the grey waters of the Hamoaze. The crew bent to their oars, the quay receded. Raoul kept himself from looking where they were going, for indeed the impulse was strong on him to leap, bound as he was, into those unfriendly waters. To keep it down he tried, not for the first time, to make himself believe that on arrival at the prison-ship he should find awaiting him an order from the Transport Board for his restoration to parole, that he should set foot on the hulk only to leave it again. Three weeks was long enough, surely, for some step to have been taken; Lord Fulgrave was a peer, a Privy Councillor, he had heard—and he himself an innocent man.

But when at last he lifted his eyes and had his first sight of the hulks, lying out in mid-stream like a string of giant blots on the water, his heart died within him. It was hard to believe that any good fortune could be waiting in those black sarcophagi. Yet every one of them had been in the past one of the most beautiful things that man has ever made, and the nearest to a living being—a full-rigged ship, splendid in majesty and motion. Now, stripped, dismasted, like birds without wings or trees demolished by the axe, they were not only lifeless but degraded, even less honourable in their immobility than the slave-brig buffeted by the rollers of the Guinea coast.

Except for some slight difference in size, a horrible uniformity reigned in these floating prisons, moored each behind the other for mutual surveillance. Each had a couple of jury masts, with one yard; round each, nearly at the level of the water, ran a gallery for the sentries; in each the boats were all drawn up save one, secured to the raft at the foot of the accommodation ladder by an iron chain. The pinnace's crew took her to the third of the hulks; it was, so Raoul found later, the *Ganges*. They were herded out of the boat; he went up the last of all, so hustled by the impatient marine behind him that, pinioned as he was, he almost fell. And as he mounted the ladder he knew, knew in every fibre of him, that there was no order of release here. For a second he looked up with hungry eyes at the gull sailing effortless overhead ere he stumbled on to the dark deck which opened before him.

Three quarters of an hour later, deprived of his uniform and clothed in a hideous and ill-fitting orange-yellow garb branded with the great T. and O. of the Transport Office (an ignominy which he had never anticipated) Raoul des Sablières stood in the lower battery of the *Ganges* gazing, with a sick horror, through an atmosphere in which he could scarcely breathe, at its half-starved and half-naked population. The battery was only about thirty feet by forty; it was so low that a tall man could not stand upright, and the only light and air came from a dozen or so small ports about eighteen inches square. In this space, furnished only with a bench running round it and four in the middle, were penned between three and four hundred beings in various stages of misery, disease, and degradation—his future companions.

It was the hour for a meal, and the hungry inmates of this inferno were clustered into groups round some great iron pots into which, like a pack of savages, they were ravenously dipping their tin cups, or even their hands. Of knife or spoon there was not a trace anywhere. . . . Well, he would starve rather than do that in their company. And as he stood there half stupefied with the clamour, watching the throng of evil faces, some of which, no doubt, had, when their owners first entered this place, been as unbranded as his own, Raoul felt as a drowning man may feel whose fingers can no longer grip the spar which has kept him afloat. It would be profanation to think of Juliana Forrest here; he had better forget her. That pure kiss of hers which he still carried would wither in this atmosphere; for here—one could feel it instantly—was not misery merely, but depravity.

A hand touched him on the arm, and, looking round, he saw an elderly man clothed in nothing but a pair of old breeches.

"A new arrival, I take it," he observed in a voice which retained traces of education. "Does not the look of the soup make your mouth water? To-morrow we shall have dried fish that has been going the round for months, because, since even we cannot eat it, we sell it back to the contractor again. But you—those clothes are new—you can stake them for a great deal; and have you not a watch or some trinkets or other? I'll play you for your watch——" His hand shook on Raoul's arm.

It was here as in the prisons then—the unhappy creatures gambled away their very rags, the very bread out of their mouths. But before Raoul could make any reply he was seized by the other arm, and the face of a damned soul, yellow and leering, was looking into his.

"Ah, another recruit!" it chuckled. "And where, my fine fellow, do you think you are going to sling your hammock to-night?"

"By a scuttle—if I am to be alive in the morning," answered the young man, half choked already.

"I daresay! Places near the scuttles are all taken, you——" The leer became more pronounced. "But for money, for a great deal of money——"

"I have no money," said Raoul.

"Then you can sling your hammock in hell, for all I care!" snarled the purveyor of breathing-spaces, and, aiming an ineffectual kick at him, turned away.

"Mr. Rowl"

*

It was, indeed, where Raoul slung it, and where he lay all night gasping, and thinking, sometimes saying to himself, "O God, how am I going to endure this . . . how can I?"

Part III
The Making of a Wildcat

Tight Shoes

"You shall be willingly supplied with such conveniences for the night as this cavern will afford."–Rasselas, chap. xxi.

On the edge of the road which runs from Tawton in South Devon down to the little port of Stowey there was growing in the summer of 1813 a certain gigantic elm, larger and more stately than its fellows. For some two hundred years it had duly thrown its quota of shade over the heads of the travellers and countryfolk who passed below it, though but few of these had been conscious of its separate identity. The sudden death of this tree, however, was to attract more attention than its long and serviceable life had ever done. For on the evening of the eleventh of August in that year, a windy but not excessively windy day, the cables which for so long had moored the great elm to the soil were snapped without warning, as is the way with its kind, and, with a vast crashing and rending, it fell, and–since the hour was too far advanced to begin sawing operations–lay where it fell, presenting an impassable barrier to all vehicles on the Stowey road, and a pleasing test of gymnastic ability to the young of the nearest cottages. By them "the day th' girt ellum blawed down" would be agreeably remembered; and Captain Hervey Barrington, R. N., of "Fairhaven," Stowey, was to remember it also.

He was at this moment one of the descending passengers of the stage-coach plying twice a day between Stowey and Tawton, which conveyance, having received no previous warning of the downfall of the elm, had just come to a rather indignant standstill before the prostrate giant, and this at seven in the evening. Some of its occupants–indeed, all who had any baggage worth mentioning–were favouring the alternative of returning in the coach to Tawton and spending the night there. But Captain Barrington, who had only been to that little town for the day on business, was not encumbered in this way, nor did a three-mile walk in the least dismay him.

161

"Mr. Rowl"

Very soon the bulk of the great elm, sprawling like Goliath across the road, was exercising, not without laughter, the returning Stoweyites, farmers or well-to-do fishermen for the most part. "Us'll have to climb un, for sure!" "Or creep on our bellies beneath un." But Captain Barrington surveyed the noble tree with a tinge of regret; and was meanwhile conscious of the voice of the guard behind him addressing someone still in the coach.

"I shouldn't advise you to go on to Stowey to-night, Miss—a matter of three or four miles 'tis. Why not goo back wi' us as far as Tawton? If so be as you couldn't get a room to yourself at the 'Lion,' you'd get a bed to yourself for sure."

The only person in the coach who could be addressed as "Miss" was a girl in grey already there when Captain Barrington had entered it at Tawton, a girl to whom his attention had subsequently been drawn—indifferent though he was to the sex—mainly because she seemed so desirous of attracting none, sitting very demurely in her corner, her face almost invisible under the gauze veil depending from the front of her small poke bonnet. But he had quite forgotten about her again till he now heard her reply hastily, "No, thank you, I must go on to Stowey."

The slight foreign accent piqued Captain Barrington's curiosity sufficiently to cause him to turn his head, and thus he got a glimpse of the speaker where she stood, above his level, at the top of the steps, looking down at the guard outside. She had put back her veil, and her face was more clearly revealed now—handsome, striking even, rather than beautiful, a little hollow in the cheeks, where burnt a somewhat hectic colour, but not timid like her demeanour, not shrinking. And he wondered for a moment who she could be; just possibly a member of some French Royalist household.

"Very well, Miss," said the guard. "I daresay some gentleman going to Stowey will carry your valise for you, and, as for company, there's Mrs. Stratton as lives at Stowey. She've started already, if so be she've got past that old toad of a tree."

"Thank you," said the girl again, and still, as it seemed to Hervey, hurriedly. "I will not trouble anybody; my little valise is not heavy. And no doubt I shall overtake this lady."

She descended, helped by the solicitous guard, Captain Barrington having moved away for fear of alarming her with proffered attentions. Better to leave her to Mrs. Stratton. Moreover, at this moment he happened to enquire from a rustic standing by what steps were going to be taken to ensure that no chaise or horseman should collide with the fallen tree after dark. None, that the rustic knew of.

"What, you are going to leave a wreck in the fairway without buoying it!" exclaimed Captain Barrington indignantly. "Not with my consent!" Striding off to the nearest farm, he soon returned with Farmer Cadman and half-a-dozen lanterns, and it was not till he had seen them lighted and strung on either side of the obstacle that he himself set off on his homeward way.

At present on half pay and likely—for all that promotion had come rapidly to him—so to remain, owing to a mishap at sea for which he was not responsible, Captain Barrington, a bachelor, lived in a comfortable house by the river about a mile on the hither side of Stowey, looked after by an excellent and commanding housekeeper and her husband, who had been his coxswain. For though Captain Barrington's spinster sister, a good eighteen years older than himself—he was one and forty—also dwelt near Stowey, the two had never joined their domestic forces, though the theory was that they were going to do it some day. Perhaps they secretly knew that they were at heart too dissimilar for such an arrangement ever to be successful, that Hervey was too "set" in his ways, and Miss Lavinia too free with her tongue, and too much of a quiz. But they were very good friends, and each had a room assigned and always ready for occupation in the other's house; in fact, Miss Lavinia was arriving this very evening at Fairhaven to spend a couple of days there en route to Exeter. For all her teasing tongue, nobody understood better than Miss Barrington how his inactivity fretted her brother, how savage was the resentment at the injustice which had laid him aside in time of war for a blunder which was not his. The wound went too deep to be often handled, but it stung always.

It was stinging now as Hervey Barrington walked along in the soft

Devonshire twilight. He had the road to himself, for the business with the tree had delayed him by quite twenty minutes, and all the other wayfarers were a mile or so ahead of him by this time. All but one, that is, for as he turned a corner he saw dimly, some forty yards ahead, the figure of a woman carrying something, and it looked like that of the foreign girl. She was walking with a limp, and at sight of her Captain Barrington's curiosity was revived. Even if she were lame how had she contrived to spend so much time covering so little ground, to have lagged so far behind everyone else? Had she stayed behind on purpose? Well, she had already struck him as wishing to avoid notice, but it was strange that at so late an hour she had not preferred to avail herself of company on the road, not to speak of someone to carry her valise. And, despite the limp, she was not walking so slowly as to have been unable to keep up with stout Mrs. Stratton, for instance.

At his present pace Hervey could not avoid overtaking her in a moment or two, and he should then feel bound to offer her his escort, whether she wanted it or no. It was not fitting for a young woman, a stranger, to be on a lonely road by herself at this time of day.

Before he was up to her the foreigner had heard his footfalls and half glanced round, quickening her pace a little. But in another thirty seconds he was level with her.

"Madam," he said, raising his hat, "it is not right that you should carry that baggage of yours. I beg you to allow me to do it for you."

The girl did not stop. She walked on with the limp and said, as if she meant it: "Sir, you are very kind, but no, it is not necessary. The valise is truly very light."

"But you—you are walking with difficulty already; you are fatigued," observed Hervey as he kept pace with her. "And you still have more than a couple of miles to go. You really must permit me." And, respectfully but firmly, he, too, possessed himself of the handle of the disputed object.

The fingers which held it tightened for a moment, then relaxed their grip, unwillingly. "You are indeed kind, Sir," murmured their owner as she relinquished her burden, but there was no real gratitude in her tone. She had, however, spoken the truth about the little portmanteau, for it was light—extremely light. Hervey began to wonder what was her destination in Stowey; he could not think of any of its inhabitants who were at all likely to be expecting such a guest.

"You are visiting friends in Stowey, I expect, Madam?" he said tentatively, excusing his question to himself on the ground that he would ultimately have to learn to what house he was to escort her.

"No," replied the traveller after a moment. "I go to an inn, is it not?"

"An inn!" said Hervey, still more surprised. "None of the inns at Stowey, Madam, is very suitable for a lady, and the 'Dolphin,' a better-class house, is temporarily closed. The others are only fit for sailors and such-like."

"Sailors will not hurt me," she murmured.

Her voice sounded dejected, or so Hervey thought. And she was most indubitably lame; she was hobbling.

"I must insist on your taking my arm," he said, somewhat masterfully. "You will never reach Stowey at all without assistance."

And the girl seemed to think so too, for, after a moment, she took the proffered support without looking at him; that is to say, she leant her hand, not much more, upon it, and they proceeded for a little in silence. Side by side with her, Hervey could not see her face because of the poke bonnet.

"You have already walked to-day, perhaps, Madam?" he suggested, as the weight on his arm gradually increased. "Or do you think it is possible that there is a nail, or a stone, in your shoe?"

"No," said the girl rather shortly. "I fear there is no nail, no stone. It is not for that reason that they hurt me."

"But would it not be well to make sure?" persisted Hervey, really sorry for her, since he could see that she was suffering. "Or will you not at any rate sit down on this wall and rest a little?"

For the road, no longer tree-shadowed on either hand, had been for some minutes following the Stowey river, whose outgoing tide lapped along the foot of the low wall on their left.

"Yes, I will sit down for a small moment, Sir," agreed the girl quickly, and she sank down without more ado on the stone parapet.

"You are, I take it, a stranger to these parts?" observed Captain Barrington conversationally.

"Yes," replied the traveller, after a moment's pause. "I come from York-sheer."

"From Yorkshire!" exclaimed Hervey involuntarily. Surely she was not trying to pass herself off as English? "Ah, you mean in this moment, of course. For I perceive that you are——" Then he stopped; he had no wish to appear prying.

But, to his regret, he saw that he had already given that impression; he had already caused alarm. "You mean, Sir," said the girl in a would-be calm voice, "that you see I am . . . not English. Oh, Sir—Señor—no, I am Spanish—but for the love of God do not betray me!"

"But, my dear young lady," said Hervey soothingly, "how and to whom should I betray you? You have a perfect right to be Spanish, and, being Spanish, to travel in England. Come, now, there is no cause for agitation—except possibly about those shoes of yours. I will withdraw a little, and you can take them off, and see whether something cannot be done to ease them."

He turned as he spoke, and, going a pace or two along the road, looked out over the darkening river. This was an odd encounter.

"Well, now, is that better?" he asked, coming back after a minute or two. The shoes, however, were not yet on again. He could discern them lying in the dusty road. The girl was sitting with her hands in her lap.

"When they are off it is better, yes. But I do not know whether——"

"Whether you can get them on again," finished Hervey with a smile. (Why did women always have their shoes too tight?) "If you will allow me——"

"No, no!" cried the girl, evidently affrighted, and, as far as he could see, tucking up her feet under her petticoats. "No, Sir, I will contrive . . . You see, it is not that they are too small"—how feminine! ladies, he knew, always said that—"but that the shape, the English shape——"

"Ah yes," said Hervey. "Of course. You bought these in England. Perhaps that was unwise."

"Many things are unwise," responded the girl on a deep, tragic note. "That I am here at all is unwise, but, Dios di mi alma, what else could I do?" She stifled an unmistakable sob. "But I shall soon be gone." And, bending down, she struggled feverishly with her footgear, Captain Barrington rather uncomfortable in this sudden and unexplained rush of emotion, and she evidently too much carried away by it to care whether or no the gentleman who had so considerately turned his back during the doffing of her shoes watched the process of resumption.

At last she stood up. "Now I will go on, Sir. I am now better." She hobbled a step or two, with little ejaculations under her breath, and then supplemented bravely, "–if I do not think of them."

"And if you take my arm again," suggested Hervey, tendering it.

She took it, leaning a little harder this time, and said, as they started: "Suppose I take altogether off my shoes, and go without them? As go the peasants in my country?"

"No, Madam, you could not possibly do that," replied Hervey. "This road is much too stony." They went on a little in silence, till he, having revolved the idea for a moment or two already, continued: "I have a better plan. My own house is now only half a mile distant, for I live well this side of Stowey. Now, if you would allow me to offer you hospitality for the night—"

"Señor!" exclaimed the Spanish girl, evidently deeply affronted. Her hand stiffened on his arm.

"I assure you, Madam," said Hervey hastily, "that my housekeeper—my name, by the way, is Barrington, Captain Hervey Barrington of His Majesty's Navy—"

But at that the hand was withdrawn altogether. They both stopped.

"My sister, too," began Captain Barrington anew, "will be—"

"Ah, your sister lives with you," interpolated the unknown, and, the hand returning, they took up their march again. Hervey did not think it worth while to explain, but enlarged a little on the pleasure it would give Miss Barrington to receive the footsore traveller and (though he did not say this) to tease him afterward for his knight-errantry.

"So you will accept, will you not, Madam? I assure you," he proceeded with a certain stiffness, "that I regard you with all the respect due to a member of your sex, and particularly to one who is, for the moment at least, unprotected. In order to prove, indeed, that I desire in no way to take advantage of you, I will cause my sister to come down to the garden, if you wish, and there make you known to each other, so that you can satisfy yourself of my intentions. For indeed you will never reach Stowey to-night, nor, as I say, is there any inn there quite suitable to your requirements."

The Spanish girl stood still once more. She clasped both hands to her breast and looked away over the river. Hervey had an uncomfortable suspicion that she was imploring the Virgin for guidance—really quite unnecessarily. When she spoke, the words were charged with feeling.

"Indeed you are too kind to an unfortunate. Unprotected—*Madre di Dios*! it is not for the moment only that I am unprotected. Shall I tell you my poor little story, Señor Capitan?"

"There is no need unless you wish," replied Hervey gently. (But he was curious all the same.)

"But yes, if you are so noble as to receive me under your roof I must tell you. In a few words. Again I will sit on this kind wall." She did so, and stooping, tugged off the shoes which were not too tight. "Señor, I am the wife—the deserted wife—of an Englishman like yourself, an English officer."

"Is it possible?" said Hervey, gravely astonished. He sat down on the wall beside her. "How did he desert you—where did you meet?"

The Spaniard made a gesture. "You ask where? Ah, Señor, in a terrible place—in Badajoz, in the storm of Badajoz."

"Good God!" exclaimed Captain Barrington. "You were in Badajoz when we took it last year!"

"With my poor father, yes. He was killed. Me the soldiers were dragging away—your soldiers . . . they were enraged at the resistance of the French . . . me, a Spaniard, your friend . . . when *he* saw me. Señor, he saved me . . . he loved me . . . he married me—that is to say——"

168

"Yes, I understand," murmured Hervey rather awkwardly.

She made another gesture. "But no, Señor, I think you do not! It is true that I was not married by the rites of my own Church, but of his, for I am married by the priest, the—what do you call him in your tongue?—the *capellan* of his regiment."

"The chaplain. And what was his regiment?"

The girl hesitated. "The English names are so difficult," she said deprecatingly.

"Try!" said Hervey.

She addressed herself visibly to an effort. "Mi *marido*—he was in what you call—the Light Brigade."

"Ah, yes. But what regiment? A brigade is not a regiment."

"Not?" queried the soldier's wife innocently.

"Was it the Rifle Regiment—the Ninety-fifth?"

"Yes, that is the name." She resumed feverishly. "We live in Badajoz a little . . . oh, how I am happy! But he will not take me with him on campaign; he leave me there. For a time he write to me. I find out always where he is. Then he writes no more. I think he is dead. I write to the Coronel; no, Tomás is not dead, he is gone to England; he is sick. And to me not a word! I wait. No letter . . . how to tell you the pain I suffer! At last . . . I have a little money, I sell my jewels, I go on board a vessel, I come in England. I travel to the home of my husband. Señor, he denies me! He says, No, I was never married to him—I was only a poor girl to amuse him! Vaya! I am to go back to Spain—he is finished with me!"

"What is the scoundrel's name?" demanded Hervey indignantly.

"Ah, no, I shall not tell you that!" She flung out her arms to the night. "Though I never see him again, though he treat me so cruelly, I love him—in Badajoz!"

"I see," said Hervey rather drily, the more so that the passion of the last words had caused an uncomfortable sort of thrill to pass along his spine. "But, Señora, you are in all probability really married to this man. In fact, I do not see how else it could be if the chaplain of the Rifle Regiment. . . . It would be perfectly easy to ascertain."

At that the abandoned wife clutched his arm—but not to welcome the suggestion. "No, no! If he cast me off it is finished. No, I go back to Spain. I leave him free."

"But, dash it all!" cried Captain Barrington, wishing that she would liberate him at all events, "the man himself, scamp that he is, won't be free—if by free you mean free to marry someone else. If you are his legal wife, as I feel sure you must be, you are still his wife whether you return to Spain or stay in England. And, by the way," he added, "how were you proposing to return to Spain?"

The ecstasy of self-sacrifice appeared to have died down as suddenly as it had arisen, and, having already (to his relief) relinquished his arm, the deserted lady said, with a sublime disregard of bathos, "Now I put on my shoes again," and did so. It was not until she was on her feet, and had once more accepted her escort's arm, that she answered his question. "To return to Spain I will find a little ship at Stow-ee."

"Indeed you will not!" returned Hervey rather sharply. "Who told you such a thing?"

"No little ship for Spain at Stow-ee! *Ay di mi!*" lamented the fair traveller. "Then I come all this painful way for nothing. Alas, how I am unfortunate!"

"We must consider your plans in the morning," said Hervey hastily, apprehending tears. "I can no doubt be of some assistance. But, if you will pardon the enquiry, how did you come to England in the first place? At what port did you land?"

"I have forgotten its name," replied the girl. Then, quickly taking herself up ("I knew she was lying," thought Hervey, pleased at his perspicacity) she said, "No, no, I now remember. At a place called Gos-port."

"Gosport! Then you came in a troopship!"

"Was that so wrong, Señor Capitan? I came as best I could. The passage was offered me . . . I paid nothing." Very oddly, there seemed to be a suggestion of laughter in her voice now—or was it tears fought back? The next moment she stumbled and gave a little cry, hanging heavy on his arm for a second. "A stone . . . no, Señor, it is nothing. I can go on. It is perhaps not much farther now?"

"No, fortunately. But I am afraid that this walk has meant a good deal of suffering for you."

"No, no," she murmured, "for I have found a friend so kind, so sympathetic!——" And for the first time the other hand joined its fellow on his arm, and both gave that support an unmistakable pressure.

Now Hervey Barrington had not the slightest desire to receive from this emotional Spanish female any evidence of her warm southern heart in return for his hospitality. Yet, as he could not withdraw his arm, the only measure he could take against such a risk was to change the conversation.

"When I was in Spain——" he began—and had quite a gratifying success. The joint pressure on his arm relaxed, and the second hand went away again.

"Ah, you have been in Spain," observed its owner slowly, and almost as if the information were not to her taste.

"Yes, just before the war," answered Hervey. "I travelled with a Spanish friend in Catalonia and Valencia."

"I do not know those parts," said his companion hastily, as if she were rebutting an accusation; and for the rest of the way became rather silent, except for an occasional tired sigh. Captain Barrington was glad when he could at last announce, as a house loomed up by the side of the road, between them and the river: "Here we are at our destination."

Departure of the Señora Tomás

"I am not a princess, but an unhappy stranger who intended soon to have left this country."—Rasselas, chap. xxxviii.

Though on one side Fairhaven, a house of moderate size, bordered directly on the road, a garden stretching to the river surrounded it on all the others, and it was into this garden, by a side gate, that Hervey, in his anxiety to show himself no Lothario, now conducted his guest. In the middle of the lawn was a fine old mulberry tree, and under the mulberry a garden seat constructed out of the timbers of the *Halcyon* sloop of war, which had been Lieutenant Barrington's first command. Upon this relic Hervey invited the Spanish traveller to sit, while he summoned his sister. "Like putting her in quarantine," he thought, as he entered the house from the garden and ran upstairs.

A minute later he was down again in the spacious hall calling "Mrs. Jeremy! Mrs. Jeremy!" and then, receiving no answer, ringing a bell.

It was impossible to be more immaculate, more spotlessly and stiffly becapped, more suitably clad in a high-bosomed grey gingham that showed her ample but shapely contours, than Mrs. Hannah Jeremy, to enter with more of the air of the all-competent but respectful housekeeper, or to drop a slight curtsey of more dignity.

"Did you ring, Sir?"

"I did. Where is Miss Barrington?"

"She has not come yet, Sir."

"Not come!" ejaculated her master with more stupefaction than the news seemed, on the surface, to warrant.

"No, Sir."

Hervey's thoughts went to the garden seat. With no sister forthcoming, as promised, the girl would think he had been lying . . . as indeed he had been, tacitly, when he allowed her to suppose that Lavinia lived with him. It would look as if he had deliberately entrapped the stranger. "You don't think, surely, Mrs. Jeremy," he said in dismay, "that Miss Barrington has changed her mind, and is not coming to-night at all?"

"I couldn't say, Sir. We have heard nothing. But it is getting late. I have had to put supper back, for if you'll excuse the liberty, Sir, you are late yourself."

"Yes, I know that," responded Hervey, his brain busy. "There was an accident—the road blocked by a tree—and I had to walk from Cadman's Corner." Of course, there was always Mrs. Jeremy in the house to play propriety; what he disliked was having to confess to what must look like calculated duplicity. As he stood silent, his hand at his chin, wondering how he could get out of this admission, Mrs. Jeremy observed in a voice noticeably prim and frigid:

"I don't know whether you would wish me to acquaint you with it, Sir, but there's a very awkward thing occurred. How long she's been there there's no telling, having only just seen her myself, but there's a female—and seemingly a young female—sitting in the garden, Sir . . . and at this hour, too!"

Hervey made a gesture which appeared to signify that as many females as pleased might sit in his garden all night. Actually it meant that there was no need to tell him of a fact which he knew already, but Mrs. Jeremy did not thus interpret it, and she proceeded:

"How she come there I can't conceive, nor what she's doing, sitting there on the *Halcyon* as bold as brass—I might almost say lying there, saving your presence, Sir, for she's put her feet up off of the ground!" Had Mrs. Jeremy announced that the stranger had removed the major part of her clothing her voice could hardly have held more reprobation. "I wish I had told Jeremy to keep an eye on her from the pantry window."

"It is not necessary," said Hervey, groaning inwardly. Hang Lavinia and her unpunctuality! But he was master in his own house (if sometimes at the cost of effort) and he faced Mrs. Jeremy boldly.

"The young lady in the garden, Mrs. Jeremy, was left there by me. She is an unfortunate Spanish girl who has been deserted by her husband, an English officer. She was walking into Stowey, like myself, from Cadman's Corner; she is lame from—from fatigue and too tired to go any farther; so, counting on Miss Barrington's presence here, I offered her hospitality for the night." (Here Mrs. Jeremy permitted herself an inarticulate exclamation.) "Now—I don't know what I'm to do! If Miss Barrington doesn't come at all I suppose I must hand the poor girl entirely into your charge—that is to say, if she will now consent to stay here."

"I think you will find, Sir," responded Mrs. Jeremy with unusual tartness, "that the young person—Spanish, you say?—won't raise any difficulties about sleeping in a gentleman's house, whether there's another lady there or no! It's my belief she'll be only too pleased if there's none!"

"Mr. Rowl"

"Nonsense, Mrs. Jeremy!" said Hervey sharply. "You know nothing whatever about the girl. She only consented to come when she heard of the existence of my sister. I don't know what excuse I am to make to her for Miss Barrington's absence. You will have to come out into the garden with me, so as to show that there is at least a respectable woman at Fairhaven."

"Much obliged, Sir," said Mrs. Jeremy, with a movement of the head which approached perilously near a toss. "As I said before, being Spanish" (impossible to reproduce what Mrs. Jeremy put into this word) "she'll likely come in the more readily if she don't see a respectable woman, she sitting there as if the garden belonged to her already!"

Hervey was now really angry. "Mrs. Jeremy," he said sternly, "you are forgetting yourself. You ought to be ashamed of such insinuations! Now listen. When I have persuaded this poor girl that she need fear nothing under my roof, you will get the spare bedroom ready for her at once; and I think that as she is tired, and I am . . . alone . . . the best thing will be for her to have some supper taken to her up there before she retires. Do you understand?"

"You really mean her to sleep the night in this house, Sir?"

"Did you not hear the orders I have just given you, Mrs. Jeremy?" enquired Hervey, very quietly, but with an unmistakable quarterdeck inflection.

"I beg your pardon, Sir," said his housekeeper, quelled and flushing slightly. "And you wish me to come out with you now to see the young per—lady?"

"Yes. That is to say, come out on some pretext in a minute or two, after I have explained the situation to her. You can ask me, for instance, at what time I would like supper."

When he got into the garden again Hervey realized with quite a shock how dark it had grown, and the oddity of leaving a guest—a lady—to sit outside in the more than dusk. Still, it had been done entirely for her own sake, and fortunately this was a warm evening, an evening full of the scents of the flowers in the little garden, and of the murmur of the outgoing river.

A bat was wheeling over the relic of the *Halcyon*, but the seat, to Hervey's surprise, was empty. Had the Spaniard taken fright and departed? He searched the gloom and, descrying a shape by the steps which went down to the river, hurried towards it. The Señora was sitting on the low wall.

"This river must be beautiful, if one could see, Señor Capitan," she observed, as he came up to her. "You have steps here—a boat, I perceive!"

"Yes," said Captain Barrington, for he did keep the skiff of his small sailing cutter moored at the foot of the steps, but in the gloom it was quite impossible to see it from where the lady sat, and it struck him that curiosity must have led her down the steps to investigate. But he had not come to talk about his surroundings or possessions.

"Madam," he began uncomfortably, "I must present my deep apologies. I ought to have made myself clearer on the road just now. My sister does not live with me, she visits me from time to time; and, though she should be here to-night, the fact remains that she has not yet arrived."

In the silence which ensued, this speech sounded to its maker most unconvincing. And the Spanish girl gave a quick sigh. It was too dark to see her expression; but she surely was not contemplating going on to Stowey after all, disabled as she was? He would reason with her, plead with her, before he allowed her to do that.

But after a moment she spoke. "Señor Capitan," she said in a low voice, "it is not possible for me to walk farther, even though the Señora your sister do not arrive this night. So . . . I throw myself upon your chival-ree."

So long as she did not throw herself upon his breast Hervey was quite content with this acceptance—though it was a good deal readier than he had anticipated. He was even rather touched by its simple dignity. But then, in the semi-darkness, as he stood before her, he felt his hand seized in both of hers, and, before he knew what she was about, she had sealed her committal to his honour by carrying it towards her lips. Halfway she suddenly seemed to think better of it, and Hervey, intensely disliking the prospect of having his hand kissed by a woman, deduced with gratitude that he was spared this supreme embarrassment owing to the opportune arrival of Mrs. Jeremy, with the prearranged query, made in her best style, "At what hour would you wish supper to be served, Sir?"

*

Mrs. Jeremy disappearing the instant they were in the house, Captain Barrington himself was the only person available to show the girl to her room, which, doubting in any case if it were yet ready to receive her, he had no intention of doing. He therefore suggested that she should remove her bonnet in the hall, if she would forgive the lack of ceremony. She assured him in her pretty broken English that there was no need to apologize for the so handsome apartment, but she did not hasten to comply, and sat down as she was, with her dangling veil, in an armchair near the hearth, placing her feet, in the purgatorial shoes, upon the overblown bead roses of a convenient footstool. She did, however, loosen her cloak, and presently it slipped altogether from her shoulders. Hervey had thought to see her face more clearly in the glow of the candles which Mrs. Jeremy had already lit, but, between the height of the sconces, and the poke of the bonnet, there was as much shadow upon it as illumination. He did discern, however, that she was high-coloured for a Spaniard, and not so very dark, after all . . . yet not of the fair Spanish type, either. Perhaps she had a mixture of some other nationality.

One might be able to tell that from the way she spoke her native tongue. Speaking Spanish very fairly himself, and with a good accent, Hervey wondered now why he had not addressed her in that language before. Probably because her English was so adequate. Well, better late than never.

"I am afraid that you must be exceedingly tired, and hungry also, Señora," he observed in his best Castilian. "I assure you that I greatly regret this delay in offering you rest and refreshment."

He saw her colour spread. She was surprised, not unnaturally, at his tardy revelation of his accomplishment. She answered him, however, not in her own tongue but in his.

"Ah, you speak Spanish, Señor! My congratulations!"

"Allow me to return them," said Hervey, this time in his own language. "It is remarkable for a Spanish lady to speak English." ("And to cling to it so persistently, too," he thought to himself.)

The Señora flushed again and moved in her chair. "You are very kind. Yes, I speak it so much with Tomás . . . and now in your country . . . that I have almost forgotten my own language."

But, reflected Hervey, she and her Tomás cannot possibly have spent long enough together for her to acquire such a mastery of English. She must have known it before. . . . And an unaccountable desire to hear her talking Spanish persisting in him, and his own command of the unfamiliar tongue reviving more quickly than he expected, he went on to ask her in that speech what she proposed to do about returning to Spain, since he could assure her that it was not feasible to voyage thither from Stowey. And who had so misdirected her as to inform her that it was?

The questions seemed oddly to confuse the Señora Tomás. The colour which had risen disappeared—except on her cheeks, where it did not vary.

"I pray you not to talk Spanish to me," she said in an uncertain voice, looking away. "It is cruel. It reminds me . . . of too many things. . . ."

And then an extraordinary, a stunning conviction broke upon Hervey Barrington. He leant forward and fixed his guest with a steady gaze.

"You ask that because you do not understand what I say! You cannot reply in your own language—you are not a Spaniard at all!"

The bonnet trembled for a moment. Then its occupant returned his searching, condemnatory look in silence, with an effect of measuring him in her turn; after which, with a gesture of abandonment, she put her hands before her face and bowed her head. Her thin shoulders heaved a little, and there was a sound like stifled crying, but not much.

Hervey had risen. "Well, Madam?" he enquired stonily after a moment.

A further silence, and his guest raised her head.

"It is true," she said quite quietly. "I have lied to you. I am not Spanish. I am French."

"You have lied to me—you acknowledge it!" repeated Hervey between his teeth. "All that story about Badajoz, that——" He clenched his hands, restraining his language with difficulty, remembering that, in spite of everything, she was a woman. "All that was lies, then?"

"Yes," she said, still in that very quiet, emotionless voice. "I wish I had not . . . had to lie. I did not like doing it . . . and I might have known one does not deceive a man like you."

"Did not like doing it!" repeated Hervey wrathfully, as certain episodes of the deception came back to him. "You enjoyed it, you——" Once again he checked himself.

But she looked up at him with a sad, limpid gaze. "No woman as heartsick as I am, Captain Barrington, could enjoy anything at this hour," she returned sorrowfully, "and no woman with a heart at all could enjoy deceiving an honourable and generous man."

"We will have a truce to compliments, if you please," said Hervey grimly. "Instead you will give me an explanation, less of your being French, than of why you passed yourself off for Spanish—I imagine, though, that I must now prepare myself for another cock-and-bull story. I suppose that you will tell me next that you are a French Royalist, an *émigrée?*"

The girl shook her head with a faint smile. "That would indeed be more convenient for me. But this time I will tell you the truth. Ah, I wish I had done it before!"

The complete change in her manner, her hopeless tone, her utter abandonment of feminine wiles, the very way she sat surrendered in the big chair began to have some effect on Hervey. He felt it and removed himself farther off. "Why did you not, then?"

"Because I was afraid. I thought that to acknowledge myself French—an enemy—was too dangerous. I fancied I could pass myself off as Spanish. But I only know a word or two of the language. And the story I told you . . . Ah, do not be angry, Monsieur! I must have some story to account for my presence in England!"

"I must congratulate you on the one you served up to me," observed Hervey sardonically. "Your talents are wasted in private life. But perhaps you are an actress, in your own country?"

Looking down, she shook her ringlets. "No, Monsieur. I live very quietly in the provinces, with my parents. But I have deserved that you should reproach me. I have been very foolish . . . I think my best justification is to tell you my real story . . . if you will listen to it now?"

"I will listen."

"You are generous indeed, Captain Barrington." She paused a moment; then, as it were, drew herself together. "My name is Adrienne des—" But here, at the outset, she checked herself, and looked across at him reflectively. "No, perhaps I will not tell you that. But everything else I will tell you. . . . I had, Monsieur, a brother, fighting in Spain—fighting against the English, yes, but fighting like a gentleman, for I think all your soldiers have said that of us. Besides"—her head lifted itself a trifle—"he is a gentleman. But he was captured and brought to England, and made a prisoner on parole. And then, Monsieur, an atrocious thing happened, for some intrigue against him led to his being accused, unjustly, of having broken his parole, and he was sent to prison. He tried to escape from the prison—was that unnatural, Monsieur?—and for that he was sent to the *pontons*—the hulks." Hervey, who was watching her rather surreptitiously, saw her bite her lips at that ill-omened word, and put her handkerchief to them for a moment. "You know what that means, Monsieur . . . and he was an officer!"

"Yes. Go on," said Hervey. At the back of his mind he was conscious of how much better she spoke English now that she had renounced her Spanish nationality. Curious.

"Monsieur, he is my only brother—my twin brother. My parents are old and *tant soit peu royalistes*. When Raoul and I were children we lived for that reason in England; in short, we were *émigrés* in those days, so I might well have called myself an *émigrée* just now but that I have done with deception." ("Ah, that," thought Hervey, "explains the excellent English; then she must have been mangling it on purpose just now!") "*Eh bien*, I said to myself, some of the friends of my childhood may be alive still, in London, and if only I could find them they would help me; they would remember Raoul, they would do something to right this horrible injustice. So, I came to England." Seeing Hervey about to interrupt, she held up a hand. "Monsieur, you, a sailor, know that it *can* be done—but I do not wish to implicate any one by telling you how."

"Yes, very well," said Hervey, interested despite himself, and not least of all by the different manner in which this girl told a true tale. "I accept that. Go on, Mademoiselle."

"In London I cannot find these old friends; they are removed or dead. I have no one to help me. I cannot go to any man and ask for help. Although I was playing a part this evening you will acknowledge, I hope, Monsieur, that I did not solicit your assistance; au contraire, I tried to escape notice."

"Quite true."

"All that I can permit myself to do then is to go to the Transport Office in Dorset Square and to make enquiries about my unhappy brother. They look up registers and the like, and they tell me he is at Plymouth, in the prison ship the *Queen*. They give me no hope of his release, but they say I may go and see him. At least that is something. I take the coach to Plymouth; I go in a boat to those . . ." Her voice broke suddenly, and she clenched her hands together.

"Yes?" said Hervey gently. No place for a woman; what had she seen?

With an effort Adrienne went on. "It is a déception—a mistake. Raoul is not there . . . was never there . . ."

"But if the Transport Board——" began Hervey.

"Oh, Monsieur, they have so many names of unfortunates on those registers. . . . And I saw some of them . . . men like the dead! They tell me, the officers of the *Queen*, that it must be a mistake for the *Queen Caroline* at Portsmouth; that my poor brother must be there. And so I am going back, and I pray God that I find him at Portsmouth, even in one of those terrible ships, because—because——"

"Because what, Mademoiselle?" asked Hervey, and he came and stood by her.

For one moment the dark-ringed eyes, heavy with sorrow and fatigue, looked up at him. "Because I have the thought that he may be dead, and that they would not tell me!" And with that her self-command gave way entirely,

180

and, burying her face once more in her hands, she sobbed helplessly.

Hervey Barrington was far from being a hard-hearted man. Before this grief and these unmistakable accents of sincerity he ceased to resent the fact that an hour ago this girl had been fooling him with a pathetic fiction, more especially because the present narrator did not seem the same person at all as that pseudo-Spanish minx. What a pity she had ever tried that game; it was so unnecessary. No man with a grain of feeling could have stayed her, or done anything to her, technical enemy though she were, on learning of her errand. And the poor creature had actually visited those unpleasant places . . . in vain.

Meanwhile she sobbed on and on, while he tried to offer suggestions about Portsmouth, and about what he could do himself in the way of enquiries. But she still had her face hidden, and he was almost bending over her when Mrs. Jeremy reappeared to say that the bedroom was ready, and that she had set supper for the lady there.

In the presence of a domestic, Mlle. Adrienne made a more determined effort to pull herself together. She dried her eyes and stood up.

"I will wish you the best boon I can, a good night's rest," said Hervey kindly. "In the morning we will talk about what is to be done. Meanwhile"—he sank his voice, though Mrs. Jeremy was waiting a considerable distance away, at the foot of the stairs—"meanwhile try to forget Plymouth and what you saw there."

The shadow in the French girl's eyes deepened.

"I can never do that," she responded gravely, "not in all my life. But I thank you, for myself and for my brother Raoul, too—if he lives. I would kiss your hand, Captain Barrington, but I know that you would not like it." The half smile that came with this, like a gleam of sun after rain, suggested that when she was not tired and overwrought she had a very sweet one.

"Mademoiselle," said Hervey, "I think it should be the other way about." And on an impulse, regardless of the presence of Mrs. Jeremy, he took her hand and raised it for a moment to his lips. "Good-night."

"Mr. Rowl"

Departure of Her Successor

"I was weary, and hoped to find in sleep that remission of distress which Nature seldom denies."—Rasselas, chap. xxxviii.

The room on the second floor to which Mrs. Jeremy preceded Mlle. des Sablières was large and comfortable. It had two windows, now discreetly curtained, looking out on to the road. Mrs. Jeremy was large, too—that she could not alter—and she was usually very comfortable also . . . but not now.

"This is your room, Miss—Madam, no doubt I should say," she announced with extreme frigidity. "The bed is well aired. Your supper is on that little table; soup I've given you, and a cold chicken wing, knowing as young ladies have not much appetite, particularly when fatigued after a journey *from heaven knows where!* And here is your—baggage, Miss; that, I understand, is all you have. And now if you'll excuse me I must go and see to the roast for the Captain. I wish you a good night, Miss." She withdrew, and the temperature sensibly rose.

Mlle. des Sablières, who had looked at her mutely during the delivery of this speech, raised her eyes to heaven as the door closed. "*Mon Dieu!*" It was all she said; she proceeded with no loss of time to action, always so much more important than speech. The first thing she did was to sit down on the nearest chair, pull off her shoes and fling them petulantly and with a look of hatred one after the other across the room; the second, to hobble to the door and lock it; the third, to draw up a chair to the table, take the cover off the bowl of soup, and, without waiting to spread a napkin, drink off about half its contents in one draught. Midway she set it down and surveyed the rest of the collation with a gradually falling face: the wing of cold chicken, the slice of bread, the small pat of butter, the remnant of apple tart and the tiny jug of cream, all very daintily set out upon a tray; after which, taking a spoon, she consumed the rest of the soup slowly by means of that implement. She then drank a glass of wine with a good deal more obvious gusto than the less appreciative sex usually exhibits (but then she was alone), sighed, looked fondly at the wing of chicken, and began upon it with a forced deliberation. . . . Even so, in eight minutes there was nothing whatever left of the elegant little supper save the chicken bones, as bare as if a colony of ants had been at work on them, and one glass of wine, with which Mlle. des Sablières, leaning back in her chair with her stockinged feet stretched out straight in front of her, then proceeded to conclude the not very substantial meal.

After holding the empty glass for a moment or two in her fingers, and looking at it regretfully, she put it down with a sigh, and, taking up the tray, considerately put it outside the door, relocked the latter and then, candle in hand, made a careful tour of the walls of the apartment. The only other door was a small one covered with wall-paper, of the kind that commonly leads into a cupboard or powdering closet, and this one did no more, as the explorer satisfied herself. She returned, therefore, and began to take off her dress—presumably a new one, since her fingers seemed unused to the fastenings, and it was some time before she stepped out of it, in her white underdress. Evidently, too, she regarded it with the reverence due to a new gown, for she spread it out, with what seemed exaggerated care for so simple a confection, over the back of a chair. After this she removed, with the same precision, an object of which some ladies, it is known, do divest themselves upon retiring, but these, as a rule, of an age more advanced than Mlle. des Sablières.

The removal of the high-piled ringlets, thus laid en masse on the table, revealed her own short hair, of approximately the same dark-brown colour. She next unlocked the famous valise, took from it an instrument which she laid by the wig, went over to the washstand and vigorously washed her face, and then, returning with a hand-mirror from the dressing-table, scrutinized the result by the candles, feeling her chin and upper lip critically. Her ablutions had had a somewhat singular effect upon her complexion, for the mirror showed all her brilliant colour gone.

Suddenly the fair traveller put down the glass and yawned violently, stretching her arms to their fullest extent, and causing an ominous cracking sound in the bosom of her tight-fitting underdress. A look of alarm crossed her face, and, using an expression of a kind with which a gently nurtured girl should not be familiar, she slowly unfastened the underdress also, and let it slide to the ground. And with that there was nothing of Mlle. des Sablières left . . . only a very near relation of hers, slim to leanness in shirt, thin breeches, and stockings, with a lock of damp hair clinging to his forehead and a face which, now that the paint was gone, showed its true hollowness under the cheekbones and round the jaw—the face, too, of one tired to death, though at the moment it wore a faint and transitory amusement as its owner looked down at the circle of white lying round his feet.

That dress, the money in his pockets, his presence here as a practically free man, Raoul owed in the first instance entirely to Juliana Forrest. She had got him out of the hulks, as she had vowed she would—employing for the purpose one Creedy, who combined in Plymouth the occupation of ship chandler and escape agent. Had Raoul realized earlier how deeply she was implicating herself in what now ranked as a felony, he might have hesitated to accept his freedom, but the truth was that, though for two months he received letters from her by the ordinary channels, adjuring him to keep up his spirits and assuring him that he was not forgotten, he supposed her, in the absence of any hints to the contrary, to be continuing her campaign by legitimate methods. Then, yesterday morning, as he was taking his turn, in heavy rain, at hauling up the casks of fresh water from the boat which daily brought them from the shore, one of her crew whispered something in his ear. There was no time to question or to argue; only, in the downpour which no doubt had something to do with the relaxed vigilance of the sentries, to slip as directed into one of the empty casks lying on its side in the barge. But not until he was safely in the cellar under Creedy's shop did he, still bewildered, discover that that individual had been for two months in Miss Forrest's pay awaiting this chance. . . . It was too late then to refuse the gift; the best way of showing his gratitude was to use it, and get himself as speedily as he could, by means of Creedy's directions and her money, to Start Bay, where the smugglers would run him over to France.

Raoul stepped out of the underdress and folded it neatly up. Well, here he was, on his second night of freedom, under the roof of an English naval officer, of all men in the world, and though in the first instance only the more than discomfort of those damned shoes had driven him to accept this hospitality when it was pressed upon him, he had not been slow to realize that, if he had been tracked as far as Stowey, this was probably the last house where the authorities would ever dream of searching for him. He was really very glad that he had not to run the gauntlet of the unknown Miss Barrington's eyes to-night; Captain Barrington, indeed, had evidently no suspicion of his sex—really it was almost a shame to have taken such advantage of his good-nature—but "Adrienne's" possibly over-rouged appearance had not seemed to find favour with the housekeeper. Creedy, who at Miss Forrest's suggestion had fitted him out in woman's attire, had also provided him with the means of touching up his pallor and thinness into something more femininely presentable; and it was when Raoul, thus embellished, had beheld himself in Mr. Creedy's looking-glass that the likeness to Adrienne had suggested to him the whimsical idea of impersonating her—an idea which he subsequently discarded for exactly the reason he had given Captain Barrington, that to avow oneself French was too hazardous. . . . Even in the wearing of a petticoat elsewhere than at private theatricals there were risks which he had not anticipated; before ever he had got clear of Plymouth a half-drunken sailor had tried—tried very hard—to kiss him. . . . This sailor to-night, thank the saints, had shown no signs of that desire, and heaven send it never visited him, for the most discreet embrace could hardly fail to lead to discovery, even though the grey gown had been carefully padded to simulate a roundness which Raoul's own person was very far from possessing.

Still, he must have made rather a convincing girl to have scored such a histrionic triumph as to impose his second story on his host immediately after the discovery of the falsity of the first. But it had not been difficult to throw the accents of sincerity into the account of what, after all, was only too sadly true—his own case. Yet he saw now that he had let himself be a trifle too much carried away over the business of the deserted Spanish wife. He must guard, in future, against allowing the humour of a situation to take hold of him like that. Heaven knew that there was little enough to laugh at in his own . . . though of course to masquerade as his own sister had its amusing side. . . .

Sleep, the sleep of profound fatigue of mind and body, was pressing on him now like a feather-bed. It was almost shameful to be so tired with so little cause, but the horrible existence of the last two months had sapped his strength unbelievably, and the long duel with Captain Barrington had been a great strain. He dragged himself to the table and took up the razor. No; he dared not shave when he was so weary, for he might cut himself, which in the circumstances would be suspicious. He would do it early in the morning; he never had a stiff growth. . . . He lurched to the bed, and sitting down upon it, began to unfasten his shirt.

Peste, the feminine night-rail which he really did carry with his razor and a few other necessaries in the little valise was still in it. It was absurd to put it on; it seemed to him a very absurd garment altogether, but it afforded him a chance of getting out of the clothes he wore by day. In a moment he would rise and fetch it . . . but just for a second or two. . . . He gave another mighty yawn and fell sideways against the pillow; the next instant he had instinctively brought his feet up on to the bed. *Ciel!* was there anything like a good bed after . . . He stretched out his legs, thrust a hand under the excellent down in which his head was sunk . . . and never moved again.

*

"La, Miss Lavinia, 'tis you after all then!" exclaimed Mrs. Jeremy, opening the hall door. "And I just about to dish up supper for the Captain; we made sure by this time that you wasn't coming."

The tall cloaked form of Miss Barrington stepped briskly into the hall. "I rather thought so myself, Hannah, at one time. I started later than I should, then the pony cast a shoe and had to be walked two miles to the nearest forge and the smith knocked up. Is my brother in a very bad temper? Put my portmanteau down there, Jacob, and get back as fast as you can, or your mother will think that I have either eloped with you or sold you for a slave."

And as the door shut behind the grinning youth Miss Barrington began to divest herself of her cloak. "I'll not wait to go up to my room now, Hannah, and do you for God's sake go and set supper on the table without more delay, or we may find ourselves in irons!"

"Oh, Miss Lavinia, what things you do put into the Captain's mouth, to be sure!" exclaimed Mrs. Jeremy, half shocked, half smiling. "Let me take your cloak and bonnet, Ma'am. Supper is in the breakfast room, because the dining room carpet is repairing, and so I thought—*Yes, Ma'am, you may well ask what that is!*"

For Miss Barrington, having taken off her bonnet, was smoothing down her hair, when her glance fell on something grey lying in a huddle on the seat of the big leather chair by the hearth. Picked up, it resolved itself into a lady's hooded cloak.

"I thought I was the only woman to use this hall as a dressing room," observed Miss Barrington, surveying it. "But it seems that I am not!"

"No, Ma'am," returned Mrs. Jeremy, almost bursting. "There's a female—a Spanish female—in this house . . . *sleeping* in this house . . . that the Captain brought in this evening . . . picked her up in the road he did . . . she's got over his kind heart . . . and what does a gentleman like him know of her sort . . . *painted*, Miss Barrington, and——"

A door opened upstairs and Hervey's voice, mildly sarcastic, called down: "Mrs. Jeremy, if you are unable, through pressure of work, or of conversation, to carry supper upstairs, ask Jeremy to do it for you."

Mrs. Jeremy put her hand over her mouth and fled. "'Through pressure of work'?" said Miss Barrington to herself. "Work for the Spanish female, I suppose. What is Hervey about?—My dear brother," she called up, "it's I am the culprit, with my abominable lateness. Don't come down, I am coming up—and so is the supper." With a very light foot for her fifty-nine years and her stately form she ascended the staircase and received her brother's kiss at the top. "I have left my cloak, too, in the hall," she observed, smiling sweetly—"I mean, my cloak and bonnet, too, in the hall. I am sure you don't mind."

"No," replied Hervey quite innocently, "why should I, my dear Lavinia?" He opened the breakfast-room door. "I hope you do not object to supping here? The dining-room carpet——"

"Yes, Mrs. Jeremy told me," interposed his sister cheerfully. No doubt Hervey wished to know whether Mrs. Jeremy had imparted some much more interesting news, but that was just what she was not going to reveal. It would be far more amusing to watch Hervey's efforts to nerve himself to do it, and to see in what terms he would convey the information when he succeeded. Lavinia Barrington, on the brink of sixty, still possessed an unquenchable zest for the humorous and cared not how she gratified it.

But why indeed should Hervey have to find a way of announcing the presence of his protégée, when possibly that protégée was already waiting to sup with them? But no—one glance round the sitting room showed that no dark-eyed Castilian or Catalan was there—no high comb, no mantilla, no shawl. A second revealed the fact that only two covers were laid. Hervey was discreet, then; he had banished the Andalusian maid to her room.

The candles in the branched silver candlesticks, when in a moment or two the brother and sister sat down to the belated repast, revealed what a handsome woman Miss Barrington was, her face untouched as yet by any of the disfiguring lines of age, but only by those that testify to character. Her hair perhaps had never been so beautiful as now in its silvered abundance. She had always been handsome; she had always been courted; she had always jested at her suitors. But twenty-five years ago the man she had loved had married another woman and then died.

It was not until the end of the meal that Miss Barrington's ears were gratified by the avowal for which they had been delightedly waiting.

"I had a most curious adventure on the road this evening, after that tree had forced us all to leave the coach," began Captain Barrington. "I fell in with an unfortunate French girl who had been to Plymouth to see a brother of hers in a prison-ship there."

"French, did you say?" asked Miss Barrington in a surprised voice.

"Yes, why not? The majority of the prisoners are French."

"Curious," murmured his sister. "Yes, go on."

"Hers was a sad little history," said Hervey, and proceeded to relate it.

"Most pathetic," agreed Miss Barrington at the close. "What did you do, Hervey?—I know! You paid the girl's coach fare to Portsmouth, which I expect was what she wanted . . . though I should have thought that one seaport town was as good as another . . . I expect she has a good many of those 'brothers'!"

"For shame, Lavinia," said Hervey, reddening. "Why are you aspersing a girl whom you have never seen? Do you suppose I don't know a female of that sort when I see one?"

"Well, my dear Hervey, I don't feel sure that you would." And as her brother made an angry gesture she said pacifically, "You must forgive me, for, as you say, I have not seen her, and never shall now, I suppose."

"Yes, you . . . you will have the chance to-morrow," murmured Captain Barrington, fidgeting with a fork. "I asked her . . . she was so footsore . . . in short, she is in the house to-night . . . Knowing that you would be here," he added, a little incoherently.

Miss Lavinia made no comment at all, just because she knew that he would be expecting one. She merely looked across the table at him and allowed her smile to broaden enjoyably—more enjoyably to herself than to the Good Samaritan at the other end. After a moment she said lazily, "Mademoiselle is in the spare bedroom, I suppose? May I ask, in that case, what you have done with the Spanish girl? Is she occupying your dressing room, or is it the other way round?"

"Spanish girl?" stammered Hervey. "There's no—Then you knew all the time, Lavinia!"

"I know that the Spanish damsel has left her cloak in the hall. Is Mrs. Jeremy, who seems to be aware of her presence, and to have made notes of her appearance, ignorant that you have ensconced a French lady also in this hitherto blameless house? Of course, I hardly wonder that you did not care to tell her, but you may be quite certain that she will soon find out where you have hidden the other member of your . . . seraglio. Really, Hervey, you to set up as Grand Turk in this fashion."

"Lavinia, oblige me by ceasing to talk nonsense," said her brother rather sternly. "You let your tongue run away with you, and your witticisms amuse nobody but yourself. There is only one young lady in this house; the misunderstanding about her nationality arose because she foolishly gave herself out at first to be Spanish, fearing to say she was French; but I soon discovered . . . that is to say, I discovered . . . that she was not Spanish. You shall see her to-morrow and be satisfied that she is not a woman of bad character, and you can speed her on her way to Portsmouth. Meanwhile, I should be obliged if you would drop this meaningless and offensive jesting about her."

Miss Lavinia made a moue. Then she rose, came to her brother, and deposited a kiss on the top of his head. "I will, my dear. But can I not see your pretty Puritan—I mean your respectable Huguenot—to-night?"

"No, I am afraid not," replied Hervey, glancing at the clock. "She retired to her room an hour ago; I expect she is asleep by now. You must wait until to-morrow."

*

"But I don't want to wait until to-morrow!" said Miss Barrington inwardly when, not long after this, she found herself in her own bedroom—and that bedroom adjoining the apartment of the fair unknown. It was so unusual for Hervey to show any interest in the sex other than that demanded by ordinary politeness that she was curious to see this girl, though at the back of her mind she knew quite well that it was only his humanity which had led him to offer her hospitality. She really almost wished it had been some warmer feeling.

Now a former owner of Fairhaven—the same who, apprehensive of house-breakers, had furnished the lower part of the house, on the side facing the road, with a series of iron spikes—had seen fit to cut an entrance from the room now Miss Barrington's into the powdering closet which was properly the appendage of the next. Miss Barrington, therefore, had an easy means of access to the latter apartment if she chose to use it, and surely it was almost her duty to go in and see if her brother's protégée had all she required—assuming, of course, that the latter was still awake. Indeed, if she were, ought not Miss Barrington to put in an appearance for that brother's own sake, lest the respectable Huguenot should be thinking her very existence a mere invention of her host's?

Fortified by these excellent reasons Miss Barrington thereupon went quietly into the powdering closet. And lo, duty and desire still rode together, for when she closed her door of the cupboard behind her, Lavinia Barrington was aware of shafts of light penetrating all round the other one which led into the spare bedroom. The visitor therefore was still awake . . . or else (for there was no sound of movement) had fallen asleep and left the candles burning, a source of danger which it was one's duty to remove. So Miss Barrington tapped at the door confronting her, very gently at first, then louder. There was no response, so she opened the door a few inches.

Yes, the candles were all burning. As Miss Barrington herself was still in the cupboard, she could not actually see the bed, away on her right, but in her line of vision was the grey dress, disposed over a chair. It certainly looked very modest, almost Quakerish. Yet on the table by it, full in the candlelight, lay something which gave its modesty the lie, according in fact much less well with the damsel of her brother's imagination than with her of Miss Lavinia's own—a wig. This wig interested Miss Barrington very much indeed, and she emerged on tiptoe from the closet in order to survey the occupant of the bed . . . and then remained as immobile as Lot's wife.

On the bed—and in no sense in it—with his stockinged feet towards her, lay a young man in his shirt and breeches fast asleep; so fast that after her momentary petrification Miss Barrington ventured to tiptoe nearer to verify the astounding fact. But there could be no doubt of it.

He lay on his side, almost on his face, at the edge of the bed, the edge nearest to Miss Barrington, his left hand tucked under the pillow, the right hanging down towards the floor. It looked as if he had flung himself there too tired to finish undressing. . . . Undressing! Miss Barrington's eyes, suddenly sparkling with mirth, went to the grey gown, and then returned to the masquerader. There was no getting over the fact. Hervey's distressed

Franco-Spanish damsel was a young man, and a personable young man at that, though rather thin. From the way he was lying she could only just see the profile pressed into the pillow; it was true that it was finely cut, and she saw long dark lashes, and a little close-set ear, but (particularly when combined with a man's shirt open at the throat and a pair of grey nankin breeches) it had no suggestion of the feminine about it.

And it was on this good-looking young scamp that Hervey had been squandering his compassion! Miss Lavinia put her hand over her mouth. She must remove herself before she could give vent to her mirth. But first . . . Going cautiously to the door of the room she tried it and removed the key; then she hastily caught up in succession the grey dress, the woman's wig and—this brought her nearest to the laughter she was staving off—the razor which, as she now saw, lay in such telling proximity to it.

At the cupboard door she took a fleeting backward glance. The sleeper had not stirred, but the pose, the shape, everything about him looked even more masculine than before. How could Hervey have been such a fool! was Miss Barrington's inward cry as she sped through her own room to acquaint him with the full measure of his folly.

Captain Barrington had not yet gone to bed. He was still in the breakfast room, reading the last number of the *Gentleman's Magazine* by the light of one of the branched silver candlesticks from the supper table. The window was open, and in the silence, above the lazy monotone of the river, could be faintly heard the eternal struggle out on the bar.

"Who is that?" he asked, without turning his head. "You, Lavinia?"

"Yes," answered his sister. "I have brought down something to show you." Laying the wig and the razor on the table behind him, she advanced into the light of the candles with the grey gown over her arm. "I thought you might like to see this," she observed pleasantly, and held it out before him by its sleeves.

Hervey stared at it with a frown, and then glanced at her face—the face of one in the grip of secret merriment. "I thought I had begged you to refrain from jesting on that subject," he said. "And why, if you must go into the girl's room, need you bring her dress away with you?"

"For you to see, my dear chivalrous brother! For you to gaze on, Don Quixote, because it is the last you will ever behold of your damsel in distress. This gown . . . and this!" She stretched out a hand and added the wig to her exhibition. "Pretty curls, are they not? They do not altogether match the genuine article though, I fancy."

Like an automaton Hervey had slowly risen to his feet, his eyes as though they beheld a basilisk. "What on earth . . . Has the girl gone?—But she could not go, wanting . . ."

"Yes, she could," broke in his sister, struggling with her mirth. "She could vanish in the way that hard-pressed ladies sometimes did, I seem to remember, in heathen mythology. Some nymph or other, I know, turned herself into a laurel. This nymph has taken the shape"—she threw down dress and wig and once more picked something off the table—"the shape, Hervey, that requires this o' mornings!" She flashed the razor open and burst into a peal of laughter. "Oh, Hervey, Hervey, how could you be so misled? I said I was not sure you knew the kind of woman you had befriended. . . . There he lies, on your best spare bed, in his shirt and breeches, and there, judging from the way he is sleeping, he will lie till morning. I should like to see his face when he wakes and finds the means of continuing his nymphhood taken from him. . . . What are you doing, Hervey?"

For while she laughed and teased, Captain Barrington had gone into the darker portion of the room, and she now heard him opening a drawer. Yet when he came back into the light it was not what he carried in his hand so much as his face which caught Miss Lavinia's eyes and held them. For perhaps the first time in forty years she felt a little frightened.

"Is that loaded, Hervey?"

Her brother did not answer, but the fact that he examined the priming was an answer. Then he lifted his head, and out of the lips whose familiar lines were all altered asked peremptorily:

"How did you get in? Had he not locked the door?"

"Yes, but I went in through the powdering closet. That does not fasten; the bolt is broken. But I took away the key of his room and locked my door on the outside."

"Is the key still in the lock—your key?"

"No. I . . . I think I brought that away too. Yes."

"Give it to me!"

"I will if you will put back that pistol."

"Give it to me, please!"

And slowly Miss Lavinia brought out a key from her pocket and laid it on the table.

"Is that the key of your room or of his?—I'll have both, please!"

"Hervey . . . he's only a boy . . . and looks so tired!"

For the first time in his life her brother exploded into an oath in her presence. "Not too tired to fool me—twice over—thrice over—not too much of a boy to pay for it, as he shall!" The words came out like missiles.

"But, Hervey, you can't murder him—here, in your own house!"

"Murder?" exclaimed her brother on a strange, high note. "Of course I am not going to murder him. But he is a French prisoner escaped from the hulks. . . . I see it all now . . . and I am going to send him back whence he came!"

"But you cannot send him back to-night, brother!"

"I never said I should. But I am going to let him know it and——Give me the other key!"

"Oh, Hervey," pleaded his sister in a most unusual tone, "why go up to-night at all, as you can do nothing, and he cannot get away? Why not wait till morning?"

"No, he cannot get away . . . but there are things I can do," responded Hervey grimly. "Give me the other key at once, and send Jeremy up to wait in your room in case I need him. Do you hear?"

"But, Hervey," protested Miss Barrington as, rather flushed, she reluctantly produced the second key. "with that large pistol you cannot possibly need Jeremy as well in order to master one half-starved lad from the hulks! If that is where he comes from I can understand better why he——"

"Will you mind your own business, Lavinia?" broke in her brother savagely, and pulled at the bellrope. "If Jeremy has gone to bed he's to get up at once. I may not want him, but I intend him to be handy, in your room. Do you understand? And you will kindly stay down here." He put the pistol in his pocket, took one of the candelabra, and left the room.

Miss Lavinia stood a moment irresolute, looking from the closed door to the grey gown in a heap on the table, and in that moment unfeignedly regretting, if not her discovery, at least her too hasty and facetious announcement of it. It was that, no doubt of it, which had helped to blow Hervey's fury to such white heat against the culprit—her emphasis on that point of which he must be only too stingingly aware, that he had not merely been deceived, but ludicrously deceived. On a sudden impulse she started for the door, but ere she reached it, it opened to admit the large form of John Jeremy, the solid and faithful and bearded, and instead of going to the rescue upstairs she perceived the uselessness of such an attempt, and conveyed to him instead his master's instructions.

The ex-coxswain received the transmitted orders with his usual ready obedience, at once impassive and slightly surprised.

"In your room, Miss Barrington? Yes, to be sure. Well now, an escaped French prisoner! 'Tis likely he'll fight like a hell-cat!"

"I don't think so," said Miss Lavinia rather sadly. "I fancy you will have an easy task, Jeremy." And to herself, left alone once more, she said, "I wish now that I had never gone into that room! Yet it was a diverting situation . . . though I suppose one could not expect Hervey to see it in that light. . . . I do hope he will not use that pistol! What did he mean he was going to do to him?" And though at last she sat down and took up the *Gentleman's Magazine* and held it open at the "Historical Account of Burnham Church, Kent," she was listening all the time for the sound of a shot from upstairs.

The Battle of the Spare Bedroom

"All imposture weakens confidence and chills benevolence. When the sage finds that you are not what you seemed, he will feel the resentment natural to a man who . . .

discovers that he has been tricked."–Rasselas, chap. xlvi.

The dreamless sleep in which Raoul was sunk was still dreamless, but not
so deep as when Miss Lavinia had made her incursion into his bedchamber,
for a slight sound echoed down to him where he lay in oblivion as at the
bottom of a well. And though the sound was not actively registered by his
mind, it disturbed him, and with a muttered exclamation he flung up his arm
and turned over on to his back. The movement jolted him still nearer to
consciousness, so that his body, at least, realized the space and comfort of
what it was lying on, after the cramped hammock in suffocating darkness and
too close companionship; and at last the fully sentient Raoul himself became
aware that he was surrounded by light, air, and silence instead of the usual
noisy, fetid gloom in which he slept. He opened his eyes with a start and
remembered where he was—and saw that he had most reprehensibly left the
candles burning when sleep overtook him.

But surely there was a fresh source of light in the room, by that cupboard
door? Raoul turned his head to see . . . and his heart stood still within him.
There, a branched candlestick in his left hand, stood Captain Hervey
Barrington, looking at him with an expression there was no mis-reading. In
his other hand was that which very effectively backed up the expression.

"If you move, I shall fire!" he said briefly.

But the words were not out of his mouth before Raoul was off the bed and
at the door . . . to stay there. The key was gone. Backed against its panels, his
breath coming fast, his hands clenched, he faced the levelled pistol again.

"Yes, that place will do as well as any other," observed Hervey coolly, and
without removing his eyes from him or lowering the barrel he set down the
light on the nearest table. "Now, make over everything you have—plans,
papers, money. *I know what you are!*"

The bitter shock had not deprived Raoul of his wits, and they worked
quickly. Since Captain Barrington could not have come in through this
locked door—even though, now, presumably, he had possessed himself of the
key—there must have been another entrance to that cupboard after all. If he

could only get him to move away from it! . . . Raoul gave what had all the appearance of being an involuntary glance towards the little valise lying on the centre table—even, at the risk of a bullet, made a tiny, instantly checked movement towards it. His manœuvre told, though Hervey did not abandon his post.

"Bring that thing here!" he commanded.

But Raoul did not move. "Is it likely? Go and get it yourself! You cannot terrorize me with that pistol, because I do not care whether you shoot me or no."

Hervey gave a very disagreeable smile. "I shall take great care not to kill you outright, and, as I am a dead shot, I can hit you exactly where I please—break your leg for choice. I shall count five; I do not threaten twice. One, two, three——"

An excuse for altering his tactics was just what Raoul wanted now. He went slowly and with apparent unwillingness to the centre table, Captain Barrington keeping him covered the while, and took up the valise.

"Bring it over here and put it down by the candlestick. Now take out all its contents, one thing at a time, and lay them beside it."

Watching his moment, Raoul removed a clean shirt, a brush and comb, a pair of stockings, and began to take out the nightshift. Then, suddenly flinging this at his captor's head, he made a spring past him for the cupboard door. But Hervey was on the watch too, and a boxer, and as he saw the white folds coming at him he sidestepped, grasped Raoul by the throat with his left hand, and hurled him off with such violence that the young man was spun back as far as the foot of the bed, his shirt ripped to the waist.

"It is no good trying that!" said Hervey contemptuously. "Besides, my man is in the other room now." He raised his voice. "Jeremy!"

"Here, Sir."

"Stand by to stop him coming through, if he tries it again."

"Ay, ay, Sir."

And, assured of his reinforcements, Captain Barrington viewed with a sardonic indifference the dash his quarry then made for the further window, the feverish way in which he tugged aside the curtains, threw up the sash and thrust his head out.

"Is there light enough for you to see what is waiting for you down below there?" enquired Hervey. "I hope so, because I don't particularly want your corpse impaled on my railings." His tone, however, did not suggest that the contingency would greatly trouble him, and he turned, keeping no more than half an eye on the suddenly rigid figure by the window, and tipped out the few remaining articles in the valise on the table. But, except for a purse with a little silver, he drew blank; the fellow—who must have more than that—had tricked him again.

As for Raoul himself, his vision of escape by the window had indeed been brief. It was no wonder that Captain Barrington had not opposed his opening it. There was light enough for him to see what was waiting for him down at the bottom of the bare, creeperless wall—the horrible chevaux-de-frise of long spikes turned in every direction, impossible to escape by jumping or dropping. And climbing down was out of the question, for there was no foothold of any sort, not even a pipe. He remained there without moving, despair in his heart, while the soft, inflowing night air mocked him with its associations of space and freedom.

"Come, turn out your pockets without more ado," came Captain Barrington's voice harshly. "It is no good deferring the inevitable."

Give up without a struggle his only means of procuring liberty, give up at his bidding Juliana's smuggled money! All the concentrated horror of the place from which her devotion had succeeded in extricating him rushed past Raoul in a hurricane of memory and resolution. He would never let himself be sent back alive! But, if ever he succeeded in leaving this house which he had so foolishly entered, without money or disguise or even adequate clothing his plight would be hopeless. And yet how could he avoid having the money taken from him in the end?

He loosed the curtain which his hand was gripping and faced his captor.

"Haven't you any pity, Captain Barrington?" he asked in a low, difficult voice.

"None," responded Hervey. "You worked out the vein too successfully this evening—damn you!" he added almost inaudibly.

It was true; Raoul knew it. He had been too successful for pardon. And yet—what else could he have done but pit his wits against the Englishman's?

"It is of no use thinking of any more moving stories to play off on me," resumed Hervey, bitter mockery in his tone. "You cannot expect to fool even me any more. Nor," he added, as Raoul seemed about to speak, "is it any use telling me your own. I will not listen to it."

"You have already heard it," said Raoul rather unsteadily. "Except that I changed the name of the hulk. I was in the *Ganges*."

"Indeed? Well, it will be pleasant to return to familiar scenes. Though I suppose the ship's Black Hole will receive you for a while first. Have you sampled it yet?"

Raoul came forward a little. He was as white as his torn shirt.

"If you think I am going back alive to that hell, Captain Barrington, you are mistaken!" His voice shook, but speech poured out of him so hot and fast that it was impossible to stop him. "You can stand there, in no danger of cruelty yourself, and use words which prove that you know to what you are condemning a fellow creature! I would not send my worst enemy to a prison-ship . . . no, not even the man whose practices sent *me* there! And what have I done to you? Did you expect me, directly you addressed me, against my will, on the road, to tell you exactly who and what I was? My God, you would not care how many lies you told if you were fighting for your life—yes, for your life! I was strong and well when I went to the *Ganges* . . . but go through even a few months of that degradation and starvation, and see what you are like at the end of them, and whether you would not almost sell what soul is left to you rather than endure them again! And I am a prisoner of war, an officer like yourself, taken in fair fight as you may be some day. . . . No, you *shall* hear me! My name is Raoul des Sablières, a captain in the Third Hussars, and I am by rights a parole prisoner, but first I was sent to Norman Cross on a false accusation, and then to the hulks for attempting to escape from an imprisonment which I had never merited. Would you not have done the same? Why should your country treat me as a criminal?"

"Because," said Hervey, a certain merciless satisfaction in his eyes, "she happens, like most civilized nations, to regard the breach of military parole as a crime. Your case, I see, is plain, Monsieur Raoul des Sablières—and only too common amongst your compatriots. I really wonder at the leniency which sent you to Norman Cross instead of direct to the hulks. That is the more fitting place for a parole-breaker!"

"I am not a parole-breaker!"

"For what were you sent to Norman Cross, then?—No, I don't want to hear another farrago of lies, thanks; I have lost interest in your inventions. I only want——"

But Raoul broke in stormily. "I see, there is no justice in England, and it is useless to plead with any Englishman in uniform! You too, you do not know what it is to suffer injustice—you are of those who dispense it! If you knew a little——"

"That is enough!" Hervey stopped him, his face suddenly darkened. "I have listened to sufficient falsehoods; I am not called upon to hear insults. Hand over your money and papers, and we will conclude this interview. In the morning you will be taken back to the *Ganges*, to find what scope you can for your peculiar talents."

He had had the pistol in his hand all this while, though he had dropped the barrel. With these words he raised it and once more covered his prisoner. "Now, please!"

Raoul put his hands behind him. "You can rob me, Captain Barrington," he said slowly, coldly, and rolling the rs more than was habitual with him in English, "because I am in your power in your house to which you invited me . . . but I think you will not send me back to the *Ganges* to-morrow."

"Indeed?" retorted Hervey with an appearance of interest. "And how are you going to prevent me?"

"*Ainsi!*" said Raoul between his teeth, his hands coming forward very suddenly; and he launched himself at his enemy like a panther.

He was so quick that he took Hervey by surprise and got within the pistol's guard; his hands sought Captain Barrington's throat, and for a second or two they really wrestled, Hervey being hampered by the cocked pistol, which he feared to drop lest it should go off, and which he was equally determined not to use. Nor would he have called to Jeremy, but that worthy, hearing trampling feet, burst unsummoned through the cupboard; and at that, Raoul, seeing that he was going to be taken in the rear, relaxed his grip. This was Hervey's opportunity; he also let go, stepped back a foot or two, and his left fist, shooting out like lightning, landed a punishing blow on his assailant's mouth. Raoul's arms went wide, he reeled and would have gone down if Jeremy, hurrying round, had not caught, or rather, captured him.

"All right, Jeremy—though I didn't need you," said his master. "Can't he stand? Put him in that chair and when he comes to you can turn out his pockets. No, not yet—wait a moment."

The ex-coxswain deposited Raoul, unresisting and half dazed, in the chair in which he had sat to eat his supper. Hardly knowing what he did, the young man put his elbows on the table, his head between his hands, and stared at the splashes of blood from his mouth as they appeared on the inlaid rosewood. Finally he reached out a shaking hand for the napkin which still lay there and held it to his lips.

It was not consideration in Hervey Barrington which caused him to leave his prisoner time to recover—far from it. He had been so deeply humiliated himself, his self-esteem had taken so intolerable a wound, that if, as he guessed, it would humiliate as well as anger this young trickster to have his last hope taken from his own person, he should not suffer that ignominy hardly knowing what was happening to him.

To ascertain whether he were still in that condition or no he came over to the table and spoke to him.

"You brought that blow on yourself!" he said harshly.

Raoul raised his head. His eyes were extraordinarily bright. He removed the blood-stained napkin and said, as distinctly as he could for his cut and swollen lip, "Why did you not fire . . . like a gentleman?"

"Ah, was *that* what you were after?" exclaimed Hervey, a light breaking on him. "No, my friend! And in any case let me tell you that I don't believe in these heroics. You will have got the better of them to-morrow." He made a sign to Jeremy. "You can search him now."

The order brought Raoul, unsteady as he was, to his feet again, and his glance at Jeremy was such that that worthy mariner hesitated. Raoul then turned the look on Jeremy's master.

"What right have you to take my money?" he demanded fiercely. "I never asked you to bring me into your house!"

"If you will give it to me it will not have to be taken from you," was all that Captain Barrington replied.

"You will get ten guineas reward for betraying me," went on Raoul, tense and quivering. "Isn't that enough? And you do not run any risk . . . two of you . . . armed. . . ."

"What are you waiting for?" said Hervey sharply to his henchman. He had reddened. "The money must be in his breeches pocket."

This was obvious, since the torn shirt could now conceal nothing. The faithful Jeremy made to fling his weight upon the defiant figure, but before he could lay a finger on him Raoul had snatched up the nearest candlestick, which was tall, and of heavy Sheffield plate, and had aimed a savage blow with its base at his head. It missed and took the sailor on the shoulder. The next moment its giver was backed against the far wall by the window, clutching the candlestick like a mace.

"You will have to divide that ten guineas, Captain Barrington!" he called out.

But Jeremy, whose temper was roused by the blow, gave him no second chance of using his weapon. In the twinkling of an eye it was twisted out of his hand, and he himself pinned against the wall by sheer weight, his arms, in Jeremy's powerful grip, spread out on either side like those of a fruit tree. But even then, though he had him helpless, Jeremy could not search him, for he had not a hand to spare for the operation; moreover Raoul was still struggling hard to the best of his very limited ability.

"Keep still, ye wildcat!" said Jeremy, and gave him a hack on the shins with his solid footgear. "You'll have to help me, Sir," he called over his shoulder. "He'm like an eel!"

"Do, Captain Barrington!" laughed Raoul wildly. "Don't let your servant do all the kicking!—Take your beard out of my face, damn you!"

And Hervey had to come and help, after all, in what he suddenly felt was a sorry affair. The Frenchman might have the spirit of a wildcat, as Jeremy had called him, but he had little physical strength left to back it up; indeed, after Hervey had torn the packet of notes out of one breeches pocket and a few papers and a map out of the other, the captive said in a changed voice to Jeremy, who still held him pinned against the wall, "If you will let me go now . . . I will not do anything . . . I . . . I . . ." He frowned and shut his eyes.

Hervey looked up from the notes he was examining by the centre table. "Let him go, Jeremy," he said abruptly. "It would be a nuisance if he were to faint." Jeremy dubiously relaxed his grip. Raoul opened his eyes, clenched his hands, and guiding himself by the wall, reached the window where the cool air was still coming in gratefully. He sank down on its very wide, low sill, and put his head against the side. Everything was finished, and he, too.

"Is this money your own?" came Hervey Barrington's voice after a moment.

Why talk about it any more? But Raoul roused himself. "It has not been stolen . . . until this last five minutes," he replied without moving. His captor had in his hands too Juliana's letter to him at Norman Cross, which he had treasured as a sort of talisman, and some of her brief later ones also.

Hervey finished his examination and looked across at the motionless figure on the window seat. What was he going to do with him for the remainder of the night? The safest plan would undoubtedly be to tie him up. But that would mean manhandling him again, and he had had enough of that; for he found, to his surprise, that the prospect of mastering him once more rather sickened him. The first heat of his fury, indeed, was gone now. He pondered, with a frown, the feasibility of leaving him loose. Escape by the window was impossible, and he could run that very heavy chest of drawers in Lavinia's room against the cupboard door from the other side.

Raoul suddenly turned his head. "May I have my pocket handkerchief?" he enquired in a lifeless voice. His pockets had been rifled of that too, and it lay on the table. It was obvious why he needed it.

"Yes, if you will come and fetch it," replied Hervey, who wanted to get him into the light again for survey.

With a stifled sigh the young man rose and came, noiseless in his stockinged feet, the blood coursing anew down his chin from his lip. Hervey's eyes were drawn by one or two trickles on his chest, a good deal exposed by the now even more torn shirt. . . . Leanness of that degree was almost emaciation. . . . No, shame forbade any more rough handling. He would have to take just one precaution, however, in case that window proved too tempting, despite the chevaux-de-frise below.

"Come here, Jeremy." He led the sailor aside and whispered to him, while Raoul, with his head bent, dabbed slowly at his lip with his recovered handkerchief. For the moment his brain felt empty of thought or plan—besides, what use planning without a penny or even a coat to cover him? His body ached all over. He only wanted to sleep. Soon he would be able to . . . unless Captain Barrington meant to have him removed and locked up this night? It was too late, surely. He went back to his place in the dark corner by the window and sat down again patiently. "Juliana, he has taken your money away . . . your money, curse him! I can do nothing now. . . ."

"I want you to come away from that window, please," said Captain Barrington's icy voice once more. "There is something to be done in that corner.—You can start there, Jeremy. Shut the window first."

And once more Raoul obediently got up and came away.

"Sit there, where I can see you."

It mattered little where he was now, so Raoul sat at the table in the middle of the room, an elbow on it, and his handkerchief still pressed to his mouth. And suddenly he caught the eyes of his enemy looking at him, hard and cold, yet with something in them he could not read. He straightened himself, and defiance began to tingle once more along his veins.

"Well, I hope you are satisfied with your revenge," he said. "By the way, it is not usually considered chivalrous to strike a woman."

Hervey did not condescend to answer, and removed his gaze to the window, where Jeremy, mounted rather precariously upon a chair, was beginning to take down a curtain.

"And how much," went on Raoul jeeringly—"how much were they worth, your protestations and your mythical duenna of a sister, when the first thing you did was to force a midnight entrance by a secret door into the bedroom of the girl who had thrown herself upon your chivalry?"

This imputation, at least, was more than Hervey Barrington could endure in silence.

"It was my sister herself who discovered you, and informed me," he said curtly, and half turned his back.

Raoul shrugged his shoulders. "As I was asleep I naturally cannot tell whether that is a 'farrago of lies' or not! However, I am glad to think," he went on, leaning back in his chair, "that I did not kiss your hand. But you——" He did not need to finish, for he saw the angry red mount into Captain Barrington's cheek, and he broke off into a laugh himself. "Which did you really prefer, the señora or my sister? I have a sister, you know!"

"Take down both curtains, idiot!" said Hervey to the window. Raoul turned, and for the first time beheld what was happening there. His eyes lit up.

"I am not worthy of curtains in my prison?" he enquired. "Or is it a regular . . . déménagement? But you must allow me to assist. Your hired bully does not seem skilful."

"Sit down!" thundered Hervey. And, as if this had been a command to him, the unlucky Jeremy, stepping off the chair, became entangled at that moment in the released curtain, and he too sat down—very heavily—upon the floor. Raoul gave one wild little yell of laughter and, bending forward, buried his face in his hands and shook for a second or two. Then he raised his head expectantly in time to see the coxswain get up ruefully, rubbing himself, and went off into another fit. It was genuine laughter, if a thought hysterical.

"Now the other window," said Hervey crossly.

"You will not allow me?" asked Raoul, looking up. "I am not so heavy; the floor would suffer less."

Hervey disregarded this; but it became too much for him when, Jeremy proceeding under his direction to dismantle the bed, Raoul deliberately moved his chair so that he could have a good view of the operation, which he punctuated by a running commentary of remarks, ostensibly to himself.

"It really is a *déménagement*—but what an hour for it! I have always been told that the English are mad. The sheets . . . the blankets . . . the mattress too!" (for this also was being rolled up by the perspiring Jeremy.) "I suppose that is to be burnt because I have lain upon it. But I am not verminous now . . . no, not in the least! How clever—he will tie it up with the bell-pull. But how will the good man get all that through the door? Tiens, he is leaving the napkin. . . ."

"Will you be quiet!" broke in Hervey savagely at last, for his henchman was getting so flustered under this fire of ridicule that the mattress burst from his grasp, and he had to assist him to re-roll it. "You young fool, can't you see that I am putting myself to all this trouble merely to spare you? Do you think I am going to leave you loose in a room with the means of letting yourself down from that window to your hand, and with a convenient mattress to throw on the spikes, if you were so crazy as to risk death or mutilation out there? If I left these things I should have to tie you up hand and foot . . . and I make a sailor's, not a landsman's, knots!—Put those things through into Miss Barrington's room, Jeremy; she will not be sleeping there to-night; and I will come and secure the cupboard door.—Now, do you understand, mountebank?"

"Yes," said Raoul. He stood up. "You are indeed kind to spare me a night in bonds, and to take away from the bad child the means of doing itself a mischief. I suppose I must set it against your having also taken away my liberty . . . and refused to take my life. . . . Never mind, Captain Barrington, I daresay I can find a means of getting rid of that, if the worst comes to the worst . . . and although you do not believe in heroics. I wish you good repose!"

Hervey gave him a long, stern look, and without a word turned on his heel and went towards the cupboard.

"Your walk," observed Raoul softly after him, "reminds me strongly of that of my dear and faithless Tomás!"

The door of the cupboard slammed. A moment later came sounds of a heavy object being put against its farther door. Raoul stood motionless, listening. When all sounds, even in the passage outside, had ceased, his figure relaxed, and he turned and sat down somewhat suddenly, and stared at the floor, his head between his fists. He remained in that attitude for a considerable time. . . . Then, after a glance at what had once been a comfortable bed, he curled himself up like a boy in a large chair, his head on the arm, and lay there perfectly still. He was tired to the point of exhaustion—and more than tired. Now and again a long sigh shook him, but there was no other sound; and when, about an hour later, the moon was able to look in at the uncurtained windows, he had straightened himself out a little, and she could see his upturned, sleeping face. And she tried, first, to smooth out the contractions in it with the same silver touch which had revealed them, and then, pitying this haggard Endymion who was dreaming, not of Dian's kiss, but of the realms of the dead, she withdrew her light behind a bank of cloud, and the room sank again into darkness.

The Cruise of the "Kestrel"

"He now felt a degree of regret with which he had never been before acquainted . . . and he was long before he could be reconciled to himself."—Rasselas, chap. iv.

The household at Fairhaven might have been "put about" the previous night as never within living memory, Miss Barrington, despite her protests, sleeping in her brother's room, and Captain Barrington in his dressing room, Miss Lavinia's own room "all upside down and full of curtains and mattresses and bell-ropes," these permutations on account of the presence of a French hussy alleged by Jeremy, when he at last sought the connubial chamber, to be a young man. Yet even this spiritual and physical turmoil had no power to make Mrs. Jeremy late with breakfast next morning.

But brother and sister alike ate her excellent fare rather silently. Hervey had told Lavinia overnight as much as he had a mind to, and he did not amplify his information this morning, nor, curiously, did Miss Lavinia animadvert in her wonted style either upon the humour of the situation or upon his share in the epic of the spare bedroom—of which she had already wrested a fuller version from John Jeremy. She was in truth regretting with all her heart that she had let Hervey into the secret of her discovery; for one thing she fancied she could have had a much better laugh at him afterwards if she had allowed him, all unsuspecting, to despatch Mademoiselle on her way to Portsmouth; for another the lad himself would not now be on the point of return to that horrid captivity from which he had employed so much ingenuity to escape.

It was true that Hervey was not displaying any great haste to inform the authorities of his presence, but she knew that it was useless to try to move him from the performance of what he considered his duty. And, any vindictive feelings apart, no doubt it was his duty to deliver up the fugitive.

Miss Lavinia glanced at the clock as she rose from the breakfast table, and opened the casement window on to the jasmine and climbing rose. Down below, the little square garden lay smiling in the August sun, refreshed to a new greenness by a heavy dew, and sending up the invisible incense of stocks and lavender. The mulberry tree hung its ripening fruit over the old teak bench; sparkling and singing and very blue, the river poured by; a couple of wagtails were taking excited little runs over the grass. Farther on were the clustered houses of old Stowey, pricked with masts, but from here the actual mouth of the estuary could not be seen. Hervey's sailing boat, the *Kestrel*, was tugging gently at her mooring buoy in mid-channel. What a morning to go back to prison—and such a prison!

"Has your captive had anything to eat yet?" asked Miss Barrington casually as she picked a sprig of jasmine.

Her brother was turning over the pages of a nautical almanac. "No, I don't suppose he has," he answered in an indifferent tone.

"Then, if you will forgive my suggesting it, would it not be as well to send him up something, if he has later to take the journey back to Plymouth, or even to go to the lock-up here. . . . I don't know what your plans are," she added half apologetically.

"'Send him up something,'?" repeated Captain Barrington, laying down the almanac. "You talk, Lavinia, as if Mrs. Jeremy could go in carrying breakfast as to a guest. Do you know that your 'poor tired boy' fought like a demon last night, and that it took the two of us to hold him?"

Now Miss Lavinia did know this, but she was making great efforts after discretion—perhaps not altogether successfully, since she objected: "But, even if he is such a desperate character, surely Jeremy could venture in, provided that you were there to protect him—with your pistol!"

Captain Barrington's face darkened, and he turned to his almanac again.

"Surely you cannot really think it is too dangerous to go in?" resumed his sister, still with that unusual note of pleading in her voice. "And to give him an extra dose of starvation when you know it is what he is going back to—I have heard that the food in the prison-ships is almost uneatable—to do that just because you are . . . annoyed . . . with him is so unlike you, that I am sure it can only be because you have forgotten that you have given no orders."

"Why do you think it is so unlike me?" asked Hervey. He had his back turned and was fidgeting with his book. "You do not know of what a man is capable when he is—annoyed—as you call it. I did not know myself until last night," he added, in a voice so low that his sister did not catch it. "But it is quite true," he concluded, turning round, "that I had forgotten the question of food. I will rectify the omission."

"I was sure you had," said Miss Lavinia, and as he rang the bell she smiled at him like a grey-haired angel.

But Hervey did not take the pistol when he accompanied Jeremy to the prisoner's room, for he had learnt the uselessness of that weapon in the hands of a man who is determined not to use it to kill, does not wish to use it to wound, and knows that as a threat it has no power whatever. He would not have gone there at all but that it was, plainly, necessary that someone should unlock and guard the door for Jeremy, encumbered as he was with a tray and liable to be sprung upon.

However, the prisoner did not spring on John Jeremy when he entered. He did not greet him in any way whatever, as Hervey, outside, holding the door just ajar, was aware. He heard Jeremy deposit the tray upon something; after which there was dead silence for a moment, and then his gruff voice, with a note of alarm in it:

"Cap'n Barrington—please to come in at once, Sir!"

Hervey's own heart gave the most unexpected twist in his breast. The boy had somehow cut his throat or hanged himself! Why had he not foreseen this? He went in, so sure of it that he did not lock the door.

The large form of Jeremy seemed to obscure everything. "He's gone, Sir—he's not in the room, unless he's in the wardrobe yonder."

Gone? Yes, by George, the window was open! But that was suicide also—God knew that that had been made clear. No, he must be in the room somewhere—under the bed, in the powdering closet. . . . The open window was merely a ruse, and Jeremy was a fool—and he too. He snatched the key from the lock outside and fastened the door.

"Have you looked under the bed?"

No, Jeremy had not. He did it there and then, while Hervey wrenched open the door of the big mahogany wardrobe. Quite empty. He was hiding in the closet, then. Could he possibly have pushed aside the barrier and got into Lavinia's room? They would soon see.

They did. The closet was as empty as the wardrobe, and the far door immovable. Yes, the captive was, indubitably, gone. And since he had been deprived of all, even the most makeshift means of letting himself down from that high window, and there existed on that bare wall no natural ones, he must have jumped, or let himself fall. In that case—

Hervey Barrington, who had fought at Trafalgar, turned white. He was for a moment on the point of ordering Jeremy, who was still gazing round the cupboard, to go first and look out of the window. But it was he himself who had driven the boy to it, and he must face the consequences of his action. He went over to the open window, stood for a second or two, and then put his head out.

He had already in his mind so vivid a picture of that light, half-clad body transfixed on the hellish invention below, that the fact of there being nothing there did not convey itself immediately to his brain. And when it did, it seemed so incredible that for a flash he thought his eyes were playing him a trick.

"Jeremy, come here!" Serious and heavy-footed, Jeremy came. "There is nothing, after all, on those spikes, is there?"

Jeremy looked out. "No, Sir, nothing. He must 'a' jumped clear of 'em somehow."

They stared at each other. Then Hervey, leaning back against the wall, passed his hand over his eyes.

"There's not a rag on 'em, Sir, not a mark, so far as I can see," continued Jeremy, his head out of the window again. "Unless someone's took him off 'em, he never fell on 'em at all."

"But . . . he couldn't fly!" said Hervey, feeling an odd disposition to laugh. Once more he looked down that naked wall. "There was nothing we had forgotten in the room, was there, that he could have used?"

And then to Jeremy, the slow-witted, came the solution. "Begging your pardon, Sir," he said, touching him on the arm, "seems to me he've gone up, not down. Put your head out again, Sir, and you'll see as he *could* have got up, being active like, and hard put to it."

Hervey looked. Yes, by standing outside on the window ledge a man of moderate height could certainly manage to grasp the leaden rain gutter which ran along just under the roof. But he would have to be very athletic—or desperate—to pull himself up by that alone; added to which a gutter of that sort was not so firmly fixed in place as designedly to carry such a weight. And this one had been up for many years.

"Good God!" said Hervey, staring up at it, and then down at the spikes. How could he have trusted himself to so horribly inadequate a support with those points waiting down below all the time!

"No doubt he helped hisself a bit by the corner here, Sir, where the wall juts out," proceeded Jeremy, developing his discovery. "Got his feet against it, or his knees. A nasty climb, though, Sir—makes your blood turn, in a manner o' speaking—and his weight has brought away the gutter a little. Lucky for him it didn't break loose altogether."

"Yes," assented his master shortly. He had had enough of that gutter, and straightway abandoned the contemplation of it. "But when once he was on the roof," he continued, "he would find no great difficulty, I imagine, in climbing down the other side of the house, into the garden, because of the ivy."

"Child's play to this, Sir," pronounced Jeremy, bringing his head in again. "But, for all we know, he'm on the roof still."

"I doubt it," said Captain Barrington. "But I suppose we had better make sure. We will not, however, take his route there."

They emerged, indeed, in a more prosaic manner by the trapdoor in the attic provided for the purpose, and, as Hervey had expected, found neither the fugitive nor any traces of his passage. Scanning the view of the river and the countryside afforded by their present elevation, John Jeremy gave vent to a wonder as to where the "wildcat" was "tu" now, and his master wondered also. Not far away, probably; he would never get any distance in that scanty and torn attire and with no money. He was bound to be recaptured sooner or later, for all that he had risked a horrible death to win clear of Fairhaven.

And now it was his business to go out and, by setting the hounds on his trail, carry out last night's threats and complete his own revenge.

But the minutes went by, and still Captain Barrington stood there on the roof with his hands behind his back. For over the grinning visions which had been so hot in his brain last night, the vision of the "Señora" and her mythical love and desertion (the Señora he had so decorously and absurdly left in the garden); of the "sister" and her even more successful onslaught on his sympathy and credulity—memories which made him grind his teeth over his own gullibility—there was scored, palimpsest-wise, another picture, of a dazed figure with a bleeding mouth caught in Jeremy's unsparing hold. Surely, in that savage hour upstairs, he had settled his account with the culprit!

Yes, the business of informing was too distasteful. Let the Government find and catch its lost prize if it liked. After that crazy climb he was not going to join in the hunt. The boy was too game. . . . Yet it must be confessed that to this *volte-face* of Hervey Barrington's there contributed also—since the motives for any resolve are seldom unmixed—a faint dislike to owning that his prisoner had given him the slip, and an absolute horror of having to acknowledge that he himself had, in the first instance, been completely duped as to that prisoner's sex. For now he saw (and wondered at his tardy perception of it) that this fact would certainly have to be revealed, or how should he account for the Frenchman's presence in his house at all?

He turned quickly round. "Jeremy," he said in his quarterdeck voice, "as long as an escaped French prisoner was under my roof it was my duty to hand him over to the authorities, and I should have done it this morning. But, all things considered, I do not intend to inform them that he has been here and has escaped. His whereabouts will be discovered quite soon enough. So, not a word to any one outside the house about last night's business. I do not choose to be the subject of idle gossip. Is that clear?"

"Ay, ay, Sir," replied John Jeremy, and saluted him among the chimney pots. "Am I to tell Hannah the same, Sir?"

"I will see Mrs. Jeremy myself on the matter," replied his master, walking towards the trapdoor.

"Curious thing, Sir," observed Jeremy, half shyly, rubbing a hand up and down his trousers, "but she won't, in a manner o' speaking, believe me when I say the—the young lady which she saw was a young man."

"Won't she?" returned Hervey rather grimly. "We will have her up, then, and show her the climb he did." "Me taking down them curtains has upset her proper," observed Hannah's spouse. "I doubt if she'll make much account of any climb till they'm back in their places again. . . . Let me go first and hold the ladder, Sir."

*

And as Captain Barrington had decreed, so it was at Fairhaven. Mrs.

Jeremy, indeed, when she had received her orders, remarked (but not to their giver) that *she* had no desire to gossip about a French hussy having been brought after dark into the house, and Miss Lavinia, with her own accusing conscience, was only too delighted to obey the order to hold her tongue, though it was more than probable that the precaution would be useless.

But no news of the fugitive came to Fairhaven, and Hervey, though he kept his ears open in Stowey that afternoon (he could not, naturally, put any questions) heard nothing. He had no idea in what direction the young man had gone in his forlorn endeavour; evidently not across the river, or he would surely have taken the skiff, of whose convenient presence he was, as Hervey remembered, very well aware. It was Miss Lavinia who made the only discovery worth mention—and even that led nowhere—which was, that a large stem of ivy had been torn away from the wall of the house about ten feet from the ground on the garden front; and it seemed quite probable that this minor catastrophe marked the path of the "wildcat," and that he himself had accompanied the ivy, and added a more or less severe fall—though upon grass—to his other disabilities.

Miss Barrington started for Exeter next morning, and Hervey, left alone once more, found his mind dwelling, with ever less appreciation of his own part in it, on that scene in the spare bedroom. Yes, he had behaved like a brute. He did not blame himself for having detained an escaping enemy, nor for having deprived him of his only means of further flight, his money . . . though it was deuced awkward to know what he was going to do with it now that he had it, since he had resolved not to inform the authorities of the owner's presence and escape. (Lavinia had suggested the poor-box; but that did not seem quite the right destination for someone else's banknotes.) The letters taken from the captive, as a cursory glance had shown, were from an Englishwoman. Hervey did not read them. If the young man were recaptured, and he got to know of it, he would try to return them to him; perhaps his money too. He knew his name—or at least the name he went by; the letters bore it also.

But as to believing his story of injured innocence—no! The boy was too

214

clever, too good an actor . . . but he did wish that he had not given him that unnecessary and ferocious blow. A spectator would have said that it was thoroughly justified, and dealt in self-defence. Hervey knew that it was neither, and was aware of what exactly had inspired it, though he did not wish to name the feeling. If only he had not been so blind at the outset, had drawn the right conclusions from what now seemed so obvious; the height, unusual in a woman; the voice, too deep; the reluctance to attract attention. At bay upstairs, in his proper attire, the masquerader had looked so much younger and slighter—and so much more spent. That accusing picture was before him again; he turned his gaze away from it.

Late in the afternoon, having succeeded in banishing the scene and its protagonist from the surface at least of his mind, and seeing the prospect of a fine evening, he decided to go for a sail.

The *Kestrel* paid off slowly, under mainsail and jib, her owner at the helm, but very soon Fairhaven was left behind, and the first river-huddled houses of Stowey were slipping past; old dwellings which looked as if they had sprung up by natural growth on their piles or ancient tide-greened walls.

"Not many craft in the river to-day," murmured Captain Barrington.

"I see a Brixham trawler over there," grumbled his satellite. "What be doing here, I wonder?"

"Come to sell fish, probably."

"Stowey men can catch their own fish, I rackon," replied Jeremy indignantly. "And look at the berth he's put hisself in!"

Hervey smiled. "I see a vessel ahead which has chosen a worse. When did that schooner run ashore on the Whalesback?"

For, half a mile or so farther down the river, on the invisible shoal which was the bane of Stowey harbour, lay a large schooner. Her tilted hull and masts gave her an odd effect of floating at an angle. But Captain Barrington was aware that she was not floating.

"Grounded two days ago, Sir, in the neap. Have to wait for the next spring tide to fetch her off. Dunno where she hail from. Her crew's all gone ashore. . . . Topsail now, Sir?"

"Mr. Rowl"

"Not yet," replied his master, though they were past the harbour, where Stowey river widened to the dignity of an estuary before it gave itself to the sea, and here he commonly shook out the *Kestrel*'s extra plumage. But this evening he was content to slip gently along with what sail she was carrying, his eyes fixed ahead on the mild unrest of the bar, thinking of that calamity of his own which was woven in such unfading colours on the arras of his mind. It needed but a touch to set the tapestry swaying, and the whole scene would spring to life again. And the stranded schooner there in the sunlight had done it, though it was an uncharted rock, not a sandbank, which had sunk H. M. S. *Suffolk* that dark October night off the Scillies. The court-martial had acquitted her captain, who was indeed perfectly blameless, condemnation being pretty equally divided between a faulty chart and the sailing-master . . . but Hervey Barrington never got another ship. Was it likely—a man who had lost a 74? And very shortly afterwards in 1811 came the flimsy pretext on which he, at thirty-nine, experienced, competent, and ambitious, was put on half-pay . . . in war-time. He might be blameless—but he had lost a 74.

And yet that voice had said the other night with such indignant scorn, "You do not know what it is to suffer injustice—you are of those who dispense it!" Did he not! Why else was he here now, idly steering this little craft, all that was left him to command. . . .

He roused himself from his bitter and useless contemplation. John Jeremy, sitting sideways on the weather coaming, was contemplating him, and Hervey's reserve fretted even under his gaze.

"That schooner looks berthed for a month," he observed in a matter-of-fact tone, gazing at her as they approached the sandbank. Broken water indicated the shallow, but no sand was visible. "We will go to larboard of old Whalesback for a change." (From habit he nearly always took the right-hand channel.) "Really I hardly know this side of the river. Who has got old John Wood's farm now—that is it, is it not?" he asked, pointing over the dancing water at the solitary-standing farmhouse, about a furlong from the edge of the river, which they were just leaving behind them.

"Ay, Sir, it is. A nasty, low-lived, ill-conditioned set there now, from all I hears—three brothers of the name of Willis. Foreigners they be," said Jeremy, meaning, of course, not true Devon men. "Will you have top-sail up now, Sir?"

"In a moment. The 'foreigners' seem excited about something," observed Hervey, craning his neck to look behind him, as a sudden outburst of shouts and yells came clearly over the intervening quarter mile or so of water.

"Likely their bees has swarmed on one of 'em," suggested Jeremy unemotionally. Standing amidships, he gazed back, shading his eyes with his horny palms. "No, they'm chasing one of the hands—wi' pitchforks tu. He'm running for dear life—making for the river. Do'ee look, Sir!"

Hervey brought the *Kestrel* farther into the wind and let her hang, twisting himself to see. Something of an agitating nature was certainly taking place at the abode of the brothers Willis. Eight or ten men, with a woman or two among them, had suddenly poured themselves out in a stream from behind the previously quiet farmhouse, shouting, yelling, and, most of them, brandishing either a stick, a hoe, or, as Jeremy had discerned, the deadly pitchfork. Hervey's eye caught the pursuers first, and then was aware of the pursued, a slender, scantily clad figure which, with only a few yards' advantage of the foremost, was running like a deer for the water.

Captain Barrington gave vent to an exclamation. His mouth tightened. "Stand by, Jeremy; I'm going about."

The *Kestrel*'s already wavering sail flapped, she rolled, hesitated, and then obeyed and began to make for the scene of the drama. Even as she came about, the fleeing figure had reached the water's edge, and, stumbling a little, waded in waist-deep and then struck out vigorously. A redoubled shout of rage went up from the pursuers, and one, with a yell, hurled his pitchfork at the swimmer. The rest contented themselves with imprecations and stones from the foreshore. Hervey Barrington, standing up at the helm, was shouting too: "Stop that, you brutes—stop it, I say!" but his voice, even if it carried to the ears of the infuriated group at the water's edge, had no effect.

Meanwhile the swimmer, his head a dark object amid the splashes of the fusillade of stones, none of which, luckily, seemed to be reaching their mark, forged slowly on towards midstream, using the overarm stroke, but always with the same arm. Although he was not swimming quickly he was drawing away from the *Kestrel* as well as from the shore, and Hervey's eyes were so keenly fixed on that head and arm as not to notice that the wind had fallen into one of those sudden little lulls common in a harbour, and that the cutter was now making very little headway indeed.

"He's swimming very oddly," said Captain Barrington aloud. "I wonder if those devils did get a pitchfork into him after all. . . . And where is he making for?—He'll never get over to the other side. If he has any wits left he'll make for the stranded schooner—ah, I suppose he doesn't know there's no one on board. . . . Damn it, the wind's dropped!"

Jeremy, already conscious of this fact, brought his gaze back from the peak of the mainsail. "Is it him, Sir—the Frenchy?"

"Of course it is. We will pick him up, if we can. Topsail, Jeremy, as quick as possible."

But, even in the short time it took to set the extra sail it began to seem a little doubtful if they would be able to accomplish this design. Hervey, hauling on the topsail halyards, knew instinctively that the swimmer, now almost in mid-stream, was in difficulties. He cursed himself for having stood staring instead of getting the rest of the canvas on sooner. However, in a moment or two the *Kestrel* responded to the new impetus, and began to cut through the water as if she knew what was required of her and rejoiced to do it. But for all that the outgoing tide (not his own efforts now) was sweeping her quarry away from her and round the other side of the Whalesback. Hervey could see that he had abandoned the effort of swimming, and, devoting his energies merely to keeping afloat, had thrown himself on to his back. Shouts came from the disappointed group on shore as, midway between them and the shoal, the *Kestrel* shot past on the now fresher breeze, but Hervey did not even turn his head. "Prisoner . . . French prisoner!" came to his ears. "Let them bawl!" he thought disgustedly.

But from where he stood at the tiller the French prisoner was no longer visible; he had disappeared entirely round the northern point of the shoal.

Hervey swore. But next moment the *Kestrel* also was past the point, and he looked over his left shoulder. No, the young man was still afloat, but struggling. "Ready, Jeremy!"

Like a bird checking in flight the *Kestrel* went about, rounded the bubbling, sucking sand, and was chasing up the deep water the other side. "Hold on one moment more!" shouted Hervey to the half-swimmer, half-flotsam a few yards ahead on his starboard bow. The topsail was already down, the jib coming in under Jeremy's skilled hands; in another second or two the mainsail itself came down with a run.

Even then, as was almost inevitable, they overshot him a little, but he had enough wits left in him to understand what was happening, and as the big boat glided by, he made an effort to fight her wash and get alongside. Leaning over, Hervey threw him a rope, and, rather to his surprise, the young man compassed a few painful strokes and seized it as it trailed past him.

"Excellent!" shouted Hervey. "Hold tight now!" and he began to haul in. The *Kestrel*'s way was spending itself; in another moment or two she would be stationary, except for the tide. "And only just in time, too," thought Captain Barrington, as hand over hand he pulled in the rope, not very fast for fear of jerking it out of the hold whose only strength lay probably in its desperation—and which was, he saw, a one-handed hold to boot. "No, I don't think you need go overboard, Jeremy," for that mariner already had his coat off. "Hold on to the slack of this so that I can use both my hands to get him in. We must be careful that we don't overset in doing it. Here we are!"

He was alongside, yes; sodden, and panting, and exhausted almost to the point of unconsciousness. But as Hervey leant over the side to clutch him the half-closed eyes under the plastered, dripping hair, opening, met his, and into them shot the next instant such a look of horror and aversion as turned Hervey cold.

"You . . . *you* . . . No!" gasped Raoul des Sablières, loosed his frantic grip of the rope, threw up his arms . . . and went instantly under.

Half-stunned though he was with the shock of it, Hervey made a quick mechanical grab at the disappearing body, but in vain. The next second a resounding splash announced that John Jeremy, for once not waiting for orders, had entered the estuary, and John Jeremy swam like a porpoise.

"Wait till you see where he comes up," said Hervey quietly. He was very pale. In another moment something reappeared a few yards away, something that now had no more volition of its own than a drifting spar. With half a dozen powerful strokes Jeremy reached and secured it, and was shortly treading water alongside, holding the inert head and shoulders out of the water, while the rest of the lax body showed a disposition to be sucked under the cutter's keel.

"Will this—whatever it is—hold, I wonder?" muttered Hervey, twisting one hand into something white, fastened across the almost bare breast like a scarf, "Yes, I think so. . . . Now—one, two, three!" A heave, a jerk, a grab at the trailing legs, a certain tilting and rocking on the *Kestrel*'s part, a moment's uncertainty and balancing on the gunwale, and Captain Barrington had got his prisoner back again.

Revenge and Hervey Barrington

"The consciousness that his sentiments were just and his intention kind was scarcely sufficient to support him."–Rasselas, chap. xvii.

By the time that John Jeremy had scrambled on board once more, shaken himself like a huge Newfoundland, and come thudding aft, his master was no longer occupied in treating the rescued man as a case of drowning, but was listening to his heart.

"I am sure he cannot have swallowed much water in the short time he was under," he observed, looking up at his henchman. "He has only collapsed from exhaustion, I think. All the same . . ." He glanced down again at his recovered captive.

The young Frenchman was indeed a sorry spectacle as he lay there unconscious, quietly drenching the bottom boards to an extent which was surprising in view of the small amount of clothing left on him by this time.

He had his breeches—and those torn at one knee—portions of his shirt clinging to him, the scarf-like object by which Hervey had hauled him in, and absolutely nothing else, for shoes and stockings alike were gone from his cut and bleeding feet. And when Hervey slipped his hand under the wet, heavy head a diluted little crimson trickle began to course over his own wrist, and he saw that a stone had struck the swimmer near the right ear, though the damage done did not appear to be serious.

"Yes, the most important thing, I fancy, is to keep him warm," he went on, lifting his prize a little. "I'm afraid there's no brandy on board, worse luck. Get that old boat cloak of mine from the locker forward; the spare jib too would not come amiss." And he began stripping off the soaked rags of shirt, discovering in the puzzling scarf, when he unknotted it, a close resemblance to one of his own huckaback towels. Another discovery was the greatly swollen and discoloured state of one of the limp wrists—the result of more rough handling, perhaps . . . like the big bruise on one shin and that disfiguring cut on the lip which showed up so vividly, so reproachfully, on the surrounding pallor. (And *those* marks had not been the work of an excited rabble who scarcely knew what they were doing.)

"I take it, Sir," observed Jeremy, handing him the boat cloak, "that you don't intend giving him up to them Willises?"

"I do not," replied his master shortly. He finished wrapping up his capture, rose to his feet, and looked across to the other shore to see if the individuals in question were still watching and still expectant—to find, somewhat to his astonishment, that he could not see the shore and farmhouse at all. The *Kestrel* was so near the shoal that the bulk of the careened schooner entirely blotted them out.

At this discovery a very unexpected idea came to Hervey Barrington, and he demanded of Jeremy whether at the actual moment of getting the Frenchman aboard they had been screened by the schooner as they were now. He could not himself tell, since his back had been towards her all the time.

"Ay, Sir," replied that mariner, "we was. I happened to notice particular, and she were nicely to lee of us. Them Willises over there couldn't have seen a thing.—Don't you want 'em even to know, Sir, in a manner o' speaking, as we pulled him out?"

"No, in a manner of speaking, I don't," returned Hervey, compressing his lips and doing some very rapid thinking. He unfolded the spare jib and spread it completely over the motionless figure at his feet. "I shall keep the affair in my own hands now. Get the sails up, and we will stand over to the other side—within hailing distance, that is—and tell those savages that the French prisoner sank before we could get to him—sank under our very eyes and did not come up again, and that as the tide is running out fast it is not likely that his body will ever be recovered. Do you understand?"

A slow, appreciative grin spread over his myrmidon's broad countenance. "Lord love you, Sir, yes. And they'll believe you when you sings out who you is. And then . . . shall we put back home?"

"It's what I should like to do," replied his master, glancing down at the sailcloth, which looked rather like a pall, "but it would seem rather too suspicious if we did, since we were so plainly standing out to sea before, and only came about to find out what was going on. No, we will beat out to sea for a little while, and then, when the light has faded somewhat, bring the Frenchman in and get him to bed. To-morrow will be plenty of time to tell the constable about him."

*

And Captain Barrington's bold lie, shouted in an authoritative voice to the still expectant Willises and their retinue from a safe distance, was evidently believed without hesitation, to judge from the angry dejection which it caused. "No doubt they were after the ten guineas reward, the ruffians!" thought Hervey Barrington to himself, as the *Kestrel* once more swung seaward—and incontinently felt his own cheeks burn. Two nights ago he himself had been taunted with having the same ignoble aim.

When they were well away from the shore he stooped and turned back the jib. Provided they kept him warm, the unavoidable delay in getting him into a bed would surely not do the fugitive much harm, for he was young enough to fling off the effects of exhaustion, and he should have the best of care that night. But when the sail was withdrawn Hervey was uncomfortably startled by the aspect of the face at his feet, so desperately white and pinched against the folds of the boat cloak.—And, by Gad, what a fool he was!—there was some brandy in the forward locker, some that had been there for a long time. Even as he thought of this and determined to get it, there was a movement in the prostrate figure, the closed eyes half opened, the lips said something in French, and an arm extricated itself from the boat cloak.

"Come and take the tiller, Jeremy," called Captain Barrington, "and keep an eye on him. He's coming to." And he himself went quickly forward to the little cuddy and hunted for the brandy bottle.

He had just laid his hand on it when he was aware of a sudden commotion in the stern, a shout from Jeremy, followed by a cry, a sort of sob of anguish; and coming hastily out he saw what looked like a tussle going on. Amazed and angry he hurried aft. But whatever had been happening was over when he got there, and Raoul des Sablières, freed entirely from the boat cloak, now lay in a huddled heap at Jeremy's feet.

"What on earth have you been doing to him?" demanded Hervey sternly, stooping over the thin, bare shoulders.

"Nothing, Sir, but pull him back," replied Jeremy earnestly. "He come to, like, and look round, and seem to see where he is, and then I think he sees you, Sir, and he gives hisself one heave and gets hisself half over the gunwale before I knows what he is about. So I ketches hold of the nearest bit of him I can grab and pulls him back—what else was I to do, Sir?—and when I lays hold of him he sings out and tumbles back like that. That's all I did, upon my oath, Captain Barrington. He'm light-headed, sure, to try to throw hisself overboard after all your trouble, Sir!"

Light-headed? If so, his resolve to fling away his life rather than return to the prison ship was all the more innately steely. This was the second—no, the third attempt. Decidedly it had been no figure of speech, that threat. . . . Hervey was half afraid to touch him now, but—mercifully, perhaps—Jeremy's rough method of salvation (no doubt he had unwittingly caught him by the damaged wrist) had thrown the captive back into semi-consciousness. He evidently did not know who it was that wrapped him up again, first putting his own coat on him this time; but the pain of having his injured arm slipped, however carefully, into the sleeve, made him catch his breath sharply.

"*Laisse-moi, laisse-moi, tu me fais mal!*" he said indistinctly and without opening his eyes.

Hervey buttoned the coat over him and put the brandy to his lips. "Just drink this," he said persuasively.

"*Je voudrais être tranquille,*" murmured the young man. "*Dormir . . .*" His voice died away. He could swallow, however, and Hervey got some brandy down his throat and rearranged the sail under his head. Good God, what a wreck the boy looked! Two days had done it—two days without food, no doubt (since he had no money) without shelter, almost without clothes. And was he to be handed over to justice to-morrow in this condition, thrown into the lock-up at Stowey in the company of drunken and quarrelsome mariners and masterless men?

Hervey rose from his knees and sat down by Jeremy in the stern-sheets, and in a low voice bade him listen to his instructions. As he had so successfully drowned the fugitive he proposed to keep him drowned a little longer. Bates, the constable, would be only too glad that Captain Barrington should look after his lawful charge for a few days until the latter recovered from his immersion and exposure; he would see Bates to-morrow and make that right with him. The rabble at the waterside farm would be dispersed by now; if not, he must run the risk of their discovering his trick. "So we will stand in at once, Jeremy," he concluded, "and get home as soon as possible, though I am afraid, by the way the wind has dropped in the last few minutes, that we shall not make Fairhaven very quickly."

He was right. By the time they had worn ship and gone five minutes or so, at no great speed, upon their homeward tack, the breeze had still further died down, and they were barely moving over the water. And, as Hervey now became aware, shivers were running over the figure at his feet, half conscious or asleep though it seemed to be. There was nothing further that he could wrap round him now.

"We cannot waste time like this," he said in an undertone to Jeremy. "We must get out the sweeps and pull in."

A look of dismay crossed that individual's countenance. "Don't 'ee remember, Sir, as I took 'em by your orders last week to have 'em releathered, and 'tain't done yet?"

"So you did," said Hervey. "What a misfortune!" He bit his lip.

"We'm making some headway, Sir," said the steersman consolingly, "and likely when sun sets we'll get a breeze."

"Yes," said Hervey, "but meanwhile . . ." After a second's hesitation he knelt down, lifted Raoul des Sablières into his arms, and sat down on the bottom boards with him across his knees, holding him close to see if the contact would warm him, and praying that he would not open his eyes and recognize him.

His prayer was heard. After a while, too, the young man ceased to shiver; he even buried his face in silence against his enemy's shoulder. And so the *Kestrel* dawdled homewards under the hues of coming sunset, and Hervey sat with his victim's damp head against his breast, and wished his work undone, despite a mocking voice that whispered to him: "You are grown deuced squeamish all of a sudden!" Yes, that might be; but he had been deuced brutal first . . . and all because he had been made to feel ridiculous. That did not seem to matter now and, since the masquerader had paid dearly enough for his mumming, and he himself turned with so much disgust, to-day, from his own figure as memory showed it to him, he resolved, looking down on that brine-tangled hair, that he would write to the Transport Office, and try to get the boy's case investigated; for it seemed to him that behind the two desperate attempts of the last hour to be done with life there did really, perhaps, lie some great injustice suffered. And if that were so, the authorities might be persuaded to order him back to the lesser hardships of a land prison.

Truly Hervey Barrington had done with revenge. But his revenge had not yet done with him.

By this time his position had become somewhat cramped; but when he shifted it a little the head on his breast moved too.

"Are we nearly there?" suddenly asked its owner, in a dreamy voice. And as Hervey hesitated, not knowing what to reply, Raoul went on: "Surely we are off the coast of France now . . . we have been so long at sea. Let me look!" and he made an effort to raise himself.

"No, no, lie still!" said Hervey, involuntarily tightening his grasp. "All is well; you will soon be . . . where you wish." ("God forgive me!" he added mentally.)

Raoul gave a long sigh of contentment and fell back again. But after a moment he went on, rather less clearly, "You are very good to me, to take me after all, now that I have no money. But I will pay you somehow, never fear! A man at some place . . . I forget . . . two men . . . they took it all away. . . . Tiens, it is strange," he added reminiscently, "but when I swam out to you I thought I saw his face in the boat. . . . Am I ill that you hold me like this?"

"You had a long swim," replied Hervey, rather hoarsely, transfixed by the fear that he would look up and recognize him. . . . Yet what other course was open to him? He could not have left the fugitive to drown, and the lie which had been told him was for his very life's sake. But somehow Hervey wished it had been any other lie.

Raoul roamed on, less coherently still. "Yes, I swam twice. And my wrist . . . it hurt too much . . . I think it is broken . . . I fell . . . a long time ago, climbing somewhere . . . there was ivy. *Mais que m'importe? Maman me le guérira.*"

And with these words he relapsed into silence again. Hervey, looking cautiously down, saw with relief that his eyes were shut once more; saw too, with a pang to which he could not have put a name, that there was a smile on the disfigured mouth. It would be his task to break that dream.

The trend of this conversation had by now penetrated the mind of John Jeremy, and, bending forward to his master's ear, he enquired if he had rightly apprehended that "the Frenchy" imagined the *Kestrel* was taking him to France? And Hervey, corroborating this deduction, impressed on his henchman the distasteful necessity of keeping up this delusion lest they should have trouble again with the fugitive, a course which Jeremy cordially approved, for, as he muttered, the lad was a proper wildcat.

The afterhues of sunset had changed from rose to saffron, from saffron to palest green, and the fair star was trembling over the last bank of cloud in the west, before their destination came in sight. The "wildcat" lay very quiet in Hervey's hold, only babbling now and then in his own tongue of France and of his mother, and occasionally of someone called Lenepveu and the port of Morlaix, but with so much incoherence that it was plain he was half light-headed; so that it might be hoped he would not yet recognize the trick which, out of sheer mercy, was being played on him.

But if he did, how on earth should they persuade him to enter the skiff and be landed? He would certainly jump into the river first, and another immersion would probably finish him off. Hervey cudgelled his brains over this problem, whose only solution seemed to lie in bringing the *Kestrel* right in to the garden steps. He had occasionally done this at high water, though he had all a sailor's dislike of scraped paint, but it was not high water now, or anything like it, though the tide was making by this time. He turned his head and consulted Jeremy.

Yes, Jeremy, after survey, thought it might just be possible—with luck; it was better, he opined, to try it than to risk having the skiff upset. Slowly, carefully, therefore the *Kestrel* glided toward the steps, and Hervey, who had temporarily laid down the passenger in order to lower the sail, bent rather apprehensively over him to rouse him from his state of semi-coma.

"We are going to land you now—but before you go any farther you must have a good night's rest in . . . in the house to which we are taking you."

"*Nous sommes arrivés—on est vraiment en France?*" exclaimed the young Frenchman joyfully, and he tried to sit up in the bottom of the boat, Hervey hastily moving out of his field of vision. But next moment he relapsed with an exclamation and put his hand over his eyes. "*La tête me tourne; j'ai le vertige.*"

"Shut your eyes then, and trust to me," said Hervey quickly. This was an unexpected piece of luck; and it was without a twinge that he heard the *Kestrel's* keel scrape horribly over the rocks at the bottom of the steps. "Now, lend a hand, Jeremy!"

Together they got the half-dazed fugitive over the side and up the steps, by which time it was sufficiently apparent that he was not only giddy, but quite beyond recognizing his surroundings, as Hervey had feared. Clinging blindly to his guide's arm he followed his instructions with a rather uncanny obedience, and though at the top of the steps Jeremy relinquished his hold in order to tow the bumping *Kestrel* by means of the skiff to her moorings, Hervey had no difficulty in piloting his charge up the garden by himself. He chose the grass rather than the path out of consideration for the bare and lacerated feet, but indeed it was like steering a sleep-walker who neither saw, nor felt, nor spoke, but only smiled in his sleep and manifested a patient docility and confidence which cut Hervey to the heart.

At last they were in the hall which had witnessed the metamorphosis of the Spanish girl into the French, and now saw a still more startling transformation. But Mrs. Hannah Jeremy, who happened to be there as they entered from the garden, was not aware of any transformation, for she had no idea that in the half-drowned apparition which her master was supporting she beheld the memorable visitant of the night before last. But she was so startled at what she saw that she gave a slight scream.

"Lord have mercy!" she ejaculated. "What's this—who is it?"

"A . . . traveller," replied Hervey, for Raoul's problematical benefit. "But he is ill. Get the spare-room bed ready at once—at once, there is not a moment to lose. Up with you, and we will follow."

One more comprehensive glance did Mrs. Jeremy cast on the two figures, then she mounted the stairs more quickly than Hervey had ever seen her.

Much more slowly, and with a great deal of assistance, Raoul des Sablières likewise ascended. But on the landing, just before the three shallow steps which led to the spare bedroom, even the automatic obedience came at last to an end, and but for his captor's encircling arm he would have crumpled up and slid to the floor. Hervey thereupon lifted him bodily and carried him in his arms over that threshold.

Mrs. Jeremy had not quite finished making the bed, so Captain Barrington deposited his burden in the big chair and went to utter a hasty word of warning.

"I picked him up out of the river, Mrs. Jeremy; he was drowning—had been chased by some brutes with pitch-forks. He's the Frenchman who escaped two nights ago, and, being confused in his mind, he thinks I have brought him back to France; but he understands English perfectly, so be careful what you say."

"*Pitchforks . . . drowning . . .* mercy on us!" exclaimed Mrs. Jeremy; but Hervey had the impression that the rest of his admonition had gone like wind over her head. As she tucked in the blankets she took a quick survey of the pitiful figure trailing in the big chair. "Lord save us—his poor feet! And his mouth—whatever have they been doing to him? . . . He must have a hot drink, and I'll pop a brick into the oven. One moment, Sir, while I do that." And before Hervey could stop her she had whisked out of the room.

He was so afraid of undoing his successful work that he carefully avoided the neighbourhood of the chair and went over to the window. But in a very short time he was alarmedly aware that the sleepwalker was showing signs of returning animation and of conjecture. He had pulled himself up a little, and, flushed and coughing, was looking round the room. Hervey, guilt-ridden, shrank further into his corner. Raoul passed his hand once or twice over his eyes, and then, to Captain Barrington's great relief, Mrs. Jeremy reappeared with a kettle of hot water in her hand, and the young Frenchman fixed his gaze on her. Their encounter that night had been so brief that Hervey thought it improbable the one-time guest would recognize her.

Very businesslike, Mrs. Jeremy fetched a basin and knelt down by the chair.

"I'm going to bathe these feet of yours, my dear," she announced gently, and Raoul, coughing again, lay back and let her do it.

"Is Jeremy in yet?" asked Hervey from behind the chair.

"Just come in, Sir.—Dear sakes, here's a nasty cut!—As I came up there was someone at the front door, and I left him to answer it."

"I hope to goodness——" Hervey was beginning, half to himself, when there came a solid knock at the bedroom door. Obviously Jeremy in person, so his master went out on to the landing to see what he wanted.

"If you please, Sir, there's a sergeant of marines downstairs."

"A what!" exclaimed Hervey, thunderstruck.

"Soldiers, Sir, from Plymouth, a sergeant and a couple of marines—the sergeant asking to see you at once, along of this escaped French prisoner what's drowned, him having heard as how you had witnessed the affair, Sir."

For a second or two Hervey was dumb. A search party from Plymouth already! He had never contemplated this—a very different business from dealing with the local constable. "Marines," he repeated slowly. "You did not, I hope——"

But this was one of Jeremy's bright days. "No, Sir," he replied complacently. "I says nothing but, 'No doubt Cap'n Barrington will see you if you'll step inside.' 'We comes from Plymouth,' he says then, 'bin a-looking for this prisoner since Tuesday; a most desperate character, he says, escaped from the *Ganges* prison ship.' And then he swears a bit, saving your presence, Sir, because the man's drowned, and all their trouble for nothing."

"Did you corroborate—I mean, did you say the man was drowned?" asked Hervey quickly.

"Not I, Sir. And for all the sergeant knows I've bin in the garden since morning a-pickin' of cabbages."

"Where is the sergeant?" asked Hervey, his heart sinking lower and lower.

"In the hall, Sir. The marines stayed outside. Seemed to me it was best to let him in willing-like."

Hervey nodded. "Yes, you are quite a diplomat," he said, but mirthlessly. "I will go down and see him. You did very properly in not committing yourself about the drowning, because now I shall have to extricate myself somehow from that lie." He mused a moment, his hand on the bannisters. "Tell me, Jeremy, do you consider that, with the tide running out as it was, it would sound plausible, especially to a man who probably doesn't know the river-mouth, if I said that though the Frenchman sank and I believed him drowned, I found him shortly afterwards cast up alive on the Ledges—you know where I mean?"

"Why, yes, Cap'n Barrington," returned Jeremy admiringly, "and just about where he would have been—like the man as was washed overboard from the Falmouth barque near the Whalesback last winter. Couldn't say as that mightn't well have been, Sir, seeing as I suppose you'm got to account for the Frenchy's being in the house, and then give him up."

"Well, what else can I do?" asked Hervey, more of himself than of Jeremy. "What else can I do?—Tell your wife in there the bed will not be needed after all; she's not to put him into it. But she must find him some clothes—some warm clothes—and she had better bandage his feet before he leaves." And with bent head he started to go very slowly down the stairs.

And as he went he felt that he would sooner be going to face arrest on his own account. But, instead of that, he was going to surrender the boy who had lain helpless in his arms for the last hour, whom he had not allowed to die by the merciful clean death he had chosen, but whom he had lured by a heartless trick under his own roof again . . . a boy almost dead from exhaustion and ill-usage.

And yet again, what choice had he? Even if he had not worn the King's uniform himself it was felony now to assist the escape of a prisoner of war; though indeed it was not the very remote prospect of transportation which weighed with him, but the certain wreckage of his own deeply threatened career. For he had by no means given up hope of his restoration to the active list; he had influential friends who considered him most unjustly treated, and held that the time would certainly come when he would be reinstated. It would never come if he followed his instincts now; he might as well send in his papers at once. Moreover, personal considerations quite apart, it was his plain duty as an Englishman to do what he was going to do.

Down and down he went, as slowly as an old man. A broken enemy, his victim already, enticed into an illusive security, and then immediately, in cold blood, handed over to . . . what? Pah, it sickened him!

But perhaps he could at least prevail on the sergeant to wait for a couple of days before taking the prisoner off—to wait till to-morrow even. The fugitive could not be dragged away to-night; it would be his death warrant. Yet he was, technically, still on his feet, and the man would be perfectly within his rights in insisting on his removal. It depended, then, on the personal character of this sergeant of marines whether an appeal to him would be of any use.

And the moment he set eyes on him Hervey knew that it would be of none.

"I Have the Honour to Report . . ."

"Is there such depravity in man as that he should injure another without benefit to himself?"—Rasselas, chap. ix.

He came forward, saluting with much respect, as Captain Barrington descended the last stairs into the hall. It was not likely, of course, that he would show anything else to a naval officer of Hervey's rank. But he had a hard, brutal mouth, a hard eye.

"Sorry to trouble you, Sir," he said briskly. "Your man has no doubt told you what we've come about."

"Yes," said Hervey. There was no use in beating about the bush. "This matter of the French prisoner, I understand. How did you come to connect me with it?"

"Like this, Sir," responded the sergeant. "Having tracked him on Wednesday nearly as far as Stowey—he was got up as a girl, cunning young devil—we lost trace of him, owing, I fancy, to an accident to the Tawton coach that evening. He seems to have disappeared entirely after that—thrown off his woman's gear, no doubt. And we went off on a wild goose chase as far as Widdeford. Thinks I then, finding it a false track, my gentleman's perhaps lying low in Stowey or near it all the while, waiting his chance of a boat—no doubt there's a bit of smuggling goes on there. So I brought my party back. But hardly had we got back to Stowey before a farm lad comes up to me in a hurry and says they've got a suspicious character at their farm, down by the mouth of the river, on the other side; had already come there yesterday evening, when he sold his shoes for a meal, and now again, begging for another and offering to work for it. The first time they had thought nothing of it, but before he came the second time they had heard as there was a prisoner escaped from Plymouth, and a party after him. So (by what this boy says) this time they had locked him up in a barn, all ready for us to nab—thinking the reward as good as in their pockets, I reckon. Down the river again we went, Sir, and . . . got there too late. My fine fellow had taken the alarm, broken out, made for the river, and . . . well, I suppose, Captain Barrington, you know best in what port of Davy Jones's locker he's likely to be now. For they told us at the farm that it was you, Sir, in your sailing boat, as saw him drown . . . trying to pick him up, I daresay, Sir?"

"Yes," said Hervey slowly, "I was trying to pick him up. But I was . . . too late." He suddenly perceived that the door from the garden had been left open when he had brought in the drowned man not half an hour ago. He went over and shut it.

"Well, Sir," continued the marine, "as things are, if the young devil had drowned when he swam the Hamoaze on Tuesday, as it's thought he did, it would have saved a deal of trouble, besides being a warning to the others. It has happened with an escaping prisoner before now," he added explanatorily, "that his dead body has fetched up on a mud bank, and a few weeks of him laying there, with only the gulls to attend to him——"

"You don't mean to say," broke in Hervey, turning round at the door in disgust, "that his body would be *left* there, on purpose!"

"But when you shoot a pole-cat or a weasel, Sir, you nail him up as a warning and don't think nothing of it!"

"I imagined we were speaking now of human beings," retorted Captain Barrington freezingly.

"If you were in command of a prison ship, Sir, you'd think different, saving your respect. Stinking vermin, that's what they are. And if I had my way, I'd soon stop escaping . . . with the cat o' nine tails. But we aren't allowed to touch 'em that way, though a good honest British tar gets it as soon as look at you. . . . Begging your pardon for the freedom, Sir, you being a Navy officer!"

"Oh, there *are* some things you are not allowed to do to the prisoners, then?" enquired Hervey.

His tone evidently puzzled the marine. "I don't quite rightly know what you mean, Sir. Short of mutiny, we mayn't lay a finger on them. That's not to say they don't have some pretty stiff punishments among themselves."

Hervey was still standing by the door, looking hard at the speaker. Yes, this man would no doubt abide by the letter of the regulations, but what about his obedience to their spirit when he had the "cunning young devil," as he had called him, in his hands? No superior officer, and a sick and injured prisoner against whom he was already incensed! There was opportunity for a good deal between here and Plymouth.

"What is it you want me to do?" he asked—anything to gain time to think.

And the sergeant of marines replied promptly and as it were ingratiatingly: "If you would be so good, Sir, as to give me an account of what happened down the river, and perhaps a bit of paper—an affidavit, like—then when I get back to Plymouth there'll be no suggesting that we gave up when we might have got him if we had gone on. Because when a man's dead he's dead, and if it's by drowning no one can say the body *must* be produced, and I understand the tide was running out strong. So if you were to write it down, Sir, the captain of the *Ganges* could make his report to the Transport Office, your evidence being quite sufficient for him, particularly as he is only of lieutenant's rank."

"I see," said Hervey. All unprepared, he stood face to face with the gravest decision of his life. This man, however disappointed he might be, had evidently no shadow of doubt as to his informant's veracity, and they would take his word as unquestioningly at Plymouth, and—yes, in London too, despite the mark against his name. He stood in no immediate danger if he lied. It was when the truth came out afterwards—for it would be almost a miracle if it did not—that his ruin would be complete. Well, he had only to say, with a little forced jocularity, "After all your trouble, Sergeant, you will be glad to learn that your prisoner is not drowned (for though he sank before my eyes, I picked him up later) that he is in the house at the moment, and that, as my duty to my King and country bids me, I invite you to go upstairs and . . . take him."

The speech arranged, rehearsed itself in Hervey's brain. He saw beforehand the cruel light it would bring into those hard, reddened eyes. . . . No, it was physically impossible to utter it. Instead he asked, a little hoarsely, "How much of my . . . of what I saw . . . do you want in writing?"

"Very little, Sir," said the sergeant apologetically. "Just a few lines, and your signature, if you please. I'm ashamed to trouble you, but if I only take back a verbal report, I reckon that the authorities would write to you for confirmation of the story; but if I hand in a written one you won't likely be troubled further."

"Quite so," said Hervey drily. "Sit down then, and I will report the matter."

The pursuer sat down in the very chair occupied by his quarry during his successive incarnations two nights ago. And Hervey Barrington, seizing a sheet of paper from the writing table in the corner, "had the honour" to report on the death by drowning on the afternoon of August 13th of a French prisoner of war escaped from the *Ganges* prison ship at Plymouth, which death he had witnessed; and signed away his good name and his self-respect, asking himself all the time why he was doing it, and unable to find any answer except that he could not do the other thing. . . .

"Thank you kindly, Sir," said the marine, taking the paper with a salute and disposing it inside his tunic. "That will be quite enough to show that I have not failed in my duty. My men are waiting outside. Good evening, Sir."

Feeling no desire to have his health drunk by this man, Captain Barrington abstained from giving him a shilling for the purpose, and a minute later he and his two subordinates were marching down the road in the twilight. From his doorstep, Hervey watched them go, empty-handed. . . . No, not empty-handed; he had given them, in exchange for the boy upstairs, something very costly indeed—his signature to a lie.

Coming in again he rang the bell for Jeremy.

"I have sent the escort away again," he announced curtly, "with a written statement that I saw the prisoner drown. I was not disposed to give him up in his present condition." He took a turn up and down, while the ex-coxswain was speechless. "You realize, of course, Jeremy, what a serious step I have taken; for if it comes out in any way that I am concealing the prisoner here, even from the most humane motives, I am ruined—utterly."

"Yessir," said Jeremy, his face taking on profounder shades of alarm. "Oh, Cap'n Barrington, you didn't ought to 'a' done it—indeed you didn't!"

"I know that," replied his master grimly. "But it is done now, and I must abide by it. We must use the greatest caution that no word of the young man's presence here leaks out before we can get rid of him. Of course, if you feel that you ought to inform against me——"

"Cap'n Barrington, Sir, how can 'ee talk like that!" ejaculated the good Jeremy, deeply hurt. "Me that's been shipmates wi' you, saving your presence, Sir, since——"

"No, no, I beg your pardon, Jeremy," said Hervey quickly. "I ought not to have said that—though I am not sure whether it is not your duty to lay information, all the same. However, if it comes out, you will not incur blame, acting as you do under my orders, I must speak to Mrs. Jeremy at once, and see that she understands the situation and keeps her mouth shut. Is she in the kitchen?"

"No, Sir. She'm upstairs, terrible took up wi' the young man. I see she'm for cosseting him proper." A slight smile illuminated the gloom of Jeremy's features. "Shall I fetch her down, Sir?"

"No, I'll go up to her," said Hervey. "I am glad to hear that she has taken to him—he will certainly need care."

Up he went, and entered the spare bedroom. Not only was the fugitive ensconced in bed, contrary to orders, but the apartment had somehow taken on the aspect of a sick-room already. And Mrs. Jeremy, the complete nurse, was bending over the dark head on the pillow.

"Now, my dear," he heard her say, "do'ee lay quiet and go to sleep—you've no call to fidget like that . . . nor to cough neither.—Do you want me, Sir?"

But once out on the landing with her master she gave him no opportunity to tell her what it was he required her for.

"I've put him to bed, Sir, knowing that's what you'd wish"—Hervey's eyebrows went up, unnoticed—"and I've taken the liberty of putting on him one of your old nightshirts. But he's very feverish and restless, Sir, and won't touch the good hot milk I have for him—and yet by the body of him he's been more than half starved lately. What to do with that wrist of his I don't know, seeing as he can't bear a finger laid on it, and yet——"

"Yes, Mrs. Jeremy," interrupted Hervey, obliged to dam the stream, "but I want first to speak to you on another aspect of this matter. I have got rid of the soldiers who came here after him by repeating—in writing—my assertion that I saw him drown."

"Well, Sir," returned Mrs. Jeremy easily, "and I'm sure that was the best thing to do. I knew you would send them away."

"The deuce you did!" exclaimed Captain Barrington, staring at the prophetess. "Do you realize what a very grave step——"

But for the first time in his knowledge of her Mrs. Jeremy did not accord him her whole attention while he was speaking. "There's that nasty cough again!" she exclaimed. "Excuse me, Sir—I'll be out again in a moment." With that she whisked back into the room leaving her employer almost gasping.

"Well!" he thought grimly, "if I can induce her to bestow half the care in keeping his presence hidden that she is evidently going to lavish on the young gentleman himself, I shall be fortunate." He waited, though he hardly expected her to reappear, but reappear she did, when the sound of coughing within had ceased.

"Look here, Mrs. Jeremy," said Hervey with determination, "perhaps I have not made it clear to you that this young Frenchman is the same as he who got out from this room by the window the night before last."

"Of course, if you say so, Sir," returned Mrs. Jeremy with an air of respectful unbelief. "The . . . the person who, I am told, climbed on to the roof?"

"Yes," reiterated Captain Barrington, "the *male* person who climbed on to the roof, and who, as you see, injured his wrist over the business. That person was, and is, an escaped French prisoner from the hulks at Plymouth, and as his presence here, which I have tacitly denied, is strictly illegal, it must be kept absolutely secret, even more for my own sake than for his."

"I was never a gossip, Sir," replied Mrs. Jeremy with great dignity, and, her master answering briefly that he was aware of it, she suggested that he should come in and have another look at the rescued man.

But that Hervey declined to do, lest he should be recognized, and the Frenchman try to climb out of the window again. He had better not enter the room, and only hoped the ex-captive would not remember the room itself.

"Lord, Sir," replied Mrs. Jeremy, "he's beyond that now. He has no idea where he is, I'm sure, beyond being thankful to be in a bed, poor young man. Very feverish he is, and——"

There was no point in hearing all that again. "Well, do your best for him," cut in Hervey hastily. "And remember, not a word about his being here!" With that he retired from the interview.

A cold and not particularly appetizing supper was served to him a little later by Jeremy, whose spouse was evidently too much occupied with the new arrival to provide anything hot. Hervey, however, did not grumble at this absorption; he had an absorption of his own, if it came to that. For though he sat down afterwards with a book, he could not read; he meditated on what, with his eyes open, he had done that evening. He sat there a perjured man . . . a fool . . . almost a traitor. Yet, at bottom, he was quite unrepentant. He knew what he would be feeling like if he had done his duty. And somehow he might be able to get rid of the fugitive later on without exciting suspicion. He took up his book and resolutely read a page.

And then Mrs. Jeremy came in.

"If you please, Sir, may Jeremy go at once for Dr. Hills?"

"Go for Doctor Hills!" exclaimed Hervey, turning round. "No, certainly he may not! You don't grasp the situation yet, Mrs. Jeremy—that's evident. If that young man's presence gets known in Stowey—don't you understand? I thought I had sufficiently explained my delicate position."

"Yes, Sir, and I'm sure I wouldn't wish you to get into trouble, but a doctor he must have."

"A doctor he can't have," reiterated Hervey. "He must do without one." And, thinking that this decree sounded harsher than he intended, he added: "You see, if the authorities knew that he was here, they would have him off back to the hulks in no time. So the precaution is really for his own sake."

Mrs. Jeremy looked down and pleated her spotless apron, a sure (and rare) sign of distress.

"He'd better even go back to the hulks, Sir, than be taken out of the house in a coffin." And she sniffed.

"Don't be absurd, Mrs. Jeremy!" But she had alarmed him. "The young man has got a touch of fever, no doubt, from the exposure, but a day or two's care—"

"It's more than that, Sir, begging your pardon. It's more like what my own brother died of, after three days—begun in just the same way, with a terrible fit of shivering (it come on when you was having your supper, Sir) the whole bed shaking with it. And now he's coughing and crying out with the pain of it every now and then, and that changed already you'd hardly know him. If you can say what to do for him without a doctor, Sir, I'm sure I'd be only too thankful—but I don't know!"

Hervey put down his book and went upstairs.

It was quite true. Des Sablières did look most alarmingly ill, and, in the short time, was extraordinarily changed. He lay curled up on his side with a hot flush on one cheek, breathing very fast, and his air of lassitude had given place to one of intense disquiet. Every now and again he was shaken by a short, dry cough, which seemed to give him great pain. Mrs. Jeremy went to him. His eyes, with their bright, strained glance, followed her as she moved.

"*Maman, j'ai tellement mal!*" he said, like a sick child. "*Maman—*"

Mrs. Jeremy, bending compassionately over him, took his restless hand between her own and stroked it.

"What does he mean, Sir?" she asked in a whisper. "Is it anything I can do?"

"You are doing all you can, Mrs. Jeremy," replied Hervey, biting his lip. "He wants his mother." He turned away. "I am going for a doctor."

" . . . But not for Dr. Hills, who attends everybody," he added mentally, as he ran down the stairs. "And any doctor's presence here will have to be accounted for somehow . . . I have it! I will see if I can dig Alexander Touchwood out of his shells and fossils. People hardly realize that he is a doctor, yet I believe that, for all his eccentricities, he was very well thought of before he gave up his practice. If he will undertake it, nobody would think anything of *his* visiting here."

*

"Yes, but you see, Touchwood, I had rather you knew nothing, for your own sake," he was repeating a quarter of an hour later, in that gentleman's phenomenally untidy study. "Heaven knows that it isn't that I fear your discretion. If you'll only come and look at him and ask no questions——"

"My dear Barrington," said the geologist, shutting up Brander's *Fossilia Hantoniensia*, "you might give me credit for some human qualities. I'm not a fossil myself, if I do collect 'em. Curiosity, my dear fellow, curiosity about my neighbours' affairs lodges here"—he thumped his lean breast—"just as much as in any old maid. I'll come, as you ask me . . . but I'll come quicker if you will tell me why I am to have my eyes blindfolded, and swear secrecy on a skull and crossbones, and write a prescription in blood!"

Half annoyed, Hervey laughed. "I never made any such ridiculous stipulations," he replied. "I only thought that if I were run in for what I am doing——"

"Ha!" exclaimed Mr. Alexander Touchwood in a joyful tone, and he rose with alacrity from his crowded table. "Just what I was wanting, something to take my thoughts off the follies of Werner and the Neptunists in general. I should like to be run in with you, Barrington; you'd be so dignified over it. Now out with it; why are we likely to share a cell in Newgate?"

"Have it your own way, then," said Hervey, and gave him the particulars of the cruise of the *Kestrel* and what she had brought home from it. The Frenchman's previous residence under his roof and his method of leaving the

240

latter he decided for the moment to suppress.

Tall, bright-eyed, prematurely wrinkled, Mr. Touchwood listened with attention. "To put a name to your crime, it sounds more like body-snatching than anything else. And you say your good housekeeper is alarmed at the young man's condition?"

"I am alarmed myself," confessed Hervey. "But if you will be so extremely kind as to come and have a look at him——"

"I can't cure with a look, you know," returned Mr. Touchwood, lifting an old coat off a heap of dusty books and tipping some ammonites out of a depressed hat. "Gad, it's touching, the faith you laymen exhibit! And what if I *have forgotten all I ever knew?*"

Des Sablières was worse than when Hervey had left, his breathing still quicker. There was a stain, too, on the pillow. The opponent of Werner dropped his bantering manner the moment his eyes fell on him, and his face became grave.

"This looks as if we had our work cut out," he observed in a low tone.

At the end of a brief examination he led Hervey to a corner of the room. "I shall stay the night here, Barrington, if you'll allow me." He was purely the doctor now.

"Is it as serious as that?" asked Hervey, considerably taken aback.

"It is very serious indeed, my dear Barrington, and won't be a short business either—if he pulls through, that is. Of course he may go off the hooks within the next day or two, but we must hope for a fight. Only he doesn't look . . . but you can never tell."

"What is it?" asked Hervey unhappily.

"Congestion of the lungs—and a bad case of it. It's only just beginning too, poor fellow."

The Sapphire Necklace and the Major of the Buffs

"It soon appeared that nothing would be done by authority. . . . But the Princess would not suffer any means, however improbable, to be left untried. . . . As one expedient failed, another was suggested."—Rasselas, chap. xxxiv.

"Mr. Rowl"

There were those of his acquaintance who continually enlarged upon the physical likeness between Frederick William Forrest, third Viscount Fulgrave, and Arthur Wellesley, Marquis of Wellington; but even the most indulgent had not gone so far as to hint at any similarity in character. And indeed it was agreed among them that Lord Fulgrave, despite his eagle nose and fine presence, would have made but a poor show at commanding even a regiment in the Peninsula, since he could not, it was suspected, control one young lady, and she his own daughter.

Juliana would have been very angry had she known of these strictures, for she was extremely fond and proud of her handsome father, and no one had ever heard her show him anything approaching disrespect. But she could not avoid knowing that he was far from being as Roman a parent as his nose seemed to denote. She might get from him her good looks—with the merciful exception of the nose in question—but her strong will she drew from the distaff side, though her mother had been so long dead that Juliana did not recognize the heritage.

She was sitting now, at half past four in the afternoon, in a bow window of their house in Grosvenor Square awaiting the return of Lord Fulgrave, who was engaged upon a quest for her. Juliana certainly could not accuse him of lukewarmness over this not yet accomplished desire of hers, the release of M. des Sablières, and often and often she told herself, and her parent too, what a good father she had.

But if Lord Fulgrave had known everything, he might not have returned the compliment. He might, he did know, the story of the prank which had brought about such a train of unfortunate consequences for the young Frenchman (not to speak of leading his daughter to break off her own engagement); and he fully approved her determination to get injustice righted. But he did not know that Juliana, disgusted at the evasive attitude of the Transport Office, which "regretted that nothing could be done at present," had been, since June, in communication with an escape agent at Plymouth, and very little suspected the reason why she never wore her sapphire necklace nowadays. How could he imagine that the gems were (or had been) in the custody of a low-looking individual who dwelt at the sign of three balls in Cheapside, or that Juliana, heavily veiled, was in the habit of calling every week for letters at a little stationer's in Mount Street. Or that these letters, in a sufficiently illiterate handwriting, were from a man in a back street of Plymouth who signed himself "your loving Aunt," and that, with a few variations, they usually contained something of this sort:

So far, my dear Neice, my atempts to procure you a maidservant have not bin successful, the Girl not bein able to Leave her present Sitation. But I shall not fail to inform you when She can do so and then I have a Sutable gownd for her to travvel in.

By this time Raoul des Sablières had made acquaintance with that loving aunt and the suitable gown, but of this Juliana was not yet aware; indeed, she was uneasy because for a fortnight there had been no letter for her at the stationer's from this affectionate (and expensive) relative of hers. Juliana had no qualms about her course of action in itself, since she conceived it a sacred duty to free M. des Sablières at whatever cost, and she had only slight intermittent ones about having kept this nefarious manner of accomplishing it a secret from her Papa because she thought (quite rightly) that the knowledge of it would have disturbed him. But she did have some searchings of conscience over the manner in which she had established contact with Samuel Creedy. For this purpose she had availed herself of the services of a devoted London admirer, Mr. Charles Methuen; but she had at least been perfectly open from the first as to the only reward he could expect for them—her sincere and undying gratitude. And for this guerdon alone the besotted Mr. Methuen had posted down to Plymouth, had engaged in various questionable negotiations, and had finally established communication (prepaid) between the object of his hopeless admiration and a gentleman who, unlike the much suspected Zachary Miller, did really drive a genuine and profitable trade in escapes, and who, so far, had been shrewd enough to avoid detection. But the risks to himself were undeniably so great that he could ask a proportionately elevated price for his services. Hence the disappearance of Miss Forrest's sapphires.

And not for one moment did Miss Forrest grudge the jewels, but, as she sat there in the window staring at the flowers in the jardinière, she was wondering whether she had not parted with them to no purpose whatever. It was now thirteen weeks since M. des Sablières had started from Norman Cross for the hulks, and nine since she had engaged the good offices of Creedy. The latter, it is true, had warned Mr. Methuen that the business might take months; one had to be so careful and so "fly"; however, the lady being so free with her money would make things easier. Not being a fool, Juliana sometimes wondered whether she had not been too free with it, and whether Mr. Creedy would not continue till the end of time merely to report that the girl was unable to leave her situation—although he would not get the final instalment of his price till Miss Forrest knew that he had succeeded.

So the weeks went by and "Mr. Rowl" was still entombed—caged up with the lowest of the low. No word of complaint, indeed, was to be found in the couple of letters, grateful and brief, which she had received from him since the *Ganges* had engulfed him. They pierced Juliana all the more for that. . . . Yet when the first came to her she had been a little afraid to open it. How many times since that day at Norman Cross had she not speculated, with hot cheeks, on the interpretation which he might have put on her forward behaviour, which was still a source of wonder to herself. She, to give a kiss at all—to give it unasked—and to give it to a Frenchman! . . . But she need not have been afraid. Whether or no he understood her impulse (which she scarcely understood herself) there was nothing in either of his letters which could be construed into a reference to it. Her answers also were brief and restrained; she was so afraid of putting the authorities on the track of Creedy's efforts.

But, after all, Juliana was telling herself this afternoon, even if Creedy failed, she had now a second string to her bow and a much more respectable one. Once she was sure of its efficacy she would write off to her loving aunt and tell him that she had changed her mind and would not require a domestic from Plymouth. The idea of this alternative plan had only come to her ten days ago, when she had heard, by pure chance, that the captain of a French privateer had recently been released from prison and allowed parole because of his humane treatment of some English prisoners previously in his hands. And suddenly, like a heaven-sent memory, had come to her M. des Sablières' brief reference, on that fatal day by the stream, to his having stood between a wounded British officer and the savage Poles at Albuera. Surely, for such an act as that, the Transport Office would release him from the hulks!

But how to identify the officer, and how to get his evidence? She did not even know his regiment, much less his name. But a call at the Horse Guards by Lord Fulgrave soon produced both. The regiments cut up by the French cavalry charge at Albuera proved to be the 3rd, 48th, and 66th Foot. Now it appeared that of the officers of the 3rd—The Buffs—who were captured, one, a Major Brackenbury, escaped soon afterwards, and when at length he succeeded in reaching General Hill's division at Villa Viciosa he was known to have said, in reporting the infamous behaviour of the Polish lancers to the wounded, that he only wished he could meet and show his gratitude to the French hussar who, at great risk to himself, had saved him from their further brutality. As it was, he was so badly wounded in the head that he was never able to return to the hardships of a campaign, and he was at present on light duty at the dépôt at Canterbury. Lord Fulgrave wrote to this officer with the idea of going down to Canterbury to see him, but there came a reply from Major Brackenbury stating that he himself had just come to London on leave, that he would be only too delighted to answer any questions, was putting up at an hotel in Jermyn Street, and would call upon Lord Fulgrave at any hour convenient to him. On which Lord Fulgrave went off to call on him instead, promising Juliana that he would bring him back to dine, if he were disengaged.

Miss Forrest got up and looked out of the window. Papa was late; it was nearly dinner-time already. How long would the Transport Office take to move this time? Why had she not heard from Plymouth? Would she have to reveal her own mole-like activities if—

Wheels at last. Her father's chariot, and—yes, two gentlemen getting out of it.

*

A couple of hours later the pleasant soldierly looking man with the long scar from scalp to cheekbone was gone again, having dined with them and told his tale. To-morrow he would go to the Transport Office and repeat it there. He was confident that something could be done—should be bitterly disappointed if it could not, or if, when they were confronted, as they must eventually be, he could not conscientiously identify his rescuer in Miss Forrest's protégé. For, as he pointed out, it might have been someone else whom Captain des Sablières had saved; he believed there had been some other cases of the kind.

But Juliana would not acknowledge such a possibility. It was "Mr. Rowl" who had risked his life to save Major Brackenbury—for he had risked it, leaping from his horse and standing, sabre in hand, over that officer as he lay on the ground disabled and blinded with blood, to protect him from the lancer's onslaught. Finding that his furious remonstrances were of no avail, the young hussar had thereupon sprung forward, avoiding the lance point by a miracle of agility, had seized the Pole's horse by the bridle, and, raining blows up at the rider with the flat of his sword, had literally beaten him off. Then he had knelt down by his foe, tried to wipe the blood from his face, and had said, in a voice still shaking with indignation (and, to Major Brackenbury's surprise, in good English) that he hoped he would remember the scoundrel was no Frenchman. Moreover, ere he vaulted on to his horse again and galloped after his squadron he had told a couple of infantrymen to take the prisoner to the rear with all consideration for his state. It was small wonder that Juliana had a picture which she was able to contemplate with great satisfaction for the remainder of that day. . . .

*

It was Lord Fulgrave's custom, on most afternoons, to take a short siesta in his own room. But the day after the Major's visit he wandered in search of a book into the smaller library, found it very snug there, observed a comfortable winged armchair—more comfortable, by gad, than his own!—and dropped into it.

Already that morning he had received a note from Major Brackenbury, saying that his call at the Transport Office had been most satisfactory, that the Commissioners had been impressed with his testimony, and were about to take steps in the matter. Presenting his respects and compliments to Miss Forrest, he desired she might be informed of this happy prospect.

There had not been much delay in informing Miss Forrest, for she had almost snatched the letter from her father's hands. Juliana and her Frenchman . . . and her remorse . . . and her determination to get him released . . . all so violent and disturbing . . . dear girl, it was in her spirited character . . . he would not have her changed, no, he would not have her changed. But this young man, now—it did occur to a father, even an easy-going one, to wonder what he was *like*. . . . So his lordship began to wonder . . . with the result that his book was shortly on the floor, a handkerchief over his face, and quiet reigning in the smaller library.

But about this time Peters, the second footman, was reluctantly admitting into the hall a small, shabby individual who asked for her Ladyship the Honourable Miss Forrest. This person was obsequious in his manner and démodé in his dress; he also squinted. Peters was not drawn to him, and what he could be wanting with the Honourable Juliana passed his comprehension; but the visitor maintained that her honourable Ladyship would be extremely vexed if he were dismissed without delivering the message with which he was charged, and which he refused to entrust to the ear of Peters or any one else.

Not liking to leave him in the hall, Peters cast about in his mind for a place to bestow the caller not too exalted or too richly furnished for his low estate and doubtful honesty, nor yet too humble to be entered by Miss Forrest if she really did accord an interview to this Person. He decided upon the smaller library, which would fulfil both these requirements, and where, in addition, he could turn the key on the visitor. So the Person was shown in there, told haughtily that he might sit down, and was left, locked in with the last being into whose presence Peters would knowingly have ushered him.

At first, indeed, the visitor was unaware in what august company he found himself, since the high winged chair effectually hid its occupant from the gaze of any one entering the room, so, making his way to the chair on the other side of the fireplace, he sat meekly down . . . to be glued to his seat by the discovery which he then made about the opposite chair. Next moment too the veiled sleeper stretched, yawned, mumbled something, took the handkerchief from his face and revealed—Lord Wellington.

The Person seemed to dwindle as he sat, his hands clutching the seat of his chair, his eyes fixed. . . .

Lord Fulgrave sat up.

"Who the devil are you?" he demanded, "and what are you doing in my library?"

"Sir Arthur . . ." faltered the little man, squirming on his chair, the muscles which otherwise would have pulled him on to his feet paralysed by terror.

"My name is not Arthur," retorted Lord Fulgrave indignantly. "You have come to the wrong house.—Ah, I see. . . ." Unconsciously he stroked his nose, not ill pleased. "Your acquaintance with Lord Wellington seems to date from some years back," he remarked. "But my name is Fulgrave, Lord Fulgrave, and I should be glad—dashed glad," he added, as he took in his visitor's appearance more fully, "to know what you are doing here!"

The Person cleared his constricted throat. "If you please, my Lord, I have come to see her Ladyship, Lady the Honourable Miss Forrest."

Lord Fulgrave leant forward. "You have come to see my daughter!" he exclaimed incredulously. "My daughter! What about?"

"If it please your Lordship," said his vis-à-vis, moistening his lips, "I can only tell that to Lady Forrest."

The Viscount Fulgrave eyed him with dislike and scorn. He made a sound between his lips indicative of these feelings. "Then you can get out at once! My daughter has no secrets from me!" And he rose and went to the door.

"What's this—what the devil's this? Who has dared to lock this door?"

"I . . . I think the footman who admitted me," said the little man nervously. He too, at last, had risen.

"The footman lock you in with *me*! He must be mad!" Lord Fulgrave strode to the bell-pull, then dropped it without ringing. "Look here, my man, you need not think that I shall permit you to see my daughter, but before I allow you to leave the house I insist on your telling me what you have come about."

To be locked in indefinitely with Sir Arthur Wellesley's nose was too much for a fellow captive's resolution. "It's along of this maidservant from Devonshire as her Ladyship was wishing for," he said, his little light-lashed eyes darting furtive glances at the aristocratic visage; encouraged by the blank expression thereon he was emboldened to add, "Your Lordship wouldn't be troubled about a little matter like that."

"I certainly don't know anything of it," agreed his Lordship, who was not indeed in the habit of engaging his own female domestics. Nor, for the matter of that, was Juliana, such affairs being in the hands of Mrs. Webber, the housekeeper. But, whichever of them had manifested this desire for a maid from Devonshire, she seemed to Lord Fulgrave to have gone to a curious stratum of society to gratify it. He was puzzled.

"Are you any relation of the girl's?"

"No, my Lord."

"What's your name?"

"Drane, Sir—my Lord; Joseph Drane."

"Well, Mr. Drane, if that is your errand, I think you had better see my housekeeper." And Lord Fulgrave again put out his hand to the bell-pull.

"I do beseech your Lordship," said Mr. Drane, clasping his hands, "to let me see her Ladyship. She—she will be terribly put out if she don't see me, I assure you."

This prediction seemed to Lord Fulgrave very wide of the mark.

"Has Miss Forrest ever seen you before?"

"No, my Lord."

"Is she expecting to see you?"

"No, my Lord. There should have been a letter from Devonshire, but—but there was a hitch about sending a letter, so I was to come and give her Ladyship a message."

"A message from whom?"

Mr. Drane was silent, and shifted on his feet.

"Come, come, don't you know? A message from the girl, I suppose, or from her relations?"

"Yes, yes, my Lord, that is it—from her aunt. Your Lordship is quite correct."

And if Mr. Drane, after his mutism, had not been so stumblingly eager to assure him of this, Lord Fulgrave might have been more satisfied. As it was he gazed upon him with a growing frown.

"I must get to the bottom of this," he declared, and this time he did ring the bell. But even as he rang there came the sound of a key turning in the lock. "I left the man in here, Madam," said the voice of Peters, and Miss Forrest herself entered the room.

News from Plymouth

"The price was no subject of debate. The Princess was in ecstasies when she heard that her favourite was alive, and might so cheaply be ransomed."—*Rasselas*, chap. xxxvii.

Juliana's eyes fell immediately upon Mr. Drane, and the momentary bewilderment in them was succeeded by a look of comprehension. "You have come, I suppose to—" she began eagerly—and then perceived that Mr. Drane was not alone. "Oh, I did not know that you were in here, Papa," she said with obvious discomposure.

"No, my dear, it is evident that you did not," returned her parent with meaning. "But I think it is just as well that I am."

It was plain that Juliana did not share this opinion, nor Mr. Drane either.

"I understand," resumed his lordship, "that this Mr. Drane has come about some matter of engaging a maidservant from the country. If I may say so without offence to him, I think you or Mrs. Webber choose strange intermediaries for such a business. I imagined—not that I know anything about it—that such negotiations were usually conducted through the medium of a female."

Neither party gave assent or dissent to this. Mr. Drane was looking agonized.

Lord Fulgrave turned to his daughter. "Who is this man, Juliana?" he demanded, with a manner which, joined to the Arthurian nose, caused Mr. Drane's legs suddenly to tremble beneath him.

"I suppose that he came to bring me a message," replied Juliana with fair composure. "I . . . had better tell you, I think, Papa, because it is a matter in which you are interested too. I hope that this . . . this gentleman brings me news from Plymouth—*Plymouth*, Papa!"

"Yes, your Ladyship," put in Mr. Drane encouraged. "News from Mr. Creedy."

"Oh!" Juliana's face lit up; she took a step forward. "Is it good news at last?"

"Yes, your Ladyship."

"Then tell us about it! My father will be delighted to hear it too. Listen, Papa," she said, and clung to his arm.

Mr. Drane's demeanour, though still deprecatory, became touched with the consciousness of merit. "Creedy sent word to me, my Lady, being his brother-in-law, because he did not like to trust the post this time. I was to tell your honourable Ladyship that the . . . the person in question was got away and brought to his house as arranged; it was the afternoon of the 10th. Creedy rigged him out as you suggested; he looked fine, he said, and no one would have told him from a girl; he left early next morning, and must have got clear away, or Creedy would have heard else. Creedy gave him a map, Miss—my Lady—and every penny of the money provided for the purpose, and ventures to think it may be counted a good clean job, and not dear at the price."

"No, no!" cried Juliana, her eyes shining, "not dear at any price. Papa, Papa, do you understand? He's got away—he's free—he's out of that horrible ship!" Still hanging on his arm she raised a glowing face to his unresponsive one. "It is almost too good to be true. And those are all the details you know, Mr. Drane?"

"That's all the message Creedy sent me, Miss."

"But why, if M. des Sablières escaped on the tenth—a week ago to-day—has there been this delay in letting me know it?"

"The message had to be passed on like, Miss, from one to another," replied Mr. Drane mysteriously. "Slower than the post, that is."

"I understand. And how soon, after leaving Plymouth, would he get away altogether?"

"That would depend, my Lady, on whether he had to——"

"Am I to understand," broke in Viscount Fulgrave in his House of Lords manner, "that your Frenchman has escaped from the hulks just when it seems clear that, owing to Major Brackenbury's intervention, the Transport Office is on the point of releasing him on their own initiative? That seems to me singularly unfortunate!"

"Oh, Papa, do not be so prudent!" cried his radiant daughter. "I daresay the Transport Office would not have moved for weeks, and every——"

"It seems to me singularly unfortunate," repeated his Lordship. "And I should like to know how the young man has contrived to let you know about it? Who is this Creed, or Creedy, who 'rigged him out' and provided him with money? A British subject?"

"I suppose so," said Juliana lightly.

"Then I hope he does not realize," said Lord Fulgrave with majesty, "what an unpatriotic, what a shocking thing he has done; I hope he did it in ignorance! But ignorance will not save him from the penalty of his misconduct if it is found out. Glad as I should be to know that the young man was released, I do not like to think that any Englishman is so lost to shame as to connive at his escape for money—since that is evidently what it comes to, this 'job cheap at the price'! You, Sir"—he addressed the diminishing Drane—"beware what you are about! This Creedy has committed felony—it is clearly so laid down by last year's Act—and he stands in imminent danger of transportation!"

"But only if someone informs against him," protested Juliana, recalled to a somewhat nervous attention. "And you would hardly do that, would you, Papa, you who realize the horrible injustice of M. des Sablières' imprisonment!"

"That has nothing to do with the behaviour of this Creed, or Creedy," retorted his Lordship with truth. Once more he addressed Mr. Creedy's representative. "Situated as I am, feeling a compassionate interest in this young Frenchman, it would be unbecoming in me to take any active steps against this man in Plymouth. But I warn you, I warn you, Mr. Drane, that you are both playing with fire. Tell him that I say so. You may go!"

From Mr. Drane's appearance during these last two speeches one would have imagined that he would now bolt gladly for the door. But he did not. He shuffled his feet, looked down, round, and finally at Juliana.

"Would your Ladyship give me a word alone?" he murmured.

"Certainly not!" replied her father. "Have you not delivered the message with which you were charged by this . . . miscreant?"

"Yes, my Lord," said Mr. Drane meekly. "But there still remains"—he gazed agonizedly at Juliana—"the little matter of the money . . . the small balance . . ."

"The balance!" exclaimed his Lordship. "Money—whose money? And what has that to do with us?"

"It was I who found the money on M. des Sablières' behalf for Mr. Creedy," announced Juliana hastily, and very pink. "It is true that there does remain a small balance due to him, which I had forgotten for the moment. I will fetch it, Mr. Drane."

And she went quickly out of the room before her father had recovered from his stupefaction sufficiently to stop her, and so light-hearted that the coming reckoning with him did not trouble her much. But she likewise hastened back because she did not know what, in her absence, Papa might not say or do to the poor little man.

Indeed on her return Mr. Drane's feathers were still more drooping; he looked like a small bird dishevelled by tempest and yet holding on to his twig.

But he was the only occupant of the room, at which Juliana was rather surprised and yet not surprised.

"His Lordship's not gone to set the runners on me, has he, my Lady?" he quavered. "He spoke to me something cruel, and I can't think why I was put in here with him!"

"Neither can I," confessed Juliana. "No, I do not think he will take any steps against you; but you must remember that all this has been a great shock to him, for he knew nothing at all about the matter. You are not to imagine that he did," she added rather haughtily.

"No, my Lady, I could see that. Very unfortunate it come out before him, but I couldn't help that. Thank you, my Lady. I'm sure I wish your Ladyship very good health . . . and you'll be able to keep his Lordship from saying anything about Creedy, won't you, my Lady?"

Lord Fulgrave was walking agitatedly up and down his study when, thinking it best to seek him at once, his daughter entered.

"Juliana! I cannot credit it! My own daughter involved in a felony! And I who was threatening this person in Plymouth with the rigours of the law! . . . This Drane may go and lay information against you, Juliana."

"I don't think he will, Papa. You frightened him too much on his own account."

"It would be a good thing if I could frighten you, Miss! Do you know that you could be put in the pillory for what you have done?"

To which Miss Juliana very unsatisfactorily replied that she should have deserved this punishment, not for having provided the money to get M. des Sablières out of the hulks, but for having sent him there in the first instance.

"Juliana," said her father, drawing up his commanding form, "I find your extreme preoccupation with this young man almost unbecoming."

"I am sorry to hear that, Papa. I assure you that I was never in the least preoccupied with him until I injured him."

"Then I am afraid that I must look to see this undue interest of yours continue, for I repeat my conviction that his escape, for which you appear to be responsible, is very unfortunate at this juncture, and may be found to have injured him still more. And how, pray, did you find the money—was it a large sum?"

"I sold my sapphires," replied his daughter succinctly. But, as her father uttered an exclamation of incredulity and horror she went on quickly, her face clouding as it had not at his reproaches, "Papa, do you really think it is so unfortunate, his escape? If Major Brackenbury's testimony really had any effect, I was going to write to Creedy and tell him to cease his efforts. I did not know that he had already succeeded."

"But how did you get into communication with Creedy in the first place? Does he know who you are? Did his letters come here, or . . . Juliana, is it possible that you have stooped to a clandestine correspondence?"

"But, Papa," said Miss Forrest, a dimple appearing, "that, surely, can only be a matter of reproach if it be conducted with a lover? And Mr. Creedy, as he was described to me——"

"Who described him to you? You have had a go-between in this!" cried Lord Fulgrave. "Who was it—that creature Drane?"

"No, somebody more presentable," said Juliana. "Mr. Methuen kindly went down to Plymouth for me."

Lord Fulgrave stared wildly as he discovered more ramifications of crime. "Good God! Methuen drawn into it too! Juliana, I scarcely know you for my own daughter! And we are all in the hands of this Creedy and his accomplices, if he chooses to blackmail us. I can never hold up my head again!"

And he sat down and took the fine head in question between his hands.

"Oh, Papa," said Juliana penitently, "I am sorry if you feel so deeply over what you are in no way responsible for. But I am sure Creedy is too cautious to risk exposure; we shall never hear of him again. Darling Papa, I was *obliged* to do it. I could not sleep at nights knowing what M. des Sablières was undergoing through my fault."

"I hoped you would have learnt a lesson over that affair," lamented her parent. "But no, you are as wilful as ever! You told me that you were obliged to show Mulholland that you were not in subjection to his whims—and look at the results. What the results of this may be I don't like to think. I have been very weak with you. You want a husband, Juliana, to keep you in check . . . but if you indulge in many more of these extraordinary proceedings you are not likely to get one.”

Having regard to the number of her suitors both parties knew this to be a mere rhetorical threat, and it passed without comment. Juliana sat down on the arm of the chair.

“Well, I am not anxious to leave you, Papa,” she observed in a resigned voice.

“That I can quite understand,” replied his Lordship. “In no other man's house would you be allowed a tithe of the freedom which is allowed you in this.”

“Then I had certainly better stay in it,” retorted Miss Forrest with composure. “And now I will tell you everything, dearest Papa.” She slipped an arm round his neck. “I had no intention of keeping you in the dark for ever, you know.”

“No—only until there was no chance of my putting a stop to your actions,” groaned her sire. “Well, proceed. . . .”

Juliana's confession ended in the customary way—in absolution. She was genuinely sorry that her father should feel himself involved, through no fault whatever of his own, in what he considered a most reprehensible transaction, and that no assurance of hers of her entire readiness to take all the blame, if necessary, consoled him at all. How could she take the blame in the eyes of the world, he asked? He spoke much, and justifiably, too, of the situation in which she had placed him with regard to Major Brackenbury and his efforts, which would now be rendered useless; what, he enquired, was the good of all this to-do about Poles and gratitude when his daughter had stultified it by her previous machinations? There was not much that Juliana could say in reply, but she did begin to feel that it was perhaps a pity she had rendered the “Poles and gratitude” move of no avail. Yet, after all, M. des Sablières had now been free for eight days, and it was surely better actually to be free than merely to have the prospect of freedom, and then probably only of freedom in a modified form—restoration to parole. Perhaps before very long she would receive a letter from France; for she would not allow herself to dwell on the possibility of his being recaptured. It would be her doing that he was given back to his mother and his sister, and . . . Was there really no other lady to welcome his return?

But she realized, too, that she could at best only receive a letter, if ever she got that. She would never see him again in person now. By saving him in this way she had banished him; whereas, had he been saved through the agency of Major Brackenbury, he would have had to come to London for identification. But now, if he had got away, it was good-bye to him.

. . . Unless, perhaps, years hence, when the war was over—if ever it was—she should travel in France, and, passing perhaps through the Orléanais, where he had said that he lived . . . She saw herself travelling there, after her marriage. But travelling with whom? Especially since her late unfortunate experience, she did not feel sufficient predilection for any man mentally to fill that vacant place beside her in the chaise which rolled along the straight, unknown roads of France. A chance meeting years hence. . . . Would she even know him again?

Long after she had dismissed her maid that night Juliana sat staring into the mirror. But it was not her own image that she saw.

*

"Papa," said Juliana, coming to his study next morning "if you think I ought to write to Major Brackenbury——" But her father was not there.

She wandered round, waiting for him. It really was awkward about Major Brackenbury. . . . Where was Papa? After a moment or two, finding that he did not appear, she went to a bookcase, hunted about on the lower shelves and pulled out a large thin volume which she carried to a table in the window and opened. It was an atlas; and in view of Miss Forrest's preoccupation with a certain young man who was, or had been, making his way eastward from Plymouth, it was very natural that she should consult it.

Only, oddly enough, it was a map of France over which she was poring, and her finger, after some fairly wild excursions, was resting firmly on the town of Orleans.

She hastily removed it as the door opened. But it was not her father, it was a footman.

"If you please, Madam, Major Brackenbury is in the drawing room asking to see you at once."

Major Brackenbury in person! What was she going to say to him? Her instinct was to make a clean breast of the whole business, yet at the same time to suggest that, if the Transport Board were ignorant of the escape, it was unwise to check any benevolent impulse in them. In any case she must tell him the truth.

Major Brackenbury—in uniform this time—was standing rather stiffly in the middle of the great drawing room, where the statuary which flanked the tall windows showed white against the heavy crimson curtains. As he advanced to meet her Juliana saw that he looked very grave. He knew what had happened, then, and was displeased.

"I am afraid that I must prepare you for some bad news, Miss Forrest," he said, and his tone was not one of displeasure but regret.

Juliana paled a little. "I think I can guess it. It is that M. des Sablières has escaped, been recaptured, and that the Transport Office are now going to refuse him, on account of his escape, the justice which is his due. Oh, what a crowning piece of ill fortune!" And she smote her hands together in a sudden gust of rebellion.

Major Brackenbury looked at her, then he looked away.

"Yes, he has escaped; but he has not been recaptured. There is no fault to find in the attitude of the Commissioners. They were on the point of despatching instructions for his being sent to London for identification. . . . But this unfortunate enterprise of his . . ." He stopped.

Juliana closed her eyes. In that sunlit room the most deadly presentiments seemed to swarm round her, cold, mothlike things. "Yes, this unfortunate enterprise. . . . Please do not keep me in suspense!"

"It is so difficult to tell you," murmured the Major unhappily. "And God knows I am sorry enough on my own account as well as on yours. The fact is, that though des Sablières has not been recaptured, the Transport Board can do nothing further for him. . . . Can't you guess why, Miss Forrest?"

Then the moths fluttered right into Juliana's brain. Yes, she could guess, and she did not need to embody her guess in words. She sat down in the nearest chair and put her hands over her face.

"Miss Forrest," came the soldier's voice solicitously, "this has been a great shock to you. May I ring for some wine—or for your maid?"

Juliana removed her hands and mutely shook her head. Major Brackenbury stood in a shaft full of golden motes, like a heavenly messenger; but his scarlet coat hurt the eye.

"You are trying to tell me that he preferred death to recapture," she heard herself say in a dull voice.

"Substantially, that is true, I am sorry to say. He was drowned on the afternoon of the 13th, while attempting to evade pursuit by swimming the Stowey river near its mouth. The official report of the escape and . . . and its fatal termination was only received yesterday at the Transport Office from Plymouth; but I am afraid that there cannot be the slightest doubt of its truth."

Juliana suddenly stood up; the roses of the carpet swam a little. "Oh, *how* I am punished!" she said in a very low voice. "It was I who contrived his escape. If only, only I had left him where he was! . . . Major Brackenbury, it can't be true! I can't believe it—it must be a false report!"

"My dear Miss Forrest," said the Major of the Buffs, "I only wish I could think so. But I am afraid there is no chance of that. The tragedy was witnessed. . . . Pray do not take it so to heart; if you had to do with his escape you acted with the best intentions. Oh, I am indeed grieved about it, deeply grieved!"

But Juliana had left him and gone to one of the lofty windows. She felt so cold—as cold as the marble nymph beside her. Tears did not come, though there was cause enough for them. . . . It was her hand that had lured him to that river, just as on that day in March. . . . She began ineffectually to plait the curtain fringe. Drowned . . . drowned on the verge of freedom. . . .

"Mr. Rowl"

Major Brackenbury, in the middle of the room, embarrassed, compassionate, hesitating whether to approach her, looked round with an air of relief when the door opened. It was Lord Fulgrave.

"I have only just been informed, Major, that you——" he began, and saw his daughter motionless at the window with her back to the visitor. "What's this?"

Major Brackenbury told him, adding, almost in a whisper, "And the saddest part is, there seems no doubt that, subject to my identification of him, the Transport Office was prepared to recommend the unfortunate young man for complete release and a cartel back to France."

"Dear, dear," said Lord Fulgrave. He glanced at the window. "My poor girl!—What, are you going, Sir?"

"For the present, my Lord." He too glanced at the window. "Make my adieux for me, if you please. God knows how much I regret that I can never now pay my debt."

He was gone, and Lord Fulgrave approached his daughter. "Juliana, my dear . . ."

Juliana turned round. Her father had never seen her so white and still. "Papa, I think I am a murderess!"

"Oh, nonsense, my love!" said he, shocked. "I am as grieved as you, but we must not take extreme views like that."

"I have been nothing but his evil genius all along," said Juliana, looking into some invisible distance, her eyes dilated. "And now at last—though I thought I was doing him a service—I have killed him!"

Lord Fulgrave, just a trifle alarmed, drew her arm within his own and patted it. "Come into the study, dearest child, and if you want to talk about it to your old father, we shall be undisturbed."

At that, suddenly, she kissed him, clinging closely to him; and, putting his arm round her, he drew her away from the marble population of the drawing room. In his study he put her into his own chair, smoothing her hair as if she were a child, and thinking apprehensively, "I believe she ought to cry—she ought to cry!" But Juliana leant back with her eyes closed, and for some time said nothing; then, without opening them, she observed, "I am fully punished now, Papa, am I not?" and he knew not what to reply. Some minutes later she got up, and began to walk about the room clasping and unclasping her hands. "If only I could see him once, just once, to tell him how bitterly I am grieved, how bitterly I repent!"

"Well, perhaps, my dear," said her father, stirred to an unwonted flight of fancy, "perhaps he knows it, after all." He made a hurried mental calculation as to what unseen sphere would be inhabited at the moment by a departed Papist (presumably des Sablières was a Papist) and, feeling uncertain because of this queer, unprovable Purgatory of theirs, returned to safer ground. "While he was alive, at any rate, poor fellow, he must have known that you did your very best for him."

Juliana, who gave no signs of having heard these attempts at consolation, had stopped in her walk. She had come to the table in the window which still supported the open atlas. This she made as if to close, and did not. "I borrowed your atlas, Papa," she said in a choking voice, and before Lord Fulgrave could recover from his rather alarmed surprise at this abrupt change of topic, she had flung herself sobbing beside it, her arms outflung across the map of France, her head upon it too, and her tears making inappropriately damp the departments of Creuse and Haute-Vienne.

"Will He Hate Me Still?"

"For some time after my retreat I rejoiced like a tempest-beaten sailor at his entrance into the harbour. . . . But . . . I have been for some time unsettled and distracted: my mind is disturbed with a thousand perplexities of doubt."—*Rasselas*, chap. xxi.

The *Kestrel* was gently swinging again at her moorings in the river which reflected the blue above; even the pair of wagtails were once more making their excited and jerky darts over the little lawn, oblivious this time of human presence. Perhaps indeed they were hardly aware that a man was sitting on the seat beneath the mulberry tree, because he sat so still, with an elbow on the arm of it, and a hand over his eyes.

"Mr. Rowl"

"It won't be a short business." No, indeed; centuries long it seemed already. Was it really only a week to-day that Hervey had first stood with Alexander Touchwood beside that bed in the spare room? And since then he had been beside it with him so often . . . and oftener still alone, listening to the difficult breathing, trying to shut his ears to the scraps of delirium, with their broken revelations of horror and suffering, the agonized entreaties for air . . . air . . . he was stifling in this place . . . why would they not open a scuttle and let in a breath . . . just one breath for a moment! or at other times when the fevered mind was haunted by that crazy climb from the window, when it became apparent what a strain it had been on nerve and courage, when the dreamer thought that he had to do it again and shrank from it, crying "I can't—I can't!" and no one, not even the good and untiring Touchwood, could get through the mists of delirium to tell him that he need not: when life seemed to be burning itself out to no purpose, fighting a remorseless foe that must win in the end, the foe that he, Hervey Barrington, had hounded on to the attack. For the voice was always at his ear, "If he dies, you will have killed him."

And this had been going on for a week . . . and the fight was still being waged. But it was plainly a losing battle; indeed Touchwood had said this morning that the boy could not possibly last another twenty-four hours at this rate; it must end to-day one way or the other; either the crisis must come or his heart would give out, and he was afraid, now, that the latter alternative was much the more probable, and that they had all better prepare themselves for it. Hervey was trying to do this now under the mulberry tree, where only nine days ago the Señora Tomás had sat and given umbrage to Mrs. Jeremy. . . . He was trying to look at the situation dispassionately: to tell himself that, after all, he had only done his duty in making des Sablières a prisoner in the first instance, and that since then he had saved him from drowning, endangered his own career and reputation for his sake, and cared for him not less vigilantly than if he had been his own son or brother. And yet, illogically, the sense of guilty responsibility remained as strong as ever. If des Sablières died, he died through his agency. . . .

Moreover, des Sablières knew it and—worse still—supposed his captor to be gloating over his suffering. This was no conjecture; he had said it with his own parched and discoloured lips when Hervey, coming in very early the first morning to see how he did, had observed in a rather horrified voice to Touchwood, "He is still in that pain, then?" And des Sablières had turned his brilliant, tortured eyes on him and gasped out, "Yes, you are . . . getting an even better revenge . . . than you had hoped . . . Captain Barrington!" On which Hervey, after standing for a moment like a man struck, had gone out of the room.

A little later, when Mr. Touchwood came out to say that he was going to try if cupping would give relief, he had found Hervey pacing up and down the landing in uncontrollable agitation, had been seized by him, had the complete story poured into his astonished ear, and been implored to try to disabuse his patient's mind of that most dreadful idea, that his rescuer had been pleased to see him in pain. But the moment had gone, perhaps for ever; Raoul's mind was too clouded thereafter for explanations, and very soon he recognized Hervey no more; though in the many hours to come in which Captain Barrington watched and nursed him the latter never felt safe from recognition, and tried always, as far as possible, to keep out of range of the eyes to which sight might suddenly be restored.

This unfortunate episode had made the strain of the past week much heavier for Hervey than for any of the others, though, as far as actual nursing went, Mrs. Jeremy had spent more hours at the bedside than he, in spite of the fact that she had her other duties to attend to as well. Her devotion had been wonderful, and sometimes Raoul had seemed to know her when he knew no one else; he knew at least that she was a woman, and more than once had called her "mother." It was she who had contrived to keep him quiet while the broken wrist was set. She was with him now; in an hour's time Hervey would take her place; the doctor would be back again before that.

Captain Barrington got up; he had been sitting still so long that he was almost stiff. He walked slowly over the lawn to the river wall. He was conscious in a way, of the glory of the morning, even of the snowy gull balancing itself out there on the *Kestrel*'s mast, but he was thinking how paltry, now, seemed his own great decision of a week ago which he had thought so momentous, against the greater which would be made to-day. And yet the life in the balance was only that of an unknown young man, and an enemy.

Hearing a step as he stood there, he turned his head . . . and knew that the decision had already been made. It was Mrs. Jeremy, come to fetch him before his time. And he knew what the decision was; for she was crying.

"Oh, Sir . . . come and look at him . . . beautiful he lies there, my lamb—you wouldn't credit it . . . like a miracle—asleep."

"Asleep!" repeated Hervey in an almost inaudible tone. His face was grey. "Do you mean really asleep, or . . ."

Mrs. Jeremy made a final dab with the apron and her bosom heaved. "Sleeping like a child, Sir, as the doctor said he might if the whatever it was happened. . . . I can't help crying, it seems too good to be true! . . . Will you come back with me, Sir; I daren't stay away, but I thought you would wish to know . . . and you look as pale as a corpse yourself, Sir . . . tired out, I'm sure . . . but oh, Captain Barrington, isn't it wonderful?"

*

Till he had seen him, Hervey would not believe it. But it was true. He had his hand under his cheek like a child, and drew a child's even breaths.

"When he wakes," thought Hervey, looking down at him with half incredulous eyes, "will he hate me still? I suppose he will never know how I feel about him now."

For, being an Englishman, he knew he would never be able to tell him; indeed he felt ashamed of the emotions which were his as he stood there apparently unmoved, while on the other side of the bed Mrs. Jeremy was unrestrainedly murmuring "Bless him!" with the tears still running down her face.

A little later Mr. Alexander Touchwood, as jubilant over the issue, he declared, as if he had made some discovery that would silence the geologists of the opposite school for ever, was letting fall his opinion that, when he came to himself, the young fellow would probably retain only a very indistinct recollection of the beginning of his illness—and as to events before his escape from Fairhaven well, he would realize now that he owed Captain Barrington his life.

"I shouldn't see it in that light, if I were in his shoes," replied Hervey drily. "Yet, though I have no wish for gratitude, I should prefer him not to hate me. When he is awake I shall keep out of his way as much as I can until I am sure."

But when his turn came for vigil in the sick room it was not possible, with so small a staff of watchers, to refuse it, even though the miraculous and healing sleep had broken. It seemed very quiet in there, now that the unending fight for breath was over; and des Sablières himself was so quiet, lying flat in the bed "like a Christian at last," as Mrs. Jeremy had it, mostly with closed eyes and with no expression on his face beyond that of utter weariness at rest. Once or twice in the time that Hervey sat by the bedside the sunken eyelids lifted, and the tired grey gaze flickered over him, but no emotion of any kind was visible on the tranquil features and Hervey was reassured; Touchwood was quite right, the boy had forgotten.

*

But Raoul had not forgotten; far from it. Even in the intense lassitude of mind and body which weighed him down after his battle for life, even in the strange floating contentment of rest and quiet and freedom from pain—for both lassitude and content were his at one and the same time—there was a shadow. He recognized Captain Barrington and knew perfectly who he was. To him he was associated with one scene only, the scene which had taken place in this very room, how long or short a time ago he was not sure. And now Captain Barrington had somehow got him into his clutches again.

The exact method he had employed was not clear to the young man, who remembered little with any coherence since his pursuit by the population of the riverside farm, but the fact of his enemy's success remained. One could not get away from him; he loomed up and filled all the horizon. He had gloated over him, Raoul, when he was ill; he came now from time to time to keep an eye on him, or sent his man, who had kicked him and held him helpless that night, to watch him. Only with the kind and motherly woman who had nursed him so devotedly—was she the housekeeper?—did he feel that he was not being spied upon . . . though she too must have her orders.

But the convalescent was not at first physically capable of treading continuously this dismal road which led from an unpleasant past to an equally unpleasant future. Nature strongly desired him to live in the immediate present, and saw to it that he should so live; either sleeping for hours, or spending uncounted time in an agreeable stupor, just content with the touch of the fine, cool linen sheets, or the sun coming into the room. His eyes would follow Mrs. Jeremy about with a lazy, pleased attention; her delicious soups and jellies were the events of the day, and for her, however languid he felt, he had a little smile, and generally a weak word or two of thanks. But when Captain Barrington or his man was in charge of him he pretended to be asleep (angrily conscious sometimes, in the former case, of a humiliating desire to withdraw himself entirely beneath the bedclothes).

Yet he gave Nature the slip now and then. At times he would once more be standing outside on the ledge of that very window now before his eyes, his hands gripping the gutter above him, his heart thumping against his ribs, his shirt sticking to them, his shoes slung round his neck by a purloined towel, trying not to be so acutely conscious of those nerve-shaking spikes below, and knowing that in a moment his life would hang, in the most literal sense, on the stability of that narrow leaden, trough above him. . . . Or he would feel the ivy stem give way once more, and himself slipping with it . . . clutching . . . falling . . . landing with his wrist doubled back under him, and crouching there on the grass in the dawn, sick with the hurt of it, telling himself that he had only wrenched it, and that the pain would go off. . . . How cold the river had been when he plunged in, and how longingly he had looked at the little boat which prudence warned him not to take, lest it should betray his route. . . . Yes, and how cold the wood on the other side before sunrise, and how he had shivered there in his thin wet clothes as he lay hid in the

266

undergrowth! By evening, indeed, when he had cautiously worked down the river toward the coast, he had long been dry, but so hopelessly faint and hungry that necessity had driven him after dusk, to the Willises' farm, on the chance that its inmates had not yet heard of the hue and cry after him which Captain Barrington must certainly have raised.

And the Willis family, to whom he represented himself as a smuggler in difficulties with the preventive men, had been more surly than suspicious; their ears were too dull to detect an alien accent in his excellent English. In exchange for the fugitive's too-famous shoes and his stockings they gave him a meal, but they could not be induced to part with any old footgear in place of them. All he could extract in addition was a dirty bit of sacking and some directions which turned out to be far from precise. Yet the visit of this penniless and half-clothed young man had struck out a spark of romance in one unlikely breast; the same young man, lying in his bed a fortnight later, passing the scene in review, still smiled at the recollection. Barefooted now, and with his piece of sacking over his shoulders, he had not gone far along the darkening road, before an ugly, hulking farm girl came running after him with a mighty hunch of bread and cheese. Half timidly, half roughly, she thrust this upon him "fur thy journey, lad." Then she saw his left wrist all muffled up in the towel—how vain had been Raoul's hope that tying it up in the huckaback would ease the persistent ache of it—enquired in her uncouth speech what was the matter with it, and finally converted the towel into a sling.

After his recent treatment at the hands of Captain Barrington this unexpected and unmotived kindness so moved its recipient that he rendered his benefactress the only return in his power; and though in the past he had thought little of making this payment when necessary—and even when unnecessary—it was, on this occasion, made at real cost, for the girl was not only very ill-favoured but dirty. He shut his eyes therefore, and held his breath when he kissed her.

The result of his salute was surprising, for, after a moment's stupefaction, the maiden burst into tears, and the astonished Raoul went on his way rather hastily, half fearing that some rustic Corydon would appear and fall upon him. (But now he thought that his reluctant kiss had probably saved his life.)

After that, disaster on disaster; ill-judged short cuts in the dark, full of stones and brambles; enormous fields which, to the wanderer's bare feet, seemed entirely devoted to the cultivation of thistles, causing him to regret even his hated shoes; a dawn which found him not only back nearly at the point from which he had started earlier in the night, but with a fast-growing incapacity for exercising choice or movement of any kind. His head was aching horribly; once or twice he nearly lost consciousness; and it was clear that his condition was not merely due, as he had first thought, to the inflamed and painful state of his wrist. Having vainly tried to eat the bread and cheese, he lay down under a hedge and wondered what would be the end of this. . . . Somehow, by afternoon he had crept back to the farm, and, hardly knowing what he was doing, implored them to let him stay there a little, offering to pay for this privilege by working for them later on.

Had he not been half light-headed he might have realised that there was something odd behind the changed manner of the Willis family, the alacrity with which they greeted him and agreed to his proposal, and the speed with which they ushered him into an empty barn and brought him food and cider. He could not eat, but he was very thirsty. Between the heady cider and his own exhaustion he was soon asleep on a mound of hay, and never heard the bar slide into place outside.

It was its removal which woke him an hour or so later, that and the hurried entry of his Dulcinea. Her frightened face, as she bent over him and shook him, enlightened him as quickly as her stammering words, and he dashed out of the trap just in time to avoid the pitchfork prongs for which he conceived an aversion far deeper than ever English bayonets had roused in him. If one of the Willis brothers had not seen the girl go in and guessed her errand, he might even have got away without being chased, though it was hard to know to what shelter. . . . Then, the swim he had thought his last . . . a boat making for him . . . thereafter fog, with an endless choking illness . . . till the emergence of Captain Barrington once again.

Illness, broken wrist, foolhardy climb and all, he had only been like a squirrel fruitlessly turning a wheel in its cage when he tried to get away from that man. And so, on the fourth day of his convalescence, Raoul decided to ask a question of the tall, unusual, semi-jocular doctor. From him he might find out how much longer he was going to be allowed to remain in Paradise before being sent back to hell. He was not going to give Captain Barrington the satisfaction of hearing and answering that enquiry.

But he had to wait till the following day before he saw the doctor alone, when Mr. Touchwood informed him that he was getting on famously, and would be a credit to any practitioner, much less to one who had abandoned medicine as long as he had.

Raoul half smiled, and said languidly, "You have been good—too good. Was it worth while to take so much trouble?"

Mr. Touchwood raised those eyebrows of his which were always on the move. "What do you mean, young fellow? Surely, at your age, you are not so cynical as to be tired of living."

"That depends on what you call living, does it not?" returned the young man. The colour began to come into his face, for everything was an effort, and he dreaded the result of this one. "I should like to know how long I am to stay here?"

"In bed? Well, I couldn't promise——" began Mr. Touchwood.

"*Mon Dieu*, no, not that!" said Raoul with a spurt of irritation, for he suspected that his question was being evaded. "I mean, how long before Captain Barrington tells them to come and take me back to the hulks?"

"Tells them to come and——My dear boy, you may set your mind at rest, he isn't going to do that at all. No, I assure you. When you are well enough he will, I believe, wink at your escaping . . . but send you back after this, never! Don't you worry your head about it!"

A lie, a palpable lie! As the door shut behind the doctor Raoul cursed below his breath. Why could not Mr. Touchwood be straightforward and tell the truth? Because he probably had Captain Barrington's orders not to do so! Yet how could Captain Barrington think that he, Raoul, would believe such a manifest absurdity as that he would allow his prey to escape.

Hadn't he been escaping when he came across Captain Barrington's path the second time—hadn't he? Had he not swum out to the friendly boat when somehow Captain Barrington . . . What was Captain Barrington doing in that boat with the men who were taking him to France? Or was that . . . were they . . . a dream. Which was a dream and which was real? . . . He *had* been in a boat. . . . Clutching at the sheet he began to grope feverishly in the mist. How, if he had been in the smugglers' boat going to France (as he seemed to remember) could he be here back in Stowey, in Captain Barrington's house? He had never envisaged the difficulty in this way before. . . .

Then, suddenly, the mist parted . . .

The sweat poured off Raoul with shock and rage. Captain Barrington had deliberately tricked him, lied to him, used his necessity as a lure, got him here by the most heartless of falsehoods. . . . He had taken all that trouble to entice him back so that he might have the satisfaction of the last shot in their duel, so that he might do as he had threatened that night. Wink at his escaping, indeed! He was waiting . . . waiting for the day when he could announce to him, in that cold voice of his, "You will be taken back to the hulks to-morrow morning, making acquaintance with the Black Hole first, I imagine."

But he should not have the last shot—no, by God! Utterly helpless as his captive was, he could fool him yet. He saw the way clear. It would not probably take very long to carry the business through; the plan only needed resolution. . . .

The Last Shot

"I suppose he discovered in me, through the obscurity of the room, some tokens of amazement and doubt; for after a short pause he proceeded thus: 'Not to be easily credited will neither surprise nor offend me.'?"—Rasselas, chap. xlii.

Mrs. Hannah Jeremy was in her element these days—much more so than was her spouse, during the short sick-room vigils to which he was committed, wherein he interpreted the command to "watch" the patient so painfully and literally that he sat immobile, his hands planted upon his knees, his body bent slightly forward, and his eyes glued upon the prostrate form, in the attitude less of a sick nurse than of a determined yet rather nervous man keeping an eye on a temporary quiescent wild animal. And indeed on one occasion when Mrs. Jeremy came down and reported with rapture that "her lamb" was sleeping like a child, Jeremy, unable to control himself, said with a snort, "Lamb indeed! Precious little you knows about him, Hannah! He've the sperrit of a tiger-cat, as I says to the Captain."

Mrs. Jeremy might be excused for expressing horror at this callous and almost blasphemous view, for to her the patient had shown no sign of this alleged spirit, and she regarded him as her especial property. What joy, therefore, for one who was a finished cook, as well as an indefatigable nurse, to devise and carry out the most tempting invalid dishes. And she had been doing this for five days, to her own—and plainly also to Raoul's—satisfaction, when on this sixth morning she was able to announce to him (calling him alternately "my dear" and "Sir" because, though she had enquired his name from Captain Barrington, she could make nothing of it) that the doctor had said he might have an egg for breakfast if he fancied it "a beautiful brown egg from one of our own hens."

Brushed and tidy and propped with pillows, her "lamb" looked in the direction of the window and said calmly, "I do not wish for any breakfast this morning, thank you, Madame."

Mrs. Jeremy surveyed him apprehensively. Used as she was by now to his general fragility of appearance she instantly decided (and as it happened rightly) that he had passed a bad night.

"You are feeling a little sickish this morning, perhaps?" she suggested. "But maybe it will soon go off, and then——"

"I do not feel in the least sick, thank you," returned Raoul firmly. "But I do not wish for any breakfast all the same."

Mrs. Jeremy, though disappointed, was too good a nurse to persist. "He'll be all the more ready for his next meal," she reflected. "I'll bring it earlier than usual."

Spending particular care on its preparation, she did so; but to her real dismay this time, her charge politely but quite firmly declined it.

"Come now, my dear," she said coaxingly, "just a couple of spoonfuls—just one spoonful—to please me!"

"No, thank you," said the young man, resolutely shutting his white lips.

"You must eat something, Sir, or I shall have to tell the doctor about it!"

"I am not hungry to-day," was all her patient's reply to this.

In vain did she tempt him at intervals with further delicacies. He expressed regret, but would not touch them. No, he had not a headache. All the same, he was very silent, and whereas the day before—in the earlier part of it, at least—he had talked to her as much as his strength permitted, he now lay mute or slept. Mrs. Jeremy was on pins till the doctor should arrive, but for some reason Mr. Touchwood did not pay his visit till the late afternoon.

"So you've lost your appetite, young man," he observed, informed of the latest crisis. "I can't allow that, you know. Let me see your tongue."

Raoul exhibited it.

"H'm," said Mr. Touchwood sagely. "Possibly the Iceland liverwort decoction is not suiting you. Stop it for the present," he said to Mrs. Jeremy. And as he was going out he beckoned her on to the landing. When she came in again she surprised a strange secret little smile on the invalid's face.

However, he must be hungry by seven o'clock, she thought; and the doctor had advised her to offer him nothing in the interval, a prohibition which went sorely against the grain. At half past six, however, the appetiteless one roused himself sufficiently to say, "Please do not bring me any supper, Mrs. Jeremy, for I shall not be able to eat it if you do."

Even to Mrs. Jeremy's indulgent ear there was more a suggestion of "I will not" than "I cannot" in his tone.

"But, my dear life!" she burst out, "whatever is the matter with you? Is it that you don't fancy my cooking?"

"Your cooking is delicious," murmured Raoul with his eyes shut.

And there was so much sincerity in his voice that Mrs. Jeremy was visited by a new and startling idea. He was, of course, a Papist . . .

"Is it, Sir," she asked a little timidly, "that to-day is one of the days when . . . when your religion forbids you to eat anything?"

The mutineer's eyes opened, rather startled; for a second they looked amused. "Would you feel easier in your mind if you could put it down to that?" he enquired.

"No, I don't know that I should," replied Mrs. Jeremy somewhat tartly, feeling indeed small respect for a creed which could require anything so silly of an invalid. "Come, Sir, it's twenty-four hours now since you've had bite or sup. I'm sure your religion—if that's at the bottom of it—can't ask you to do more than that!"

"Oh, yes, it might," responded Raoul, and again he had that cryptic little smile.

"But you'll be really ill again in no time if you go on like this!"

Raoul pushed away the bedclothes in which he was huddled. "Do you think so?" he enquired in a tone of real interest. "Then I am sorry if it means more trouble for you again, but . . . *heureusement que ça ne durera pas longtemps*," he added to himself. "Please do not give yourself this trouble at least, for I cannot eat anything if you bring it to me." And he pulled the bedclothes up again.

Quite baffled, Mrs. Jeremy surveyed all she could see of him with great disquiet. There was only one thing left to do, and she did it.

"Won't eat—hasn't taken his meals all day?" queried Hervey, looking up from a letter he was writing. "You mean, I suppose, that he has no appetite? Why?"

"I believe he's hungry enough, Sir, really," responded his troubled housekeeper. "I gather—but I'm not sure, Sir, from his answer when I put it to him—that it's a matter of religion with him . . . being a Papist, no doubt, with all those feasts and fasts and what not."

"That's nonsense," said Hervey firmly, for he had been long enough in Spain to know that it was. "A sick man does not have to fast. If he told you so, it was to cover the real reason. . . . He must be feeling too ill to eat and does not wish to acknowledge it."

"Doctor Touchwood said, Sir, that he could find nothing wrong with him. No, I'm afraid it's some maggot he's got into his brain.—It couldn't be, could it, Sir," said Mrs. Jeremy in a sudden tone of horror, "that he thinks there's poison or something in the food? I've heard of sick folks having queer fancies like that . . . but that would be such a terrible thought to have!"

"No, no." said her master, "I don't think it can possibly be that. Don't worry, Mrs. Jeremy; I'll go up myself and see if I can find out what's wrong."

But he looked worried enough himself as he left the room. This was a most disconcerting turn of affairs; what could be at the bottom of it? Perhaps, although he seemed to have forgotten, the convalescent had now remembered the past, and was not disposed to let it be cancelled by his captor's present behaviour and intentions—of which latter, as Hervey had learnt yesterday, Touchwood had apprised him. (And he was glad to know that Touchwood had done this, for otherwise he would have had to do it himself some time.) But surely des Sablières could not carry his detestation of him so far as all at once to refuse to eat under his roof!

He went in. The light was beginning to fade. The insurgent was lying turned away from the door, on his right side, his splinted arm stretched out along his body. For a moment Hervey thought he must be asleep, and stood in silence; then Raoul moved his head, saw who was there, and immediately moved it back again.

"I am sorry to hear," said Hervey without preamble, still standing where he was, at some distance from the bed, "that you have had nothing to eat all day."

Raoul made a slight movement of the shoulders, but no verbal reply.

"Why is it?" asked Captain Barrington after a second.

"Because I am not hungry, thank you."

"But, unless there is some cause for it, you must surely be hungry by now."

"I am not hungry. Presumably, then, there is a cause for it. But the cause concerns myself alone."

"On the contrary, if it concerns you it concerns me," replied Hervey mildly.

"I wish you would tell me what it is. If it is anything that can be put right I can easily send again for the doctor——"

It was as if he had touched a spring. Raoul turned over in the bed—slowly and painfully indeed, and yet with an effect of flinging himself over. "Yes, so as to patch me up the sooner!" he said with startling vehemence. "What a blow my illness must have been to you—since even you couldn't pack me off to the Black Hole when I was delirious!" Here he struggled up on to the elbow of his damaged arm. "You wouldn't let me die before, in the river . . . . you lured me here by a lie, a heartless lie—so that you could have the satisfaction of——"

"Stop!" cried Hervey, waking from his petrifaction. "You are quite mis——" but Raoul swept on without pause, his eyes dilating, his other hand clenched and beating on the coverlet. "But you shall not have the satisfaction of sending me back again . . . even *now*, Captain Barrington! There is only one thing that I can do against you . . . and I am doing it . . . and I shall die here . . . in a bed, and not in . . . not in . . . ." His voice suddenly wavered.

"For God's sake, boy, listen!" cried Hervey in high distress, but the feverish access of strength had already spent itself, and before he could get to him Raoul had fallen back on the pillow panting. Yet when Hervey stooped over him he still had force enough to fling his right arm over his eyes as if to shut out the sight. And at that Hervey abstained from attempting to make him swallow the wine which he had hastily poured out.

"Would it not be better," he said quietly, "if before denouncing me you waited to know what my real intentions are? I thought you knew them. I am not going to give you up when you are better—or at any time. On the contrary, I shall do my best to help you to leave England."

The arm came away. It was trembling. "Are you tricking me again?" asked its owner faintly. "Haven't you had enough of that? You can't expect me . . . to believe you."

"I think I can convince you," said Hervey steadily, even sternly, though his heart was wrung to think what unnecessary suffering his own or Touchwood's ineptitude had caused. "Directly I had got you here that day—helping myself by a lie, I admit, but a lie whose sole purpose was to prevent you from attempting to drown yourself again—a party of marines from Plymouth came to the house in search of you. I lied to them also—said you were drowned . . . reported the fact in writing, and sent them away. And so, particularly as I hold the King's commission, I am bound for my own sake to uphold my lie. I cannot give you up now if I would. . . . Does that convince you?"

Raoul stared up at him, so shaken, so ashy-faced, that Hervey now put the glass of wine to his lips, and the recalcitrant drank some without remonstrance, probably indeed without knowledge.

"*You sent away the marines!*" he stammered incredulously. "*You mean to keep me . . . till I can get away?*"

"On my word of honour as a gentleman. . . . Now, will you think better of it, and let Mrs. Jeremy bring you up some supper?"

Raoul shut his eyes and nodded, biting his lip hard. But two tears, the product of weakness, hunger, agitation, and relief, began to steal down under the closed lids. Hervey did not know whether to curse himself or Touchwood for the misunderstanding, but he was desperately sorry for the havoc it had wrought; more sorry still when he heard, as he reached the door, that the boy was actually sobbing. But his was the last presence that could comfort him.

"It is all right now," he said to Mrs. Jeremy downstairs. "Just a misunderstanding—he thought I was only waiting till he was well enough for me to give him up, so he had evidently resolved to starve himself in order that I never should." And as Mrs. Jeremy gave an exclamation of horror he said with a wry smile: "There is something of the wildcat about him. . . . Get him supper; he has promised to eat it." But he sighed heavily as he returned to his writing.

Mrs. Jeremy was more than relieved at the obedient and indeed appreciative consumption of that supper; as she had guessed, the rebel was really very hungry. He was also extremely pale and subdued, but had a smile for her; like a child that has been naughty, has undergone reproof, and promised to be good. When she settled him for the night (not oblivious of a slightly damp pillow, though she said nothing) he enquired rather wistfully whether she forgave him for being so ungrateful to her for all her care, and, giving her a glance that went to her heart, caught her hand and carried it to his lips.

"Oh, my dear," said Mrs. Jeremy, rather overcome, "you mustn't do that! It's been the joy of my life to see you better. If I had only known that you didn't understand about the Captain! Still you know, between ourselves, men are sometimes so . . ." she sought vainly for the word, "what I mean is, they don't always explain themselves."

"And 'between ourselves,'?" said Raoul with the glimmer of a smile, "I suppose you don't consider me a man. It is true; I think I have to-day behaved like a baby."

*

"So the soldiers actually came to the house after me, Mrs. Jeremy, and Captain Barrington sent them away?"

It was next morning, after an excellent breakfast (including a brown egg) that Raoul, watching Mrs. Jeremy as she dusted the room, put this query to her.

"Yes, my dear," replied the good lady, continuing to dust.

"But what exactly did he say to them?"

"Told them you was drowned, I think."

"But, Mrs. Jeremy, why?"

"Why? Because he didn't want them to take you off to those nasty hulks again."

"But," objected Raoul, "two nights before, that was just what he——" He knitted his brows. "Mon Dieu, que c'est extraordinaire!"

Mrs. Jeremy stopped. "Is that French, Sir, you're saying?" she enquired with sudden interest.

Raoul nodded.

"A very difficult language, I should think." She came towards him, duster in hand. "And yet when you were ill you talked a lot of it." There was something of admiration in her tone.

"You see, I learnt it when I was young," explained Raoul, amused.

"And speaking of the French language," went on Mrs. Jeremy, "reminds me that now you've got your appetite back all right, Sir, I can ask you what's been on my mind this day or two, and that is, what you'd wish me to call you. Not but what I've asked the Captain already, but I can't get my tongue round that!"

Raoul continued to be amused. "Where I was before, Mrs. Jeremy, the good woman with whom I lodged, and others of the English too, used to call me 'Mr. Rowl.' It is—that is to say it sufficiently resembles—my Christian name. You had better call me that as you cannot manage the other."

"But I should feel it a liberty to call you by your Christian name, Sir," said Mrs. Jeremy, hesitating.

"Ma foi!" exclaimed her patient; "then I wonder you do not feel it a liberty to wash me! I do not care a straw what you call me, dear Mrs. Jeremy. But stop that dusting for a moment, I pray you; I wish to speak of Captain Barrington."

"Well, Sir, if you'll allow me, I had rather finish first."

Raoul cleared his throat. "You know, I have not got rid of my cough yet, and I feel that if you continue to dust now it will come back much worse." And he did his best to lend colour to this prediction.

"There's not enough dust in the whole room for that, Sir!" exclaimed Mrs. Jeremy indignantly. "Though, of course, I have not been able to turn it out thoroughly with you so ill; and if I thought that . . ." Her eye kindled. "After all, it would not do you any harm if I were to spread a sheet over you and——"

"Miséricorde!" ejaculated Raoul. "And then you would take the carpet up! Shades of Miss Hitchings! No, no, I withdraw my cough; there is no dust. I was only trying to coerce you."

"Oh, was that all?" said Mrs. Jeremy doubtfully, for the word was new to her. "Well, Mr. . . . . Mr. Rowl, I won't put you to the trouble. What is it that you want to know about the Captain, poor dear gentleman?"

Raoul raised his eyebrows. "Why is he so much to be pitied?"

"Well, Sir, the worry he's had, and the state he's been in about you these last ten days! I assure you, Mr. Rowl, he could not have taken on about you more while you were so ill if you had been his own son. I don't suppose you were in a condition to know the hours he's spent out of his bed nursing you. And the anxiety he's been through! I heard him say to Mr. Touchwood one night that if you died he should never forgive himself. And the day you took the turn, well, he was like a different man—though he didn't say much. That's not his way. Oh, if ever any one had a kind heart, it is Captain Barrington, for all he knows how to be severe sometimes."

The colour had been ebbing and flowing over Raoul's face in a remarkable way during this speech, and he now regarded the bottom of the bed in silence for a moment; then he said: "Thank you, Mrs. Jeremy. If you want to put a sheet over me, I shall not object—in fact, I think it would be rather appropriate."

"No, no, my dear, I'm not going to do that," said Mrs. Jeremy, on whom the fluctuations of colour had not been lost. "You just lie quiet a bit now, while I get on with my work; I'm not sure that I ought to talk to you so much."

And Raoul obediently lay quiet against his high pillows, knitting his brows but not saying another word. But when Mrs. Jeremy had finished he said, "Will you please ask Captain Barrington if he would be good enough to come up and see me?"

"Now, Mr. Rowl?" asked Mrs. Jeremy doubtfully.

"Yes, now—that is, if it is convenient to him."

Apparently it was convenient, for about five minutes later Captain Barrington appeared.

"You wished to speak to me, I hear?" His tone was purely negative—neither pleasant nor unpleasant.

"Yes, please," said Raoul, just a trifle breathlessly. "Thank you for coming up. Won't you sit down?"

Captain Barrington complied, choosing a chair at some distance. Raoul was sufficiently supported by his pillows to look across at him with ease, but he found himself instead studying the manner in which his own left wrist and hand were bandaged to the splint, a thing which had not previously much interested him. The truth was that he felt all at once abysmally shy. And Captain Barrington gave him no help. Was it possible that he also was suffering from malaise? No, he did not look like it when Raoul glanced at him surreptitiously under his lashes; he merely looked stern. . . . It was rather like charging artillery.

"I should like to apologize, Sir, for what I said to you last night—for having misjudged you as I did. I spoke in ignorance, as I hope you realized."

Captain Barrington looked at him. "I did realize. And I blamed myself severely that you had been left in that condition. I understood from Mr. Touchwood that you had been told of my intentions. Evidently there was some misunderstanding, which I can only ask you to forgive, since it caused you so much distress."

Raoul crimsoned to his hair. Was this a deliberate allusion to last night's childish breakdown? All the more would he deprecate sympathy now. "There was no misunderstanding," he replied rather curtly. "I did not believe Mr. Touchwood when he told me, that was all. So it was my own fault."

"Well," said Hervey still more drily, "having regard to our past relations, I do not blame you for that incredulity. All the same you must try to believe it now. Unless by ill fortune your presence here is discovered, you will not return to the hulks. I hope to be able to keep you until you are sufficiently recovered to stand a fair chance of getting away, and I shall do what I can to assist you in that."

"But, in God's name, why?" burst out Raoul, bewildered by the contrast between this undreamt-of generosity and the manner in which it was announced, by the disparity between this Captain Barrington and him of his memories, so different and yet, it seemed, so fundamentally the same.

Captain Barrington did not answer that query. He looked at his watch and got up. "Is that all you want to know?"

"I don't really want to know anything," said Raoul, twisting on his pillows. "I want to apologize, as I said, and to thank you."

"To thank me!" broke in Captain Barrington, and for the first time there was emotion of some sort in his voice. "Thanks from you to me would be rather a farce, would they not? . . . I did not mean anything offensive by that," he added hastily, for Raoul's face was again suffused with colour. "I merely meant, What have you to thank me for?"

"No, you meant, I think," said the young Frenchman, looking straight at him, and the colour fading rapidly, "that, as you pointed out last night, you cannot give me up now if you would. By yielding to a momentary weakness, which by this time you bitterly regret, you find yourself saddled with . . . with the necessity of upholding your own lie, as you put it. In that case would it not have been better to let me go on with what I had begun yesterday?"

It would have taken someone older and in better physical condition to read aright Hervey Barrington's expression then. "If I gave you any impression of regret," he said at last, "it is incorrect. I merely used the argument about the impossibility of now giving you up to stop you in the madness you were set on yesterday." And here he walked away to the window, the famous window of the spikes and of Raoul's climb, and stood there for a second with his back toward the bed. Then, half turning, he went on in a manner which suggested that each sentence was being forced out of him: "I cannot help it if you do not believe me, but I have never for one moment regretted my lie to the sergeant from Plymouth. . . . I would do the same again. . . . I acted then, as I am acting now, with my eyes open and not . . . not against my inclination. . . . I used you that night you came with unnecessary brutality, as you must be aware"—a long pause—". . . and I ask your pardon for it."

For a second the bed seemed to heave beneath its startled occupant. Had he heard aright? . . . For perhaps fifteen pulsating seconds after the voice at the window had ceased Raoul was really speechless; then he drew a long breath and found words.

"Captain Barrington, you are a gentleman . . . I may tell you so? . . . For myself, I remember nothing of that night, now. And therefore you will let me thank you for . . . for all that has happened since?"

Even Hervey's curious reserve was not proof against an olive branch, so much larger and greener too than he had ever expected, held out in this way.

He had confined his hopes to not being hated; but now that with such difficulty and, as he was conscious, in so ungracious a manner, he had got out his apologia, he felt that the effort had unsealed something in himself as well as in his antagonist. He *could* take his victim's thanks, and, looking at their giver, propped up there gazing at him with eyes too big for his face, he knew that they were sincerely offered. Slowly he crossed the room and stood beside the bed.

"If it were not for me, des Sablières, you would not be in a situation in which you had to thank me for anything. You would not have a broken wrist, nor have been half drowned, nor have passed through a dangerous illness."

"But how do you know that, Sir?" asked Raoul, looking up at him with the suspicion of a smile. "There are other ways in which I might have acquired all those experiences. Besides, you had your duty to do. I was an escaping enemy." He looked down, and traced out with one finger the raised pattern on the quilt. "Will you allow me to say that I think the whole of our . . . misunderstanding . . . is due to a woman—to the lady of the tight shoes?" And, as Hervey made a movement, Raoul lifted his eyes, purged of all mockery, with only a rather rueful merriment in their grey depths. "Captain Barrington, she is dead and is not worth remembering. I never liked her very much; it was necessity which drove me to her company. Could we not bury her? And then, perhaps . . ." He stopped.

The slow flush which had risen there died away from Hervey's face. "You are right," he said, not without difficulty. "It was . . . that business . . . which angered me so. But now I will not think of it again. Our acquaintance shall begin from to-day . . . if you will."

"Bien sûr, je le veux," said Raoul simply, and his hand came into the Englishman's.

"I expect," said Hervey, loosing it suddenly as if it occurred to him that it might break, and looking from it to its owner rather dubiously, "that we had better stop talking now."

"But I love to talk," replied Raoul, smiling fully this time.

"No doubt you do, young man," commented the voice of Mr. Alexander

Touchwood, for Hervey had left the door ajar, and there he was, just coming in. "And pray what are you and the Captain discussing?"

"A funeral," answered Raoul, his eyes shining. "An unregretted death and a very deep grave. . . . Doctor, do you know that I have the most enormous appetite to-day?"

*

That afternoon Mrs. Jeremy brought up a little package. "The Captain's had to go to Tawton, Mr. Rowl; he's sent you this."

When he was alone Raoul opened it. It contained his money and Juliana's letters, and a line from Hervey Barrington:

I should like you to know that these letters have not been read by me. As for the map, I can give you a better one when the time comes.

Raoul lay still after that, the tears in his eyes again. It seemed like a miracle. The English—what a strange and wonderful race they were. A dictum of his father's came back to him. "When an Englishman does a good action he is generally more ashamed of it than of a bad one." Yes, a wonderful race. But the most wonderful member of it was a woman.

He put Juliana's letters carefully under his pillow, but the banknotes were all on the floor by the time that Hervey came back from Tawton and found him fast asleep, wan but peaceful.

Part IV
A Month of Miracles

Several Discoveries

"I perceived that I had every day more of his confidence."–Rasselas, chap. xl.

The revelation that people are other than you had fancied them is always interesting, and only the practising cynic will demur to the opinion that they are very often found to be not worse but better. On these lines, in the course of a couple of days, did Captain Hervey Barrington, R. N. and Capitaine Raoul des Sablières, 3ième Hussards, make surprising discoveries about each other. Hervey's previous conviction about his captive was not so much that he was a "wildcat" of a pretty well unbreakable spirit (for he had enough acumen to allow for the part which circumstances had played in bringing out this quality) as that he was too histrionically gifted ever to be sincere. Raoul's main idea of Captain Barrington was not that of brutality incarnate (for he on his side was far too acute not to know how bitterly he had angered him, and to allow for wrath so intense blazing suddenly out into savagery) but of someone hard and implacable as granite.

Now Hervey, to his surprise, found himself in the company of a young man of a particularly sweet and gay temper, and of an engaging simplicity of demeanour. And somehow he knew that this was the fundamental, not the superficial, des Sablières. And Raoul—the discovery was rather slower—found in his ex-captor a remarkably feeling heart, which, for all his efforts, he could not disguise. It showed as he listened to the tale of Raoul's luckless adventures after he had scaled the roof, the recital of which was early drawn from the adventurer; it showed still more clearly a little later when, on being questioned, Raoul revealed something of what he had been through in the hulks, and spoke of the scanty and often uneatable food, and the consequent perpetual hunger; of the swarming vermin, of which, since there was no soap and bathing was never allowed, the cleanest prisoner could not rid himself; of the poisonous atmosphere in which the captives slept, so foul that the guards who opened the portholes in the early morning always jumped hastily back to avoid the stench thus liberated; of the six-foot-square Black Hole at the bottom of the hold, ventilated merely by a few tiny apertures about the size of a sixpence, and visited by a sentry only once in twenty-four hours, and where men sometimes went mad or died; and of the callousness of certain of the officers. Worst of all was the terrible degradation of character which took place with so many of the inmates, forced association with whom was the chief misery of the place for any decent man.

And Captain Barrington, walking in agitation about the room in which he had once taunted the speaker with the fate which awaited him on his return to the *Ganges*, could only say indignantly that he was sure the British public was unaware of these scandals, and that, if they only knew, his countrymen would insist on better conditions. With this belief Raoul's experience of the English character led him to agree; indeed, he gave it as his opinion that a great deal of the suffering in the hulks was quite contrary to the Government's intentions, and due to the rascally contractors, who not only cheated the unfortunate prisoners of food and clothing, but swindled the Admiralty as well.

The unpalatable truth about the hulks, however, was not the only shock to his racial self-esteem which Captain Barrington was destined to receive. Rather stiffly (being far from oblivious of the fact that he had once refused point-blank to listen to it) he next asked for the story of Raoul's initial misfortunes, and was given it, Miss Forrest's name alone being omitted, and she simply referred to as "Mademoiselle." By the end of the tale of Sir Francis Mulholland's ingenuity Captain Barrington was staring at the narrator horror-struck.

"I could not have believed an English gentleman capable of such a dastardly action!" he exclaimed. "—Not that I disbelieve you, des Sablières," he added hastily.

Raoul, rather tired, lay and looked at him reflectively, wondering why he should now be as implicitly believed as formerly he had been doubted. But to ask the Englishman why would only be to disconcert him still more. So he shut his eyes instead, and, without meaning to, fell asleep in that sudden uncontrollable fashion in which oblivion descended upon him nowadays.

Since the interment of the Señora Tomás, however, he had been progressing steadily towards recovery. That too-ingenious lady's very tomb seemed forgotten now. But as for Mlle. Adrienne, it was not long before her impersonator was telling Hervey about the original. And there came a day when, to the surprise of both of them, even the ghost of the Señora stood between them and was proved harmless.

It was Hervey who evoked her, perhaps unintentionally. Surveying the convalescent critically one morning, ere he dropped into a chair by the bed, he observed: "I really think you are beginning to get a little flesh on your bones at last."

"Flesh!" exclaimed Raoul. "Mrs. Jeremy makes a prize cattle of me!"

"'Cattle' is a plural noun, des Sablières," observed his host smiling. "That's the first time I have ever heard you make a real slip in your English—except of course when you were——" For one second he paused, and then went on without a stagger—"when you were uttering the sentiments of the lady from Badajoz."

"Yes," said Raoul rather indistinctly, lowering his eyes.

"Why did you make the Señora talk so?" pursued Hervey.

Raoul shot a quick glance at him. "I . . . ma foi, je n'en sais pas trop! I think I could not help it. When I thought I was . . . celle que vous savez . . . I found I could not speak English so well, that is all."

Hervey's mouth twitched. "Well, before you impersonate her again I advise you to take lessons, not indeed in English, but in Spanish."

"And perhaps," suggested Raoul with a penitent expression, "in truthfulness as well!"

"I'm afraid," returned Captain Barrington, "that the Señora would never be closely acquainted with that virtue."

"And yet," said her originator apologetically, "she was not so . . . so untrue as you may think, Sir—at least I have heard that some English ensign of the Light Brigade did marry a Spanish lady after you stormed Badajoz."

"Oh, that tale was not pure romance, then? What regiment was he in?"

"I do not know, Sir. Not having met it in the field, I am ignorant of the composition of the Light Brigade."

"Then you made a deuced good shot when you gazetted your . . . hero . . . to the Ninety-fifth!"

Under his dark lashes Raoul looked at the speaker with an indescribable mixture of compunction and devilry.

"Oh, pardon, Captain Barrington, but it was you who did that! I was very grateful, I assure you, for your suggestion."

Hervey stared and then broke into a laugh. "Yes, on my soul, you are right! It was my own suggestion to the damsel who seemed unaware of the difference between a regiment and a brigade. She had parts, that lady." A corner of his sister's mantle fell upon him as he added, "It is to be hoped that the real ensign has not behaved as badly to his wife as your scoundrelly Tomás—of whom it seems I had the doubtful honour to remind you."

Raoul grew red. "No, no," he said uncomfortably, "I am sure he was not like you. But I was enraged, you see, when I said that——"

"Not without cause," interrupted Hervey, dropping his bantering tone. "And I don't mind admitting, des Sablières, that . . . afterwards . . . I admired your pluck for snatching the last word in the way you did that night. We had not left you any other weapon, I'm afraid."

Raoul shook his head deprecatingly. "But of that Tomás I am ashamed. I had to tell you some story, it is true—though you never asked for one—but . . . I wanted an excuse for sitting on the wall a little longer, out of those abominable shoes, and . . . you forgive me?—I could not help enjoying the tale. Only when you said that I was really married did I not enjoy it quite so much. . . . And now you have avenged yourself a hundred times by all this. . . ." He waved his available hand round the room. "I think of it every day as I lie here, and I am smitten to the heart!"

"I wish you wouldn't think of it, then," said Hervey. "Read a book or go to sleep when you feel like that. Nobody wants you to——"

"To behave like a girl," finished Raoul. He clapped his hand over his mouth. "*Oh là là! que je suis maladroit!*"

And his face was so comical that Hervey laughed too.

*

With Mrs. Jeremy, of course, there had never been any need for reconciliation or rapprochement. Had he not been her "lamb" and her property from the beginning?

Raoul could not be ignorant of this gratifying fact, but so much the less could he be expected to divine her obstinate separation of his personality into two distinct entities, one of which was still repudiated by her. He discovered this mental peculiarity, however, one fine afternoon when, waking to find "Madame Jérémie," as he had taken to calling her, sewing by the open window, he was inspired, after looking at her in silence for a little while, to ask, in a far-away voice, "whether it was a dream, or whether it had really happened just now?"

"Has what happened, my dear?" enquired Mrs. Jeremy, putting down her work and looking over at him indulgently. Perhaps he had been dreaming, poor young gentleman, that he was back with the mother for whom he used to cry out when he was ill.

"Your kissing me," replied her patient with an intensification of his rapt manner. "I am afraid that it can only have been a dream—I only wish I could think . . ."

"As if I should ever do such a thing, Mr. Rowl!" exclaimed Mrs. Jeremy, positively bridling.

"Would it be so unpleasant an experience?" queried the young man, looking very innocent. "Now that M. Jérémie shaves me so beautifully? It is true that I had much rather have been awake. . . ."

Mrs. Jeremy took up her work again. "You talk a great deal too much nonsense, Sir!"

"I know when you would not have kissed me," observed her tormentor. "When I had on that uncomfortable grey gown and the beautiful complexion. You would rather have slapped me, I think."

Down went the sewing again. "Don't speak about that baggage!" ejaculated

Mrs. Jeremy. "When I think of her and her brazen face, imposing on a good kind gentleman like the Captain, my blood fairly boils!"

Raoul stared a moment, and then burst into laughter. "But, Madame Jérémie, it was I all the time! . . . You don't mean to say that you still think it was a real girl? I can assure you that my blood boils too when I think of that meagre if elegant little meal you brought me up, when I could have eaten all that roast of the Captain's to which you so cruelly referred."

"What I brought was quite enough for the young person," said Mrs. Jeremy stubbornly, resuming her sewing.

"But no, it was not! I assure you that it was not. And it was all that she had to support her during her climb out of the window—yes, and its insufficiency was probably the reason why she fell and broke her wrist. For this is her wrist, Madame Jérémie! . . . Come, you cannot really disbelieve me. And if I am not the lady, where did she go to? What of Captain Barrington's reputation?"

"I don't wish to discuss that hussy," declared Mrs. Jeremy, "but it's not in human nature to believe——" She broke off abruptly, and stood up as Captain Barrington himself appeared in the doorway. "Yes, Sir, he's awake; please to come in, Sir, if you wish."

Yet if, apparently, it was impossible for Mrs. Jeremy to concede the same identity to the fevered and half-drowned young man whom she had put to bed in the spare room on that Friday evening and the painted hussy who had vanished from the same apartment on the previous Wednesday night, there was one subject on which her credulity was unlimited, and that was "Boney" and his doings. She would swallow any libel against that bugbear of the English nation; on discovering which Raoul naturally exercised his wits in finding food for so entertaining a propensity.

One morning he had imperceptibly led her to the point where she exclaimed, "And so people don't get married in France nowadays, there being no churches left, and no clergymen!" (For twenty years ago she had heard of émigré priests, but of the Concordat of 1801 never.)

Raoul was pleased, because now he could administer a greater shock. "Oh, no, you are quite wrong there, Madame Jérémie. One does marry—a great deal. My last wife——"

Mrs. Jeremy, the most sure-handed of women, dropped the broom she was wielding. "Your–wife . . . your *last* wife. . . ."

"Didn't you know that I was married?" asked Raoul with elaborate carelessness. "Why not–I am nearly five and twenty."

The reasonableness of this consideration further disconcerted his victim. "But," she protested, remembering, "you were married before, you say–you have been a widower, already, at your age!"

"Oh, no," said the young man, gazing at the ceiling, "I am glad to say I was never that. And indeed," he added thoughtfully, "even if one of them had died, I could hardly describe myself as widowed, because there would always remain the other two. You see, we are allowed three."

"Three what?" demanded Mrs. Jeremy, her head turning.

"Three wives. It is the Emperor's wish."

Mrs. Jeremy sat down heavily in the nearest chair. "Mr. Rowl——"

"I daresay you don't believe me," went on Raoul, with an air of great candour. "But I will tell you all about my wives, if you wish. I wonder that I have not mentioned them before, for I am very fond of them all–Julie and Anastasie, and Claudine the newest one. It is true that I have not seen any of them for nearly three years, and it is possible that by now some of them, if not all, have been confiscated."

"Confiscated!" breathed his listener.

"Well, you see," explained the romancer, wondering how far he could go, "there is the future population of France to consider–that of course is why the Emperor wishes . . . and one cannot complain if one is absent so long. I daresay I shall easily find some more. But I should like to tell you about Claudine."

Mrs. Jeremy rose to her feet. "Mr. Rowl," she said in strong indignation, "I can't but think that you are jesting. If not, all I can say is–well, really I'd rather not discuss it with you." And indeed she was quite red.

"But don't you want to hear about Claudine?" asked the invalid with an ingratiating smile. "She had the most beautiful——"

"I'd Clodeen her!" said Mrs. Jeremy. "And you too, you young jackanapes, if I thought it was true! Three!"

"Madame Jérémie, that's not respectful," said Raoul lazily. "And surely Bonaparte's wishing me to have three wives is not as disgraceful as his habit of eating children—and you know that that is true, don't you?"

"Get along with you!" responded Mrs. Jeremy, breathing a sigh of relief, as her lamb's guile was revealed. "Making game of me like that! I don't believe you are married at all . . . and I pity your wife when you do get one!"

"My ideal wife," began Raoul unrepressed, "would be the lady with the wig who——" but Mrs. Jeremy went out and shut the door. And while he was still smiling to himself over his late success Captain Barrington's tread and that of the doctor were audible outside, and his thoughts were diverted from the subject, not altogether pleasantly, by Mr. Touchwood's unbandaging and manipulating his wrist; though he managed to keep up during the operation almost his usual flow of persiflage, desiring to know, for instance, whether, supposing the wrist remained stiff in perpetuity, it would gradually turn into a fossil—for he always expressed a great wish to be instructed in geology.

"One thing that won't easily turn into a fossil, young man," replied Mr. Touchwood, "is your tongue, I fancy. Or your spirit either," he added, as he finished re-bandaging. "There, I sha'n't have to hurt you like that again, I hope."

"And when may I get up?"

"All in good time," responded Mr. Touchwood, as he generally did to this query.

*

There was, however, one person in the household who was not subjugated by the young man upstairs, and that was John Jeremy, late captain's coxswain of the *Suffolk*. He was not hostile, but he was bewildered and inclined to be injured. Why Captain Barrington had turned round as he had, running himself thereby into a danger which still threatened him, was a complete mystery. It seemed too as if the young beggar had done nothing but get him into hot water, from the time when his master had called him to account in the *Kestrel* for hurting the blessed wildcat when he saved him from drowning himself (and secretly John Jeremy, though not inhumane, thought it would be better for all parties if he had succeeded in his attempt) down to yesterday, when Hannah had given him the rough side of her tongue because the razor had slipped when he was shaving his lordship. (For John Jeremy still performed that office, and performed it with much of the immense solemnity and subdued nervousness of the first occasion of all, when he had said humbly to the young man against the pillows, "I asks pardon if I've not done it well, Sir—me not being used to shaving the Captain, as always shaves his self, nor I haven't never shaved a gentleman in bed before.")

But Raoul, who had never set out to subjugate anybody, had no desire to wean the seaman from his rightful allegiance. He guessed quite well why the good mariner looked upon him with distrust, and but thought the better of him for it; it was because Jeremy knew that a French prisoner's presence at Fairhaven was a standing menace to his master.

Raoul could not forget it either. This house, which was heaven after the past, could not harbour him for ever . . . and what if Captain Barrington did have to pay dearly for his generosity? The thought tormented him at times; yet he was still bedridden and could not get away. Moreover since he had not been traced here three weeks ago, why should he be traced now, when he was drowned and forgotten? Thus Captain Barrington, when he had broached the question to him. But the possibility was there.

Another trouble was, that from beneath Captain Barrington's roof he dared not write to Juliana Forrest as he longed to do. Not that he imagined she would be anxious about him. Creedy, he knew, would soon acquaint her with the news of his escape, if only to get the residue of the money which, he had informed the fugitive, was now due. (Raoul had tried in vain to find out what was the total sum expended, having a firm intention of repaying it somehow.) And as Miss Forrest had, most evidently, abandoned her siege en règle of the Transport Office, she would not have heard of his supposed drowning; it was unlikely to be in the newspapers, and even if it had come to Creedy's ears he would not be very anxious to pass on the fact to her. No, he longed to write to Miss Forrest for other reasons. But, not having Creedy's facilities for private communication, he could not do it, lest the letter should fall into the wrong hands. So, since he could not tell her what he felt, he thought of her the more.

And about Captain Barrington he thought continually: why he had done what he had done for his sake; why he now believed what he, Raoul, said; why he was not married; why he was on leave so long in wartime? (He had tried to discover the last from Jeremy, and Jeremy had replied, quite snappily for him, "A man must have a rest some time, even from sinking of French ships!") Further, why his face in repose was so stern and sad? Raoul decided in the end that Captain Barrington had a secret grief. Probably he loved, or had loved, in vain. The lady had married another . . . was dead . . . had eloped . . . had jilted him at the altar. He longed to question Mrs. Jeremy on the point, but delicacy restrained him.

He did not, however, feel any hesitation in questioning the good lady about that half mythical sister of Captain Barrington's who was so largely responsible for his present situation.

*

What nobody at Fairhaven realized was that Miss Barrington would shortly be at hand to answer for herself, since, for reasons of her own, she was shortening her stay at Exeter by a full six days. Thus she descended upon Fairhaven en route for her own home on the other side of the river six days before she was expected there. Hervey, indeed, had not been thinking about her return at all; the ten days which had passed since his prisoner and he had shaken hands having given him more immediate occupation.

Aware of her departure from plan, Miss Barrington was therefore neither hurt nor surprised to find, when she arrived at her brother's door, that he was out, and Mrs. Jeremy likewise. She was conscious of a strange—but surely erroneous—impression that Jeremy had no great desire to admit her; at least he displayed no alacrity about the business (but then John Jeremy was never instinct with that quality) and he scratched his head with a puzzled air as he looked at her baggage.

"Mr. Rowl"

"Be you gwine to stay, Ma'am?"

"Yes, a night or so," responded Miss Lavinia. "—Unless there is any reason why I should not," she added. "You have not, I trust, got smallpox in the house?"

"Smallpox? Lor' no, Miss Barrington; whoever said so?" exclaimed Jeremy, looking alarmed; then, gathering by the visitor's face that the query was not meant seriously, he added, but without a smile: "I'll bring your portmanty to your room in a minute or two, Ma'am. For, if you'll excuse me, I've got summat to see to in the kitchen, Hannah being out." And, eyeing her again with that slow, curious, half distrustful look, he vanished.

"Jeremy is becoming a cook," thought Miss Barrington as she went upstairs, "and culinary cares are weighing upon his spirits."

Miss Barrington's bedroom at Fairhaven was supposed to be ready for occupation at half an hour's notice, and, since Mrs. Jeremy was out, Miss Lavinia took off her bonnet and cloak and herself began to remove the shrouds from the furniture. Thus employed, she soon detected that something was missing from the room—the little inlaid table by the bed, which Hervey had brought her as a present from Spain. What an odd thing . . . and yet perhaps not so odd after all, considering the confusion in this room at her last visit. What had become of that unfortunate young Frenchman, the cause of its disorganisation? She had often thought of his fate during the last three weeks, but she had seen nothing in the newspaper, and had not received any letter from Hervey. Perhaps he had got clear away, as she could not but hope.

No! she was not going to submit to being deprived, for no reason, of her little Spanish table, and, if Hannah had taken it into the spare bedroom, she would soon have it out again. So Miss Barrington went resolutely through the powdering-closet—the fatal powdering-closet—to investigate, remembering as she went her previous incursion into the spare bedroom, and what had met her eyes when she got there. . . .

It becomes therefore a question for psychologists whether her mental preoccupation with her former shock tended to heighten or to alleviate her

294

D. K. Broster

second one. Miss Lavinia herself inclined afterwards to the first alternative. At all events, so she averred later to her brother, she staggered and clutched her hand to her head like any heroine of romance, and her heart stopped beating—"absolutely ceased, my dear Hervey! And I said, aloud I believe, 'Good God, am I going mad, and is that to be my end?'?"

For there—but this time well in the bed, not on it—there he was again, the same young scamp, lying motionless in something the same attitude, save that to-day she could see more than his profile. And there was her vagabond table by the bedside, laden with a glass, a spoon, a bottle or two, a portion of jelly, and, rosily ensconced on a mat of their own leaves, two—or, more correctly, one and a half—of Hervey's incomparable nectarines, those nectarines for which duchesses might have sued in vain, and of which she, his dear and only sister, received a bare half-dozen in the course of the summer. Their presence here was as astounding and as eloquent as that of the runaway. If Hervey gave him *those*——

As once before, Miss Lavinia ventured nearer. The occupant of the bed was sound asleep . . . again. Yet he was not quite the young man of her first discovery, who had looked thin and tired indeed, but not wasted or transparent. Since she last saw him Hervey's wildcat visitant had clearly been very ill. But how in the name of Fortune. . . .

Deciding that, if not insane already, she certainly would soon become so unless she took steps to obtain information, Miss Barrington crept from the room in search of Jeremy (the door not being locked this time) and met him mounting the stairs, carefully carrying, not her baggage, but a covered bowl on a tray.

"Stop, Jeremy!" she said imperiously. "You can put down that turtle soup, or peacocks' tongues, or whatever it is, for a moment—he's fast asleep—but if you don't tell me how he got here again and what has happened you may as well order a coach and four for Bedlam at once!"

*

Every time that Raoul came to his senses in this pleasant room, this heavenly bed, these lavender-scented sheets, it was a fresh shock of bliss to

295

him. Yes, once again he was really here in decency and comfort, and not——He moved, gave a little sigh of utter contentment, and then became aware that the door handle was turning somewhat hesitatingly. He remembered that he was for an hour or so under the guardianship of Jeremy, and that Jeremy was always rather timid in discharging this function and required encouragement.

"Come in, Palinurus," he said—for it pleased him to air what remained of his classical knowledge on one quite incapable of appreciating it, and who, though it had been explained to him that this appellation was the name of a Trojan pilot, remained quite unaffected by its—as Raoul considered—extraordinary appropriateness.

But there came in instead a very handsome grey-haired lady bearing a bowl on a tray.

Raoul flushed up to the roots of his hair—that hair which, as he was instantly and painfully conscious, must be extremely untidy. Shaved he had been that morning—by Palinurus—but he felt in no state to receive a strange lady.

"I must apologize for intruding," said the newcomer in a very pleasant voice, as she set down the bowl by the jelly and the nectarines. "I hope you will allow me to replace John Jeremy till his spouse returns. I am Lavinia Barrington—Captain Barrington's sister, of whom I think you must have heard when . . . when you were here before—though you may have doubted her existence."

The rather hollow grey eyes went over her, and a little smile came into them. "We were to have met in the garden that evening I think," murmured their owner. "I hope, Madame, that you are so kind as to excuse my present condition. I did not know that I was to have the honour . . ."

"Nobody knew," said Miss Barrington frankly, "least of all I myself.—Now, about this soup? You are ready for it—can you manage with that bandaged wrist? Then I think a little rearrangement of pillows first." She tucked them under him. "Is that how Mrs. Jeremy does it? There—can you hold the bowl so?" And she sat herself down to watch the consumption of its contents.

"What is the stuff like? *Can* Jeremy cook? Ah, I expect it is really of Hannah's compounding."

"It tastes indeed like the soups of Mrs. Jeremy," replied the invalid, lifting his eyes from it. "She cooks divinely. Miss Barrington, I am spoilt in this house—you cannot figure to what an extent! Not to speak of owing Captain Barrington my life."

"Tut!" said Miss Lavinia, "you came very near owing him the opposite, I fancy. Or rather——Do you know, my dear young man, that I am the cause of all your troubles . . . as a woman generally is of a man's?"

Raoul seemed to ponder this. A trace of a smile appeared; it had a kind of secret quality. Then he observed politely: "I hope that I should welcome anything at the hands of a lady," and addressed himself once more to the bowl.

"Your nation has always been gallant," observed Miss Lavinia, smiling in her turn, "but I assure you that the coals of fire which you are preparing to heap on my head have already been preceded by the ashes of penitence. In other words, I was afterwards extremely sorry that I had betrayed you to my brother.—But a woman's repentance always comes too late. Haven't you found it so, Mr.—Rowl?"

"I?—No," said the young man, momentarily taken aback. "I have not made any philosophic reflections on the subject.—Do you think, then, Miss Barrington, that it is better not to repent at all?"

"For a woman, perhaps, since the result is always so ineffectual," pronounced his visitor.

"Ah, no, not always!" said Raoul quickly. "No, I cannot allow that." And he finished the soup.

"And have you made any philosophic reflections about a man's repentance?" enquired Miss Lavinia, as she took the empty bowl from him.

There was certainly meaning in her tone this time, and Raoul coloured faintly. "No," he said, his eyes lighting up, "those are cold things—reflections. For undeserved goodness one has only—gratitude."

("This is all very extraordinary," thought Miss Lavinia, "and I don't wonder that Jeremy could give me no coherent account of what has been taking place. Of course, Hervey has the best heart in the world, but still . . .")

"My brother has gone to Tawton, I hear," she remarked, casting a side glance on the symbolic nectarines.

"Yes. He has the goodness to do a commission for me—to buy me some clothes," said Raoul with half-concealed elation. "To-morrow I am to get up for a little."

"More clothes!" exclaimed Miss Barrington. "—You reject then that elegant grey gown of which you were so careful, Mademoiselle?"

The young man in the bed gave her a look which said so much that Miss Lavinia's heart warmed towards him. With a little further acquaintance they would understand each other perfectly.

"I regret that I never saw you in it," she went on. "Perhaps some day . . . I believe that I have it in my room still. I have half a mind to get it."

"But you must not let Mrs. Jeremy see it," said Raoul, smiling. "It might give her a *coup de sang*, that costume."

"I trust then that she has not made away with it," said Miss Lavinia. "I would never forgive her!" She got up with her surprising ease of movement, and went incontinently through the closet into her own room.

She had to open and shut a good many drawers in the chest where she had laid the dress and wig the morning after the battle, and in the middle of her search suddenly heard Hervey's voice in the other room.

"Ah, my sister is not here then?" (Did he not sound relieved?) "But you will have her and Mrs. Jeremy fighting over your body now, I expect, my boy. Have you slept at all this afternoon?"

"Yes, thank you, Sir," replied the invalid, while Miss Barrington caught her breath. "My boy!" and Hervey's tone . . . and the young Frenchman's when he answered him! Miracles had been going forward in that room!

And by even that brief contemplation of them she deprived herself of the mischievous pleasure of having her first meeting with her repentant brother in the presence of his former victimizer and victim, for by the time she got through the cupboard the bedroom door had shut behind him.

D. K. Broster

Juliana's Immortelles

"The Princess and her favourite embraced each other with transport too violent to be expressed, and went out together to pour the tears of tenderness in secret, and exchange professions of kindness and gratitude."—Rasselas, chap. xxxviii.

The sun of the September afternoon poured cheerfully into Hervey Barrington's meticulously tidy dressing room, where he was changing into riding clothes. He was going to Tawton on business—not by coach this time. Yesterday Lavinia had returned to her cottage, having stayed four days at Fairhaven. Hervey had observed to her that it was clear why she had prolonged her visit beyond the couple of nights for which he was usually privileged to entertain her, and asked how Mrs. Jeremy had borne this preoccupation with her especial property.

"Mrs. Jeremy's property?" queried his sister, flashing at him one of her quick glances. "Isn't he rather yours, Hervey?"

"It is I, certainly, who am responsible for him, if that is what you mean," Captain Barrington had replied. But it was not what she meant, and he knew it; and even now a smile curved his resolute mouth as, having settled his stock before the mirror, he went to the window and looked out.

His dressing room was one of the few rooms in Fairhaven which overlooked the little walled fruit garden at the side of the house. However, it was not his espaliers that he was contemplating now. On the plot of grass in the middle was a couch, and by it a book lying face downwards. But the occupant of the couch was at this moment standing meditatively in front of a laden plum tree which was displaying its treasures against the warm stone of the wall.

Raoul called this little fruit-ringed garden his parc or sheepfold, for here he and his sofa had been installed for the last two afternoons, on condition that he never strayed out of the enclosure—he was under engagement not even to return to the house without first ascertaining that the coast was clear. But, so successfully had his presence at Fairhaven been concealed, that, beyond taking certain obvious precautions, one did not trouble much about the prospect of discovery. From his window Hervey watched the selection of two of the ripest plums, and the convalescent's slow return with them to his couch, on which he stretched himself out luxuriously. Exactly a month to-day since he had been smuggled into this house. How Hervey was going to get him away when he was fit for it he had not yet thought out; he only knew that he had no desire to hasten that moment. How odd that seemed!

He left the window, and had drawn on one riding boot when there was a knock, and Mrs. Jeremy appeared, announcing that a lady and gentleman from London desired to see him on business, and were at this moment in the morning room. She held out a tray, and Hervey, taking up the cards which lay thereon, read with puzzled eyes the names of Viscount Fulgave and the Honourable Juliana Forest.

*

It was not hope which had brought Juliana to Stowey. She had been driven here, after twenty-four haunted, miserable days, by the longing to hear on the spot what details were known of the tragedy witnessed, as she gathered by the coast-guards, and, if M. des Sablières' body had by this time been recovered, to be sure that it had fitting burial. For in his death, as in the last painful months of his short life, she felt that she was the only person in England to care for him.

Yet, on the other hand, the very shortness of that life was due to her, to her initial waywardness, which had set in motion the whole fatal train of events, as the unthinking loosening of a pebble may end by causing a whole cliff wall to slide downward in an avalanche of disaster. So acute and so persistent was her distress that her father finally snatched at any method of alleviating it; and though he thought the present method both morbid and inconvenient—for he had threatenings of gout at the moment—he offered to take her down to Stowey on this melancholy errand. They had arrived this afternoon, and made their way to the coast-guard station, only to be told, in the soft Devon tongue, that it was not the coast-guards, but Captain Barrington up to Fairhaven who had seen the Frenchman drown, and that no, the body had not come ashore yet, likely never would. So to Fairhaven they had come.

And in the pleasant, casemented room where she was to hear the last act of the tragedy she had written Juliana sat and wondered whether this old retired naval captain (such her father had said he must certainly be) would show annoyance at their coming; would refuse details, or . . . give too many. And as she heard the door handle turn she felt a sudden doubt of her courage, a sudden wonder at her temerity. . . .

Compared to the veteran she had expected, the somewhat stern, good-looking man who came in was young. But, young or old, those eyes had seen Raoul des Sablières die . . . and she could not take her own from him all the time that her father made themselves and their errand known, and asked Captain Barrington for details. "The . . . the body, I gather, has not been recovered?" he finished.

For all her mental anguish, Juliana could not avoid noticing the colour which mounted at that to Captain Barrington's face.

"No," he said a little indistinctly. "I . . . I doubt if there is now any chance of it." He turned away—for he had not sat down—and murmuring something about a draught, closed the casement window. Then, fixing a very clear and steady pair of eyes on Lord Fulgrave, he said: "You were sincerely interested in this young man, my Lord?"

"Sincerely," replied his Lordship, with a glance at his daughter. "I did my best to obtain his release from the hulks. Had he not escaped and lost his life in so doing, I should have succeeded, for it appears that he had rendered a signal service to a British officer at Albuera, and the Transport Board were prepared to recommend him for an unconditional cartel. But now, of course . . ."

"A cartel!" exclaimed Captain Barrington in evident astonishment. "He would have been released altogether?"

"That was certainly intended. He had saved the life of this officer—a major in the Third Foot. But before the Commissioners could take the necessary steps came the melancholy news of the young man's death."

Why did Captain Barrington look so strange—so much more than merely surprised? But Juliana's eyes, in her pain, wandered at last away from his face . . . only to encounter a sharper pang. From where she sat she could see the wide river that had drowned "Mr. Rowl," all blue and sparkling under the September sky. Now she did not want to hear those details she had come to hear . . . it hurt too deeply . . . she cared too much—more, more than she knew. Oh, why had she come?

"You . . . you astonish me very much," she heard Captain Barrington saying, and then he seemed to come to a stop.

"It is indeed very regrettable that the young man should no longer be alive to profit by this favour," observed her father.

"You are quite sure, my Lord, that it really would have been extended to him, had he lived?—Forgive my pertinacity!"

"From what I was told, Sir, I feel convinced of it."

"Then——" began Captain Barrington, and stopped again. Suddenly he put a curious question. "My Lord, are you disposed to admit that there may be occasions when a man's duty to his country conflicts with the claims of humanity?"

"I suppose there may be such occasions," replied his Lordship cautiously.

"Then if, in the case of this young Frenchman, who is reported to have been drowned——"

"Reported!" interjected Lord Fulgrave. "But was it not you yourself, Captain Barrington, who reported it? Was your report then based only on hearsay?"

"Yes, I *did* report it," admitted Captain Barrington, "but——" He hesitated, and a spasm of relief darted through Juliana. He meant that he had not, after all, witnessed the tragedy with his own eyes . . . and, after all, she need not hear of it. But the speaker was going on again:

"If I were to tell you, Lord Fulgrave," he said squarely, "that this young Frenchman had been rescued, hidden and cared for through a serious illness by an Englishman who ought no doubt to have made him over to the authorities, but who could not bring himself to do this, what would be your opinion of that man?"

But Lord Fulgrave had no opportunity of stating his opinion, for his daughter was on her feet, stretching out a hand to Hervey Barrington. "Is it true, Sir," she implored, "is it true, or only a possibility, that he is not . . ."

Hervey turned to her. "It is quite true, Madam," he replied soberly. "He is alive and——"

It was he who caught Miss Forrest as she swayed, transferring her quickly to her father's care, and ringing the bell violently for Mrs. Jeremy. Then supervened a period of the attentions of that good lady and smelling salts—at one moment there was even borne to Hervey's nostrils, he having discreetly turned his back, the odious smell of burnt feathers; and during the time that he thus contemplated the *Kestrel* at her moorings, he lost any remaining doubts as to Miss Forrest's identity. She was, of course, the unnamed lady of Raoul's story; and it seemed hardly necessary for it to be apologetically whispered into his ear by her father, as it presently was, that the news of the young man's being alive after all had proved too much for her, she having taken the sad affair so much to heart. Swoon and explanation, however, confirmed him in his resolve to remove the veil from his own conduct—or misconduct; he could not keep Raoul from these good friends of his and from the prospect of release because of the possibility of risk to himself.

At last Miss Forrest, apologizing for her foolishness and the trouble she had caused, and declining Mrs. Jeremy's suggestion that she should repose herself in Miss Barrington's bedroom, appeared fully recovered, and Hervey caught her whisper: "Ask him, Papa—ask him how—and where—and who . . ." And Lord Fulgrave obediently approached him.

"Will you tell us the rest, Sir? Who, for instance, is the man you spoke of, who showed so much charity? You need not be afraid of our ever breathing a word about his—humanity."

Hervey Barrington had turned round. "Thank you, my Lord, for the assurance. Since the man in question wears His Majesty's uniform he is doubly grateful for it. He has the honour of speaking to you at this moment."

Never in his life had he made so dramatic an announcement. "You, Sir!" exclaimed Lord Fulgrave. "Then you did not see him drown—you saved him!"

"Yes," said Hervey rather curtly (he did not love the histrionic). "What else would you have a man do?"

"Quite so—but you appear to have done a good deal more than that! Captain Barrington, I should esteem it a privilege——" He held out his hand.

"This is a felon's hand, my Lord," said Hervey, and for the first time he smiled.

"Tut, tut!" said the condemner of Creedy, and he wrung it. "And are we to understand that you have the young man still here, under your roof?"

"Well, he is actually in the garden at this moment. I will have him summoned; or perhaps . . ." he hesitated.

"I think you said, Sir," put in Juliana, leaning forward, "that he had been ill?"

"Yes, very ill, and he is still weak, though quite well again. If therefore his Lordship would give himself the trouble to come with me into the garden, the stairs being somewhat trying to a convalescent . . . Yet doubtless Miss Forrest too would wish . . ." He looked from one to the other.

Yes, Miss Forrest did wish, and announced herself as perfectly able to accompany her father to the garden. Indeed, she had now the most lovely colour; so Hervey gave her his arm. And as they left the house she said to him in a low voice: "Captain Barrington, I hardly dare let myself believe it. Yet, since it must be true, how is one ever to thank you?"

"By not saying a word about my action to any one, Miss Forrest," replied Hervey Barrington, and lifted the latch of the little door in the wall.

*

"Raoul," said Hervey's deep voice, penetrating a very fleeting dream, "here are two visitors to see you. Don't move—they will excuse your not rising."

He stood back, and Raoul opened his eyes, half sleepy, half startled . . . and saw who one of them was. The colour rushed over his face, he made an inarticulate sound, and tried to get off the couch. But her companion—he must still be half asleep, it could not really be Lord Wellington!—prevented this disobedience by coming close and holding out his hand.

"How do you do, Sir? I am exceedingly glad to learn that you are not drowned, as we thought. And here is my daughter, who is in the same case. We came to . . . ah . . . lay a wreath on your grave, and find—most happily—that there is no necessity."

"Sir . . . my Lord . . ." stammered Raoul, utterly confused and dizzy. Whether this tall gentleman with the nose were real or a remnant of a dream, she was real, and was looking at him with a little rainbow of a smile. How could he answer coherently or speak to any one else . . . or even to her? And she said nothing, but only looked at him with that heavenly kindness.

Hervey had by now brought up a rustic chair. "Sit down, my dear," said the gentleman, and Juliana obeyed. "Perhaps I ought to introduce myself," he went on to the young man, "for your good friend here probably does not know that I have not previously had the pleasure of meeting you, though indeed you have been much in my thoughts these last months. I am Lord Fulgrave."

Again Raoul tried to get out thanks, again he failed to produce anything coherent. But Lord Fulgrave by no means waited for either.

"And I may give myself the satisfaction of telling you, Sir," he pursued, "since you are fortunately still alive, that I have been able, by following up a happy suggestion of my daughter's, based on something you once told her, to procure—however, I think she shall inform you of that herself." He seemed in high good humour—as indeed he was, on Juliana's account. "I see—ah—that you have some fine espaliers over there, Captain Barrington. Fruit-growing greatly interests me. . . ."

Hervey said something; and their voices receded . . . died out of the garden altogether. Between these four fruit-laden walls, under the blue roof, there was only Juliana Forrest . . . who had come all this way to see him. She had on a muslin gown the colour of an apricot, with little silver lines . . . she was not looking at him now, and a silence had fallen. Was she thinking of the close of their last meeting? As if he should ever presume on that angelic gift of hers! He slipped off the couch on to one knee, took her hand, and bending his head kissed it passionately, without words.

"For more than three weeks I have believed you drowned," said Juliana in a little thread of a voice, and trembling. "I only heard just now, and the joy . . . the relief——" She turned her head away and put up her free hand to her eyes.

"You thought that!" said Raoul in deep distress. "I hoped—I was almost sure you would not hear it. . . . I have longed to write to you, but there was Captain Barrington's safety to consider."

Juliana Forrest turned her head back, careless that two tears were coursing down her face. And seeing him still kneeling there, so thin and altered—"Please, please, Monsieur des Sablières, lie down again! Indeed you should. . . . Oh, to please me!"

To please her he would at least sit upon the couch. And indeed he felt a strange swimming in the head. Notre Dame de Bon Secours come to visit him . . . or come to bury him? Perhaps he was dead and in Paradise already (only that seemed unlikely). But here certainly was a denizen of heaven. And he might—he must—address her.

"I am grieved indeed that you should have heard that," he said again, and stole another long look at her. ("But are you really?" asked a little voice within him. "If she had not heard it, she would not, probably, be here.") "How did you learn it, Mademoiselle? Surely it was not in the newspapers?"

If Raoul was a prey to varied emotions, his visitor had to control even more varied. He whom less than an hour ago she was mourning as dead was alive, and was here within reach of her hand; and she had great news for him. Also, the last time they had met she had . . . But, in presence of matters so much more vital, that memory had scarcely room to raise its head and make her blush.

"No, it was not in the newspapers," she answered. "I heard because—oh, Monsieur des Sablières, I have good news for you—the prospect of a cartel!"

"What!" exclaimed Raoul, gripping the edge of the couch.

"It is true," said Juliana seriously. "But for your escape—my doing—you might be in France to-day. Even now, I suppose, it only needs your identification by this officer, and the Transport Office will recommend you for it."

"Identification?" stammered the young man, his head whirling. "What officer?"

"The officer whose life you saved at Albuera—Major Brackenbury of the Buffs."

"But—I never heard his name! And you, Mademoiselle, how did you know anything about him?"

His amazement was very sweet to Juliana. At last she had accomplished on his behalf something that was not merely reparation. "That day by the stream," she began, looking at him with a really radiant smile—and with that told him the whole story of the quest of Major Brackenbury and his gratitude.

"My God!" said Raoul, gazing at her almost stupefied. "And you have done that for me—that too!"

But, after all, Juliana had been too lately and too long under the shadow of the misfortunes which she had brought upon him so easily to forget them. She looked away, and it was with rather an unsteady voice that she said: "Whatever I do, I can never make up for the harm I have caused you. Even if you shortly receive your freedom, as I hope you will, nothing can give you back these last months, or make up to you for what you have suffered—through my doing. All your life you will remember that the folly of an English girl sent you to—that."

"And that her unexampled courage and devotion saved me from it again," said Raoul, "—more than saved me! Oh, Miss Forrest, if you could only know how you appear to me, you would cease to torment yourself with this unnecessary remorse. You bring me this great gift, return to my own country, and you think I can have room in my heart for the shadow of a reproach? A *vrai dire*," he added, and his voice sank, "I think that in my heart at this moment there is room for only one feeling—wonder at your incredible goodness in coming all this way to ask the last tidings of a poor prisoner who had crossed your path . . . If I were the ghost I might be, Mademoiselle, and saw you standing at my grave, and though I knew, as I do know, living, that you had spent so much time, so much effort, so much gold to help me, still the immortelles in your hand would outweigh all else. You have come yourself, when you did not even know that I had a tongue to thank you!"

With an emotion so contagious as this Juliana had never before been in contact. She turned a little pale.

"You exaggerate, I think, Monsieur des Sablières," she said in a rather troubled voice. "And let us discuss now how we are to proceed about the cartel. If you were to come back with my father and me to London——"

"Come back with you!" exclaimed Raoul as if he had not heard aright.

"You think it would not be safe?" asked Juliana, mistaking his tone. "But you have only to prove your identity—you are practically a pardoned man!"

Ah, would it be safe—in a different sense? To sit by her side for two days—to sleep under the same roof; it might be intoxicating, but would it be safe? Yet, had it meant Huntingdon Gaol, he would do it . . . if he were really to have the chance of it. . . .

"I will discuss it with my father," Juliana was going on, "It seems to me that it would be the best plan." She rose. "I think I hear him returning. We might come again to-morrow to see you about it; we are staying at the 'Dolphin.' And I have so much to hear. You have been ill, and nursed here, by Captain Barrington—not only ill, I see, but injured?"

Raoul had bent his head. Why must she go? But if she came again to-morrow perhaps he could bear that this should end.

"Yes, I have a great deal to tell you about Captain Barrington, and what I owe to him . . . and a great deal to hear too, if I may. It amazes me that you can have found that officer—and it was nothing, what I did. Are you sure it is not a mistake?"

Juliana shook her head. "Major Brackenbury did not call it nothing, I assure you. Yes, Papa, I am ready."

And Raoul walked in a dream beside her to the garden door, where Lord Fulgrave and his host were standing. Lord Fulgrave shook his hand.

"I am sorry to see that sling, Sir," he remarked. "But I hope it will be many a day before you have your foot in one, which is where mine will be to-morrow, I am afraid. Gout."

"In that case," said Raoul, "how can I express my sense of your Lordship's goodness in taking this journey?"

"I am very glad I did," responded his Lordship, looking at him kindly. "Yes, to-morrow, Captain Barrington, we will discuss ways and means for getting this young gentleman his due."

"I shall have pleasure in waiting upon you, my Lord, as I suggested," replied Hervey—and was instantly aware of a hard, almost vicious grip on his arm from behind. "—Or," he added hastily, "in welcoming you here."

"Yes, that would admit of a full council of war," responded Lord Fulgrave. "Provided that my enemy has not attacked me.—Till to-morrow, then, Monsieur des Sablières."

"—But you mustn't show yourself yet, you know, my dear boy," said Hervey quietly, putting a hand on Raoul's shoulder, for the latter was manifesting every intention of escorting Miss Forrest to the carriage.

"My faith! I was forgetting," said Raoul, a trifle taken aback. "No, I suppose not. *Au revoir*, then, Mademoiselle."

It was as he raised her hand to his lips that the full memory of their last parting came like a tide upon Juliana, dyeing her face for a moment. Heaven grant he were not thinking of it too! . . . But surely the news she had brought must have obliterated the recollection!

She went to the carriage hugging that quite illusory consolation.

Relinquishing a Dream

"At last he began to fear lest they should be discovered. . . . He therefore took passage in a ship to Suez."—Rasselas, chap. xv.

When Hervey came back from escorting the visitors to their carriage the occupant of the *parc* was still standing just inside the garden door like a man in a trance. Hervey smiled at him.

"Well, Raoul?"

"I am still . . . rather overwhelmed," confessed Raoul—and he looked it. "*Her* coming like this . . . and the cartel. Have you heard of that? It's like a *conte de fées.*"

Hervey slipped his arm in his and began to lead him back to the couch. "I don't need to say how delighted I am, do I, my dear lad? But why have you never told *me* of this British officer at Albuera?"

"Because there was really nothing to tell. I kept a Polish lancer from spearing him, that was all. I never even knew his name. And now it seems that, thanks to Miss Forrest's good offices—and Lord Fulgrave's, of course—I have merely to show myself to be sent back to France! It's astounding!"

It was not unnatural that he should go on in this vein for a little, and Hervey had no wish in the world to stop him; he was too rejoiced himself. Yet before long an unpleasant little thought was tapping like a woodpecker in his own brain: "What is to become of me when my illegal share in this happy event is revealed? No one, not even the boy himself, seems to be going to give a thought to that!" But he was ashamed of this selfish reflection, and, lest he should betray any preoccupation with his own safety, abstained from reminding the fugitive for the second time that he ought not to show himself yet, merely announcing that, to his regret, he must hurry off to keep an appointment in Tawton. He should probably be back late. "So remember Mr. Touchwood's orders, Raoul," he said as he left him; "bed at nine o'clock sharp. Pleasant dreams to you to-night!"

Raoul did not feel sure about the night, but he had one here and now—an enchanting day-dream, in which Juliana sat beside him still, and he was able to say all the things he had left unsaid; and in which he thought at first much less of the great news which she had brought him than of to-morrow, when she would come again and he could gaze at her anew.

But after a while he did think of it, absorbedly. Could it really be that he was practically a free man, about to be sent back to France, after all his struggles and shifts, by the British Government itself? He saw the news arriving at Les Sablières, and Maman reading his letter in her bedroom with the old-fashioned furniture, and running with it to his father in the library of the château, under the portrait of that forbidding-looking ancestor in the buff coat who had fought with Turenne. And then they would both tell

Adrienne, perhaps in the orchard, where she would be supervising the harvesting of those apple trees that he and she used so assiduously to climb. . . . And then, a little later, there would be his mother in his arms, his father saying that he was not ashamed of him, and Adrienne hearing how he had impersonated her . . . And to make this dream true he had only to present himself at the Transport Office to meet this grateful major of the Third Foot and establish his identity. . . .

Raoul, lying with his hands behind his head, suddenly became so still that the robin which he had been trying to tame did alight for a moment on his foot, and cocked its head at him. But the young man never even saw that this signal favour had been accorded to him. A thought like a dark cloud had suddenly obscured the golden horizon. It was not so simple as all that! How could he go and present himself at the Transport Office and establish his identity without terribly injuring Hervey Barrington?

A month ago he had been reported drowned—by Captain Barrington himself. How was it that he had not been drowned, and where had he been all the time? He would not tell the authorities, of course—not even if they refused the cartel in consequence—but the danger was that they would find out. And if they did, they would find, not only that Captain Barrington had concealed him for weeks, but that he had deliberately told a lie to cover his action—and told it in black and white in an official report! The discovery could hardly harm *him*, since even at the time he was destined for a pardon, but for Hervey Barrington it would mean utter ruin. And was he to go lightly off to France and leave him to that?

Raoul suddenly became very nervous. Suppose someone was to look over the wall now and see him—suppose some inquisitive stranger were to come into the garden? To think that he had only been stopped by Captain Barrington from walking openly out to Lord Fulgrave's carriage! He shivered, rang the bell at his elbow, and got off the couch; and, when Mrs. Jeremy appeared in answer to this summons, demanded to enter the house on the plea that it was getting cold; on which he was led back and scolded for not having rung earlier. But the offer of a fire he refused, saying that he should soon go to bed; and so laboriously ascended the stairs to the morning room.

Once alone there he took up a book, threw it down, sat in the window seat, looked at the estuary, the *Kestrel*, the opposite shore rosy with the sunset. This must be talked over . . . but with whom? Hervey would say, "Go and claim your freedom; never mind about me." Juliana Forrest, who had brought it to him, would hardly urge him to throw it away. . . . Oh, what was he to do?

For some twenty minutes he sat there thinking it over, till all at once he heard Jeremy's heavy foot pounding rapidly up the stairs, and the coxswain put his head in.

"Oh, you're here, Sir? I—"

He was out of breath. "Come in," said Raoul from the window seat. "What is it?" Then, seeing his alarmed discomposure, he got up. "Not an accident to Captain Barrington, I hope?"

"No, Sir," said Jeremy. "Worse!" He came nearer and dropped his voice. "Mr. Rowl, *they've heard!*"

No need to ask what, or who "they" were. "Great God!" said Raoul. "Are they after me? But I am—"

"Nay, not after *you*," interrupted Jeremy contemptuously. "After him, because of you! . . . When I were out this afternoon," he went on, still breathlessly, "I fell in wi' one of the coast-guards and stopped to pass the time o' day. And after some talk he says, 'Sims to me there'm a great interest took sudden in that French prisoner as was drowned here last month,' says he. 'Why, whatever dü ee mean?' says I, feeling like a man do when he see a squall coming sudden out of the nor'east and him carrying too much sail—'whatever dü ee mean, Jan?' 'Why,' says he then, 'only this afternoon there was a lady and gentleman from Lunnon askin' about him, and we sends them on to Cap'n Barrington, as saw it happen, and blow me if now on top o' that there ain't a Navy lootenant asking the very same questions, only more of 'em, where the prisoner come from, just whereabouts he were drowned, whether it was thought there was any smugglers aiding and abetting of him—and so on. So I says to him: 'You go and see Cap'n Barrington, Sir;

he'll tell you all there is to know.' 'Yes, I'm going to see Cap'n Barrington in any case,' says he."

"Well?" asked Raoul, who was oddly breathless too, as Jeremy paused.

"Arter that," resumed Jeremy, "I come back as fast as I can and finds out from Hannah that no Navy lootenant ain't arrived. . . . Ah, but don't you go flattering yourself, Mr. Rowl—he's been here right enough, five minutes ago!"

"And what happened?" asked Raoul, feeling slightly sick.

"He asks for Cap'n Barrington; I says he'm away from Stowey, won't be back till late. At that he looks a'most as if he meant to wait, but I weren't going to let him into the house. So he says, looking grimlike, that he'll come again in the morning, seeing as he must see Cap'n Barrington in person; nor he wouldn't leave no message. Had some kind of a paper in his hand too, but he put it back in his pocket and goes off, looking . . . well, as an officer looks when it's a matter of the bosun's mate and the cat-o'-nine tails."

"He was probably some friend or acquaintance of Captain Barrington's," urged Raoul, though he did not believe it.

Captain Barrington's coxswain snorted. "Precious few of them as I don't know by sight, one way or t'other. And moreover, when I asks him if he'll leave his name he says, No, it's not known to Cap'n Barrington.—No, no, Sir, he'm come from the Admiralty to make enquiries; perhaps to take the Cap'n back to Lunnon. Take my word for it, they've heard *something*—else why should he a' gone asking all these questions of the coast-guards? and now the Cap'n's got to answer for it all!"

Raoul sat down again, turning whiter and whiter.

"I've always said," went on this new Jeremy, now so fiercely loquacious, "that he didn't ought to have done it—and him as it were under their Lordships' displeasure already, though he was acquitted at the court-martial—and quite right too, for if ever——"

His hearer was on his feet. "What in God's name are you talking about? What court-martial?"

"He haven't never told you why he's on half-pay—on the shelf?"

"I didn't know he was on half-pay. I thought he was on leave—you gave me to understand so!"

"Leave! an officer like him—in wartime!" said Jeremy scornfully. "No, he'm eating his heart out these two years, and all along of the *Suffolk* lost off the Scillies through no fault of his; and if ever there had been a chance of his getting another ship, as was always said he would, because he left the court without any sort o' blame being put upon him, well, it don't look much like it now, do it, harbouring a French prisoner and lying about it, as I always said he were crazed to do? And now, if it's been found out—"

He made a short dramatic pause, during which Raoul subsided once more on to the window seat and put his head against the mullion, speechless. So this was the explanation of the sad sternness of Captain Barrington's face in repose. And, for his sake, he had weighted the scale against himself still further. . . .

"They always say as it's bad luck to save a man from drowning," resumed the sailor darkly. "He'm sure to do you an injury in the end!"

Raoul got up, steadying himself by the sill. "Jeremy, that's Captain Barrington's sailing-boat, isn't it? *Eh bien*, the moment it is dark you can start for some place on the coast—anywhere—and just turn me out there . . . as long as I am out of this house and no one sees me go nothing can be proved."

There was a feverish flush on his cheek. "You'd not get far," said Jeremy, eyeing him dubiously.

"That would not matter so long as I was not here!"

Jeremy considered a moment, "No, not without Captain Barrington's orders I couldn't do that!"

"But, you fool," said Raoul impatiently, "he would never give them. Don't you know him better than that? This must be done unknown to him, before he returns."

"But he'd soon see the *Kestrel* was gone," objected Jeremy. "And a sailing-boat's easy tracked by other folk."

"Then what are we to do?" asked Raoul. "You want to get rid of me at once, I suppose, just as much or more than I want to go? But I cannot walk far—it is no good pretending it. I cannot hire a conveyance here. Couldn't you row me somewhere in the little boat?"

"The skiff? I've got her bottom up in the garden for caulking of her seams—she'm leaking a bit—couldn't go rowing no distance in her."

"Get another boat, then, from somewhere!"

"And have to answer a mort of questions! . . . No, I'll see what can be done to the skiff atween now and dark, and maybe I can get her shipshape enough to put you across the river, Sir—that would be better than nothing."

Raoul put his hand to his head, which was beginning to ache.

"Yes, and I must go *after* Captain Barrington's return, not before. Then he will not find out until morning. Don't let Mrs. Jeremy know either. . . . What time, do you think?"

Jeremy reflected deeply. "There's no moon to speak of. Sun rises about half-past five. I'll have to slip out without waking Hannah, for she'd certain sure stop me. . . . I should say as near three o'clock as possible, Sir."

"Very well; and try and bring me some food to take with me. I will save what I can from my supper. I must have a map of some kind too; do you know where Captain Barrington keeps his?"

But Jeremy did not know. "And where would you be thinking of making for, Sir?"

"Upon my soul, I don't know," answered Raoul, and laughed.

When Jeremy was gone he hunted vainly in the bookcase and drawers for a map, and then fell to writing a note for Hervey; for there was no point in leaving him in the dark as to why he was running away. He wrote it stumblingly; it sounded to him cold and dry compared with what he felt towards him, and the message he asked Hervey to convey to Miss Forrest more inadequate still. He supposed he should leave this note on his pin-cushion like a heroine of romance.

Acutely depressed, he went upstairs, undressed, and got into bed; he must not excite Mrs. Jeremy's suspicions. It was the last time she would bring him a meal; the last time he should have her comfortable presence beside him. And apparently he was not to enjoy even that bittersweet consolation, for it was his fellow conspirator who brought him his supper.

"I got Hannah to let me do it," he whispered, so absorbed by intrigue that the bowl of soup nearly slid off the tray on to its destined recipient. "Now if you'll be ready, Sir, from two o'clock onwards, I'll come so soon as I can give Hannah the slip. I've bin overhauling the skiff——"

The door opened. "What are you worrying Mr. Rowl about that boat for?" asked the voice of his spouse, as she came in after all. "He isn't interested in that. Now, Mr. Rowl, you eat up your soup, or you won't be looking your best if the beautiful young lady comes to see you again to-morrow—you stayed up too long as it was. . . . What are you waiting for, Jeremy?"

Rolling a conspiratorial eye towards the bed, John Jeremy reluctantly departed.—Oh yes, it would be funny, if it were not otherwise. . . . Raoul obediently consumed his soup, but his eyes followed Mrs. Jeremy as she went and pulled to the window curtains. "I sha'n't bring your breakfast till a bit later to-morrow," she announced. "No good comes of invalids being waked too early." Behind her back the invalid smiled a pale smile.

Presently she came and stood by him. "Well, my dear, and a beautiful young lady she is indeed.—What's that under your pillow—bread?"

"I . . . I thought I might be hungry in the night," muttered Raoul shamefacedly.

"My dear life, don't put it *there*! you'll have nasty crumbs all down the bed!" She rescued the slice. "Leave it on the table, covered over . . . but don't let me hear of your being awake in the night to eat it!"

"No, very well; you shall not hear of it," promised her charge; on which she tucked him in, saying: "Now, go to sleep—for I wouldn't keep awake for the Captain if I was you—and dream of your visitors!"

"Mrs. Jeremy," said Raoul, "will you kiss me?"

"Well, I never!" exclaimed Mrs. Jeremy. Then she saw that he was not joking or near it. "What's the matter with you this evening? . . . Well, there, my dear," she added quite simply, "to tell truth, I've often thought of doing it . . . and I daresay the beautiful young lady wouldn't mind."

After the salute and her departure Raoul did blow out the candle and try to go to sleep while he could, but kaleidoscopic visions of past and future kept forming and reforming in his brain, till at last one dominated the rest and stayed—Juliana Forrest coming to this house to-morrow, full of her generous plans, to find him fled in the night with scarcely a word, the safety she had brought him after such long endeavours flung away. Would she understand that he must do it? Surely, surely; her past conduct showed it. Yet, after all, she was a woman, and it would seem an affront to her to find him gone . . . and gone whither? To claim his freedom, in such haste that he could not wait to see her again? No, it was intolerable that she should think that, when, as far as he could see, he never would be able to claim it because of Captain Barrington; when indeed, if he were recaptured in the next few days—and the chances of that were about ten to one—he would certainly be taken back to the hulks.

But he must explain this more fully than in his message; he must write a letter to Juliana also. He relit the candle, found writing materials, began, and then paused miserably. Which would be worse for her to hear, that he, throwing away the pardon she had so miraculously won for him, was going to allow himself, most probably, to be taken back to the inferno from which she had rescued him, or that he was going to attempt to leave England without ever seeing her again?

Sitting up in his bed the harassed young man groaned and ran his hand through his hair. His conduct would surely appear to her unpardonable. Nevertheless, though distracted, he did not waver; he had no choice but to act thus and slay his hopes. . . . Hopes of what? He had none; it was only that he would give ten years of his life to see her again. . . . At any rate, the most sensible thing was to explain clearly what he was about to do, and why, and ask her to try to forgive him. He set to work, and gradually the pencil ran on hotfoot; when he saw how much he had written he was astonished, and without reading it over he thrust it under his pillow, blew out the candle and, lying hastily down, closed his eyes, for he had heard Hervey's step on the stair, and could not trust himself to speak to him.

The door opened softly, and Captain Barrington, shading a candle with his hand, came in, while Raoul lay motionless, watching him under his lashes.

"Mr. Rowl"

He crept on tiptoe to the bed, as careful as one who fears to wake a child; stood over him a moment studying him; then he and the candle vanished toward the historic cupboard. In another moment he came back with something white hanging over his arm, put the candle down, and proceeded to arrange this white object over Raoul's feet. Apparently it was the coverlet off Miss Lavinia's bed.

Raoul's heart went out to him in an almost painful impulse. No, decidedly he could not speak to him. . . . If only he had it in his power to make him more than the negative return for all his goodness which he was about to make. At least he would make that willingly—he did, he did, even though the cost was so heavy in regret, in relinquishment. . . . But what is it to relinquish a dream—less than a dream? Hervey Barrington had risked for him something much more solid than that. . . .

"Good-bye, my dear Barrington," he said within himself. "God bless you—and give you your heart's desire!"

What Miss Lavinia Brought Home

"Since, then, not suspicion but fondness has detected you, let me not lose the advantage of my discovery."—Rasselas, chap. xiv.

If you feel (and feel rightly) that part of the glamour of mushrooms is the finding of them, then, in any district where their habitat is known to others, you must get up early to secure this enjoyment and them. And that is why Miss Lavinia Barrington, who adored both, left her little house, armed with a basket, at a quarter before six on this fine but misty September morning, and betook herself to the high, dew-drenched meadows on the banks of the river.

A couple of miles or so down stream on the farther side the port of Stowey still showed half asleep, though a few unwavering columns of smoke were beginning to testify to certain household activities. In the next field, which had just been ploughed, gulls were walking along the furrows among the rooks, but these winged creatures, as intent upon their breakfast as Miss

Lavinia upon hers, were the only signs of life. Nobody else, to her satisfaction, was out after mushrooms this morning.

Or was there someone? The meadow which she had selected was rather like a green sheet pinned out insecurely between its fringe of copse at either end, and sagging into a hollow in the middle. And in the nearer copse—which was also that nearer to Stowey—Miss Barrington distinctly heard sticks crack underfoot. She glanced towards it, and the crackling instantly stopped. Probably a poacher, which she did not mind, because he would have ambitions above mushrooms.

But some ten minutes later, when Miss Lavinia, who worked methodically, was harvesting at the other side of the field, though on the same slope, she saw a man come out of the copse at the point where she had already heard the sticks snap, and begin to descend the field, keeping close to the hedge which ran between it and its ploughed neighbour. If he was a poacher, thought Miss Barrington, looking at him idly across the width of the meadow, he was remarkably well dressed for one, and he had no gun. No, he was no poacher; he was a gentleman—a young man too—and his walk almost suggested that he was drunk, which was possible, though unlikely so early in the morning. With this peculiar gait he proceeded down the slope; but when he was faced with the uphill gradient, it was evidently too much for his legs; he stopped, lurched, and, catching sight of a stile in the hedge, went and sat down hastily on the lower step, leaning his head forward in his hands. On this Miss Barrington, deciding that he was not drunk but indisposed, charitably started across the field to him. But before she got very near he evidently heard her coming, and, leaving the stile, started as hard as he could up the slope in front of him.

"Stop!" cried Miss Barrington. "Stop! I want to help you!" But, despite his obvious difficulty in walking, her quarry pushed on up the rise as though a fury were after him, and making his way through its sparse hedge disappeared in the thicket at the top.

Miss Barrington had, however, gained on him so much that she was in this refuge the moment after; and there he was, leaning against a young sycamore, his back to her, gasping.

"Are you ill, young man?" asked Miss Lavinia, approaching him. "Let me——"

He half turned, as though to ward her off, and she saw who it was. "Heavens above! Mr. Rowl!"

Mr. Rowl stared at her without speech. "For God's sake sit down," said Miss Lavinia hastily. She looked to see him pitch forward at her feet, his face was so ashy, "There, that's better." For, almost sliding down the trunk, he had let himself subside, and sat down on the dead leaves below, half supported by one hand.

"I . . . I am . . ." he said, opening and shutting his eyes several times in succession. "I am trying . . ." His head drooped.

"Yes. Never mind," said Miss Lavinia, wishing that she carried smelling-salts. "You are running away, I know. But you need not have run from me. Just sit there a little." Very tactfully she supplemented the half support of the tree with an arm, so insensibly indeed that she flattered herself he did not know it, and at the same time she laid a speculative finger on the furiously bounding pulse in the nearest wrist.

"We must go on, Sarrelouis," murmured the collapsed fugitive. "Oh! I beg your pardon!" He had raised his head, and was now looking at his companion with startled eyes. "How did I——"

"You came on your legs," said Miss Barrington, withdrawing her arm. "Most unwisely, I should say. However, here you are. . . . You grew tired of Fairhaven, perhaps?"

Raoul shifted himself to get his shoulders fairly against the tree. He had discarded his sling, but was evidently chary of using his left arm. "I was afraid that Captain Barrington was in danger because of my presence. So . . . I left."

"Admirably succinct," commented Miss Barrington, sitting back on her heels, and even in that position retaining all her dignity. "And may I ask where you are going?"

Raoul dropped his head. "I don't very well know," he admitted, fingering the leaves on one side of him. "I could not procure a map, and I find that I cannot walk far."

"You surprise me!" remarked Miss Lavinia. "At any rate, you are now coming home to my cottage to help me eat these mushrooms. The distance is not great."

"Oh, no, I could not do that," said Raoul quickly.

"I assure you I am not entirely unprotected," observed Miss Lavinia with great gravity. "I have a maid and a gardener."

But Raoul looked at her without a smile.

"And I have not been hiding you," she went on "—if that is what is troubling you. Are you not hungry?"

"Yes," avowed the young man, and his glance fell on the basket. "You would let me go on afterwards?"

"You talk as if I had captured you!"

"But I think you have," said the runaway, and his mouth did twitch a little. "I must say that it is not easy to get away from your family, Miss Barrington!"

"Come, that's more like yourself," thought his captress. "Yes," she said aloud, "I expect you will soon have my brother on your track."

Raoul shook his head. "He does not know. . . . Perhaps," he pursued, beginning to struggle to his feet, "the explanation is that I am not very good at escaping."

"Yet one way and the other," said Miss Lavinia, assisting him, "you have certainly had enough practice. I think that for the peace of this country it is time you had your exchange."

"But I believe that I have got it," returned the young man casually. "I heard yesterday. A—a pardon, in fact. But I cannot claim it."

"And why not, pray?"

"Because the authorities would be almost sure to find out where I had been these last weeks. I would sooner—yes, sooner go back to the hulks than bring disaster on Captain Barrington. As it is, I am afraid the Admiralty has got wind of something; a naval officer came demanding him yesterday when he was out, and is coming again this morning, so I got Jeremy to put me across the river before it was light, and I must get farther away—I must, Miss

Barrington! Perhaps I could hire a horse . . ."

"Yes, yes," said the lady, "we will see about all that after breakfast, and you shall tell me more about this officer. For you can trust me to be alive to my brother's danger, can't you?"

"Yes," said Raoul, looking at her in a rather bewildered way. "But——"

"But for the rest of your life you will distrust women, you mean?"

"No, no!" said Raoul hastily, and no doubt it was to prove his confidence in the sex, as well as because the ground seemed so unstable, that he took her arm with no more than a half-hearted protest, and they moved together out of the little wood.

Susan, Miss Barrington's maid, was a good deal surprised when she was told that there would be a young gentleman to breakfast, but, as she never thought of questioning her mistress's orders, it was with only a mild wonder why a visitor should arrive so early that she cooked the mushrooms. And when she had her first sight of him, lying back, very pale, in Miss Barrington's own easy chair, she decided that the young gentleman had arrived by sea, and had not yet recovered from that devastating experience.

Raoul was indeed so much at the end of his tether by the time he arrived at Woodbine Cottage, that his hostess forbade him to utter a word until he had eaten and drunk. Not till then did she ask how he had heard of his "pardon."

"Lord Fulgrave has been good enough to interest himself in my case," said her visitor with a slight increase of colour. "He came to Fairhaven yesterday, and——"

"Who?" asked Miss Barrington. "Lord Fulgrave—Frederick Forrest?"

"I . . . yes, I suppose his name is Forrest," answered Raoul. "You know him, Miss Barrington?"

"I *knew* him," said Miss Barrington, smiling at memories of her own. Poor Frederick . . . she was said to have broken his heart. "Yes, I knew him—a hundred years ago. And so he came down to Devonshire to call on you?"

"Not exactly," replied the young Frenchman. "I think it was rather to erect a tombstone to me. They thought I was drowned, you see."

"Who is 'they'?" asked Miss Lavinia like a shot. "I thought Lady Fulgrave was dead these twenty years."

"Lord Fulgrave was accompanied by his daughter," explained Raoul, striving to give this announcement an air of small importance.

"Oh, indeed!" said Miss Barrington. "May I repeat your question: Do you know her?"

The colour in the face of her vis-à-vis was sufficient answer. "I . . . she . . . it is she who . . . I mean——"

"You mean that you are betrothed?"

Raoul nearly leapt from his seat. "Miss Barrington, what are you saying! I mean that she has done for me . . . no, there are no words to say all that she has done—contrived my escape from the hulks—poured out money on my behalf—and now has got me a cartel——"

"Well, my dear Mr. Rowl," said Miss Lavinia, "then I think there only remains one thing for her to do to complete her good work—and that is to marry you!"

Instead of colouring this time the young man on the other side of the breakfast table turned rather white. "I know that you are only jesting, Miss Barrington, but out of regard for Miss Forrest I would ask you——"

"Yes, yes," interrupted his hostess. "I have a vulgar wit, my dear Mr. Rowl; my brother implied the same on the night of your first arrival. But I can appreciate your delicacy. We will not consider then the procurer of the cartel, only the fact. May I ask what it is for?"

Raoul briefly told her. "But, as I say, I cannot claim it."

"Did you say that to Miss Forrest?—It would be encouraging news for her after all her efforts."

No doubt Miss Barrington told herself that she was being cruel only to be kind, for she must have known from Raoul's face that she was being cruel.

"I did not think of it at the moment," he said. He was pricking the tablecloth with a fork. "But I cannot bring ruin on Captain Barrington, even——" He stopped, and the prongs of the fork ran right through the damask.

"Mr. Rowl"

"My dear boy," said Miss Lavinia warmly, "—you must pardon the term, for you might well be my son, you know—I assure you that I appreciate your self-sacrifice on my brother's behalf. But I think so much abnegation is not, perhaps, necessary. Listen. I suggest that you present yourself at the Transport Office, either not saying a word of where you have been since your supposed drowning, or making up a story of having been, let us say, cast up at some lonely spot on the coast, and cared for there by some unnamed poor people whom it is not worth the Government's while to prosecute. Besides, it is no crime to care for a half-drowned man, and they in no way helped you to escape from the country. As soon as you were well enough to do so you left them; you don't look so robust—with that bandaged wrist too—that doubt can be cast on that statement. How is the Transport Office going to disprove any part of that story?"

Raoul, with an elbow on the table, had been listening attentively. "I should also have to account for the manner in which I first heard of my good fortune. . . . Yes, perhaps. . . . But it depends a great deal on what errand this officer has come to Fairhaven."

"Well, that I can soon find out," returned Miss Barrington, getting up. "I will drive over to Stowey at once and see—if you will give me your word to remain here? *Parole d'honneur, Monsieur le Capitaine*—or else, the coal cellar?"

A brief smile flickered over her prisoner's face. "You leave me no choice, Miss Barrington. I give you my parole, till you return. Yes," he added meditatively, "I could always refuse to accept the cartel unless they promised not to make investigations as to my whereabouts."

"I am glad," said Miss Barrington, "to see that you are open to reason. Our first step is certainly to find out about this messenger of doom from the Admiralty. I will order my pony cart. Incidentally my brother will be glad to hear where you are, I fancy. You say you made John Jeremy put you across the river? I am sorry for him!"

"Jeremy is a faithful soul," said Raoul. "All along he has thought of his master's interests, not of mine, and quite rightly too."

"Yes, but you may be sure that his master won't hold that an excuse. There seem to be a good many martyrdoms over this affair of yours, Mr. Rowl!"

Raoul sighed and studied the carpet. He was much depressed. Miss Lavinia looked at him keenly and added, "Nor are martyrs always of the male sex, you know."

He looked up, startled. "Oh, Miss Barrington! But you know that it is not my wish to stay here and perhaps involve you too. Give me back my parole!"

"Never in life," said his hostess, tugging at the bell-pull. "You are too slippery. But you did not really think I was referring to myself, did you?—Susan, tell Jacob to harness the pony at once.—Now, come back to this comfortable chair, Mr. Rowl. By the way, have you the address of this major who owes you his life and must needs identify you?"

"He is quartered, I believe, at Canterbury."

"You will have to communicate with him."

"Yes, I suppose so."

"Unless Miss—Lord Fulgrave does so."

"I cannot expect Lord Fulgrave to take any further trouble when I have behaved in what must seem to him such an extraordinary way."

"No, perhaps you can't," said Miss Lavinia uncompromisingly. She studied him again as he stood before her, and, between her liking for him and her feeling that she owed him some reparation for the past, resolved to take a hand in his destiny to better purpose than last time. For all that, she went on to point out that, since he could find Major Brackenbury, he was in a position to carry through the business of the cartel without Lord Fulgrave's assistance at all.

But this truth seemed very little to exhilarate her visitor. Biting his lip, he merely looked broodingly at her.

"Well, I am going to put on my bonnet and set off," said Miss Barrington. "I propose that you sit quietly in this chair with a book till I return. Now remember that I have your word of honour that you will not give *me* the slip!"

"You don't think, surely, Miss Barrington," said poor Raoul in a tone of anguish, "that I *wanted* to give—anybody—the slip?"

"Except your friends in the *Ganges*, no, I don't. But you have an uncontrollably Quixotic turn of mind, I'm afraid." She patted his arm as if, however, this quality did not displease her, put cushions in the chair, a book in his hand, and departed.

And Raoul sat in her chair, leaning his head against the back, frankly wretched. Once again he had made a mess of his affairs—a supreme mess. But, once again, he did not see how he could have done differently. Yet if only he could see Juliana for five minutes to explain—a letter was so doubtful an ambassador! But it seemed to him that she would never listen to an explanation after such an affront. He knew, none better, of what she was capable with regard to a man who had displeased her.

But, if he did see her for five minutes, if she did listen—yes, even if the arrangement shadowed forth yesterday in the Garden of Eden were carried out, and he went up to London with her and her father to claim the cartel, what would be the result? Only more heartache for him. No, the sooner he got out of England the better—for other reasons than because of a distaste for captivity. Over there he could throw himself body and soul into the following of his Emperor's paling star—for how it had paled in the last twelve months! . . . For a time he sat staring moodily into the empty hearth, and absent-mindedly stroking the black kitten which had come in with Susan when she cleared the breakfast table, and which had established itself on his knee. Then they both fell asleep.

And, being pretty well exhausted and having had practically no sleep the night before, Raoul, for his part, slept the minute hand twice round Miss Lavinia's ormolu clock; though, if he had known the full extent of Miss Lavinia's activities meanwhile, it is probable that his slumber would have been less profound.

*

The door opening smartly woke him with a jump.

"Raoul—are you there?" It was Hervey Barrington's voice. "Miserable lad! What a morning I have spent! How *dared* you do such a thing!" He was over him, shaking him, and the kitten, frightened and indignant, sprang from

Raoul's knee to his farther shoulder.

"You have seen Miss Barrington, I suppose?" enquired the culprit, looking up at him rather shamefacedly. "I meant to get much farther than this, mais——" He gave a shrug, and the kitten promptly scratched his cheek. "But, for God's sake, tell me what the officer from the Admiralty wanted—if you know by this time."

Captain Barrington, apparently in a most unusual state of excitement, took a turn down the room, flung his riding whip with a clatter on the table, and said, "I do know! And never, never, as I am a living man, did a messenger bring news more ironical!" He laughed. Raoul was rather alarmed, and twisted in the chair to look at him.

"Tell me quickly! Oh, Barrington, if I have harmed you——"

"Harmed me! You have given me the wish of my heart," said Hervey, and at that Raoul almost began to fear for his sanity.

"Listen," said Captain Barrington more calmly, "and don't look so apprehensive. That naval officer yesterday who so terrified the timid Jeremy—and by the way," he added rather grimly, "I think Jeremy is timid with more reason this morning—merely came to deliver to me a letter of introduction from a friend of mine in London. The letter, however, happens to contain some news as well. Would you like to see it?" And without waiting for a reply he threw a missive on to Raoul's knee.

Raoul unfolded it and read:

My Dear Barrington:

This is to make known to you Lieutenant Fanshawe, late of the Sappho frigate, a promising young officer whom, as he has occasion to spend a few days in Stowey on private matters, I desire to introduce to your notice. He is in some sort a cousin of my wife's, so we shall be grateful to you on his behalf for the light of your countenance.

Raoul gave an exclamation. "Then the visit of that lieutenant yesterday was quite harmless—he only wished to present this letter of introduction?"

"That was all. The rest was Jeremy's guilty imagination. You fled from a shadow, you see, you scoundrel!"

"But why then did he question the coast guard about my drowning?"

"From curiosity or zeal, I suppose. He said nothing about it to me this morning. But go on."

And now, my dear fellow, I seize this opportunity of giving you a piece of good news. You may take it from me—or better still, from Charles Denison of the Admiralty, who told me yesterday—that the sun of official approval is about to shine on you once more from behind that damnable black cloud which ought never to have obscured it, and that when the new first-rate Thetis, 90 guns, is commissioned—she is all but ready, as you probably know—her captain will be one George Hervey Barrington.

Raoul sprang up, his face alight. "Oh, Hervey!" He was unconscious that he had used his Christian name. "Is it true?"

"I suppose so," said Hervey, half sitting on the table like a boy. "But go on—the cream is yet to come. Read why I am thus to be reinstated."

Raoul obeyed.

You will naturally wish to know why their Lordships have at last realized what they were throwing away by not employing you. It appears that, although your friends believed them to have your case continually under their benign consideration, they had really forgotten all about you. But you may remember, about a month ago, sending to the commander of one of the Plymouth hulks a report on the drowning of an escaped French prisoner at Stowey. This report was forwarded in due course to the Transport Office, and came up in its turn at a meeting of the Board. As chance and your good star would have it, my dear Barrington, that meeting happened—I don't quite know why—to be attended by Admiral Clutterbuck of the Navy Board. When it came to your name in connection with this document, it appears that he nearly lifted the roof off:—'What, is that fellow still kicking his heels in

Devonshire, reporting on escaped prisoners when he ought to be making 'em? By——I never heard of such a scandal!' etc., etc., all the more vigorously, no doubt, that he was partly responsible for the scandal himself. The upshot of it was, I believe, a stiff breeze at the Admiralty, terminating in their Lordships' resolution to appoint you to the Thetis, a piece of news obligingly communicated to me, as I say, by Charles Denison, who knew of what interest and pleasure it would be to me.

Nota bene: If I did not know C. D. to be an absolutely trustworthy informant, I should not be so cruel as to pass on the statement. As it is, I have no hesitation in offering you, my dear Barrington, my warmest congratulations—a little antedated, perhaps, but not much. Indeed, I fancy you had better be looking over your kit. . . .

Raoul dropped the letter and seized Hervey's hands. "Oh, Hervey!" he said again, with tears in his eyes. "Oh, my dear friend, let me congratulate you too!"

"Why," said Hervey, smiling and not unresponsive to the grip, "it is I who ought to thank you for bringing this about. If I had not sent in that lying report it would never have happened. A strange reward for something like felony, isn't it? I did a better day's work for myself than I thought when I hauled you into the *Kestrel* in spite of your efforts. . . . But you'll admit that it is a little ironical!"

"I am so delighted that I won't admit anything," cried Raoul. "Between this, and the kind intentions of the Transport Board towards me, all my thoughts of your Admiralty are rosy just now. I would decree them all haloes, *des auréoles bien dorées*. Ninety guns, and new! With so large a vessel, Barrington, you will surely have to be made an admiral!"

"It is a pity that she will not be allowed to take you over to Morlaix. It would only be fitting!"

Raoul thrust a hand into his pocket and turned a little away. "I am not so sure that I am going to Morlaix," he observed nonchalantly.

Hervey caught him by the shoulder and spun him round again. "Raoul,

Raoul, you have done enough in that line! And to think that I wondered yesterday if any thought of my position would ever strike you! I could have kicked myself for it this morning when Mrs. Jeremy brought me your letter. . . . Now, if you hesitate to claim your freedom because of any scruples about me, I——" He paused as if selecting a threat.

"What will you do?" asked Raoul with levity. "You can't make me, if I don't choose! I am my own master, *parbleu!*"

"I can take the matter out of your hands by going up to the Transport Office and telling them everything—how I lied about you and hid you. How would you like that, you crazy young—runaway? But my sister has been talking the matter over with me this morning, as I understand she has already done with you, and I think, as she does, that if you do not object to telling the Commissioners a few lies the matter can be put through without involving me at all. . . . You see, by successfully removing yourself from Fairhaven you have already severed the link between us to a certain degree. But perhaps since you abandoned female attire, you have sworn a vow never to tell anything but the strict truth?"

Raoul made a face at him. "If I tell any more lies, they shall be the lies of Miss Barrington, who is a lady of great resource. I will trust *her*, perhaps, with my conscience. Tiens, I think I hear the wheels of her chariot returning."

Hervey listened a moment; the window was open. "Yes, I hear them too. Raoul," he said with a change of voice, "I have scolded you for this escapade, though not nearly as much as you deserve, but I have not told you what I think of you for sacrificing yourself for my sake."

"But," said Raoul with a little shrug, "there is no need. As it fell out, *voyez-vous*, it was silly of me to run away. And all that I sacrificed was a night's rest."

"Was that really all?" asked Hervey.

Raoul either could not or would not meet his eyes. He avoided them by the expedient of dropping suddenly down into his former chair. "Ma foi, was not that enough?" he asked perversely, "—a whole good night's sleep! That was why you found me asleep just now—like the little cat, who had perhaps lost hers too. Where is she then?" He stooped from the chair to search for the kitten, Hervey standing and looking at him, wondering if his half suspicion of a far greater sacrifice made for him were correct. From Miss Forrest's demeanour, indeed, when he had conveyed the letter left for her and the news to the "Dolphin" this morning he had been able to deduce nothing.

Suddenly Miss Lavinia's head appeared at the window.

"Hervey, come and take the pony round to the stables for me, there's a good soul," she said. "I don't know where Jacob has got to.—No, not you, Mr. Rowl; you stay where you are, please!"

Obediently Hervey went to the window, put one leg over the sill and vanished. Raoul scrambled out of the chair again, took up the letter of good news from the table and began to re-read it, but he had not got through the first paragraph before he was aware of the door opening. The voice of Susan thereupon murmured, "Miss Barrington said in here, if you please, Miss," and someone came in—a lady.

The Marriage of Dunois

"The union of these two affections," said Rasselas, "would produce all that could be wished. Perhaps there is a time when marriage might unite them—a time neither too early for the father nor too late for the husband."—Rasselas, chap. xxix.

"Oh," she exclaimed as the door shut, "I thought no one——"

Raoul, as still as she had suddenly become, stood perfectly mute for a moment, Hervey Barrington's correspondence clutched in a tightening hand. Was he really going to have that five minutes after all? Then the room began to swing warningly round him. Horrified at this tendency, he retreated a step or two till he could brace himself against the high back of the chair he had just quitted.

"Will you . . . will you not sit down, Mademoiselle?" he stammered out.

She was lovelier than ever—as always when she flushed, he remembered it from Wanfield days. To his infatuated eyes the very clothes she wore seemed cloth of gold, though it was not at them that he was gazing.

Juliana likewise continued to look across the room at him. "I think it is you who should sit down, Monsieur des Sablières," she said gently, on which, with a final effort to show that he was not such a poor thing after all, M. des Sablières moved towards her. And speech was restored to him.

"Did you receive my letter—did you understand . . . did you, Mademoiselle? I had to do it . . . it seems it was a mistake, Captain Barrington was not in immediate danger . . . but I thought he was."

"Yes," said Juliana with the same gentleness, "I perfectly understood. Captain Barrington brought me your letter this morning. I honoured you for feeling so, and for acting as you did—to your own disadvantage."

The relief was so intense, her praise so intoxicating, that Raoul's heart seemed to stop for a moment, and he was therefore guilty, for the first time in his life, of sitting down while a lady stood; for he drifted rather quickly to the window seat and sank upon it.

"Ah, that is right," murmured Miss Forrest, and, possibly with an idea of keeping him safely there, she also came and seated herself at the other corner.

"You do really pardon my seeming discourtesy and ingratitude?" once more enquired the runaway anxiously, leaning a little towards her. The fresh air steadied him—but her proximity did not.

"I saw neither to pardon," Juliana assured him gravely. "But what I do find difficult to forgive, Monsieur des Sablières, is the small consideration you have displayed for your own state of health. For that I do think you should be blamed! And how did you, scarcely convalescent, contrive to get as far as this?"

"But I did not get so far," retorted Raoul. "Miss Barrington captured me in a little wood, and brought me here. I was not making for this house. You . . . you were surprised to find me here, I think?" he ventured.

"Indeed, I had no idea at all that I should see you," replied Miss Forrest rather hastily. "I must explain to you how I come to be here myself. The fact is that Miss Barrington is an old friend of my father's—though it had not occurred to him that Captain Barrington could be her brother, for in those days, I gather, he did not know that she had one, that brother being so much younger. Well, Miss Barrington came to call upon my father this morning at the inn at Stowey, and in the end was so kind as to carry me off to dine with her."

"Without mentioning that I was here," supplemented Raoul, in something that was between a question and a statement. "I wonder . . ." And there he stopped, suddenly realizing that a silence on Miss Barrington's part otherwise so inexplicable could only be due to strategy, and a strategy directed . . . yes, to what end? The same conviction had evidently dawned on Miss Forrest also; she became very still for a moment, and then remarked in a detached tone, "What extremely fine asters those are!"

"I had not observed them," said Raoul, following the direction of her eyes. The flowers in question, he then saw, were in a bowl on the table in the centre of the room, but he was quite able to admire them from the window seat where Miss Forrest and he were sitting, and he was sorry that she should feel it necessary to rise, go to the bowl, and bend over them as if to smell them. Even he was aware that asters had no scent. Yet he understood her need of a diversion and followed her to the table but slowly.

"My father was unable to accompany me here to-day, as he is confined to his room with gout," volunteered Miss Forrest, with her back to him, taking an aster from the bowl.

"I am extremely sorry to hear that," returned Raoul. "I feel that I am the unworthy cause of it."

"It is not a serious attack." Here she put back the aster with care, turned and faced him, and said, somewhat to his surprise: "This matter of your cartel, Monsieur des Sablières—since we have met we might as well discuss it. You explained in your letter why you felt you could not claim it, but surely we could think of some plan which would enable you to do so without involving Captain Barrington."

It leapt to Raoul's mind that Miss Barrington's scheme had probably been expounded to her in the pony chaise (which made that astute lady's silence as to his whereabouts still more remarkable). No wonder, then, that Miss Forrest did not wish to refer explicitly to the author of the plan. She went on:

"If we can do so satisfactorily, I still think that when my father is better you might accompany us to London, as I proposed yesterday. One cannot, of course, tell how long his attack may last. . . ."

As she spoke Raoul was aware of a strange, rending vision of the truth about that journey to London. Yesterday the prospect of accompanying her thither had seemed like heaven. Delusion! It would not be heaven at all—it would be the fate of Tantalus! He must not let himself be beguiled into submitting to it.

He looked down, and beheld the kitten running perseveringly after its own tail. "If you will excuse me, Mademoiselle, I think that I would—I mean, that I had better go separately."

"But why?" Evidently much surprised, Juliana faced him across the table and the flowers. "Why, Monsieur des Sablières? I thought that, travelling with my father, you would in a sense be protected from enquiry until your freedom was established. That was why I proposed it; and my father also thinks well of the plan."

Raoul looked up for a moment from the gyrations of the kitten. "You are all kindness, Mademoiselle. If I had a hundred lives, I could never repay what you have done for me."

"Then why have you changed your mind? Yesterday you approved of the plan, I thought."

To that he said nothing.

"It must be, I suppose," said Juliana slowly, and in an altered voice, "that you do not wish to have my society for a couple of days. Then evidently your forgiveness of the injury I have done you is not so complete as you pretend!"

How could she be so unseeing—and so cruel! "Juliana!" said Raoul under his breath, and with that, throwing away discretion, went on desperately, "I cannot let you think that! If you press me so I must tell you the reason, though it would be more honourable to keep silence. . . . There is only one journey in the world that I want to take with you, and since I can never take it I will travel alone now. Indeed, I would rather say farewell to you here, to-day . . . because I have less fortitude than I thought. . . . And now that I have said this, you will wish it too . . . but I hope you will forgive me because you forced me to tell you the truth."

She was, he knew, standing rigid on the other side of the table; he knew it though he was not looking at her. It broke his heart to end like this, and directly the words had burst out of him he would have given almost anything to recall them. But the best that he could hope for now was that she would be merciful, and let him go without withering him for his presumption and folly. He looked at her to see.

But Juliana too was standing with downcast eyes, and she was very pale, and twisting her fingers not at all like a goddess about to launch thunderbolts.

"I . . . I did not know you . . . felt thus," she murmured almost inaudibly. "I . . . I am very . . ."

Seeing her so clement Raoul took courage. "Do not say that you are sorry for me, for I am not—except for my own weakness in telling you. Only say that you forgive me!"

"I . . . was not going to say that I was sorry," replied Juliana. She was now nervously stripping off her gloves. "Only that I was . . . very much surprised." And immediately she sat down on the chair by the table, put her elbows on the latter, and covered her face with her hands.

By this manœuvre Raoul found himself extremely disconcerted, for it left him no prospect of her features by which to gauge her sentiments. Yet perhaps, after all, they were going to be able to part good friends; he began to have at least a hope of it. And with the hope came also to him the weak-minded idea of allowing himself a partial reprieve. Might it not be almost *necessary* to call on her father in London, even if he journeyed thither separately? Certainly it would be more courteous. He was weighing the manner in which he should make this retrograde suggestion, when, from behind the shelter of her hands, Juliana Forrest uttered these amazing words:

"What did you mean about the journey you wished to take—with . . . me?"

*

"Did you not really understand, most beautiful?" asked Raoul some twenty minutes later, when they sat side by side on Miss Lavinia's sofa. He still held her hand in both his own.

Juliana turned her head away, and her reply was evasive and incoherent. "You see, I was so astonished," she murmured. "I never thought that you . . . and then you were so modest . . . so I had to be horribly bold . . ."

"But I shall be called 'impudent,'?" said Raoul half to himself. "Your father—"

Juliana looked round. "I do not pretend that I can bring Papa to reason all at once. It will take a little time, and we shall have to be patient." Laughter and remembrance came into her eyes. "I fear he will not say, '*De ma fille Isabelle sois l'époux à l'instant!*' But in the end . . ."

Raoul loosed the hand. "He will call me an adventurer, a fortune-hunter. I suppose that, unfortunately, you possess a fortune?—Oh, have I been guilty of a *calem*—of a pun?"

"A fortune? I have, and I have not. My money is not settled upon me. Papa can cut me off with a shilling if he likes."

"*À la bonne heure!*" said her suitor with a sigh of relief. "Perhaps, however, he will leave you a guinea. . . . At any rate, he cannot so easily call me those names.—But there is another embarrassment. You perhaps succeed him—no? Why do you laugh, *ma toute belle*? I know that it does so happen sometimes, even in this ungallant country."

"Not half so ungallant a country as yours has always been, Sir," retorted Juliana. "We have no Salic law against queens in England! No, as it happens, the title goes to my uncle, since I had the bad luck not to be born a boy. Is that a disappointment? If you thought that you were going to marry a peeress in her own right—"

"The bad luck not to be born a boy!" exclaimed Raoul in tones of horror. "*Grand Dieu*, suppose you had been! What a terrible thought! . . . As for the other question, I must own that I have a prejudice in favour of a wife who bears her husband's name. Now ask me how a poor cavalry soldier is going to support a wife at all, particularly one to whom he owes the price of a sapphire necklace—did you not say sapphires?"

"How are you going to support a wife, 'Mr. Rowl'?" asked Juliana obediently.

"In the first place," replied 'Mr. Rowl' airily, "by my sword. But, secondly, on the money that my rich uncle in Orleans will leave me at his death, which will shortly occur, I think—money which I have sometimes intended to refuse because he is personally odious to me, but which I shall now make the sacrifice of accepting for your sake."

"You are very magnanimous—and absurd!" said Juliana laughing. "And as for me, you have no idea what a quantity of methods of needlework Laetitia Bentley and I learnt at school. So if we have not enough to live upon——What is the matter?" For all at once the optimistic lover gave an exclamation and sprang to his feet.

"I fear I go too fast," he said dejectedly. "Our countries are at war; I am your enemy, Juliana, and I am returning to fight once more against you over there. If every other difficulty were gone, how could we marry each other in such conditions—for I would never consent to leave you behind in England when you were my wife, and I could not well take you to France, even if you wished it."

The gaiety of a moment ago was struck from him, and the triumph; he looked tired and tragic. Juliana got up and placed her hand on his arm.

"No war lasts for ever, dear enemy," she said consolingly. "Even this will end some day. We must wait, that is all."

Raoul put his lips to the little hand. "I would wait till next century for you! But it needs two to wait, *mon cœur*. And while you wait for me . . . *ciel*, who am I that I should demand such a thing! . . . you will meet so many other men, rich, and of your own nation, a thousand times better matches than I—though hardly of a better family," he added, with a little lift of the head—"and you will regret. . . . Oh, I ought not to ask it!"

"But what if it is I who ask it of you?" returned Juliana in her soft tones. "You, who have gone to prison for my sake, and were ready to return to it in its worst form for Captain Barrington's, surely you are too chivalrous to refuse me that! Oh, Raoul," she went on, shaking her head at him, "why did you fear that I would not understand when you decided to throw your freedom behind you yesterday? Why, it is a habit with you—I am used to it! You did it again at Norman Cross when you sacrificed yourself rather than fail your comrades. . . . Yes, I have come these last months to see what you are—much better, I know, than you see it yourself!"

As if ashamed, Raoul had put a hand over his eyes. "*Mon Dieu*, I do not know through what spectacles of rose-colour you look," he said indistinctly. "*Vous rêvez—je ne suis pas comme ça!*" And then suddenly he turned on her, his voice shaking slightly. "Are you sure that this is not all a dream, Juliana—that you wish really to take that journey with me? For if it is a dream, do not let me go on dreaming . . . make it end quickly!"

Juliana took his two hands and folded them for a moment in her own, as once in prison. And, looking gravely at each other, they both saw, perhaps, glimpses of the long road they should eventually travel together. Then, gently, his arms went round her, and the kiss of Norman Cross was repaid in full.